## Praise for *The Girl*

'In *The Girl on the Page*, John Purcell tr[...]
hand and his heart in the other. It is a gripping, dark comedy of a
novel which eviscerates the cynicism of contemporary publishing
while uttering a cri de coeur for what is happening to writers and
readers this century. Through this dark comedy – I squealed with
laughter, page after page – flash questions about cultural life that
Purcell asks but leaves us to ponder' – BLANCHE D'ALPUGET, author
of *Winter in Jerusalem, Turtle Beach* and *Robert J. Hawke: A biography*

'It's like getting on a fast-moving train, or maybe a rocket, filled with
people who love books as much as you do. You cannot and don't
want to get off, but must follow every dynamic, insatiable, brilliant
character right to the stunning end' – CAROLINE OVERINGTON,
bestselling author of *The Ones You Trust, The Lucky One* and *The
One Who Got Away*

'A juicy page-turner that takes a scalpel to the literary world,
written with deep insider intel and a gleeful sense of mischief,
*The Girl on the Page* is a wickedly clever, razor-sharp satire of
lust, betrayal and ambition' – CAROLINE BAUM, broadcaster and
author of *Only*

'You could strip *The Girl on the Page* of all its publishing-
insider juiciness; what remains is a searing take on integrity,
commerce and the consequences of compromise. Purcell is a
born storyteller, having spent a lifetime surrounded by books
and having learned from the masters of the craft. *The Girl on the
Page* is moving, hilarious and ultimately heart-wrenching. It's a
love-letter to literature, for sure, to its creators and its readers.
But it's so much more than that, too' – SIMON MCDONALD, Potts
Point Bookshop, Sydney

'A rollicking, sexy read about great fiction, trashy readers, writerly egos and the industry that feeds them all' – MICHAEL ROBOTHAM, Gold Dagger winner and international bestselling author of *The Other Wife* and *The Secrets She Keeps*

'Whilst questioning the very definition of what makes fiction commercial or literary, Purcell himself brilliantly genre-straddles, moving his novel from what starts as a comic romp to a serious rumination on literary integrity, commercial realities, ambition and the importance of flexibility and compromise, both personally and professionally' – SCOTT WHITMONT, Lindfield Bookshop, Sydney

While still in his twenties, John Purcell opened a second-hand bookshop — imaginatively called 'John's Bookshop' — in which he sat for ten years reading, ranting and writing. Since then he has written (under a pseudonym) a series of successful novels, interviewed hundreds of writers about their work, appeared at literary festivals and on TV and been featured in prominent newspapers and magazines. He lives in Sydney with his wife, two children, three dogs, five cats, unnumbered goldfish and his overlarge book collection.

JOHN PURCELL

# The Girl on the Page

FOURTH ESTATE

This book is a work of fiction set in the literary world. While some of the authors and books mentioned in this book are real, all the events are purely fiction and the contents are not endorsed by any of the people mentioned.

**Fourth Estate**
An imprint of HarperCollins*Publishers*

First published in Australia in 2018
by HarperCollins*Publishers* Australia Pty Limited
ABN 36 009 913 517
harpercollins.com.au

**HarperCollins*Publishers***
Level 13, 201 Elizabeth Street, Sydney NSW 2000, Australia
Unit D1, 63 Apollo Drive, Rosedale, Auckland 0632, New Zealand
A 53, Sector 57, Noida, UP, India
1 London Bridge Street, London, SE1 9GF, United Kingdom
Bay Adelaide Centre, East Tower, 22 Adelaide Street West, 41st floor, Toronto,
  Ontario M5H 4E3, Canada
195 Broadway, New York NY 10007, USA

A catalogue record for this book is available from the National Library of Australia.

ISBN 978 1 4607 5697 3 (paperback)
ISBN 978 1 4607 1074 6 (ebook)

Cover design by Hazel Lam, HarperCollins Design Studio
Background texture by shutterstock.com
Author photo by Sarah Louise Kinsella
Typeset in Bembo Std by Kirby Jones
Printed and bound in Australia by McPherson's Printing Group
The papers used by HarperCollins in the manufacture of this book are a natural, recyclable product made from wood grown in sustainable plantation forests. The fibre source and manufacturing processes meet recognised international environmental standards, and carry certification.

*For Tamsin*

# Prologue

'Amy, what are you doing?'

I was sitting naked on his loo with his laptop. It was 4 am and I'd only met him the night before. The question was reasonable.

He'd remembered my name, which was cute.

'The edits on the new Archer,' I answered, without looking up from the screen. 'He's not mine, but a friend called in a favour.'

I saved my work to the cloud, trying to remember if he had been a guest at the book launch, in which case he'd know what I'd meant by 'the new Archer', or a member of the bar staff. One quick glance at him confirmed it for me. He was standing there completely naked – tats, six-pack, stubble, enormous package – definitely bar staff.

'What? How'd you log in?'

'I'm on as a guest. Don't worry,' I said, logging out and closing the lid, 'I haven't been going through your porn collection. I mean I would have been, but I couldn't get in. Go back to bed. I'll let myself out.'

'Are you going?' he asked, stepping forward and taking my hand in his.

I handed him the laptop and looked up. Nope, I couldn't for the life of me remember tattoo boy's name.

'If I stay, can I take a photo of your cock for my blog?'

His cock stirred and he smiled.

'Check your phone. You took a million already.'

And so that is how it is with me. I'm an insomniac. I drink way too much. I take naughty pics. I like to fuck strangers. And I'm a workaholic who will edit books on any computer I can break into.

# Chapter 1
# Wednesday, 27 July 2016

'They're here,' said Helen, who had been watching from the window of her West London terrace. Her husband, Malcolm, was standing in the doorway to the sitting room waiting for this news. He strode down the corridor and pulled open the front door.

Parked outside the house was a black Citroën estate car. A man in his late forties with sparse sandy hair was standing by the open driver's door, arms raised in a luxurious stretch. He began to yawn and then saw Malcolm walking towards the front gate.

'Hi, Dad,' he said, mid yawn, adding, 'Hi, Mum,' when he saw Helen at the door.

'Good trip, Daniel?' asked Malcolm.

'Fair,' he answered. He opened the back door, reached in, took out his tan blazer and put it on. 'The weather's better here. It's been miserable in Edinburgh. This is glorious.' He glanced briefly at the blue sky. When his gaze returned to Malcolm, he added, 'You've had the house painted. Looks like all the others now. I didn't recognise it. Lucky I remembered the number.'

Malcolm nodded and was about to say something when the passenger door opened and a woman in her late twenties emerged. She gave Malcolm and Helen a tight smile and then opened the back door and helped two little boys out. The boys stood on the pavement in matching jeans and ruby red jumpers and stared up at Malcolm. They looked like they had been woken from a nap.

Helen opened the gate and crouched down. 'Hello, boys!'

The boys stared at Helen, expressionless. After a moment, the younger of the two decided it was best to bury his face in the heavy material of his mother's charcoal skirt.

'Hello, Geraldine,' said Malcolm as he watched his wife try to coax the remaining boy into a smile.

Geraldine stepped forward awkwardly, the little boy still clinging to her, and gave Malcolm a quick kiss on the cheek. 'The boys and I have been asleep.'

'It's a long drive,' said Helen, admitting defeat with the boys and standing up. She was struck by how much Daniel had aged. He was almost twenty years older than Geraldine and it was more evident than ever. Geraldine, always attractive, had become a dark beauty. Her face was thinner and more defined. And though shy in this moment, her eyes showed that she had matured and was more herself than ever.

'We did it in seven hours,' said Daniel. 'And we stopped for lunch. The boys can watch DVDs in the back. They were great, weren't they?' Geraldine nodded. 'What's the best movie ever, Charlie?' he asked touching the boy's shoulder.

'*Frozen*,' came the muffled reply from within the folds of his mother's skirt.

'Geraldine, go in with the boys. I'll help Daniel with the bags.'

'No rush, Dad, we'll get them later. I'd kill for a cup of tea.'

Malcolm ushered the visitors into the front room, while Helen went off to make tea. Entering the room, he pointed out the train set Helen had set up on the floor for the boys. The boys clung to their parents tenaciously.

'That was once Daddy's train, Samuel,' said Daniel, leading the elder of the two by the hand, 'from when I was a little boy like you.'

Both Geraldine and Malcolm watched in silence, still standing by the door, as Daniel got down on his haunches and showed

Samuel how it worked. Charlie left his mother's skirt and went over to see, too.

When Helen returned with a full tray of tea things, Malcolm and Geraldine still hadn't thought to sit down. It became obvious to both that they had been behaving awkwardly. Malcolm hastened off to the window, passing his son and grandsons on his way, and proceeded to check the weather. Geraldine took the tray from Helen and placed it on the coffee table, allowing Helen to return to the kitchen to see to the now boiling kettle.

Once the tea was poured, and everyone was settled, the adults watched the two boys playing with the train. Daniel had remained on the floor but now turned to the coffee table to stir his tea and take a few tentative sips.

'I'm sorry we couldn't get down for Christmas. Geraldine's parents always put on a big family Christmas and the look of disappointment on their faces when I floated the idea of spending Christmas in London was too much. I know your views on religious ceremonies and thought you both wouldn't mind too much,' said Daniel, his eyes travelling from Geraldine, alone on the sofa to his right, to his mother and father, seated on his left.

Helen almost spoke. She almost said that it didn't matter. Her head and shoulders lifted almost imperceptibly, in order to speak. But it had mattered. And consciousness of this fact kept her silent.

Malcolm, thinking he was about to hear the words he knew Helen must say, remained silent, too. So real was his premonition of her speech, he'd thought he'd heard it. But only for the shortest of moments.

'We didn't handle it well,' admitted Geraldine. 'To make arrangements with you and then to break them at the last minute wasn't ...' Her words died on her lips.

Daniel gave his wife a reassuring smile. He was glad she hadn't said anything more. He knew his parents were waiting for an apology and Geraldine had almost given them one. But he knew better than anyone how much she had been dreading that Christmas visit to London, almost as much as she had been dreading this current visit. If anyone deserved an apology it was Geraldine. His parents had never made any effort to get to know her.

'It was difficult,' said Malcolm.

'I don't want to speak about it,' said Helen, instead of the words that had come to mind. These had made her feel uncomfortable. They were so ordinary. *We were both hurt*, she might have said. But she recoiled from the idea. They weren't people who said such things. Or felt such things. She was facing behaviour that was so distressingly ordinary that only ordinary speech and emotion applied. But she wouldn't stoop. Daniel and Geraldine were singularly selfish and unrepentant. To proceed, that fact would have to be agreed upon by all present. And that wasn't going to happen.

'What can we speak about then?' asked Daniel. Helen knew the tone of this question well. It never took long before the facade of the good son crumbled.

'I read your article on the library closures in Scotland,' said Malcolm.

'We both did,' said Helen.

'I don't want to discuss my writing with either of you. I was compelled to write. In my work I see first-hand the deterioration of literacy standards. But writing, I have no ambitions in that direction.'

Geraldine, alert to her husband's tone, spoke before either Helen or Malcolm could. 'Daniel said you'll be celebrating your fiftieth wedding anniversary in October.'

'Yes, we will,' answered Malcolm, unhelpfully.

'And your work, Geraldine, will you be returning now the boys are older?' asked Helen.

'I never really stopped. Clients still come to the house. The boys are very good. They know when I'm working. Sometimes they join in. I'm now thinking about running yoga classes designed specifically for children.'

Neither Helen nor Malcolm could find a reply to this. Helen wondered why she had asked. She looked down at the boys and felt none of the joy she had expected to feel. The excitement generated by the anticipation of the visit was smothered by the reality.

Daniel was adept at reading the direction of his mother's thoughts. He was not so adept at comprehending their cause. He didn't need to look at his wife to know that she'd be hurt by his parents' failure to show sustained interest in her. The visit was going just as he had expected it to.

As the silence lengthened it grew uncomfortable.

'No one would ask for you two as parents,' Daniel said quietly, looking at the surface of the coffee table. He glanced up at Malcolm and added, 'Some might, I suppose, not knowing you. Thinking they know you. But they don't know you.'

Malcolm sighed and sank back into the sofa while observing Helen closely. The expression on his wife's face pained him. With a hint of weariness, he said, 'The same old Daniel. Desperate to be a real boy.'

'Why shouldn't I want that? I know the difference now,' Daniel continued. 'I've seen what I've missed. My boys won't miss out. I won't refuse my sons the privilege of normality.'

Malcolm repeated the phrase to himself softly, 'Privilege of normality.'

'They'll miss out,' said Helen, sharply, 'just as you have. Not on the things you're referring to. Whatever your concept of *normality* is. But that doesn't matter. It really doesn't. Not these days. Perhaps not ever.' She had failed to convey her meaning. She blamed her audience. She didn't know how to talk to Daniel when he was being so wilfully obtuse. She lifted the plate of biscuits and held them out to the boys. Each took a chocolate one.

'I didn't want exceptional parents. I don't want exceptional parents. I want a normal mum and dad.'

'So you've said. An unvarying insistence since you were about fifteen. We were unequal to your tenacity. Normality, any kind,

7

was impossible in those circumstances. Every single thing we did had to be abnormal in your eyes. And then as soon as you could, you left. Moved to Edinburgh. We haven't seen you. Any of you. You would have spent more time with your dentist than us in the last twenty-five years. And now you expect *this* to be normal?' asked Malcolm, with a grim smile. He had been hopeful of some change after reading Daniel's article. The article had mentioned both Helen and Malcolm and spoke of the importance of having been brought up surrounded by books and conversation. How he had been a regular visitor to Brixton Library as a child and the impact this had had on him. But now it was obvious their shared history had been important to his argument and nothing more.

'You know what to expect when you visit us,' said Helen. 'I don't know why we come as such a shock time and time again. Isn't it time to accept us as we are?'

'No. And I don't think I will ever be able to convince you why I think this. But if you had been with us at Geraldine's family's Christmas, you would have *seen* what I mean. We all had such a marvellous time. There were twenty-five of us in total. A real Christmas, with a tree, tinsel, carols, terrible jumpers, presents and children squealing with delight.'

'It was lovely. I wish you'd been there,' said Geraldine, without conviction.

'Really lovely,' continued Daniel. 'I couldn't bring Geraldine and the boys here. They'd miss out on all that. It wouldn't be fair.'

'What did you two do for Christmas?' asked Geraldine.

'Salman Rushdie joined us for dinner,' answered Malcolm, drily.

'That's what I'm talking about! Who does that?' asked Daniel, standing.

'I'll help you get the bags,' said Malcolm, standing as well.

'We're not staying,' said Daniel.

Both Malcolm and Helen stared in disbelief. Daniel and his family had just driven seven hours and had been planning to stay a week.

'We've booked a hotel,' chimed in Geraldine. 'We've plans to see some old friends while we're here.'

'We've prepared the flat below,' said Helen. 'Separate entrance. You can come and go as you please.'

'You'll be entirely independent,' said Malcolm. 'Kitchenette, bathroom, two double beds. You'll have everything you need.'

'No, we won't,' said Daniel, shaking his head slowly. 'No, we won't.'

He bent down and lifted Samuel. The child was clutching a train engine. He rested him on his hip.

'Don't go. This is madness,' said Helen. 'How do you think any of this will get better?'

'We need to spend some time together,' added Malcolm with feeling.

Daniel looked around the room. He had seen the house before, just after they'd bought it and before they'd moved in. They'd spent money on it since then, he could see. Painted and decorated. While they'd talked he had noted the paintings, the ornaments on the shelves, the books, the two sofas, the sleek television, the coffee table. All of it appeared to be new.

'You lived in Brixton in the same squalid flat for fifty years – my entire life – and now this …' He carried the boy to the door. He looked directly at Helen, adding, 'You might have sold out earlier.'

Geraldine followed him to the door with Charlie, who wasn't very pleased to leave the train set. He started to resist and then cried. Helen picked up one of the engines and gave it to him. He wouldn't look at her, but took it all the same.

'Let them go,' said Malcolm, when he saw that Helen was following them out.

'I don't want them to go,' she said, visibly shaken.

'You think I do?'

They went to the window and watched the young family get into the car, buckle up and drive off.

'They had no intention of staying,' said Malcolm, placing his hand on Helen's shoulder.

'If we'd been different ...' she began, then sighed, knowing where their self-recriminations always led, and moved away from Malcolm and the window.

Malcolm followed.

Helen started clearing away the tea things.

'I'll do that,' he said, placing the cups and saucers on the tray.

Helen was left alone in the room. The train set needed to be put away. As she bent down to pick up the pieces, the phone rang. The handset was on the hall table.

'Hello.'

'Helen! I've been trying to get hold of Malcolm. He's not answering his mobile.'

'He's misplaced it. What's the matter, Trevor?'

'He's been longlisted for the Booker!'

'For *A Hundred Ways*?'

'Yes, Helen.'

'Hold on.'

Helen covered the mouthpiece with her hand and called down the hallway towards the kitchen, 'Malcolm. Malcolm!'

He appeared at the end of the hall.

'*A Hundred Ways*, by someone called Malcolm Taylor, has been longlisted for the Man Booker!'

# Chapter 2
# Past Engagement

'I'm serious, Amy.'

'You can't be.'

'I really am.'

He placed a little black box on the table.

'Oh, shit, you *are* serious.'

We were at the Sound Bar and had been drinking since 2 pm. It was now 6 pm and I was hungry. The bar was filling with suits coming from work. It was getting noisier and noisier. We had a booth to ourselves, thank god, but we had to sit close to hear each other.

Alan had won some big case, or something, I don't know, and had invited me to celebrate with him. I'd been avoiding his calls for about three months but needed to see his face again, so I had accepted his invitation.

You have to know that Alan is a candidate for the best-dressed man in London – he's always immaculately and expensively attired. And though he isn't strictly handsome, his self-confidence and his self-command go a long way to convincing you he is.

But we have a unique relationship. I see an Alan no one else sees. He would do anything for me. Anything. As a result, I have always treated him poorly. He is like a good Christian, always turning his head so I can slap each cheek afresh. It has become a habit, and I never tire of it. We can go months without a word and then pick up where we left off. Me taking and him giving.

And Alan had just proposed.

There was that little black box on the table.

'I am serious,' he said.

'Holy fuck.' I sat up straight.

I had been lounging in the curve of the booth with my leg draped over his knees. He moved the box closer towards me. His eyes were bright with fear and joy.

'Open it.'

'You've had this in your pocket all this time?'

'Open it.'

I picked up the shiny black box. It had weight. I tried to remember what we had been talking about before he had said, 'Will you marry me?'

I remember he had been stroking my bare thigh in the most chaste manner. It was nice. Virginal. The kind of thing he never, ever did. We were lifelong friends. It was the bravest he'd been. Most other men would have run their hand under my dress. But Alan was not like most other men.

But what we'd been saying before? A blank.

'There's a ring in here?' I asked, twisting the box in my fingers.

Alan laughed.

'Yes, I'm asking you to marry me. Open it.'

'Did you get me here under false pretences? I thought we were celebrating some boring law thing.'

'I've had this in my pocket for months, Amy.'

'I need a drink.'

I reached across the table and lifted the bottle of Bollinger out of the ice bucket. Instead of refilling my glass, I drank straight out of the bottle, but lifted it too high too fast and it flowed down my chin onto my dress.

'Dammit!'

'You're drunk!'

'You don't know what a drunk me looks like if you think this is drunk. This is Functional Amy. This is how I go to the office.'

'You go to the office covered in champagne?'

I smiled at him and said, 'Why are you doing this? Why now after all these years?'

He lifted the bottle to his lips, drank deeply then dropped it in the ice bucket upside down.

'Aren't you even going to open it?'

'A ring won't change my answer.'

'Just open it.'

I lifted the lid.

'Oh, god,' I said, with a gasp. I looked up from the ring and added, 'I was wrong. A ring can change my mind. It's gorgeous.'

'Put it on.'

'No. Alan. No,' I said, closing the lid.

'Why not?'

'For one, you're Alan. My *friend*, Alan. But more importantly, I couldn't possibly marry someone called Alan, could I? And then …'

I paused. I didn't really have my reasons defined.

He was unperturbed, and prompted, 'Is that all?'

'Isn't that enough?'

'Look at the ring again. I want you to take your time. I'll get us some more champagne.'

Before I could stop him he was up and navigating his way through the suits to the bar.

I opened the box and stared at his solitaire engagement ring. I even took it out and tried it on. He'd done well. I held up my hand to see how it looked. The band was platinum, but wasn't too heavy. The large round brilliant cut did its best to sparkle in the dim light. It had to have cost him £50,000. It was a statement of his intentions, if ever one was needed.

Though we'd been friends all our lives, he'd always had one peculiar quirk. He had always said that one day we'd get married.

As a child he'd said it. As a teen he'd said it. At university he'd said it. And yet in all that time we had never dated. We'd never even kissed. He'd never even tried to kiss me. While other 'friends' were dry-humping my leg as we watched TV, Alan never pestered me. Never tried to hold my hand, never put his arm around my shoulders. We were best friends and that was that. Nothing unusual except for the absolute confidence he had that one day we'd be married.

By the time he returned I had put the ring back in the box. I watched as he poured two more glasses of champagne.

'I saw you looking at it,' he said, as he handed me my glass. 'And saw you put it on your finger.'

'You were always so adamant we'd get married one day.'

'Yes, I've known for years. But a few months ago I dreamt you were married. I woke up heartbroken. And though I realised it had been a dream, I felt sick, a kind of vertigo, at the thought my dream could come true at any time. So I finally decided I had to do something about it. I bought the ring, but since then you've been impossible to contact.'

'You don't expect me to say yes, do you?'

'You have before.'

These three words stopped me in my tracks.

'What do you mean?'

'I've asked you before.'

'And I said yes?'

He nodded.

'We were engaged for three days,' he said.

He wasn't someone who made up stories.

'We were lovers for two of those days,' he added.

Lovers? Alan and me? This was madness. Mine, not his. He was as solid as a rock. I was the damaged one. But I never thought I was this damaged.

'When was this?'

'It was five years ago, after Max.'

After Max. After Max. After Max. 'Don't say another word. I don't want to talk about that.' I slid around the booth and stood up. 'I need to go to the loo.' I pushed my way through the suits, leaving Alan with his little black box.

When Max threw me out of our flat I was a mess. No, that doesn't quite describe it. I'm a mess now. That was far worse. I just wasn't. I was a negative. I no longer existed.

Max had been the guy. The One. We'd met at university. Nothing before, and nothing in the future, will ever be as good. And I had fucked it.

After crying until dawn on the street in front of the flat I'd shared with Max, I crawled into the forefront of Alan's life, completely disrupting it. I can't be more detailed, I don't have much recollection of that time, but I know Alan's girlfriend walked out on him not long after I moved onto their couch. So I suppose I progressed from couch to bed. Alan said I didn't speak, barely ate. I quickly shed all my happy fat. He found it impossible to keep me from drinking. No matter how closely he monitored me I always found something. He used to lead me to the bath and bathe me. He washed my clothes, dressed me, brushed my hair and force-fed me when he could. He was soon exhausted. And I cried. He said I cried for hours each and every day. No one came for me. No one enquired. My phone didn't ring or beep. I had betrayed Max, and thus, the world. The world would not forgive me, but Alan would.

I had to line up in the corridor to get into the ladies'. There were three girls ahead of me before the line continued through the door. The girl in front of me was sobbing silently to herself, her shoulders shaking, while she typed messages rapidly into her phone. Loud shouting and laughter was echoing out from the men's room, the door to which was held ajar by a lookout, who was turning away men who wanted to pee.

So what if Alan had taken advantage of the situation? He had always loved me. He had been a good friend. A much better friend to me than I had ever been to him. So what if he had proposed? So what if he had fucked me when I was at my most vulnerable? I didn't even remember it.

I'd probably be dead were it not for Alan. It wasn't that I was suicidal at the time; it was because I was numb. I was negligent. I could easily have drunk myself to death or drowned in the bath or stepped in front of a bus. The only hunger I had was for hunger. I was comforted by pain. All I wanted was to disappear. Alan's presence alone inhibited me.

So Alan told me later on. But you know, it all sounds plausible. I've been like that since. Not as bad, but I know how it goes. Especially the drinking. I've lost days to drink. Woken up beside people I'd never seen before. So it sounds like me.

I had fucked up big time. I'd betrayed Max, the one person I loved most in the world, and I was utterly traumatised. No wonder I'm sketchy on the details. I still wear the scars.

My phone vibrated.

*Did you leave?*

*No, there's a queue for the loo.*

But Alan and I had never lived together. I had stayed with him for a few weeks maximum. His declaration of love had probably helped me pull myself together. Like electric-shock therapy. No wonder I got the fuck out of there and didn't look back. Thank god for repressed memories.

Not that we didn't keep in touch. We kept in touch, but as friends only. We barely spoke of my breakdown. Just enough to get an idea of how shit it was. And never once in all that time did he ever mention the engagement or that he'd fucked me.

He knew it had been wrong.

The more I thought about it the more it disturbed me. It was all pretty creepy and fucked up. Better left forgotten.

When I returned Alan had an expectant air about him. The ring was still on the table. He looked up at me and smiled an old smile. One from years ago. When we were kids.

Still standing at the end of the table, I downed my glass of champagne.

Then I slid around the booth until I was right up against him.

I had to end this.

I leant in, my hand on his thigh, my mouth close to his ear, and, being a bitch, said, 'I'm your big love, aren't I?'

Alan's eyes narrowed a little. He thought he knew me well, but I could see he couldn't get a handle on my present shift in mood. I could see him sizing up the situation.

'You always have been.'

He was sincere, I saw at once. He'd matured a lot in the last few years. Life had thrown him accolades and with them responsibilities. He'd made a lot of money. He was ready for love. He was ready to settle down.

I slid back along the seat some distance from him, and looking him in the eye, said clearly, 'You're not my big love.'

'I know,' he said.

'And you're happy with that?' He took a sip of his sparkling water and then sighed. He said something I couldn't hear.

'What?'

'I'll never be happy with that.'

I didn't say anything.

He slid around to me and said, 'I'm worried about you.'

'You have no right to be.'

'You look terrible, Amy. I was shocked when you walked in. You're so thin. And there are dark circles around your eyes. And those eyes have no life in them.'

I didn't look terrible. I looked spectacular. The lighting was bad.

'I live hard. I don't want to live any other way.'

'I want to give you a home.'

'I wreck those.'

Alan smiled sadly.

He leant in closer and said, 'I've known you your whole life. I was there when your parents weren't. I've been there when you've been blissfully happy and when you've been desperately sad, when your mind has been ablaze with new ideas and when you've cried in frustration at not getting published. You're no angel. I know that. You're more often than not a fucking bitch. You've hurt me too many times for me not to know what you're capable of. I'm not an idealist. I'm no romantic. I'm much, much stronger than Max. I can take anything you dish out. I want you in my life and I will do anything to accommodate you.'

'I'd despise myself more than I already do if I even considered what you're offering.'

'Please consider it. A home. A base. A centre. With a man who loves you.'

This is what he had come to say.

I moved away from him again. 'You really know nothing about me. If you did, you'd know that what you're offering is poison to me. If I lay down with you, I'd never rise again.'

'You do talk a lot of crap, Amy,' he said, leaning across the gap I'd made. 'You're a brilliant writer who has sold herself short. You're brilliant, period. But you've taken the easy road, the coward's path, and you know it.'

'Fuck you.'

'I blame your success. It came too easily, and too early. You haven't had to work hard.'

'I work fucking hard.'

'Not just long hours. I mean difficult hours. Challenging hours. You should be exhausted at the end of the day. But you're coasting. Yet I bet you can't sleep. Am I right?'

'You know nothing about me.'

I moved. He followed.

'I know you. A brain like yours will eat itself alive if it isn't being fed properly. You'll go fucking nuts or you'll drink yourself to death. I'm probably the only person who will say all this to you, Amy. You aren't happy and if you don't change, you're heading for disaster. It's obvious to everyone but you. You can't live as you do without something giving out.'

It was a fucking intervention.

I shuffled out of my side of the booth, grabbed my bag and stood up. Alan watched me with a pained expression. I knelt on the seat on my side of the booth and stretched across the space between us to kiss him on the lips, lingering a moment longer than friends would, then pushed my way through the crowd and out of the bar. He made no effort to stop me.

I didn't need to hear any more of that crap. He was wrong, people *had* been telling me that shit for years. I didn't need to hear it from Alan.

I'm not reckless. I'm not self-destructive. I'm not a fucking coward. I'm busy.

# Chapter 3
# #AHundredWays

'Now we're joined by literary giant Malcolm Taylor, who was among the Man Booker longlisters announced yesterday. Welcome to the show, Malcolm.'

'Thank you for having me.'

'Listeners may not be familiar with your latest work, your new novel, *A Hundred Ways*. Can you tell them a little bit about it?'

'I'm not surprised they know nothing about it. Neither my agent nor my publisher wanted to publish it. It had a very short print run and no marketing budget whatsoever. And subsequently, it's only sold a few hundred copies. To quote Hume, it "fell dead-born from the press".'

'And yet you're longlisted for the Man Booker.'

'I'm as surprised as you are. My publisher must have submitted it as a joke. I don't know.'

'What's the novel about?'

'I wanted to write a book that, like Miller's, was "a prolonged insult, a gob of spit in the face of Art, a kick in the pants to God, Man, Destiny, Time, Love, Beauty".'

'Miller?'

'Henry Miller. *Tropic of Cancer.* That was a quote. I'm not a fan of Miller, but understand his disgust.'

'And your novel? What's that about?'

'*A Hundred Ways* isn't about anything. That's why no one wanted to publish it. It's just a tiny blood clot. That's all it is. And it's travelling along an artery towards our collective brain – culture. Now I just want to live long enough to see the surprise in the eye of mankind as the aneurysm strikes.'

'That's dark. What does the title mean? What did you have in mind?'

'Nothing. I don't know. It's certainly not something I recommend anyone read. Especially if they think they're happy. "A Hundred Ways to Disappoint a Reader"? And keeping in mind *A Hundred Ways* was written before Trump, "A Hundred Ways This World is Stuffed".'

'That's a hashtag for our Twitter followers: hashtag "ahundredways", what?'

'Twitter?'

'Don't worry, Malcolm. So you'd agree with the bookies then that you've an outside chance of winning.'

'No chance. The Booker judges have it all wrong. My wife's a far greater writer than I am but hasn't been longlisted since the seventies. Her last novel was one of the finest pieces of writing ever published. Sold fairly well but was ignored by the critics – they get bored of excellence. Generally, I'm not a fan of awards. Except when my wife is the recipient. Then I love them.'

'To sum up, your wife, Helen Owen, is the real writer in the family and your novel, *A Hundred Ways*, is a blood clot, a gob of spit and an outside chance of winning the Man Booker Prize? You've sold me, Malcolm. Where do I get a copy?'

'There's probably a pirated copy of the ebook you can download for free.'

'Thank you for joining us, Malcolm. Hashtag "ahundredways".'

'My pleasure.'

Malcolm put the phone down. Helen was staring at him with her mouth open. Then they both burst into laughter.

'I won't give any further interviews.'

'It's probably for the best.'

# Chapter 4
# A Good Hard Edit

'It just isn't any good,' I said while trying to step into my knickers. The curtains were drawn and it was dark. My toe became tangled in the elastic and I toppled forward onto the bed. I laughed but Liam was silent. He hated criticism of any kind. But it was true: the new book was fucked.

'Wait, she doesn't think it's me, does she?'

Liam's wife, Gail, had accused him of having an affair and was threatening to leave him again.

'Does she?' I repeated.

He didn't reply. Which was not unusual. He was a sulker. He sulked.

'Liam, you're going to have to speak.'

Nothing.

'I came here to work, but if you're too angry to work, I'll come back next week.'

Nothing.

'At the very least, take out your anger on my arse.'

I crawled across the bed and lifted the sheet. He turned his head away, but his cock rose as my mouth took him in. He always fucks me hard after I've been critical of his writing. So I try to be critical.

I released his cock.

'You'll have to start it again,' I said. 'It can't be salvaged.'

'That's twenty thousand words,' he said, still not looking at me.

'Uh-huh,' I agreed, playing with his cock some more. 'It's shit. This always happens when you go it alone.'

'Fuck you.'

'I mean it. Commercial fiction is like driving using a sat nav. You know where you're going and you take the most efficient route. These pages have no direction at all. You're writing too fast. You're forcing it. It's really, really shit. Too shit for me to fix and I've fixed some shit in my time.'

That did it. Suddenly I was flat on my stomach and Liam's cock was deep inside me. He gripped the back of my head and was pounding me with all of his might.

We've sold millions of copies using our system. We've both got rich. I don't want anything to change.

When we were done, and he'd agreed to scrap the pages and work with me, I said, 'I'll talk to Gail. It'll be fine.'

\*

Life moves way too slowly for me. It always has.

I knew what I wanted to do when I was in my teens. I wanted to write and I wanted to work with writers. There have been three constants in my life – books, clothes, sex. And champagne. Four constants. And money. Five constants. My parents are wealthy. But too wrapped up in each other to pay any attention to me. Boarding school and au pairs raised me. My parents are both still alive, but it wouldn't matter much to me if they weren't. We barely speak. I liked having money but I wanted my own. I hated using theirs.

But I didn't want to wait. Writing takes forever. Forging a successful literary career takes even longer. It took Jodi Picoult six novels to become financially independent. I'm not a patient person now, and at nineteen I was even less so. Even before I went to university, I believed I knew the techniques that would help commercially minded writers reach their potential. I enrolled in English because that's the way things work. I needed the degree to enrol in UCL's MA in Publishing.

Those were the dullest four years of my life. My courses were not demanding. I didn't need to work because my parents insisted on loving me through their largesse. In my spare time I read and analysed every genuine bestseller I could get my hands on. I was aching to get going. If it hadn't been for Max encouraging me to write my first novel, I think I would have dropped out. Besides, the simple idea that fast-tracked my career didn't occur to me until after I had my masters.

I had just done four years' apprenticeship at university and the only way into a job in publishing was an internship. They wanted me to work for free. I joined the queue, of course. It was mortifying. I wasn't even getting to the second-round interviews. It was my attitude, one of the interviewers kindly noted. I don't think she liked the way I dressed. I'm no shrinking violet. I love looking great. I want eyes on me. I suppose I looked too good for an intern.

After months of failure, I stopped applying and got myself a job in a cafe. I could no longer stomach accepting money from my parents. I always said I'd stop living off them as soon as I was earning. I wrote to them to let them know. While waitressing one day I noticed someone had left behind a half-read copy of a novel called *Torch* by Liam Smith. I knew it was meant to be a big book. I'd read a full-page puff piece about this 'hot, young debut author'. So when no one came back to claim it, I took it home and read it. I quickly discovered it hadn't been left behind accidentally. It wasn't good.

But it wasn't terrible; it had the right elements and an excellent hero. I re-read it. *Torch* had potential.

That's when I had my idea.

The front door to publishing was effectively closed to me. So I went through the back door.

Max was still working hard on his PhD, editing UCL's paper, *Pi*, and writing articles and essays at a ferocious rate, so my nights were free at the time. If I wasn't crying over the rejection slips my first novel was accruing, I was reading through the works of Mickey Spillane.

One night I planted *Torch* on a bag of rice and started to type it out on my laptop. As I typed it word for word, I wrote notes and alternative passages – some twenty pages long – that I would eventually use when I wrote a new version of the novel. The whole project took a few months. I was an amateur and learning as I went. I made some wrong turns but I was forging the technique I still use to this day.

When I was finished, Max read a few chapters on my laptop and said, 'It is what it is,' and handed it back. Which was enough for me. I printed it out and sent this new version of *Torch* to its originator, Liam Smith.

In my covering letter, I explained that it wasn't a bad book, really. His editor had let him down, that was all. He had the talent needed to be a successful writer. I asked him to read through my version and contact me if he thought I'd done a good job.

Luck was with me. The unsolicited package arrived on the very day Liam was realising his first book was sinking without trace. He contacted me. He was bewildered, he wrote. But interested. He'd just sent his publisher the manuscript of his new thriller, *The Night*. I asked to see it. We went back and forth on email for a bit. He didn't know if he should. He didn't know me. After a day of silence, when I thought I'd lost him, he sent it through. It was better than the first book. I had been right about him. He was a good writer. But he needed me.

Knowing his editor had the book, I raced through the rewrite. I didn't sleep. But then I rarely get through the night. I am a bundle of nervous energy. Two weeks later I had my version delivered to Liam by courier. I had been brutal. I had slashed at his work and written a great deal more myself. It must have been a ball-crushing experience for Liam.

I'd also crossed out Liam's name and had written in a new one, Jack Cade. Liam Smith was a shit name for a thriller writer, I wrote. And I'd also changed the name of the hero to that of the first book, Mark Harden. It was a good name for a kick-arse hero. He'd certainly done well with that. In the accompanying notes I wrote, 'If you want to be a star, keep the same central character.' Adding, 'To be honest, the hero in the second book was essentially the same guy just with a different name.'

As painful as it was for Liam to read all these changes – and it was *very* painful, he told me later – there was no escaping the truth. The book was better. I'd made it much, much better. Pacy. Powerful. Punchy.

I included a separate letter I'd had Alan, who was a law student at the time, help me write, in which I outlined our working relationship. If Liam agreed to my conditions, I would help 'Jack Cade' become the UK's bestselling thriller writer. I also wanted him to get me a job with his publisher. He wrote back saying yes to the first condition but that he had no way of getting me a job. I wrote back telling him what to do and enclosed a contract Alan's lawyer father had helped Alan and me draft.

He didn't send the contract back straight away. I think he was waiting to hear back from his publisher. When Liam's editor sent in her edits a few weeks later – a purely perfunctory effort, he saw at once – he was devastated. The tone of her correspondence with him was noticeably different from the upbeat, excited and encouraging tone used when editing the first book. Liam had no agent, so no one was on his side. I must have looked to him like a lifebuoy flung into a cruel sea. He rolled the dice and booked a meeting with the publishing director. He took with him my edits of both books and the edits of his editor. Though the meeting did not go well – Liam got a real sense of the publisher's disappointment in his sales – he was able to leave the manuscripts with her.

Two days later a call came through. Another meeting was scheduled: Liam, the publisher and me. It had worked. Liam sent through my contract, signed. Everything was going my way. But as I made my way to the offices of Morris and Robbins, I convinced myself that this meeting would go the same way as all of my internship interviews. That failure to gain a position had shaken my confidence. And though Max had spent the previous evening and most of the morning reassuring me that everything would go my way, I was retracing steps I'd taken only a few months before. I'd applied for an internship at Morris and Robbins and had been turned away. As I entered the lobby I felt physically ill.

I hadn't even met Liam in person. Until I walked into the publishing director's office he had no idea what I looked like or how young I was. There was no hiding his surprise or that of the publishing director, Maxine Snedden. I wasn't a child; I was twenty-three. I wasn't what they were expecting. There was a moment of awkwardness. But I took a deep breath. I could do it. The proof was in the meeting. I just had to hold my own. I already knew how good I looked. The faces on the tube told me that. (I must sound terrible, but there's no point mincing words. Looking good changes outcomes.)

The best thing about that meeting was the fact that it was happening. I had been right. What I had done to Liam's books made them better. So much better that the publishing director was talking about ways to republish *Torch* under the pseudonym Jack Cade before we'd even discussed terms. It was a strange business. But then publishing is a strange industry: a weird mix of business and pleasure, passion and pragmatism. Maxine wanted to change the setting and all of the character names, but she was willing to keep Mark Harden. Liam was momentarily crestfallen when she said it didn't really matter, as the book had sold terribly. They would pulp the remainder and start again.

Maxine was all in. She was convinced the books would do well. Liam freely admitted how much of the work had been mine.

Maxine agreed to two books a year under the new name, Jack Cade, starting with my edited version of *Torch*, under a new title, *Daytripper*, and, six months later, my version of *The Night*. Maxine tried to tie us down for the third book. But I demurred and Liam followed my lead. We'd be in a much better position to negotiate on book three if books one and two did well. We shook hands on our deal. She'd send through the contracts later that week.

We stood to leave. That's when I asked Maxine for a job. She was a little taken aback.

'I'm an editor at heart,' I said. 'You won't find a harder worker.'

In one stroke I had a job in publishing, a lucrative deal with a writer I'd turn into a bestselling author, and, though I didn't know it then, a lover.

# Chapter 5
# Retirement

Helen could hear music as she climbed the stairs. She'd just come inside after spending an hour or so in the back garden. It was in a terrible state. Neither she nor Malcolm had green fingers and both were unused to being responsible for a garden. Helen did what she could do, what looked obvious to her. She had weeded the flower beds. Some things she pulled up probably didn't deserve such a fate. But she wasn't versed in garden lore.

She was climbing the stairs to ask Malcolm to mow the lawn. It wasn't a vast expanse, by any measure, but Helen couldn't manage the hand-mower they had inherited on buying the house and hoped Malcolm would fare better. Otherwise she would have to add the expense of a gardener to her ledger, which she most certainly did not want to do.

As she ascended she could recognise the nasal whine of Bob Dylan. The music was coming from Malcolm's office.

She found Malcolm stretched out on the sofa on her right as she entered. On the floor in front of him were their old turntable and two large wood veneer speakers turned to face him. The power cords and speaker cables ran untidily across the floor. An open box containing LPs was beside the sofa. The plastic sleeve and cover of Dylan's *Hard Rain* was on the floor.

Malcolm's eyes were closed and his left foot was keeping time with the beat.

The boxes of books she'd asked Malcolm to empty a number of times were still piled in the middle of the room. The floor-to-ceiling bookshelves she'd had built for the purpose, which lined the walls, were still pristine in virgin white. His desk, which she had asked the removal men to set against the windows overlooking the street, was beyond the wall of boxes and almost out of reach.

Her office was perfectly ordered. She had made it a priority, as soon as they moved in, to set up her office the way she had always wanted. Her bookcases were filled with her book collection. Neatly arranged, ordered and beautiful. There was also a collection of her own novels, all in hardcover. Her desk was set up against the windows, too, with her laptop and everything she needed; photos of Malcolm and Daniel, the boys and even one of Geraldine sat proudly to her right, her work lamp to her left. She had a printer and paper. Seated at her desk, if she craned her neck, she could just see the treetops of the park. She'd even found space to set up a sitting area at the end of her office nearest the door, with a reading chair and lamp and sofa for visitors, or meetings with editors, journalists, and so on.

Malcolm made no secret of the fact that he had loved the office they had shared for close to fifty years in their flat in Brixton. He would mention this arrangement in interviews. Always starting with the fact that, soon after they had married, they had placed two non-matching second-hand desks back to back in the middle of their book-lined study and worked opposite each other most mornings surrounded by even more books, manuscripts, notes, newspaper clippings and cups of tea. While Helen had moved on from a typewriter to a word processor, to a desktop computer and then many ever-smaller laptops, Malcolm had persisted with his patient scraping of 2B pencils across cheap foolscap paper.

The flat had been Helen's before they met. Something Malcolm never seemed to remember. She had written in that room by herself.

In their new house they each had their own office. This was something Helen had dreamt of for years. A room of one's own. Necessity had kept them in that cramped shared office. That was all. To her the romance of writing together had passed with the cessation of the impromptu sex on the desk. And that had happened soon after the talking stopped. Which was in their first five years together. Till then, their writing had been almost collaborative, but very gradually, each of them found their own voice, and took very different writing paths. In shared silence, over fifty years they, and their writing, matured.

Angered by the chaos of Malcolm's room and his obvious disinclination to do anything useful, without speaking to him, Helen started to rip open the boxes of books and, with no regard for system or order, began to throw the books onto the shelves.

She was two boxes in before Malcolm said anything – or didn't say anything, but acknowledged her presence by pulling the turntable power plug from the wall. She stopped what she was doing and turned to him.

'Well, someone's got to do it,' she said.

'I like the room as it is. It speaks of impermanence.'

'Or sloth.'

'I'm retired. There is no sloth.'

'Writers don't retire, they die.'

'I found the old turntable and our LPs.'

'They weren't lost, Malcolm. They were in a box labelled "Turntable and LPs". And these are just some of the LPs, mostly yours. Mine are in my office.'

'Yours. Mine. What happened to ours?'

Helen turned back to the boxes of books and began stacking them on the shelves again, although without the passion she had shown earlier.

'I've been out in the garden weeding. But I can't manage the mower. Can you please give it a try?'

'I only mowed it a few weeks ago.'

'So you can do it?'

'I can do it. I don't want to do it. It almost killed me.'

'You need a bit of exercise.'

'I'm retired.'

'Stop saying that. You're not retired. You just need to keep writing. Something will come up.'

'I can't write here.'

'No one could write here. It's a mess. It distresses me just to see the state of this room. We just need to roll our sleeves up and get it sorted.'

Malcolm was still stretched out on the sofa; he hadn't moved a muscle other than to pull the plug.

'Help me put these on the shelves. Getting the boxes out of the middle of the room will help. You can arrange your books the way you like later.'

He didn't move. She ripped open another box. It was filled with copies of *A Hundred Ways* sent to him by the publisher. They never knew what to do with these extra copies they sent. It wasn't like they were going to send them out to friends and family. That would be presumptuous. In the past she used to sell them to a second-hand dealer she knew. But he had long gone out of business. The charity shops had killed the second-hand market. She pushed it towards the door and turned to open another box.

'Aren't you going to help?'

He didn't answer her.

Helen then realised that this was the longest conversation they'd had since Daniel and Geraldine walked out. The acknowledgement of this made her uneasy. Malcolm always had so much to say, normally. He was never idle. Never. Seeing him sprawled out on the sofa like this was unusual. Out of character, even. She realised she had avoided conversation with him because she had been waiting for something from him.

'Have you had time to read my manuscript?' She hated having to ask, she felt physically sick saying the words, but his silence on the subject had forced her into it. It had been weeks since she had given him the manuscript of version three. Which was the only title it had as yet: 'Version three'.

'No, I haven't found the time. Besides, my opinion isn't useful to you anymore. I don't understand your recent writing.'

'This new version isn't anything like the earlier version you read.'

'That's good to hear. I'll get to it soon. I promise.'

Helen had to leave the room. As she walked to her office she recognised the opening few notes of 'Maggie's Farm', which she silenced by shutting her door. The nausea she had felt returned. She collapsed into her reading chair and stared intently at the floor, trying to steady herself.

That was her husband in the other room, the man she had lived with and loved for nearly fifty years. She was sure of that fact. And yet, even knowing that, she was equally sure that somehow, he wasn't.

# Chapter 6
# American Psycho

I had just arrived back at the office. I had a ton of work to do and regretted that third glass of wine. As I walked through the open-plan area I noted the empty desks. Every day there seemed to be more. Great people were leaving Morris and Robbins now that it had been bought out by Seelenlos, and quite a few were taking their authors with them.

It was a little depressing but also an opportunity. I was taking on some great authors who were not ready to jump. Morris and Robbins was an old and respected name and still attracted a great deal of loyalty.

If only they knew what was really going on behind the scenes.

While at lunch I received a series of emails from the new publishing director, Julia O'Farrell, asking me to come and see her on a very urgent matter. She almost ruined my lunch with Kathy Lette.

I collapsed into my chair and woke my computer. I noticed it was already past four o'clock.

'How was lunch?' asked Valerie, my cubicle buddy. Valerie has been an editor for twenty-something years. She is as weird and wonderful as they come. She has three kids, her husband plays in a covers band and her hair is blue. It has been pink, then orange and then grey, but now it is blue. And she sometimes wears socks and sandals. Not always, just sometimes. She doesn't give a fuck.

'I'm in love,' I answered, swinging my chair around so I faced her. 'Kathy has absolutely no boundaries. I was laughing the whole time. I now want to marry her.'

I offered Val my phone so she could see the selfie I had taken with Kathy – our lips pursed and cheeks pressed together.

'Is she looking for a new publisher?'

'No, she wants me to jump ship. Her agent and publisher were there as well. They want me to work with her. I told them I could work freelance.'

'It's not really your thing, though, is it?'

'Everything is my thing.'

'But even you couldn't start taking on authors on top of the ones you're looking after here. We're all swamped as it is.'

'I already do.'

'Don't take on Kathy Lette. All the best commercial authors already think the sun shines out of your arse. Don't give me yet another reason to hate you.'

'You don't hate me, Val.'

'I fucking do. Everyone does. You're fucking gorgeous, rich as fuck, and,' she lowered her voice, and leant in towards me, 'you're fucking Liam Smith, the hottest man in publishing.'

I slapped her arm.

'On top of all that, you don't need to be here, but you stay. I mean, what's not to hate? If it wasn't clear that even with all these advantages you're fucking miserable, we'd have poisoned your coffee by now.'

'I love you, Val,' I said, standing. I took her face in my hands and kissed her forehead. 'I have to go and see Julia. Something urgent.'

'You poor thing. She came out here looking for you about two hours ago. She didn't look happy. I said you were lunching with an author.'

'Thanks.'

*

'You know, Julia,' I said, as I stood at the door of her office, 'yours is the only office in this place without books. Not a good look for the publishing director.'

The corner office was large and sparse – floor-to-ceiling windows took the place of two walls. Near the door were two very low white leather two-seater sofas facing each other, separated by a glass coffee table. No ornament. The whole look was an homage to the eighties. Or *American Psycho*. On the far side of the room, facing the door, Julia sat at a steel-framed glass-topped desk. The desk was empty but for her open MacBook, a lean-looking printer and her iPhone. The only thing missing was a generous splattering of blood.

Even though she must have known there were no books in the room, Julia glanced around her office, pausing briefly to look out at the view.

'You do have a spectacular view of London.' I sat on one of the two uncomfortable moulded plastic chairs in front of her desk. 'But so do the offices above and below yours. I don't know what they do in those offices. This one is a publishing house. Some examples of the trade wouldn't go amiss. The least you could do is display a few of Liam's books. His sales helped pay for the view.'

Julia ignored all of this. It was her best defence against my shit and she knew it.

I resented being summoned to her office. She was a corporate interloper. She wasn't publishing. But she said she needed to see me face to face. I tried very hard only to have dealings with Julia via email. And she normally respected that. She hated me as much as I hated her.

Still trying to get a rise out of her, I said, 'You don't even look like a publishing director. You're management. Entirely interchangeable with management from any other business. Your predecessor, Maxine, however, was pure publishing. You could see it from a mile away. Tough as nails, too.'

Not a flutter.

Julia tapped her keyboard. The printer spat out two sheets of paper. She motioned for me to reach for them. I did.

Well, this was interesting.

In the middle of the first page was a name and address, with a helpful map marking the route from the tube.

'Helen Owen?'

Julia nodded.

I looked at the second page. Julia had put together a simple equation. In short, if Helen Owen didn't sell a fuck load of copies of her next book, Julia would have a substantial hole in her budget. Something the new German owners of Morris and Robbins would not want to see.

'May I have that?' Julia asked. I handed her the second sheet of paper. She glanced at it and then tore it into tiny shreds.

'This is why I'm here,' said Julia, placing the paper in the bin at her feet. 'To clean up messes like this.'

'What do you want me to do about it? Helen Owen isn't my sort of thing. To be honest, I thought she was dead.'

'Not dead. Not yet. I don't know what my predecessor was thinking, but the deal they gave her was ludicrous. What's worse, she's late. She was due to deliver ten months ago. It was another of Maxine's indulgences. Now it's my problem.'

'Can't you cancel the deal?'

'I'm within my rights to do so. But I believe the advance has been spent. If we were to move to get it back we would be sending two of this country's most revered writers bankrupt.'

'Two writers?'

Julia smiled. 'Her husband. Malcolm Taylor.'

'I'd forgotten. He's still alive, too?'

She nodded. 'He's just been longlisted for the Booker.'

'Oh, yeah.'

'As you know, Amy, publishing isn't what it was. Tesco and Amazon have squeezed us. The margins are no longer there. We need to ...'

'Yada, yada, yada. Get to the point.' None of this was news to me.

'We can't afford to absorb the loss of Helen Owen's advance. And we can't really afford the publicity that would be generated if we were seen to be hounding national treasures to their grave to recover that advance – though we will if we have to. To be honest, the lawyers are already drawing up the paperwork, but the best solution for everyone is still getting her to deliver.'

'I vaguely remember people talking about the deal. I wasn't involved in the acquisition though. I don't think I read anything. I really know nothing about it. Val might. I've never read her, either. Who was her editor?'

'Clarissa Munten? Recently retired.'

'Jesus.'

'You know her?'

'Everybody knows her. She actually wrote the book on editing. Set text at uni. You knew that, right?'

'Not everyone had the privilege of going to university.'

I was struck by this. I stared at her in silence for a bit, thinking about my struggle to get into publishing. 'What are you doing here? I mean, how did you get through the door in the first place? Publicity? Sales? Postroom? You baffle me. Surely people like you make much more money selling arms in the Middle East or overpriced pharmaceuticals to cancer sufferers – why the fuck did you choose publishing?'

Julia smiled again and said nothing.

I had more right to be sitting where she was. She was a usurper. God, I wanted to smash that face in. I'd slap her Mac closed and use that. Make sure the rounded corner knocked a few teeth out.

I looked around the room to calm myself. 'Publishers used to drink. It was a thing. Something you could rely on. Do you have anything hidden in a drawer or cabinet?'

'If I can ask you to concentrate for another minute or two ... Helen Owen? Will you take her on?'

'Why me?'

Julia was silent. I stared at her impeccably manicured hands as I tried to work out what was going on. Julia wasn't telling me everything.

'Are you telling me she's had no M&R support or contact since the takeover?'

'None that I'm aware of.'

'Is there anything to look at? A partial or a few sample chapters?'

'We don't have anything.'

'Surely Maxine based her offer on something?'

'My understanding is that there was a complete manuscript.'

'Was ...'

'The original manuscript has gone missing,' Julia admitted.

'You're shitting me.'

'We believe Maxine took it with her, but she denies the accusation.'

'She's with Penguin now.'

'Don't bother. We've all tried. She's very bitter.'

'And Helen Owen herself?'

'Well, according to Maxine's brief handover notes, Owen grew dissatisfied with the original manuscript and went off to rewrite it.'

'And Maxine let her?' I asked, incredulous.

'All of this coincided with the takeover. Maxine was fighting for her own survival. You remember what it was like.'

'Like the opening scene of *Star Wars*.'

Julia stared at me blankly.

'You were Darth Vader, she was ... doesn't matter.'

'Just meet with her and have a look at what she's writing.'

'You don't get it. She'll take one look at me and slam the door in my face.'

'Why would she do that?'

'I don't know … Maybe because she's like Doris Lessing and Iris Murdoch. And I help write explode-y action books.'

'I heard you did some moonlighting for Jeffrey Archer.'

'Different league. Helen Owen sits on the shelf with A.S. Byatt, Edna O'Brien and Margaret Drabble, and all of those other eminent women I haven't read enough of. And you haven't heard of. The woman is …'

'Desperate. I've spoken with her. I made it plain that she would have to work with you otherwise her life would become complicated.'

'Great. Brilliant. Good work. That's much better. Now I'll turn up there looking like a bloody bailiff.'

'I was courteous but firm.'

'Wait, did you make it clear you were her publisher? Over the phone you can sound like an automated message service.'

A slight grimace. Got her.

'Have you been drinking?' she asked.

'I've just come back from a very long lunch with Kathy Lette so of course I've been drinking.'

I don't think that was the answer she expected. For a moment she looked embarrassed. She gathered herself.

'Kathy Lette, the funny Australian? She's not ours, is she?'

'No, Penguin want me to go and work for them. Probably at Maxine's urging. She knows how good I am.'

This stopped Julia completely. I don't know if she was considering the point I wanted her to consider, that I might go and work elsewhere, or whether she was counting my misdemeanours – drinking, long lunch, fraternising with the enemy.

'Exactly. You're in demand. They need you and I need you. Helen needs you. Because you're good at this. This is what you do best. You've done this sort of thing before. Find out what Helen's writing. Steer her in the right direction. You've a talent for turning disasters around.'

'I've never done this sort of thing with the likes of Helen Owen, Julia. How the hell do you expect me to help Helen Owen? I don't think you know how this all works. Valerie would be better suited to this.'

'None of Valerie's books sell anywhere near the numbers your books do.'

'That's because she works with more literary authors. That's what I'm trying to tell you.'

'Go see her. Do that for me.'

'Can't do it,' I said, while deciding I could.

'Sure you can. What do you need? A pay rise?'

I shook my head. I needed nothing from Julia and she knew it. She was only my boss on paper. That's what made these meetings so fun.

'Who do you want to work with?'

'Now, you're really stretching. What influence do you have with any of our authors? I bet you couldn't name five of them without referring to your Mac.'

Nothing. At least she was consistent. She'd be repeating a mantra – *Never rise to Amy's taunts. Never rise to Amy's taunts. Never rise to Amy's taunts.*

'Julia, you do know that this is just a phase publishing is going through? Part of a cycle? The wheel will turn. The money men will discover their mistake again. They always do. Publishing needs risk and genius and authenticity and it needs a bit of madness, too. They'll come round and you'll be turfed out and someone more suited to the job will take your place. Someone who can read.'

*Never rise to Amy's taunts. Never rise to Amy's taunts. Never rise to Amy's taunts.*

It was after five. To get out of the office I said, 'I'll do it. I will visit her. I'll take a look at what she's written so far. But that's all I'll commit to today.'

'I won't accept a boring literary novel. I need a Jojo Moyes.'

I sat in silence a long time. I just couldn't get a hold of the idea. Julia was asking me to turn Helen Owen into Jojo Moyes. It didn't seem possible. Jojo was a friend of Liam's. I had met her a couple of times and had read and enjoyed all of her books. She was a good writer. A clever woman. Very friendly and likeable. But she would never win the Booker. Helen Owen was a writer whose name always came up when people were betting on possible Nobel laureates. The fucking Nobel. What if Helen Owen really was writing something brilliant and I shaped it into a Richard and Judy pick? If sin still existed in publishing, that would be one.

'Maxine wouldn't make a substantial offer for a book with zero commercial viability,' I said.

'The financials of M&R tell a very different tale. If you can't do Jojo Moyes, I'd settle for Kate Morton or that other historical writer. The Tudor one.'

'Philippa Gregory or Hilary Mantel?'

'Yes.'

'Okay. That's a much larger target on which to land this book. Somewhere between Jojo Moyes and Hilary Mantel.'

'I don't want brilliant. The market can't stomach brilliant. Tesco won't touch it. Think Richard and Judy pick, not a Booker Prize longlister.'

'You're revolting.'

I got up and made my way to the door. Then I stopped and returned to the desk.

'Julia, I hope you know I only say mean things because you're everything that's wrong with the world. It's nothing personal.'

I was at the door when Julia said, 'You say mean things because you can.'

# Chapter 7
# Google 'Helen Owen News'

I swung by my desk to pick up my bag on leaving Julia's office. Walking along the corridor, I took out my phone, googled 'Helen Owen news' and found the *Guardian* article at the top of the results. I'd started reading before I hit the lifts.

**Books: A life in ...**
**Helen Owen: A Path Through the Moral Minefield**

*Iesha Koury*
*Thurs 21 Sept 2015 06.50*

*As a new generation of women discovers her work, the author of* The Uninvited Guest *stops to ask, why?*

*London isn't in the best humour on the morning I've arranged to meet literary lion Helen Owen for coffee. The heavens open as I emerge from Charing Cross Station. I dash across Trafalgar Square but am wet through by the time I reach the sanctuary of the National Gallery. It is ten past eleven before I look at my notes to discover I was meant to meet Helen outside the National Portrait Gallery. I rush around and find Helen in the foyer. She too has* been caught in the rain. By the time we reach *Pret A Manger* across the road, we are both a bit of a mess.

With a mug of tea before Helen and a warm coffee in my hands we are soon chatting amiably enough. Helen shows some surprise when I let her know I've been reading her for years. She asks me my age and in the same breath says it is none of her business.

'Twenty-four,' I say, realising too late that perhaps *Pret A Manger* hadn't been a great idea. Helen doesn't look very comfortable. The rain is driving tourists in and the noise is building.

'When I was your age I had a real terror of the old. But the elderly were different then.'

'How so?'

'They were the product of a culture that no longer existed. I was in my twenties in the sixties and the elderly in my life then had been born in the nineteenth century. Their formative years were largely spent in the pre-war era. The period someone like E.M. Forster writes about. I was surrounded by people who remembered that life. They'd lived it. And made judgements based on that experience. From Queen Victoria and the horse and carriage and on through two world wars, the general strike and all that. Lucy Honeychurch might have been my elderly neighbour. Forster himself died in 1970! What changes to see in one lifetime. They were an entirely alien generation. Refugees of a kind. Stateless. Where had their world gone? I was the product of a completely new world: TV, motorways, rock'n'roll music, Sputnik and the welfare state. I couldn't even talk to the elderly. I suppose that generation might have been less frightening if my own grandparents had been alive. But all four had died young.'

As Helen speaks and warms to her subject, a light comes into her eyes, her whole face grows animated. She's taller than I expected, and her frame larger, though she hasn't an unwanted ounce of flesh on her. Her hand gestures remind me of my time in Italy. They echo her speech.

It becomes clear as we chat that Helen is genuinely surprised by my interest in her. Because I am a young woman. But on reading her early novels, I tell her, I am not struck by the differences between her female protagonists and myself, as much as I'm struck by the similarities. Their concerns – education, career, family and love – are mine. And the obstacles thrown in their path are the same as those thrown in mine – self-doubt, money, the patriarchy.

'Which just goes to show that the optimism of the sixties and seventies was premature. Not enough has changed. My books should, if progress is being made, be as alien to you as the lives of Forster's heroines were to me. Though a century apart, the novels of Forster and Austen have more in common than Forster and even, say, someone like Hemingway, who was his near contemporary. The first half of the twentieth century saw rapid change in nearly every facet of life. The second saw changes, but not so quickly, or profound. They were changes of outward appearances, largely.'

But there have been changes. Women in Western countries do have greater freedoms. And then there's the internet. I ask her what effect the internet has had on her writing.

'I don't leave the house. I used to make trips to the library. There was always something I had to look into. The library was my second home. Especially when beginning a novel. Now I just google everything. The worst effect is an obsession with being absolutely correct in every detail. It slows me down, but also deadens my writing. Malcolm is always running red pencil through these passages in my writing. He bans me from the internet when I'm revising my work. He doesn't appreciate how difficult this is for me. He is largely unplugged. Writes with a pencil. Which is probably the only thing he had in common with the late Jackie Collins.'

The 'Malcolm' she refers to often in her conversation is her husband, the writer and critic Malcolm Taylor. His 2014 book of essays on the modern London novel, The Knowledge, is seen as the new benchmark of modern literary criticism. Over the last *twenty years, Malcolm and Helen have wielded great influence over English literature and over the new generation of writers. But Helen says recent talk of them being a power couple couldn't be further from the truth.*

*'Authors are the least powerful group in the book industry. A few may get to throw their weight around, because they've sold millions of copies, but they're a rare breed. And they never throw their weight around in a way that benefits other authors. Most authors, at least the ones I've met, have no power and do as they're told. Very few only write; most supplement their writing with other work. It's a perilous existence with little financial reward.'*

*And yet, recent news would suggest otherwise. For Helen has been seduced away from her long-time publisher, Sandersons, by Morris and Robbins for an undisclosed sum, rumoured to run to seven figures.*

*She laughs when I repeat the sum. 'If only! What publisher would take such a risk on a writer with one foot in the grave? I've had a reasonably successful career. But my editor says with each new novel my readership drops because they're all dying off!'*

*Not all, I assure her. More and more young women are drawn to her writing.*

*'I've been very fortunate. Many of my novels are still in print, and from time to time they include me in a set of modern classics. Not bad. But neither Malcolm nor I have ever sold in the US. So we've never hit the big time like our friend David.' [David Cornwell, the author John le Carré.]*

*However, Helen and Malcolm recently moved from the three-bedroom flat they shared for the last fifty years in Brixton, and where, famously, they shared an office and wrote at desks facing each other, to a terrace in West London, so there might be some truth to the rumour after all.*

*I asked Helen whether she was proud of the work she had been able to produce over a long writing life.*

*'Yes, very. I'm not going to be meek and mild at this late stage.
I never set out with a plan. If a young person chose to read through
my novels I'd hope they'd prove useful. They're not going to help
them put together a piece of IKEA furniture. But I've spent so long
wandering in the moral minefield of modern life, I know many a
safe passage through. And that can be helpful, I think. Why make
mistakes you can avoid? What good is fiction if it doesn't allow you
to practise at living life?'*

*Not wanting to end our conversation, even though Helen is
showing some small signs of impatience with our surroundings,
I ask what she is currently working on.*

*'The book for Morris and Robbins. To be frank, I've lost my
way a bit. I'm in the dark with my arms stretched out taking
tentative steps. Somewhere in the darkness is a story. I hope.'*

*★ Postscript: Subsequent to this interview, German publishing
titan, Seelenlos, bought Helen Owen's new publisher, Morris and
Robbins.*

\*

My confidence in being able to turn Helen to more commercial
fiction had plummeted with the lift.

Now I was sitting on a lounge in the lobby of the building,
staring at my phone.

I called Julia.

'They gave Helen Owen a million fucking pounds?!'

There was silence on the other end.

'Hello? Julia? Just tell me. It makes one hell of a difference.'

'Yes. But it wasn't a million. It was two million.'

'Jesus! Why?'

'That's what I hope you'll find out.'

'Who knows you're assigning her to me? Julia? Julia?!'

The phone call was over.

# Chapter 8
# Leather Notebook

Malcolm had been sitting at his desk in his office for hours. It was almost four in the afternoon and he was listening to the grumbling of his belly. Helen was out for the day and he had not eaten lunch. He had been sustained by the cup of tea he had made at eleven.

On the desk was a large leatherbound notebook, opened to a page partly covered with his own clear printed script in pencil. The first writing he had attempted in the new house.

The notebook was very fine. Aspinal of London. The leather was nice to hold in the hand, to run his fingers across. Though it was many years ago now, he remembered that the box it arrived in included a printed card that read: *Happy birthday, Dad. Love, Daniel and Geraldine.*

At the time, he had been surprised by his son giving him a notebook of this kind. He must have known that Malcolm always wrote on loose sheets of foolscap paper. For notes, he always carried a spiral-bound pocket notepad and a pencil stub. These weren't recent innovations, these were lifelong habits forged in his teenage years when he first started to write seriously.

Accompanying the grumbling of his stomach were Malcolm's doubts. In order to make use of Daniel's present, he was consciously abandoning the method of sixty-something years of writing. The notebook wouldn't stay open when laid on its spine and had to be held open with his left hand. The leather binding and three hundred or so pages lifted his wrist an inch off the desk, which caused him to alter the habitual slouch and made him sit further back in his desk chair. The paper in this notebook, though of a much better quality, was coarse in comparison to his cheap foolscap. The pencil scraped across the page. And finally, the paper wasn't lined.

But he wanted to use it. It was from Daniel.

Besides, the house wouldn't let him go back to his old ways. The foolscap paper had remained conspicuously empty of pencilled words.

The leather notebook would break the hoodoo. It was Daniel's notebook he was to fill. He would write for Daniel. Not for Helen, as he had always done until now.

Helen had led him to rediscover the notebook. That day when she had tried to encourage him to empty the boxes of books in his office, Malcolm had, after she'd left, roused himself and, feeling equal parts resentful and repentant, had thrown more of his books onto the shelves: his battered Penguins bought cheap second-hand, tattered Everyman's Library editions, anonymous coverless pocket hardcovers, his Virago Modern Classics, the many hundreds of books, all in poor shape, all read before he got his hands on them. Books with a past.

On discovering the expensive leather notebook in one of the boxes, he had stepped back to look at his work but was saddened to discover his much-read books looked shabby on the pristine white shelves. Almost as shabby as the reading chair he lowered himself into. Helen had tried to throw the chair out before they moved. But he had clung to it tenaciously. Rubbed raw in some places and stained and ripped, the chair was a part of him that could not be discarded. He could not remember the chair's precise origin and he did not recall it ever being new; he supposed it had come to him second-hand. It had been in the corner of their shared office for at least thirty years, maybe more. It had been the one thing in the flat that was entirely his own.

Helen was right though. In his new office it looked out of place and, like the books, distressingly dilapidated. She had suggested getting it reupholstered but the idea had distressed him, so she had covered it with a rug.

Malcolm felt she should have waited until he was seated in the chair before she covered it with the rug. He felt as the chair and the books did, completely out of place in this new house. He too was rubbed around the edges and stained. This house was too beautiful, too clean, too expansive. And white. So white. He was a stain here. A living stain. He was almost eighty years old. He'd lived in the one place for fifty years. Fifty years. The move had been a colossal error of judgement.

The foolscap remained in the desk drawer. That Malcolm was dead to him.

Where the notebook had looked entirely out of place in their Brixton flat, it was now the only thing in Malcolm's possession that truly suited this new house.

This white purgatory.

The grumbling of his belly continued. He lifted the pencil and wrote on. This first day of writing had been productive; he'd filled page after page, but something was different. It wasn't the notebook or Daniel. It wasn't the strange light of being longlisted.

It was this: it was more than fifty years since he had written alone.

In the flat, even when Helen was out, she was there opposite him. Her papers, teacup, books and silly little knick-knacks held her place. Now she had her own office across the landing. She was gone. Everything was different.

Because of this, Malcolm had avoided writing for months, the longest he had gone without since he first started writing. He couldn't write alone, that would be admitting something. That would make it real.

He flicked through the pages he had just written and then closed the notebook.

It was real now.

# Chapter 9
# Intermission

Who wants to be woken up at 2 am by the buzz of an intercom? The street was so perfectly silent, I could hear the buzzer going off in the fourth-floor flat above. I pressed it a third time. I'm sure half the residents in the building heard it before their neighbour did.

'Oh, fuck, it's you.'

I blew him a kiss, down the camera lens. It fogged over. The street door clicked open and I pushed through it and climbed the four flights to his door. It was open. I closed it behind me, crossed the tiny flat and found tattoo boy back in bed. Stripping naked I climbed in beside him. The flat was freezing. He rolled away from me and I spooned him. He was so warm. He groaned as I put my cold hands on him.

'Sleep,' he growled.

Not a chance. He knew it, too. When my hands found their way down to his cock, it was rock hard.

\*

'Don't you sleep?' asked tattoo boy, after his alarm woke him at six. I was sitting at his kitchenette bench eating his cereal. I'd wrapped my naked self in his duffle coat.

'Nope. Too much going on.'

He didn't say anything, just stared at me with sleepy eyes.

'Hey, tattoo boy, why is it so fucking cold in this place?'

'Josh.'

'Really? Josh? Doesn't suit you. I like tattoo boy.'

His drowsy smile seemed to say he didn't care what I called him.

'It's fucking freezing!'

'Can't afford heating.'

I put the cereal down and grabbed my handbag. I dug around for a bit and found what I was looking for. Taking off the rubber band I pulled out a few hundred pounds and scrunched them up. I threw them at him.

'I'll be back for more of that cock of yours, so next time I expect some fucking heat. All right?'

'I'm your little whore, am I?'

'If you want. I don't care how you think about it or me.'

Josh didn't answer this but he straightened out the notes, smoothed them against the mattress and put them under the pillow.

'I live on champagne, too. So make sure there are always a few cold bottles of Bollinger in the fridge.'

He looked at me warily then shook off the covers and, naked, went off to the bathroom. I heard him pee and then shower. In five or so minutes he came out looking as he had when he left. There was no getting away from it. He was a perfect specimen.

'I didn't expect to see you again,' he mumbled, as he started to dress.

'I didn't expect to want to see you again.'

'You do this sort of thing often?'

'All the time.'

'I bet no one has ever left you out on the street.'

'Not yet.'

As I watched, he put on a pair of utterly filthy jeans, two unwashed T-shirts and a stained Nike hoodie, then proceeded to pull on thick woollen socks and dust-covered work boots.

'Will you be here when I get back?'

'No.'

I took off his duffle coat and handed it to him. He smiled broadly as I stood naked before him. He took his time to get the jacket on. All the while his eyes were on mine.

'You're the devil.'

I nodded. 'What time do you need to be at work?'

'Seven.'

'You can be late.'

*

I didn't leave the flat. There was no point. I'd be back that night for more. For an hour after he left I lay on his bed utterly fucked. When I finally moved I shuddered. All of my body felt electric. And it wasn't the fuck. That had been quick. He probably made it to work on time. It was how we fucked. Rabid beasts. He is so strong. He pounded me. Held me down and gave it to me. And the noise we made. I was screaming. And he roared as he came.

Then he did up his pants and left. Not a word. Not a kiss. Ruined me. Ruined. So I stayed.

This wasn't the whole truth. I mean, he knew how to fuck. And his scent was delicious. And those abs. But would I have stayed if I hadn't had somewhere else I had to be, somewhere I didn't want to go?

I wrapped the blanket around me and wandered around his flat. I looked in drawers. Flicked through an unread copy of Tolstoy's *War and Peace*. I masturbated. Ate another bowl of cereal. I opened his laptop. Then closed it. I showered.

I climbed back into bed and waited for him to return.

I was asleep when he returned. I awoke to the sound of the shower. I lay sleepily while he washed the day off him. He came to me naked and kissed me. Slipping under the covers, he held me, lay on me. He kissed me for so long I wasn't sure when his cock had slipped into me. I hadn't been kissed like that for years. These were teenage kisses, so urgent and full, then tender and lingering. And the gentle thrusts of his hips driving his cock deep. He was killing me. He knew what he was doing. When he kissed his way down between my legs I was completely undone. He toyed with me, too. Took me to the edge and retreated. When I escaped his game I came so hard that I almost suffocated him holding his head to me like a madwoman. Afterwards, he stood at the end of the bed and watched the final throes overtake me. But he wasn't done. And he was too strong for me to resist. He flung me over on my stomach and lifted me to my knees.

*

He wasn't doing anything special. This wasn't imaginative sex. I wasn't being tested. Or shocked. He wasn't someone's husband or boyfriend. It had none of the thrill of the unfamiliar or the deviant. I didn't wake up beside him in that state of aroused disgust I'd become familiar with. But here I was sitting at the end of a bar like an overprotective, jealous girlfriend watching him work. Truth be known, I couldn't let him out of my sight. So I'd followed him to his second job. It was nice to pretend to like someone. To experience the sex you get when you first fall for someone without falling for them. He reminded me of boys from the village I'd climbed over the walls of my boarding school to smoke with and kiss.

The bar was in the West End. It looked like a private bar but wasn't; the advertised prices kept out the tourists, at least those on a budget. Posh but not. Josh was kept busy enough, but it wasn't hectic. The bar work wasn't as regular as the labouring and he took what he could. He'd been saving for a trip. He liked the tips. He got generous tips. I said I bet he did.

'Barman, another,' I demanded. He made his way down to me. The way he carried himself spoke of the power of his body. He had the grace of a gymnast. Or a dancer. He was a chameleon.

He was the epitome of a labourer this morning. And now, in this environment, he looked like a rich kid trying to prove he could look after himself. The tats escaping from the edge of his rolled-up shirtsleeves just added to his appeal.

He poured another glass of champagne and placed it on the bar before me. Looking at the rising bubbles, I was reminded of Alan and his ring.

*You can't live as you do without something giving out,* he'd said.

I grabbed Josh's hand and stuffed £200 into it, saying, 'Keep the change, cutie.'

He folded the two hundred neatly and pocketed it. He served another couple of customers and then made his way down to me. Finding my glass empty, he refilled it.

'What time do you get off?' I asked.

'One, but I have a break in ten minutes,' he said with a grin.

The confidence of that grin. He was going to fuck me in the back lane, or toilet stall. I grabbed the edge of the bar. The way he was looking at me. I had to look away.

*

'You know I haven't had a regular, everyday thought since I climbed into your bed the other night? I've been ignoring work. I haven't recharged my phone. It's been dead the whole time. I bet they've been trying to contact me. I've been putting off doing something I don't want to do. The work will be piling up. But I don't care about anything. It's Friday, right?'

If it was, I had missed my Thursday meeting with Liam. First time I could remember doing that without letting him know.

Tattoo boy was getting changed again. He hadn't slept properly in days. He worked so much. He had so few hours for sleep and play. And I wouldn't let him sleep. I was rested. While he worked I slept or read *War and Peace*. At least I made him skip one night at the bar. Less for him than for me.

'I'm shattered,' he said and yawned. 'Amy, you've been wearing the same clothes for days. We'll go to your place tonight? You can get some clothes.'

'I don't need them. I'm staying here. I'm never leaving your bed. I don't need clothes. Anyway, I have all of yours. I want you to get me a job as a labourer.'

He laughed at that. 'You can stay here as long as you like. But you have things to do. You need to get back to your life.'

'I don't care about my job.' And I immediately knew this was a lie.

'But we need to rest, don't we?'

'We do. You do.' I reached out and touched his abs as he put his T-shirt on.

I knew I should have left him alone. He was exhausted. I should get back to my life, such as it was.

I could just come clean and tell him if he stayed with me he need never work again. I could buy him. Look after him like a man might keep a mistress. Keep him on call. On a retainer.

He had pocketed all the money I'd given him without comment. Perhaps he didn't mind being bought.

But I knew myself too well. This would never last. The world of fuck is not a place of permanent settlement. I'd have to talk seriously with him sooner or later and what would I find? I didn't want to know his opinions on anything.

I had to be real. I already missed my work. I couldn't put off meeting with Helen Owen indefinitely. There was no end to this other than me waking up one morning bored to death of him. This wasn't love. I know love. This wasn't it. This was a passing need. Lust, at best.

As soon as the spell broke, I'd be gone. Where would he be then?

This thought did it for me. The spell was broken. The fuck-fest was over.

I had one last question. 'Why do you have a copy of *War and Peace*?'

'It was a gift.'

As soon as he left for work, I got dressed, grabbed my things and left. I thought about leaving the rest of my cash with him, but then decided not to. I'm not completely heartless, I did give him something. I left my phone number on the title page of *War and Peace*.

Not that he would ever find it there.

# Chapter 10
# Brighton 1979

Helen was still unused to the sounds of the house. She lay in bed and listened. She'd been dreaming. The other life still lingered. The whirring noise that had woken her was not repeated. Street noise. House silence. Was it already past seven? Malcolm was evidently up and about as his side of the bed was empty. She glanced at the alarm clock. Six. She wasn't sure whether the noise that had roused her was of Malcolm's making or the neighbours'. It had sounded like some sort of motor and she couldn't reconcile this with her knowledge of Malcolm's morning customs. She might have dreamt it.

Now that she was awake there was no trying to get back to sleep. Those days had long gone. She was now lucky just to sleep through the night. She took her time getting out of bed, pausing to place herself in the week. Wednesday. Read through manuscript, again. Visit Waitrose. Hair appointment tomorrow. Then she rose in slow stages. Covers aside. Lifted torso. Deliberate swing of the legs.

Although it was August, the room felt cold. She put her feet into her slippers, stood sighing, shuffled forward, lifted her dressing gown off the hook on the back of the door and made her way to the loo. Out on the landing she paused to listen. The house was still and silent.

When she found herself in the kitchen a few minutes later, she paused again. She couldn't recall whether she had washed her hands after going to the loo, or what she had been thinking about between the landing and kitchen. As she aged she had to consciously interrupt this tendency to act habitually. She knew habit to be the enemy of creation. But it seemed the more she pushed back against these partial losses of self, the more often she found herself standing as she did now, conscious of a return.

In the time it took for the kettle to boil she had tried and failed to reconstruct the missing minutes and had tossed the tea angrily into the pot, when it occurred to her that the kettle hadn't been boiled that morning. It was only six in the morning, and though an early riser, Malcolm was never up much before this. He too had his habits. A sudden horror filled her. So sharp and bright that she gasped and gripped the kitchen bench to prevent her from collapse. But she didn't collapse. And the horror passed as quickly as it had begun. Reason had stepped in to assuage her fears. And to further convince herself that all was well, she continued what she was doing. She buttered a piece of toast, poured two cups of tea, adding a merest drop of milk to Malcolm's and a generous amount to her own. She even went so far as to stand there at the bench eating her toast and jam as she might on any given morning. This wasn't the first time she'd had a presentiment of Malcolm's death. The man was nearing eighty and had never taken care of himself other than to quit smoking in his forties.

What she had the most difficulty in doing was imagining a world without him. This wasn't just as Helen, the wife. This failure of the imagination was suffered by Helen, the novelist. Which greatly surprised her. Nothing she could construct seemed in the least possible or likely. Never had her creative efforts been thrown into such harsh light. All pains to conceive a possible future without Malcolm were fiction and only fiction. Untruths. A terrible admission for a novelist.

Malcolm's tea wasn't getting any warmer.

At the top of the stairs the whirring noise again. She hadn't dreamt it. She pushed open Malcolm's office door with her foot, as she had a cup of tea in each hand. He was standing at his desk in his pyjamas with his back to her. No dressing gown. Bare feet. The whirring ceased. She saw him lift some papers from his desk and the whirring began again. He didn't hear her approach.

She placed the cups of tea on the still empty bookshelf near the door and noticed the open top drawer of the filing cabinet which contained all of the foolscap pages of her husband's writing life. Original manuscripts, drafts, notes, sketches, short stories, poetry, journals, everything.

Over the noise of the machine, with voice raised, Helen asked, 'Malcolm, what are you doing?'

He didn't respond.

She stepped forward and looked around her husband. On top of the desk was a large black machine and into it Malcolm was feeding a slim manila folder. 'Brighton' was the only word she caught before the shredding machine swallowed the folder.

She knew what that folder contained. Brighton 1979 poems. And it broke her heart to think she would never, nobody would ever, see those poems again.

Helen shut the filing cabinet drawer. But Malcolm had another folder in his hand. She looked at his face. His expression was vacant. She touched his arm and he shook her off.

'Malcom, no!'

This time she didn't see what the folder contained. And it only occurred to her to unplug the machine after it disappeared for good.

# Chapter 11
# Seelenlos

Helen was seated by her desk in her office, an empty cup of tea by her elbow. Though it wasn't cold, she was wearing a black cotton cardigan over her white blouse. Her writing chair was turned so that she could face Amy, who was sitting on the two-seater sofa by the door. Over Helen's shoulder through the open windows Amy could see the evening sun catching the tops of the trees. Children were playing in a nearby garden. But neither woman was paying much attention to their squeals of delight as they were immersed in conversation.

Helen was shaking her head, saying, 'He won't speak to me about any of this. I don't know why. Well, I do know why. He was utterly opposed to me signing the deal with Morris and Robbins. He thought the advance obscene and questioned their intent. But the money enabled us to get out of that horrid little flat in Brixton. Something else he was unhappy about. I would have thought that after a lifetime of scrimping and saving he might like to enjoy the spoils of success. But I misjudged him on this. He thinks I've sold out. He's been absolutely miserable since we moved here.'

'But it's a lovely house.'

'It is. And as it was. I didn't want one of those modern renovations. But I don't know. Perhaps it *is* too late for all this.'

Helen twisted around and turned the desk lamp on. The room had been growing steadily dimmer.

'May I ask, has Malcolm read the novel you've been working on?'

'Yes. Well, at least part of version one, around the time I was offered the advance. He put it down then. He hasn't given me his opinion. I think he's disgusted by the whole thing. Suspicious, too. Only terrible novels are offered huge advances. I'm suspicious, too. That's why I've rewritten it twice since then.'

'Have you kept all of the drafts?'

'I have everything. I print out everything and also save every version in endless sub-folders on my laptop. It's my way. All three final versions are complete, more or less. No one has read version two or three. Both are very different from each other and version one. Version three almost killed me. I think it's good. I think. But Malcolm won't talk to me about any of this. I'd be happy to publish version three.'

'Version one, version two, version three. Do they have working titles?'

'No. None of them does. I feel completely dry. Like I've written the last book I'll ever write.'

'So M&R don't know about version two or three?'

'No, and they won't want them. They're not commercial. Like version one.'

'Version one is complete?'

'After reading version one Clarissa said I was in two minds and that the novel wouldn't be complete until I'd made my mind up.'

'Clarissa Munten?'

'Yes, my editor. We've been friends for years. She rejected version one. Told me to start afresh. Angry at this, and out of contract, I sent the manuscript on to my agent, Ted Johnson. He loved it. Thought it was the best thing I'd done in years. He'd been campaigning for me to leave my long-time publisher, Sandersons. He thought they'd become complacent. He was so convinced the book was a winner he started an auction. He played three of them off against each other until the team at Morris and Robbins made him the offer he couldn't refuse. He was so happy. He considered it his crowning achievement. But he died of a massive heart attack while playing tennis soon after. It was awful. Awful. His partner in life and business, Jeffrey Hutton, was inconsolable. He closed up the agency and moved to Spain. I've had no representation since.'

'And the deal?'

'It was done. Clarissa was furious. She said the book wasn't good enough to carry the name Helen Owen. We haven't spoken since.'

'There were people at M&R who thought version one was good enough to make a huge offer. Who were they? I believe you met Maxine Snedden? She was the publishing director then.'

'I think so. I'd have to look at my emails.'

'But you met with the team who backed the book, presumably.'

'Yes, but we didn't get along. Clarissa's comments had tarnished the whole thing for me. I told them I wanted to take it in a new direction. They weren't happy with that idea. But they relented and gave me more time. Then M&R bought Sandersons and I thought I'd get Clarissa back but she promptly retired. She was so angry with me. It was awful, too. It didn't matter because soon after Seelenlos bought out M&R and fired everyone I'd met, and all I've had from M&R since is threatening legal letters.'

'M&R is a different place since Seelenlos bought us.'

'I just want the whole thing to go away.'

'So why don't we just spruce up version one and give them that?'

'Clarissa was right. It isn't good.'

'But it's what they wanted. It's what they paid for. If they don't know the difference, why not just deliver it and move on to the next thing?'

Helen opened her mouth to answer, but reconsidered and looked thoughtful. A moment later, she turned her head towards the door.

'Here's Malcolm.'

They were both quiet and listened to the approaching footsteps.

Amy had been sitting with her right leg crossed over her left, with her leather flip-flop dangling loosely from her raised foot. Initially, she had been anxious about her first meeting with Helen. She had worn her black fitted shift dress because it was plain and businesslike, especially with the belt, and she had wanted to look professional. But as the meeting went on her anxiety had dissipated and she relaxed. Probably too much. With Malcolm coming she was suddenly conscious of how short the dress was. She shifted her bottom to the edge of the sofa, making sure her dress came with her. Then she brought her knees together, and her feet, and drew them in. To finish off the pose, she placed her hands demurely in her lap.

Helen watched this unexpected change with interest.

The door to Helen's office opened.

'I thought I heard voices. Hello, I'm Malcolm.'

Malcolm said this with a smile he hoped would sufficiently mask the surprise he felt on finding Helen with such a young woman. He almost stuck out his hand to shake hers, but thought better of it. He didn't know how young people wished to be greeted.

'Amy. I'm from M&R,' she replied, noting that Malcolm obviously hadn't updated his author photo for some years. He was not just older, but less severe. Like he had mellowed. He was certainly rounder than the images she'd found via Google. And his remaining hair was white where it had been sandy in some of the photos.

'Would you like a drink? It's almost seven. I came up to see if Helen wanted to join me.'

'I'd kill for a drink. But before we go down, may I ask what you thought of the first version of Helen's new novel? The one M&R signed?'

Helen shook her head and looked agitated.

Malcolm straightened, and looked Amy in the eye. His whole

demeanour had changed in an instant. He'd gone from genial aged husband to titan. He was all intelligence and will.

'I thought it had been written by someone else.'

'But was it good?'

'I don't know what you mean by that word. We've just met. I know what I mean by it.'

'They offered her two million pounds for the book.'

'They did. I didn't. You might want to ask them why they did.'

'I know why they did. They have a fairly simple equation to work out the value of any work. They expected the book to be a huge success. Huge.'

'Have you read it?'

'No.'

'I think we should go down for our drink then. We can't really discuss the book if you haven't read it.'

He walked out of the room. A moment later he popped his head back in. 'Have you read Helen's other work?'

'No, I haven't.'

'Brilliant.' And he was gone.

Amy and Helen didn't speak but both stood. Whether Helen was standing to lead Amy down to the lounge room and a glass of champagne, or whether she was standing to escort her out of the house was unclear to Amy.

'You're a very beautiful woman,' Helen said, catching Amy by surprise.

Amy wrinkled her nose.

'I had to say something. I feel I've been examining you since you arrived. Extraordinarily beautiful. Exceptional. May I look at your hands?'

Helen took Amy's hands in her own. 'How old they make my own look.' She turned them over and then let them go. She then stepped closer to Amy and looked more intently at her face.

'Julie Christie. Catherine Deneuve. That kind of beauty. Though you're a brunette. Lovely skin. Radiant. Beauty fascinates me, never having had it. It's beyond reason. You're compelling. You probably get this all the time.'

'No, never. You exaggerate.'

'Do I? I don't think so. You're conscious of it, too. It informs everything you do. There's an easy grace, a consciousness of perfection.'

'Please don't say anything more.'

'How else could you be as you are? I've spent my life studying people. You're entirely fearless and this must come from a place of unquestioned superiority. You have nothing to gain from anybody. What can Malcolm or I give you? You're not like us in any way. The way you spoke to him just then. Most people would lie. They'd say they'd read some of my previous novels. At university, or something. You didn't. And the consequence of this admission didn't concern you in the least. Malcolm will come around to you, as everyone eventually does. Your beauty convinces you of it.'

'You don't know anything about me,' said Amy, because she *was* conscious of the effect her beauty had on others. But here, in Helen's office, suddenly it wasn't a pleasant consciousness. Here, in Helen's office, beauty wasn't beautiful.

'I didn't know anything about you, but now I do. You haven't needed to learn the art of deception. Your face speaks only the truth.'

'Stop it.'

'Okay, then. I've gone too far. M&R have sent you. You tell me you're their "fix-it" girl. How are you going to help me?'

'I can help you deliver what they want. That's the world I know.'

'And yet you haven't read my work. Very presumptuous. I think we should talk again after you've read something of mine.'

'I've been assigned this task. I didn't request it. I don't need it. I came out of curiosity. But I see clearly now that even if I succeed, I fail.'

'There you go again. Why say such a thing? But I am reassured that you're capable of curiosity.'

'Will you email me the three versions of your novel?'

'That would be a good start. But I don't email my work. Digital copies proliferate. I like to keep a track of all copies of my dirty laundry. Can you work with printed manuscripts?'

'I tend to lose things.'

'I'm not emailing my work. Clarissa always worked with printed manuscripts.'

'I'll leave them in the back of a cab or on the tube. Let me log on to your laptop and I'll save them to the cloud. No email. They'll only be accessible to me.'

'No.'

'I can't take the manuscripts.'

'You'll have to work here then.'

'I don't keep regular hours.'

'It doesn't have to be this difficult.'

'Let me save them to the cloud. That's how I work with everyone.'

'No. Here or not at all.'

'I don't do nine to five.'

'Are you coming down?' shouted Malcolm from the bottom of the stairs.

Helen went to the door. 'Yes, we're on our way.'

\*

In the kitchen Malcolm handed them gin and tonics.

'I was just telling Amy that she's the most beautiful woman I have ever met.'

'Don't start that again,' said Amy, taking the tall glass handed to her. She was perched on a high kitchen stool. Her legs were crossed, her flip-flop dangling again. 'Congrats on the Booker longlisting, Malcolm.'

'Thanks. She's right, though. You're very beautiful. But I won't mention it again. I can see it isn't something you want discussed.'

Malcolm had thought they would go into the front room, but Helen made no move so he sat down at the kitchen table opposite his wife and leant against the wall so he could look up and across at Amy.

'We've reached an impasse, Malcolm. Amy won't take my printed manuscripts with her and I won't let her have digital copies.'

'Then she can work here.'

'That's what I said but she keeps unconventional hours, apparently.'

'The solution is very simple. Let me save the manuscripts to the cloud and I'll have them all back to you in a couple of weeks at the latest. Malcolm, help me out. You can see how simple that is?'

'Malcolm doesn't know what the cloud is, Amy. He's never owned a computer.'

Amy smiled.

'Where do you live, Amy?' asked Malcolm. 'Will it be difficult to get here every day?'

'I have a studio in Chelsea, but I rarely see it. I spend most nights with friends. I could be in the West End one night, Docklands the next. I was in Wimbledon last night.'

'And that's how you live?' asked Helen.

'I don't like being alone, but I can't commit. It's quite the dilemma.'

'How do you get anything done?' asked Malcolm.

'I don't sleep.'

'So you go from bed to bed? I don't understand,' asked Helen.

'Fuck buddies, mainly,' said Amy, unable to stop herself from smiling.

'Fuck buddies?' said Malcolm slowly, as if testing out the phrase.

'And strangers. I meet and go home with a lot of strangers.'

'Isn't that dangerous?' asked Helen.

'You'd think so, but it isn't. I've never had a problem I couldn't handle. Touch wood,' she said, tapping the wooden bench. 'It isn't all sex. I stay with friends and some of my authors, too. I have a couple of girlfriends who are very generous with their spare rooms.'

'Extraordinary,' said Helen. 'And this life suits you?'

'For now.'

Malcolm and Helen were silent. They stared at the beautiful woman sitting at their kitchen bench, trying to comprehend all that had been said in the last few moments. She was utterly, utterly foreign to them. Helen felt old and out of touch. Malcolm couldn't make sense of what he was hearing.

'It's not a good way to live. I don't recommend it. But it works for me,' she added, seeing the look of confusion on their faces. They would never understand. She barely understood it herself.

'And why have M&R sent you? I don't follow,' said Malcolm, utterly confused.

'Do you know Jack Cade?'

'No,' said Malcolm.

'Yes, he does,' interjected Helen. 'The thriller writer.'

'I made that happen. I work with the writer Liam Smith to put together two Jack Cade thrillers a year. They have been extraordinarily successful. We've sold millions of copies.'

'And you want to *put together* a book with Helen?'

'I don't, my boss does. It's only a request. If I don't think I can help, then I'll move on.'

'So presumably, you've made a lot of money out of all this. Right?'

'Yes.'

'Then why live as you do?'

'I don't have an answer for that.'

Amy had finished her drink a while ago and wanted another. But both Malcolm and Helen had barely started theirs. She got up.

'Do you mind if I fix myself another G&T?'

Malcolm started to move, but she said, 'No, no. I can manage. You sit tight.'

She made herself a strong one.

Malcolm noted she didn't put the tonic water back in the refrigerator.

'As you don't mind where you sleep, why not stay in the empty flat downstairs for a few days. You can read the manuscripts and we can go from there,' said Helen.

Malcolm shot her a look. He was finding the whole thing difficult. That Helen would even countenance this young woman advising her on anything hurt him. He studied his wife. Gone was the surety of past years. How old and fragile she looked as she sat staring longingly at this stranger, as if Amy held the answer to a long-unanswered question. It was absurd.

'Yes, read them,' he said, pushing his chair back. 'Then you'll know what you're up against.' He stood up and, passing between Helen and Amy, crossed to the bottle of tonic water. 'Or better still, read her recent novels, *The Uninvited Guest* or *More Than I Can Say*. Sublime. Or any of the older books for that matter. I can lend them to you.'

He lifted the tonic water and opened the fridge.

Helen turned her head to see what he was doing.

Speaking into the fridge as he put the bottle back in the appropriate place in the door, he said, 'Helen's work isn't for everyone. But it has its audience.' Then, closing the fridge, he turned to face Amy. 'As time has shown. Some of her books are still in print. And *The Uninvited Guest* was included in a collection of modern classics.'

Amy didn't know what to say to this. Was he implying that she wasn't bright enough to appreciate Helen's work? Or was he just defending his wife against the outstretched grasp of commercialism?

'I'm sure they're very good,' she said, trying to absorb and silence Malcolm's comments, whatever his agenda.

Malcolm took three steps towards Amy. He was kept from getting any closer by Amy's extended foot with its dangling flip-flop. He placed his hand on the edge of the kitchen bench.

'I do hope you're not an idiot,' he said, using the same tone he'd used when asking her if she'd like a drink – friendly, upbeat.

'Malcolm!' said Helen, twisting around in her seat.

'I couldn't bear it if you were,' he continued in the same tone. 'I've met too many idiots in publishing lately. Over the years Helen and I have been privileged to work with the best editors and publishers. People with a vocation. But with all this merging, with the sackings and the redundancies, the writing world has lost its best people and its soul and direction and purpose. When I meet any ambitious young person willingly entering into the business as it is now, I have to wonder. And what you've told us about *putting together* a bestselling book, I have to be suspicious of you, don't I?'

'No, you don't,' said Helen. 'Amy will be working with me, not you!'

She was quite upset, Malcolm saw.

They were all silent. Amy was stunned by Malcolm's words. So he thought she was an idiot. She couldn't speak. She uncrossed her legs and placed one foot on the floor.

'You know better than that, Malcolm,' said Helen, with great self-control. 'When they cut the head off publishing, it grows another. We just have to weather the headless beast. It never lasts. Remember the eighties?'

'And what are you then, Amy?'

Amy stood up straight and tall, and said, 'What am I? I'm successful. What I do pays the bills. How do you think publishers can afford to indulge in publishing books like yours?'

She had wanted to jab him in the chest with her index finger on the last word, *yours*, but held back. Her body had moved forward, though, and in response, half expecting the jab, Malcolm had moved very slightly back.

'Good,' said Malcolm smiling, 'there is hope. The only reason an opportunist gets upset at being called an opportunist is because they once had ideals.'

But the smile only angered Amy further. She was as tall as Malcolm and she leant in, bringing her face close to his, and asked, 'What good are ideals in the world we live in?'

Malcolm looked back into Amy's angry eyes, and asked in return, with great composure, 'What good is life without them?'

Amy and Malcolm remained in close proximity for only a moment, but his question lingered. And she saw the calm assuredness in his eyes even as she turned away leaving the question unanswered.

Amy couldn't look at Helen, so she turned back to find her drink and held it a moment, trying to gather her thoughts. Then she took a tiny sip. And then breathed.

'Look,' Amy said, turning around, 'Malcolm, be as worthy as you like, I don't care. I'm here to help Helen get out of her hole. Helen, you know what's at stake. We need to get this done and quickly otherwise they'll send in the lawyers. I can help you deliver what they want. It might not fit in with your legacy, or whatever, but it will stop you from losing all you have. You have to make a decision and quickly. Send me the manuscripts and I'll look over them.'

'I can't send them.'

'Oh, for fuck's sake! What does it matter? They're not state secrets. They're just novels. And you don't like any of them anyway. Besides, who do you think is going to get hold of them? Let's be honest, who the hell would want them?'

'Get out!' spat Malcolm, with restrained fire.

'No. You don't understand what's at stake. Tell him, Helen. Tell him what Julia told you.'

Helen was silent. Her head was lowered. She was shaking her head slightly.

'M&R want their advance back. Helen hasn't kept to the deadlines. The contract has been broken. They've been very patient, but the jig is up. They don't give a fuck who you are or what you've done. They just want their money back or a return on their investment. You're done for if we don't come up with something fast that sells a fuck load of copies.'

'So let them. Good. We don't need any of this,' said Malcolm. 'I always expected to end up freezing to death in a council flat. I was looking forward to cans of cat food for dinner.'

'Shut up, Malcolm,' said Helen. '*I* need this. They're not taking it back. This is *my* house. I won't let them.'

'Then send me the manuscripts. And I swear I'll fix it.'

'I can't send them. I won't send them.'

Amy sat back down, elbow on the counter, and rested her head in her hand. 'Then you're fucked.'

'Stay here. Just for a few days,' pleaded Helen.

Amy sighed. It was a big sigh. She tried to imagine what the next few days might look like if she stayed. She couldn't imagine it, living here, with old people. What she could imagine was returning to tattoo boy's place and hiding out for another week. That was an attractive option. *He* was an attractive option. And she hadn't finished *War and Peace*.

'Will you be a turd, Malcolm?' Amy asked.

'Probably.'

'No, he won't be,' said Helen.

'Okay, then. I'll stay. But I warn you, I don't sleep, I'm very messy, I *will* bring home strangers, and it *will* be noisy. Oh, and I *will* drink all the alcohol you have. Are you happy with that?'

'No,' said Malcolm.

'Yes,' said Helen.

# Chapter 12
# Women Writers' Guild Awards

Helen wasn't very comfortable. She had been elbowed into a corner by the pressing crowd and the din was growing ever louder. She was regretting coming. It was the night of the Women Writers' Guild Awards and she was there to read a speech and accept a lifetime achievement award. Soon after she had arrived, the small green room had started to fill up. Helen could only guess who they all were. The shortlisted authors and their partners? Agents? Celebrities? Not one face was familiar to her.

The chair of judges, a writer she had never met before, nor read, was chatting to her about the books on the shortlist, none of which Helen had read. She was surprised she'd never heard of any of the shortlisted authors. She had always tried to keep up with the literary world. She hadn't known much about the Women Writers' Guild until she was notified of her win. This admitted fact didn't faze the chair in the slightest.

As Helen stood there, she glanced over the head of her chaperone. She saw she was the oldest woman in the room by at least twenty years, perhaps thirty – she judged the majority of those present to be women in their late twenties or early thirties.

When she was in her thirties she was also one of hundreds of young writers. But few would be invited to events like this. Establishment events. What had happened to her generation, or the generations between? This room should be filled by them. They hadn't all died. Had they given up? Fallen out of favour? Or had they been shoved aside by the next generation and the generation after that? But then, she recalled sadly, so many of her peers had actually died. One after the other. Helen always surprised herself with the sudden recollection of her actual age. Seventy-seven. She might as well round up. She was eighty. Almost one hundred. She was old. Venerable.

The chair said something, and then repeated herself, louder the second time but the growing hubbub was too much for Helen. She gave up trying to hear the chair, whose name she had already forgotten, and nodded.

If this had been the 1970s, the room would have been filled with writers over fifty. Predominantly men. But there were brilliant women then, too. She'd once met Elizabeth Bowen. Only briefly, and she coloured now, after forty years, recalling the meeting. Bowen's novel, *The Death of the Heart*, had been a major influence on Helen's early work and she had told Bowen so. Bowen had been very patient with her excited talk, but had been unable to stifle a yawn. Helen had been humiliated. In such company she had always felt like an upstart. Because of her precocious success – the reviews of her first books had been exceptional – she'd been thrown into the company of giants. True giants. Writers she had read with awe. Writers who would be read forever more. Remembered and cherished. The oldest of those writers could speak of meeting Thomas Hardy.

Helen couldn't stop looking at the faces in this room. So young and attractive. All talking animatedly. The young spoke so animatedly these days. And like Amy, with the confidence of the victor. Helen had to acknowledge that youth had won, partly as a result of the battles fought against the establishment by her own generation. They had demanded to be heard. And now the voice of youth was all one heard. The young appeared to be ready-made for television.

A beautiful woman with dark skin and light eyes approached, taking hold of Helen's elbow, and must have said some witty things. The chair laughed and hugged the young woman. Helen smiled politely and was rewarded with a kiss on the cheek.

Who were all these people? She recognised no one. Not a soul, and these were some of the country's best women writers.

The room started to empty out and Helen's hearing returned.

'Would you like to sit down, Helen? You won't be called for another ten minutes,' said the chair, leading her towards a row of seats set against the wall. Helen sat and let the chair wander off. She opened her handbag and took out the notes she had written. She saw now that she had completely misjudged the occasion. Her speech was for an older audience.

An hour later Helen was seated beside the six hopeful shortlisters in the front row of the theatre. They had sat through three long speeches. The first by last year's winner, Rebecca Smith, who demanded that the wall between genre and literature be torn down; then the chair of judges – Jacqueline Roberts, they said her name was – who spoke of the quality of the three-hundred-plus entrants and the need for more ethnic diversity in publishing; and finally the MC, Spike, a comedian with a very foul mouth, who encouraged the audience to forgo reading male writers for a year to great applause. After the speeches, one by one, excerpts from the six shortlisted novels were read. The works of talented university students, they seemed to Helen.

The night had already been exhausting when Helen heard herself being introduced. Now came the flutters in her stomach. She had always hated speaking in public, and as she aged this had not changed. But she found now, even though she hated it no less, that she could do it more easily. She thought this had something to do with not caring as much about anything contemporary.

Helen listened to the speaker, someone she finally recognised and had long respected, the novelist Jeanette Winterson, who was outlining Helen's writing life. Helen heard how she had spent at least three years on each novel, apart from a prolific couple of years in her forties when she was writing a book a year – though Winterson reminded the audience that these were interconnected novellas now published together in a single volume.

And then Helen was remembered as a fierce fighter in the women's movement who championed the lives of ordinary women in her fiction. Much of the speech covered the first twenty years of Helen's career, the young woman's experience. But Helen was most proud of her writing about the experience of age. Her last five novels were the books she wanted to encourage readers to explore, but Winterson didn't mention any of those by name.

Helen rose to applause and made her way onto the stage, where she was greeted with a hug from Winterson and led to the podium. Taking a deep breath and looking long and hard into the dark void before her, Helen arranged her notes.

'Thank you, Jeanette, for your well-chosen lies. I appreciated all of them.'

Helen paused and looked at her notes. She held them up.

'I have written a speech. These are my notes. I agonised over every word of it, trying, I realise now, to overcome my unease with the idea of a gender-specific award. Listening to the speeches given tonight I realise I've been mistaken. This evening isn't what I imagined it was to be.'

There was an expectant silence. Helen was deliberating with herself. Should she speak out, or should she accept the honorary award and leave quietly? Everything was in the balance. She felt very tired. And old. So old. Nothing she had heard that evening had quelled her rising pessimism concerning contemporary society. And she felt she had no right to speak, not having been an active member in literary circles for many years now.

'I shouldn't speak, but you have invited me into this forum. I suspect because many of you haven't read my work – or if you have, haven't understood it. Which is an awful thing to say.'

Helen stared down at the faces she could see in the first few rows. All eyes were on her.

'You've given me this chance to speak and speak I must. Thank you very much for presenting me with your lifetime achievement award. To have one's works honoured in this way is a privilege few experience, though I suspect I'm being honoured for the work of my younger self who wrote primarily about the road to womanhood, not womanhood itself.

'And as I glance at the nervous faces of the six shortlisted authors seated before me, I well appreciate why – this is a young woman's award.

'I note that not one of my last five novels, each of which would have been eligible and submitted, has ever been longlisted for the award. These weren't terrible novels; each was critically acclaimed and sold moderately well. Their only distinguishing common feature is the age of the writer and the age of their female protagonists. Much has been said about the gender of writers tonight, but little, if anything, has been said about their age.

'I'll leave this point, as it smacks of bitterness and only confuses the meaning of what I wish to say, which is, if I were to have won an award such as this, an award that excludes participation by men, I would not have accepted it.'

Helen let these words sink in.

'Perhaps this is why I've never been considered? Perhaps.'

She looked away to the side of the stage where she had hoped to find a friendly face. But saw no one there.

'I've been a feminist all my life and I completely understand the need to address inequality in life as well as in the literary world. But I would rather emulate writers like Anita Brookner, A.S. Byatt, Hilary Mantel and Iris Murdoch, each of whom won the Booker having eclipsed a field of male peers, than win an award from which men are excluded.'

Helen stopped speaking. The audience had been completely silent throughout. She knew this was because her words were not pleasing them.

'But we must learn to appreciate just how little good writing is being written. By men or by women.

'If you think that writers like Doris Lessing or Muriel Spark will be discovered more often because of awards like this, you're mistaken. Awards must be given out every year but truly great writing is rare – rarer than any of us like to admit. And much of it has been written by writers facing great adversity, not the well-meant encouragement of peers.

'Men have had their run of this world since time began and yet when we look, considering the free ride they've had, few male writers are of the highest rank. Few writers of either sex have left their mark on humanity. We can't force excellence, we can't encourage it. The greatest art does not arrive with a cheerleading squad. It isn't decided by committee.

'Great writing is rare. With so little time on this planet, shouldn't we spend at least some of that time getting acquainted with the writers most often acknowledged as exceptional?

'If I have circled round and round the bright flame of George Eliot and been burnt too often, or if I have failed in my attempt to appreciate the unexpressed elements of the mind of Virginia Woolf, or if I have found too much pleasure in the guiding hand of Jane Austen, I have done so in an effort to fathom the depths of their genius.

'Every flash of brilliance in these current years is but a flash. Almost an accident rather than consistent effort. A jazz flourish rather than a symphony. And we honour these flashes. There is no growth to greatness, just bursts of inspiration that fall into place and are never built upon.'

Helen paused.

'I'm getting carried away, because as soon as I say such things I think of Toni Morrison, Marilynne Robinson, Penelope Fitzgerald,

Julian Barnes, Alice Munro, Margaret Atwood and still others. But then, of the thousands of published literary authors, these are still but a handful.'

Helen reddened. She was becoming confused. She tried to gather herself.

'And yet, which of these will be remembered two hundred years from now?'

She paused. She almost stopped. She glanced offstage again, thinking of escape.

Then, 'What I'm trying to say is that literature is a vocation, a life's work with no end and no hope of satisfaction or reward. A novel is just the by-product of the novelist's desire to understand. Understand what? Everything. Or at the very least, one thing.'

Helen felt herself wading into deep and murky waters. She wanted to return to her original point. For a moment she stared out at the audience without saying a word. She wanted Malcolm by her side.

'My husband, Malcolm Taylor, is a great writer. I think one of the finest our age has produced. He was exciting as a young writer, but he is extraordinary now. He has worked hard at it. He has never ceased seeking out the finest thinking of humankind. And even though I know what he thinks of awards, when I heard he was longlisted for this year's Man Booker Prize, I was overwhelmed with love and pride. If ever there was a writer who deserved honours in his own lifetime, it is he.'

She knew she was becoming incoherent.

'I stand here in a quandary. I was to be accompanied by my husband, but in the end he decided not to join me. He said he felt unwelcome at such an event. Of course he'd left this decision to the last minute, an hour before we were to depart, and we had quarrelled. But in the cab on my way here I tried to understand what would make my husband who has supported me in everything I have ever done — good and bad — fail to support me in receiving this honour.

'But it was on reading my speech before coming on stage tonight, and reading *in it* my own ambivalence concerning the gender-specific award, that it struck me that he was right not to come. And further, that I was wrong to come. For any event that makes a man like my husband feel unwelcome is, at some very deep level, mistaken. So if you don't mind, I think I will forgo the honour and make my way home to my husband.'

Shaking with the onrush of adrenaline, Helen walked unsteadily from the stage and, avoiding those attempting to speak to her, out of the first exit she could find. On the street she hailed a cab and, climbing in, gave her address then pushed herself into the corner of the seat and stared out of the window.

# Chapter 13
# The Lodger

Malcolm was sitting in the kitchen reading the newspaper when Helen emerged from the flat below carrying a mop and bucket.

'I was thinking of making something to eat,' he said, not looking up.

Helen glanced at Malcolm but didn't comment. She put the bucket down to close the door and the mop handle slid along the edge of the bench and collided with the wall.

He looked up briefly.

They hadn't made up after their fight the previous evening, before she left for the Women Writers' Guild Awards. And she wasn't in any mood to make up now. She felt foolish for saying the things she had said in her speech and couldn't help but blame Malcolm. His last-minute refusal to attend had rattled her. As a result she had acted the fool, slept poorly and had woken angry.

She carried the bucket into the tiny utility room and poured the water down the large sink. She rinsed the mop and wrung it out, before taking the towels out of the washing machine and putting them in the dryer.

When she returned to the kitchen, Malcolm hadn't moved.

He said, 'Can I make you a sandwich?'

'I've bought some things for lunch. Amy will be here at one,' she replied in icy tones, clearing away the tin of coffee Malcolm had left out and washing and then drying his teaspoon. 'You'll have to wait until she arrives.'

She looked around but couldn't see the coffee mug he'd used. He'd probably left it upstairs or in the living room.

Malcolm didn't say anything further. He had forgotten the young editor was coming today as his mind had been on other things. The oven clock showed it was almost one. He folded the paper twice and laid it on the table.

Then, having watched his wife wipe clean the clean benches, he said, 'You're in the paper.'

'What?' She hadn't been expecting anything more from Malcolm and turned to him. He was holding out the paper. He had folded it so the article he was referring to was prominent.

'It would appear you upset a great many people with your speech. You're as much a pariah as I am now.'

She took the paper and quickly scanned the article.

'There's barely a word about me.'

'Apparently most of the talk was on social media.'

'Well, it doesn't matter then, does it.'

'I wonder if you'll make the ten o'clock news.'

Helen turned from him with impatience. She had hoped he might never hear about what she had done. She sincerely wished she could unsay it all. If only she had read the speech she had prepared, she thought – and then coloured at the memory of the stumbling, rambling nonsense she had shared publicly.

A small vase containing the bouquet of wildflowers caught her eye. She'd bought them for the flat. To escape further comment, she carried them downstairs.

Helen had already spent the morning cleaning the flat. She now crossed the room quickly and placed the vase on the coffee table. Daniel, Geraldine and the boys were to have been Helen's first guests. She'd had the walls repainted, the floors polished and the bathroom redone with them in mind. She'd even had the tiny kitchenette fitted out with everything a young family might need.

But instead of her family Helen had prepared the flat for a comparative stranger, Amy.

She stood for a moment and looked around. The room was sparsely decorated and very white, but Helen liked it all the more for its simplicity. Everything looked clean and tidy.

She tried to imagine Daniel's boys in the room, perhaps on the sofa watching TV, but found she couldn't. All she knew of them, really, was what she could divine via Daniel's Facebook page. She couldn't even manage to conjure up the sound of their laughter.

She'd already removed all of the framed photos of Daniel, Geraldine and the boys in preparation for Amy's visit. And the toys she had brought down from the attic had been carried back up. She'd left the bottom shelf of the bookcase as it was. It was filled with picture books she'd ordered online. Amy would have to excuse this one reminder of the flat's intended purpose, she thought.

She noticed it had just turned one o'clock. She popped her head into the bathroom one last time, checking everything was as it should be. Clean white towels. A selection of creams and soaps. Then the bed. The white embroidered duvet covering was one of Helen's favourites. She had bought a few more pillows as well. It looked luxurious. Then the living area. The bouquet of wildflowers on the coffee table by the sofa gave the area a homely air.

On the bed was the reason for Amy's visit. The three manuscripts, all newly printed and tied with string.

Version one.

Version two.

Version three.

Helen viewed them with suspicion.

Left alone with Amy, the manuscripts would do all the talking.

But what would they tell her?

Helen felt exposed. She had brought this crisis upon herself. She had reneged on the deal. And she was beset by fears.

She did not want to lose her house.

She did not want to lose her reputation.

She did not want to lose the respect of her husband.

The madness of it all was that she was relying on Amy to discover a way out for her. Amy who was young enough to be her granddaughter. Amy who had not read her work before. Amy who judged the success or failure of a novel by the number of copies sold.

And yet the thought of Amy's arrival had paradoxically lifted her spirits slightly. Helen had been so alone in her trouble. Malcolm had given her no solace. The writing of versions two and three had been done in complete isolation. No agent, no editor, no husband. No one but herself. She felt lost and was a stranger to her own art. She yearned for a voice other than her own, for a companion in her crisis.

And Amy had come and she had seemed so capable, so matter of fact, so practical. Her youth, which had surprised Malcolm, excited Helen. Her abundant energy and pragmatism would help cut a path out of the woods Helen found herself in.

Helen took one last look around and then climbed the internal stairs to the house. As she reached the top, the doorbell rang.

*

Helen opened the door to find Amy standing there with her back turned, waving at a very expensive looking sports car that roared up the narrow street. It tooted twice before turning left at the nearest corner and driving noisily out of view.

It was a warm day and the sun was shining brightly. Helen shaded her eyes as Amy spun around and exclaimed, with a look of surprise on her face, 'Oh!'

Helen said, 'You're on time.' And wondered at Amy's surprise. After all, she had pressed the doorbell.

'I'm sorry. I'm not normally punctual, but Liam was in the army and does everything by the book. We've been swimming at

Hampstead Heath. It was lovely, but he knew I had to be here so he hustled me on.'

'Was that who ...?'

'Yes, that was him. The car's new. He's obsessed with driving it. Any chance. He's like my personal chauffeur at the moment.'

Helen wavered a moment. Amy was wearing little blue shorts, barely shorts at all, and a white singlet. Her bikini was showing and her feet were shod in flat sparkling sandals. And what was worse, her hair, which looked wet, was in messy pigtails. She wore no makeup and looked younger and more stunning today than she had the last time. To avoid Malcolm's raised eyebrows, Helen took Amy down the outdoor steps to the street door of the flat.

As they went down Amy said, 'I was at the event last night.'

Helen busied herself with opening the door and entered without comment.

Amy followed her in, dropped her bag on the floor and said, 'This is nice.'

Amy saw that the rectangular room was divided into two distinct areas. The furthest end was the bedroom, with a queen-sized bed, bedside tables and a built-in wardrobe. And beyond the bed, through an open door, Amy could see a small bathroom. And nearest her, bathed in the natural light of the two large windows, was the living room, with a sofa, a reading chair, a coffee table and bookcase.

Looking down at the small backpack, Helen said, 'Is that all you've brought?'

'I'll only be here a couple of days. As I said, I'm a fast worker. I do this sort of thing all the time.'

Helen didn't know what to say in reply to this, so said nothing. Instead she opened the folding doors that hid the compact kitchenette.

Amy nodded, and added, 'I'll buy new clothes if I need them.'

Helen closed it up again.

'Lovely flowers, Helen,' said Amy, bending down to smell them. She lifted her gaze to Helen and smiling, added, 'Thank you.'

Helen smiled warmly in return. The first sign of warmth Amy had won.

'There's a laundrette on the high street. And restaurants and a takeaway. And a Waitrose.'

'Handy,' she said, and regretted it. She felt self-conscious under Helen's quiet gaze.

'We had the bathroom redone,' said Helen, moving towards the back of the flat and turning the bathroom light on. 'The plumbing had been a nightmare. Everything is new and in perfect working order now.'

'Lovely.'

'Before I forget, here's your key.'

Amy followed her and took the offered key. Then there was a moment of silence.

'Is that them?' asked Amy, pointing to the three manuscripts tied with string on the bed. Helen nodded. 'Real paper manuscripts. I can't tell you the last time I had to work with one.'

'Have you ever worked with one?'

Amy smiled. She hadn't. Her whole working life had been in the internet age. Some of the older editors she knew still did their final proofreads with print. But she didn't. All that wasted paper.

'I've left the password to the Wi-Fi on the bedside table.'

Amy looked in the direction of Helen's gaze.

'I was thinking of having some lunch. I know Malcolm will be hungry. Would you care to join us?'

'I'd love to. I haven't eaten anything today.'

'I'll leave you to get changed. Take a shower if you'd like. The flat is yours for as long as you need it. Just come up when you're ready.' And with that Helen climbed the internal stairs to her kitchen.

*

Amy sat on the bed and flicked the pages of the manuscript closest to her. The flat was very quiet. Very bare. She kicked off her sandals, fell back onto the bed and stared up at the ceiling. The bed was soft. The room had a lovely fresh fragrance. Everything was nice and clean. But she felt a little disoriented. The transition from Liam's world to Helen's had been too sudden. More a collision than a transition.

One moment she was in Liam's Aston Martin, her hands down his pants while he kissed her goodbye, the next she was being shown three unpublished manuscripts by the great Helen Owen.

The sight of the manuscripts had made things real for Amy. She had become cavalier about the work she did and the privilege of working with famous authors. But, as she had tried to explain to Julia, the authors she had always worked with were entertainers. Helen Owen was in a different league. These manuscripts were in a different league. They mattered.

The short conversation she'd just had with Helen reinforced this impression. Helen had been more reserved than she had been when they first met. This time she had seemed calm and assured. This was the Helen Owen she had expected to meet that first time. A Helen Owen who had no need of her help in anything.

Amy had thought Helen might be a complete mess. Having kicked the hornet's nest last night Helen was under attack from all sides. She was at the centre of a social media shitstorm. But as far as Amy could see, she didn't give a fuck. She was her normal composed self and seemed to think nothing of it.

And I am supposed to help her, Amy thought.

She was suddenly overwhelmed by the task that faced her. Everything was going to be more difficult than she imagined. And there was no escape. She'd said she would help her. She would have to stay here a few days at the very least. To make it look like she had put in an effort.

She picked up the fattest manuscript – the one Julia wanted –

version one. She'd read it and get it over with. If it had potential that would be that.

She flicked the pages and breathed in their scent before dropping the manuscript back on the bed alongside the other two.

Amy felt like screaming. She wasn't used to doing things she didn't want to do.

She covered her nose with the palms of both hands and breathed in deeply. Gone was the scent of flowers, brilliant writing, obligation and clean bedsheets. The scent on her hands was Liam. A delicious contraband in Helen's neat flat.

'Fuck it,' she said aloud, then sat up and picked up the smallest of the manuscripts, labelled 'Version three', untied the string and let the cover page fall on the bed. From their first conversation she knew this was the manuscript Helen thought her best work in years. She allowed herself to read only the first line, then put the manuscript back on the bed.

She was suddenly filled with conviction that Helen was right, the book was good. Better than good, brilliant. She smiled at her intuition. It was madness but it didn't mean it was wrong.

But as her tummy rumbled she thought of lunch and remembered what Helen had said. *I'll leave you to get changed. Take a shower if you'd like.*

She retrieved her bag, took it into the bathroom and shut the door. A full-length mirror hung on the back of the door. Her hair was a mess in pigtails, but otherwise she looked as she might any day in summer.

Change and shower.

What had Helen disapproved of most – her obscenely short shorts or her liberally applied *eau de Liam*?

Helen was almost eighty years old. Of course she would disapprove of her shorts. They barely covered her bottom. But would she still recognise the scent of a man? Do we forget such things over time? After last night's speech, Amy wouldn't be surprised if Helen opposed sex before marriage.

Amy looked at her reflection in the mirror and tried to see herself as Helen would. There was no avoiding the conclusion Helen would come to – she, Amy, wasn't taking this seriously.

She stripped down quickly. She turned on the shower and hugged herself. Her skin felt different. She hadn't been swimming at Hampstead Heath in years. It was like childhood, swimming.

She raised her hand to her nose one last time, then stepped into the shower.

*

Malcolm was upstairs in his office when he heard voices on the landing. He stepped out and found Helen and Amy, who had changed into jeans and a T-shirt, her dark hair pulled neatly back in a ponytail.

'I'm just showing Amy around. Lunch is ready. Go down, we'll be there in a moment.'

Amy gave him a kiss on the cheek, which startled him, and then she followed Helen up the next flight of stairs.

Malcolm headed downstairs. In the kitchen he found Helen had heated some little quiches, which were still in the oven, though it was off and the door was ajar. She had also arranged a plate of cold meats and had thrown together a simple salad. There was a loaf of bread on the table as well. And small white plate with olives beside three very old jars of mustard and Branston Pickle. He thought the selection was odd. She had obviously been unsure what to prepare. They rarely sat down for lunch. It was an informal meal for them and they generally ate whatever they could put together. He usually had a ham sandwich. As plain as you like. He opened the fridge and took out an unopened bottle of white wine. He set three wine glasses on the table and sat.

After a moment, he poured himself a glass. He didn't as a rule drink in the middle of the day. But he thought he might take it up. Especially if he was to be thrown into the company of Helen's young editor.

*

'So you were there, were you?' asked Malcolm, suddenly speaking.

'It was like she'd thrown a bomb.'

Helen and Malcolm had finished eating their lunch, but Amy was still picking at the salad from the bowl with her fingers. While they had eaten, Helen had quizzed Amy about her authors, and Malcolm had only spoken when necessary, only half listening. It all sounded like gossip to him. Though he had to admit, Amy was a sharp cookie. What she'd said about Jeffrey Archer had made him laugh.

But when Amy made a passing reference to the Women Writers' Guild Awards he was all ears.

'Helen's speech? Like a bomb going off? I bet it was,' he said, pouring himself another glass of wine.

Helen put her hand over her glass, but Amy allowed him to refill hers. He placed the bottle back down empty, and continued, 'I have no idea what she said, but if I know Helen, it was brilliant.'

'No, no it wasn't,' said Amy before biting her tongue and glancing at Helen. 'I mean it was and it wasn't. On the one hand, Helen, you completely missed the whole point of the night and why there have to be nights like that, totally devoted to women's writing. But on the other, what you said about genius – how rare it is – it really struck a chord, I think. Or it will, after they stop burning effigies of you on the streets.'

'Helen the reactionary.'

'You didn't come off well either, you know, Malcolm. You didn't support her on her night of nights. They're saying you're the reason she said what she said. Some of Helen's greatest admirers are defending her because the fault was obviously yours. That you'd upset her. And that the opinions she shared were obviously forced on her by you!'

'I don't have opinions!' he said, with a mischievous grin.

Helen looked at him darkly. 'That's all you have. If you'd just come along with me, none of this would have happened.'

'If you'd told me you were going to start a riot, I would have been there with bells on. I want to read the speech, is it available anywhere?'

'No, it was nonsense,' said Helen.

'People have been sharing bits of it online all morning.' Amy picked up her phone. 'I can probably find a full transcript somewhere.' She stared intently at the phone and tapped the screen rapidly. 'Here it is. I've found it.' She held up her phone triumphantly.

'Well, that's no good to me,' said Malcolm.

Amy laughed at this, then asked, 'Is your printer wireless, Helen?'

She nodded wearily, resigned to Malcolm reading it. What did it matter after all?

'I can probably print it straight from here for you, Malcolm,' Amy said, waving her phone. 'Do you want me to give it a try?'

She stood up abruptly and they went upstairs together.

Watching them go, Helen suddenly felt exhausted. Some part of her had expected Amy to offer her an immediate solution to her problem. But of course that was impossible. And she knew it. But the hope had got her through the morning.

She looked at the remnants of their lunch, the dirty plates and glasses. She'd have to clear the table and put things away, but she didn't have the energy just yet. She sighed and, elbows on the table, rested her head in her hands.

*

'I can't get it to connect,' said Amy, clearly frustrated. She had tried everything she knew to get her phone to talk to the printer. It was a new printer, too, it should connect automatically. 'Maybe

92

if I email it to myself, I can log on to Helen's computer and log into my email and print from there.'

'Or you could read it to me from your phone,' suggested Malcolm, who had grown tired standing while Amy fiddled with the printer and was now seated comfortably on the sofa Amy had sat on during her first meeting with Helen. He rarely visited Helen's office, he realised, surveying the neat bookcases.

Amy didn't respond, feeling unexpectedly shy in front of Malcolm. She was used to reading aloud to people – she did so quite a bit at work – but Malcolm was a different audience altogether. He reminded her of the head of the English department at her school, who'd had standards too high for any child to meet.

'Or is it too long to read?' Malcolm said, offering the silent Amy an exit.

'No, it wasn't a very long speech.'

That seemed to settle it for Malcolm; he appeared to be waiting for her to begin.

Amy sat on the desk and placed her bare feet on the seat of Helen's writing chair.

She read the speech.

At one point Malcolm asked her to slow down, but overall, he thought she read it well. When Amy finished, Malcolm asked, 'What do you think of her speech?'

'I don't know. Reading it now, it seems a different speech. Last night it was outrageous. It left those who followed her at the podium in a strange position. All of their prepared speeches had made assumptions about how the evening would progress, which Helen's speech had then smashed. There was a lot of improvisation afterwards. And raised voices filled with emotion. The organisers were hurt and angry. The eventual winner of the award couldn't finish her speech because she'd written of her love of Helen's work. She broke off sobbing.'

'Do you think Helen should have kept her thoughts to herself?'

'Yes, I do. In that environment, yes. We didn't deserve Helen's speech. She was accusing us of things that just aren't true. Last year's winner was fifty-five. Not as old as Helen, but clearly not a young woman.'

'And yet, Helen has never even been longlisted for the award.'

Ignoring this, Amy said, 'The award is necessary and it is changing things. I do wish the award would acknowledge more writers of commercial fiction but having said that, there is a flow-on effect from the award. More women are being reviewed and women's writing is being taken more seriously across the board. You're a man, you don't know about inequality.'

'But Helen does. Imagine what it was like fifty years ago. I suppose you can't. But I was there. Sexism was unquestioned. Helen's parents had been progressive, they encouraged her to go to university. But both expected her to give up her career when she married. And it wasn't just the institutionalised sexism. There was her youth. And the subject of her novels – women without men. The old guard were a force to be reckoned with. The writers of the first half of the century were still an obstacle for young writers; they'd lived through the war and were above criticism. And beyond them the Modernists, in whose long shadow everyone wrote. But then every generation has difficulties peculiar to itself; the Modernists had to overcome the universal reverence for the writers of the nineteenth century.'

Malcolm paused. He had forgotten who he was talking to. Was she even listening to him? He glanced up at her. Her eyes were alert, not glazed over as expected. But he had drifted away from the topic, he now realised, and so he returned abruptly to the speech.

'I think Helen was right to speak,' he said. 'She has fought all her life. The quality of her work alone got her reviewed throughout her long career and still does. What she writes cannot be ignored. And those who do ignore her deserve to be called out on it.'

'She had been invited to speak. I think the organisers recognise what she has overcome.'

'Alone. With no help from committees.'

'She wasn't alone, though, she had you.'

'No, I had her,' said Malcolm, looking directly at Amy. 'She led and I followed. Helen was a published author before we met. In her early twenties. Not as young as Françoise Sagan, but young enough. I was in my thirties before I managed to get a novel published. Her work was well established by then and her reviews were extraordinary. I was lucky to be reviewed at all. I would never have been invited to the literary parties and the dinners if I hadn't been Helen Owen's husband. She was and is the star. And she did it all by herself.'

Malcolm stood up and crossed to the bookcase that held Helen's novels on the bottom shelf.

'These are all too perfect. They're Helen's. I can't lend them to you. Come into my office and I'll see if I can dig out my well-worn copies. If you're going to work on her book, you'll have to read a few of them.'

He led her out of the room and into his office across the hall.

Amy leant against the doorframe and examined Malcolm's room. It was a mess. She watched as he rummaged through boxes on his knees, making more mess in the process. Most of the books he was pulling out from the boxes were new to her. As were the books scattered on the bookcases. So many authors and titles she had never heard of mixed in with the usual suspects – Austen, Dostoyevsky, Proust, Flaubert. Not one recent bestseller.

The desk near the window was empty. No computer, either. Then she remembered Helen had said he didn't use one. No, Helen hadn't told her, she had read it in that article. Malcolm wrote in pencil.

'Did you ever meet Jackie Collins?' she asked.

'No,' he said, finally finding his collection of Helen's work. He sorted through them.

'You're contemporaries. I thought you might have met. What about Wilbur Smith or Danielle Steel or Robert Ludlum?'

He lifted out three of Helen's novels, balanced them in a pile on the arm of his reading chair and then struggled to get himself back onto his feet. He gave up and settled for rising to the chair and falling into it, steadying the pile of books with his hand as he did so.

'Why?'

'I've studied them closely. They interest me.'

'No, I've never met them. They don't interest me. I often find I love a novel right up to the point when its plot is revealed. Like the opening of Doris Lessing's *The Fifth Child*. The scene-setting in that novel is perfection. But when the unnatural momentum of the plot started in, I abandoned the book. I like reading under my own steam. If I do continue, the rewards are the bits between the plot, the bits an editor like you would presumably cut. That's where the heart and soul of a book exists. All the writers you're talking about reject readers like me by concentrating solely on plot.'

'But Jackie Collins sold six hundred million books in her lifetime. Danielle Steel is still writing and has sold six hundred and fifty million. Enormous numbers. Staggering. You have to admit.'

Malcolm didn't admit anything. He just stared at the young woman. He couldn't understand what any of this had to do with him.

'Wilbur Smith and Tom Clancy are only around the hundred million mark,' Amy continued, feeling it necessary to labour the point in light of his obtuse resistance. 'But then there's James Patterson. I've met him. Three hundred million. He's a very clever operator. Liam and I have learnt a lot from him. We're …'

Malcolm raised his hand and held it up like a traffic cop. 'I love Helen. I love Daniel. I love literature. But I also love baked beans. I love baked beans very, very much. Especially on a baked potato. Surely Helen and Daniel mean more to me than baked beans? That word "love" must have very different applications. So I'm a writer and James Patterson is a writer, both of us are writers. Which of us is baked beans?'

# Chapter 14
# A Work Thing

When Max called I hadn't heard the sound of his voice for five years. I hung up immediately and then cried. I don't know what happened to me. I hadn't cried like that for years. He rang again a few minutes later but I didn't answer. He left a message and I listened to it many times over, crying the whole time. The sound of his voice hurt. It was a sound from another life. Another age. Like the sound of history. Something gone forever, returning. It frightened me. The sound itself, and the power the sound had over me.

I was in Helen and Malcolm's flat when he called. Which I was thankful for. The calm white cleanliness of it. I could have been anywhere – on the street, in the arms of a lover, at the office. But I was alone. More alone than I had been for many years. And it had been good, this time alone. A quiet time with just me and Helen's words.

But now I couldn't stop crying.

I blame the timing of the call. Helen's writing had done something to me. She had been leading me to memories I would normally avoid. Asking things of me I'd prefer unasked.

I read her books, and I knew what I was up against. This was writing. I read the two battered paperbacks of her previous novels Malcolm had found for me before I read the physical manuscript of the first version of her new work. And yes, Clarissa and Malcolm had been right. The new manuscript wasn't the work of the Helen Owen they knew. But then Helen's agent and Maxine had been right, too. It was good. In the way I had grown used to using the word *good*. It would sell. It might even win some of the accolades ordinary writers win.

Her older writing, however; that was something altogether different. As were the second and third versions of the new novel. Brilliant didn't cover it. The final version was sublime. But they wouldn't recoup the money Maxine had given her. Only the first version could do that. The novel Helen and Malcolm didn't want published.

I should have let Julia know a manuscript with sales potential existed. She would have been relieved to hear it. Yet I didn't. I had been ignoring her calls and emails. I couldn't say why exactly, but it was definitely a Helen and Malcolm thing.

After the call from Max I realised I had been haunted by him this past week while living in the flat. Malcolm and Helen reminded me of Max. Helen's writing reminded me of Max. And the books did, too. Second-hand. Everywhere. And their cups of tea and their talk. The quiet in the house. The sound of people reading. The sound of people writing. The sound of thought. They were all reminders of Max. But I gave him no direct thought until that phone call.

Then he was everywhere.

I couldn't read or think. I took a shower and dressed. I tied my hair back and put on some makeup. My eyes were still puffy from crying. In jeans, T-shirt and trainers, I left the flat and walked to the tube. It was cooler than I thought and I hugged myself as I went, crossing the street to catch some sun. I needed to spend some money. It was my one antidote to Max thoughts.

I love spending money. Love it. I love having money. So much money I don't have to worry. I understand why Helen doesn't want to lose the house. After a lifetime of worrying about money she was enjoying the pleasures of material comfort. Max and Malcolm could live without it, Helen and I couldn't. Max never understood what money meant to me. He said my love of mammon was my one great flaw. He didn't appreciate my need for fine things. When I spent £500 on a rug, or £100 on some wine glasses he was shocked to his core. It offended him. When I started to make money from Liam's books he was as suspicious as Malcolm was of Helen's good fortune.

Spending money now served to banish Max from my mind. Shopping was something we never did together. The boutiques I entered on New Bond Street were as far from the world of Max, Helen and Malcolm as I could go. I spent thousands in a few hours and took a cab back to my Chelsea studio. I couldn't bear going back to Helen and Malcolm.

The cleaners had just been and the studio smelt of citrus and bleach. It might have been a hotel room or a rented apartment. I had never lived there for more than a few days at a time. It was my post box and a very expensive storage unit, really. Some of my clothes and a few mementos from my life before I had fucked everything up were in sealed boxes in the wardrobe. After Max threw me out, I never went back. I left everything – furniture, photos, clothes, paintings, books. Not that he wanted them. He had wanted nothing from me. He left the apartment, too. It was mine, after all. Yes, he threw me out of my own flat. Then it was empty, but for my stuff. It remained as it was for a year. Untouched. A Miss Havisham's without a Miss Havisham. I eventually asked Alan to sell it all for me. That's when the boxes turned up. Alan had gone through my stuff and chosen items he knew would be dear to me. They weren't. That's why they're still in the boxes.

I've owned the studio for years. Before this place there was the flat I shared with Max. Before that, I lived on campus. Before that boarding school. Before that, when I was very young, a number of different houses. I don't have fond memories of any of those. My parents are great at marriage, bad at families.

I have always much preferred other people's homes. While at boarding school I would always make sure I'd be invited to holiday with friends, and my mother and father would make no effort to stop me. I went to my parents as seldom as possible. I wouldn't know where to start making a home of my own.

Even Liam's 'office' is more of a home to me than this place. If I know Liam and Gail are travelling, I move into the office. It's a one-bedroom apartment in Vauxhall overlooking the Thames. Liam and Gail bought it in the first flush of his success, although they now live on a grand estate in Surrey. I often stay over in the office, after Liam goes home to Gail. The place is layered. The original style is all Gail, the furniture and decorations. But since she handed it over to Liam and his work, the place has been altered. The living room is an office. A big desk dominates the space, with the whiteboard on wheels we use to plot his novels. There is a large printer, too. Liam likes to bind his drafts. So they read like a book, not a manuscript. They look like cheap rip-off paperbacks. The apartment is very much a workspace. And there are books everywhere. Liam is forever researching his novels. He loves detail. He is obsessed with new technologies. With weaponry. With history and politics. If I have a home at the moment, it's that place.

I took my phone out of my handbag and played Max's message again. *Amy, it's Max. I need to speak to you. A work thing. Call me back.* No tears this time. I replayed it again. I still love the sound of his voice. He used to read to me when we were together. We'd lie in bed for hours and he would read to me. It was usually something he was reading. I didn't care. What mattered was the sound of his voice and that he was mine and that he loved me so much. I listened to the message again. The tears had stopped but I felt empty. After hearing his voice the studio seemed even more desolate to me. And I was desolate, too.

For four years Max had been the only home I needed.

# Chapter 15
# Bleach, Lemon and Death

Trevor Melville had been Malcolm's agent for more than forty years. He was now in his nineties and lived in an aged-care home in Richmond. His room was well situated, with a spectacular view of the park and the river, but he was largely bedridden. And yet he continued to look after Malcolm's affairs.

Malcolm had never been the most lucrative of his clients, but he was Trevor's favourite. He admired Malcolm and his work, which was something he couldn't say of all his clients. He and Malcolm couldn't be said to be friends, which Trevor regretted but understood. Malcolm didn't have friends. He had Helen. He needed no one else.

Malcolm had begun to be a regular visitor of late, which Trevor appreciated, as visitors were becoming rare. His client list was made up largely of estates now. One by one his authors had died off. Just as his friends had done.

So a couple of hours with Malcolm was something to look forward to. But he did worry about the regularity of the visits. There were two possible reasons for them. Malcolm knew something about Trevor's health that he himself did not know, or Malcolm and Helen were having problems. Neither possibility was particularly attractive.

In a life spent among artists, or 'creatives' as Trevor had heard they were called now, the longevity of Helen and Malcolm's alliance had been unusual. It raised many questions among his other clients and friends, none of whom had succeeded in coupling for more than a decade at a stretch. His own life was a record of depressingly regular cycles of lust, love, boredom, irritation and loss. He had enjoyed one great love. A relationship that fitted none of his normal patterns and lasted more than twenty years till the object of his affections had died. But this love had been more pain than pleasure. And was never made public.

Malcolm and Helen's partnership was something Trevor envied. In the seventies, when both writers had been at their most productive, Trevor had been a regular visitor to the flat in Brixton. He was attracted to the atmosphere of their home. Beyond the obvious accoutrements of writers – the newspapers, books and ash – there was conviction. Doubt did not visit the flat often, except in relation to their son, Daniel. In everything else, both Helen and Malcolm knew what they were about. They had direction and confidence. There was nothing they would not discuss. Their lively debates were instructive to each other and to those, like Trevor, who witnessed them, and sometimes partook in them. He never saw, nor did he imagine there to be, when he was absent, ugly, hateful disputes. The couple were companions in mind and body.

This was why he'd prefer that Malcolm was visiting him now because he thought him close to death. He'd prefer death to disillusionment.

'I've been writing,' said Malcolm, soon after arriving at Trevor's bedside.

The sun was shining through Trevor's large window, warming Malcolm's back. Behind him, Trevor could see the stately progression of a former foreign secretary across the luxurious green of the lawn on his way to the river, where it was his custom to sit in the afternoon, when the weather was fine. The former foreign secretary was accompanied and assisted and almost eclipsed by a burly male nurse, Usman, who, being of heroic proportions, was very popular with residents and management. He would lift Trevor and others as though they were small children. His great strength took the anxiety out of any necessary physical activity, something to be appreciated when even the most ordinary of human tasks could appear as difficult and as perilous as walking a tightrope across a canyon.

Their progress across the lawn was glacial and Usman had time to notice Trevor watching. He waved and smiled pleasantly. Trevor returned the gestures and Malcolm turned round in his seat.

'Is that?'

'Yes.'

'I thought he was dead.'

'He's younger than I am.'

'Tories are never young.'

Trevor laughed. 'But you're right. It's easier to assume all my near contemporaries are dead. Each obituary of a contemporary I read now is, to me, having thought them dead already, a record of a miraculous rebirth and a second death.' He paused briefly and then added, as though it had just occurred to him, 'No one bothers to talk about the second time Lazarus died.'

Trevor lifted a tumbler of water from his tray table and drank. His movements were unhurried and precise. He placed it down empty. Malcolm leant forward and refilled it.

'Perhaps Lazarus didn't die the second time,' Trevor continued. 'Perhaps he lives still. But it's unlikely to have gone unrecorded. A second death is much more likely.'

'Lazarus is overkill,' said Malcolm, emphatically. 'Conquering death once in a story is enough. John had to go and add another, in case we didn't get the point.'

Malcolm stood up and shifted his chair slightly so he could more easily turn to look out at the view.

'I've always thought it strange,' said Trevor, 'that the synoptic gospels fail to mention the miracle of Lazarus. I would have thought the occasion worth noting down by all of those present.

It isn't every day that a man raises another man from the dead. Matthew, Mark and Luke must have stepped out for a cigarette break and missed it.'

Now it was Malcolm's turn to laugh.

'What have you been writing?'

'Nothing. I don't know. Pages that have words on them. They come easily. But not like they did before.'

Trevor waited for Malcolm to continue.

'This damned Booker thing. It's unsettling. Why that book? Really, Trevor, of all my books to choose! What if it were to win?'

'It won't win. Trust me. Don't worry.'

'But imagine if it did. It would make a lot of sense in one way. It would confirm the thesis of the book. But such recognition would also underline my failure to do what I set out to do.'

'I hate that book.'

'And you're right to. So why is it getting this attention?'

'They're children playing with Daddy's loaded gun.'

'Do they know it's a gun?' asked Malcolm, eyebrows raised.

'No. But they know it's not meant to be touched. It's forbidden, thus attractive.'

'Perhaps we're out of touch,' mused Malcolm, scratching his ear. 'That's what I've been thinking. What's shocking to us might not be shocking to the young. Do you mind if I open the window slightly?'

Trevor nodded. He knew the place had an odour. Bleach, lemon and death. He could no longer smell it, but it had been overpowering when he first arrived.

'The work of the Marquis de Sade still has the power to shock,' said Malcolm from the window, 'but most books that were shocking in their day are now merely interesting historical curiosities.' He paused. 'I can't think of an example now.'

'Darkness is nothing to the blind. Your book is powerful. The Booker judges recognise this aspect, but not the nature of the power. That's all. It's everything you want it to be. Ugly, hateful and dull.'

Malcolm laughed again.

'And I read that Helen has offended every woman on earth with her speech,' said Trevor, consciously steering the conversation away from *A Hundred Ways*, a book he wished he had never read. His only defence against it was disdain. But it wasn't very effective. He thought of the book now as some sort of disease, like syphilis – a disease you catch while doing something pleasurable.

'I don't want to talk about Helen,' said Malcolm.

'That's unlike you.'

'Really? I wouldn't know.'

'Tell me about the new book, then.'

'I can't. It's darker still. Darker than anything I've written. Darker than I thought possible. I can't shake it, either. It sits upon me like a blanket wherever I am, blocking all light. There's no hope. No redemption. Nothing.'

'Can't wait to read it,' said Trevor in a monotone.

Malcolm smiled grimly. 'Try writing it.'

# Chapter 16
# They Shouldn't Be Much Longer

Amy had been asleep when the doorbell rang. She took a moment to realise it was the middle of the afternoon and she was in Helen and Malcolm's front room. On her lap was Malcolm's novel *A Hundred Ways*. Amy had removed the cover to protect it, but now it was creased. It was pristine before her unscheduled nap. One of twenty copies in a box in Malcolm's office. She tossed it and the book aside. The doorbell rang again. She stood and went to the window to see if she could see who was at the front door. She recognised the man standing there.

By the time Amy opened the front door, the visitor was returning to the front gate.

'Daniel?' she asked.

He turned, looked her up and down – she was standing there in a pair of tight low-cut blue jeans and white singlet, her feet, but for dark nail polish, bare – and asked, 'Who are you?'

'I'm Amy. Helen and Malcolm have gone to Waitrose. They won't be long. Come in.'

'Were you sleeping?' Daniel said as he walked up to the front door.

'I may have nodded off,' said Amy, smiling. She spun around and walked back into the house rubbing her eyes.

Daniel stopped to watch her walk down the hall. He scratched his near-hairless head, looked back over his shoulder at the street, shrugged and walked in.

'Do you want a cup of tea?' asked Amy as he reached the kitchen.

'I'd rather something stronger.'

Daniel took off his jacket and hung it over the back of a kitchen chair.

Looking at him as he fussed with his jacket, Amy realised none of the pictures around the house were recent. The man before her was middle-aged. His belly strained against his shirt and hung over his belt slightly. He had far less hair than in the photos.

'Espresso, beer, wine, G&T, whisky?'

'Beer. Thanks.'

Daniel couldn't take his eyes off her. His gaze fell on her behind as she opened the fridge and extracted a Beck's. She then took out a bottle of wine and spun quickly around. He turned his head, perched casually on the edge of the kitchen table and asked, 'So, Amy, who are you?'

Opening the cupboard that contained the wine glasses, she answered, 'I'm editing your mum's new book.'

'*You're* Helen's editor?'

'Yes. Does that surprise you?'

'You don't look like an editor.'

'I wonder if I should feel insulted,' she said, not smiling. She poured wine into her glass, took more than a sip then poured more in.

'Not if you don't feel it. You know what I mean, anyway. Have you met Clarissa?'

'No, but I read her book at uni.'

'That's what I mean. She's venerable.'

Amy handed him the Beck's and said, 'Let's go into the front room to wait. It catches the last sun of the afternoon.'

*

Daniel was seated on the couch where Amy had been napping. On his lap was the copy of *A Hundred Ways* and on the coffee table was an empty beer bottle. Amy was opposite him, reclining on the other couch. She was holding a near-empty glass of white wine. The sun was setting behind the row of houses across the street and Amy was coated in a warm yellow.

'They're saying horrible things about Helen on social media,' said Daniel.

'I was there in the audience. Everyone was stunned. And she just left the building after the speech. I moved in here the next day expecting her to be, I don't know, rattled or remorseful, I suppose, but she was fine. She hadn't seen any of the horrible things people said on social media. I suppose that's one benefit of being older. Neither of them has any online presence. When a journalist did get through on the phone, Helen wouldn't speak to her. You know Malcolm had already said publicly he wouldn't do any more interviews – just when the world finds him more interesting than ever!'

'It serves them both right. They're out of touch. I bet they both voted for Brexit.'

'I doubt that. Helen was wrong to say what she said, but she wasn't saying anything new. A lot of women her age feel as she does.'

'It wasn't what was said, it was *who* said it. The organisers invited her expecting her to condone the whole thing. People don't like to be schooled. Especially those who think they're doing the right thing.'

'They both deserve better.'

'Do they? You know, the last time I was in this room I said things to them I regret. But I would never admit as much to them. Or take the words back.'

'What happened between you guys? They evidently love you, this place is like a shrine. There's a photo of you in nearly every room. That's why I recognised you at the door.'

'Nothing happened. And that's probably the problem. They were absent. Even when they were present. You must know what writers are like.'

'No two are the same.'

'Helen and Malcolm are. They're almost identical twins.'

'Not the Helen and Malcolm I know.'

'They work to the same schedules, they never leave each other's side, they think the same, hold the same opinions, read the same books and newspapers.'

'Not anymore. Neither is writing consistently. They argue. Malcolm watches more TV than he reads. Helen goes out for hours without him. When she's out he might go up to his office. But at other times he might sit at that window or in the park and watch the world go by. Other than meals they live fairly separate lives.'

'Are you living here?'

'Downstairs. For now.'

He glanced around the room. 'Did you ever visit them in Brixton?'

Amy shook her head.

'I can't believe this place.'

'Neither can Malcolm. I don't get the feeling he's happy here.'

'Because she sold out.'

'Yes, that's what Malcolm thinks, too.'

'You don't think so?'

'I think writers like Helen and Malcolm should be better rewarded for their work.'

'Work like this?' he said, holding up Malcolm's book.

'You've read it?'

'It's a bitter book.'

'No, it isn't! I really hope it wins.'

'The Booker? No chance. There's always a commercial aspect to these awards. There's no money in old writers. I doubt he'll even be shortlisted. Anyway, it's an ugly little book.'

'I think it's dark, wise and funny,' she said, sitting up.

'They're always teasing horrible things out of the poor people in their books. Not that they know what life is really like. They've never lived it.'

'It's like we're talking about different people and different books.'

'Didn't you say they were going to Waitrose? Shouldn't they be back by now?'

'That's what they said they were doing.'

'I can't wait around.' He picked up the empty beer bottle and rose.

'You can't go without seeing them,' she said, standing. In the back of her mind she was trying to remember if Helen and Malcolm had said they were doing anything else while they were out. She wondered what the time was.

'I'll come round again tomorrow. I'm in London for a few days.'

He left the room and made his way down the hall to the kitchen. She followed him and watched him put his jacket back on.

'Where are you staying?'

'At the Hunter Hotel in Earl's Court. I'm here for a conference.'

'Shall I get them to call you? I'm sure they'd love to see you.'

He held up his phone. 'They have my number.'

*

After Daniel had gone, Amy ran over in her mind the last moments of his stay. It had happened so fast. Without saying anything, Daniel had taken a sudden, rapid step towards her. She was between him and the hall door, so he might have expected her to move aside. But his hand was extended, as if to take hold of her hip, wrist or waist. He might have intended giving her a goodbye peck on the cheek. But at the time, she had flinched. It was entirely instinctive. She flinched and she lifted her hands as if to fend off a blow.

Daniel's face went white, then reddened. He took a step back and then walked quickly around her and, moving very swiftly, left the house without another word.

As the minutes passed, Amy's original instinctive conviction returned. She poured herself another drink. He was going to kiss her. He was going to grab her. He had misread the signals, or had ignored them. Perhaps he was just an opportunist. He was alone with her, after all. She ran through their short time together. The only marginally provocative thing she had done was lie across the couch. But she was relaxed because she was with the married son of her hosts. The balding, soft-around-the-middle son of her hosts. She had considered him family. Safe. Entirely sexless. He reminded her of someone from a film.

Amy took another sip of white wine and fell onto the kitchen stool. She was uneasy and unsettled. He had left in anger. She felt it now. He was angry at her for rejecting him. But they had just met. How could he think …? Where do men get their sense of entitlement from?

Amy opened the fridge, took the bottle of wine and went downstairs. She wanted to be out of the way when Helen and Malcolm returned.

# Chapter 17
# Don't Fuck the Boss

I had only just arrived at the book launch at the new Waterstones on Tottenham Court Road, having headed straight downstairs to the basement, when Julia came up to me. I wouldn't have gone if I'd known she'd be there. I'd been drinking since Daniel had left and hadn't even spoken to Helen and Malcolm before leaving the house. I'd decided to have some fun. To put that prick Daniel behind me.

'Hello, Amy, you're a hard woman to find. What news?' asked Julia.

'You don't usually come to these things, Julia,' I replied. 'Val McDermid isn't even one of our authors.' Trying to shake her, I pushed through the crowd towards the bar. But before I reached it a waiter passed by with a tray of champagne. I took two.

I saw Liam on the other side of the room talking with Val and the Australian crime writer Michael Robotham. Once again, Liam was the only black man at one of these events. His success had changed nothing in publishing. He smiled and waved me over. I couldn't see Gail anywhere. Val and Michael turned to see who Liam was beckoning. I downed the first glass of champagne.

Michael was staying with Liam and Gail while he was in England. Liam loved playing host to international authors.

I started to make my way over. But Julia wasn't going to be ignored. She took hold of my elbow. The noise in the basement was deafening.

'Amy, I need to speak to you,' she said, into my ear. 'I only came tonight in the hope you'd be here.'

The second glass followed the first.

'I love your dress, Julia. Seriously, you look amazing.'

Julia seemed perplexed.

I leant forward and said into her ear, 'I mean it. You look gorgeous. Are you here with someone or on the prowl?'

I didn't wait for a reply. I had to get rid of the glasses so I made my way to the bar and left them there. The barman gave me another full glass. Julia was still with me. I knew I wouldn't shake her until she'd had her say.

Julia opened her mouth, but I said, 'The barman just checked you out.' I put a glass of champagne in her hand. 'When was the last time you let a stranger fuck you?'

Julia glanced across at the barman. He was attractive, but young. Probably not even twenty.

'Stop messing around.' She put the glass on the bar. 'You haven't answered my calls or my emails. No one has seen you.'

'You asked me to fix the Helen Owen problem. That's what I'm doing.'

'Helen has been getting a lot of press since the awards, not all of it bad. We need to capitalise. Can Helen deliver?'

'He just did it again. I've never seen you look this good, Julia. Those shoes, where did you get them?'

That's when I saw tattoo boy. I mean Josh. I don't know if he had already seen me. I turned away quickly. I had known there would come a time when I'd run into him again. I just didn't think it would be this soon. My whole body reacted to the sight of him.

'Helen can do anything she sets her mind to,' I said into Julia's ear. 'I can't guarantee success but I think there may be a way to get what you want. Maxine was right, there's great potential in the novel.'

'You're running out of time.'

'I know. I'll call you next week.'

Josh was pushing his way towards us.

I leant forward and, almost kissing Julia's ear, said, 'I know how these things work. If you want a fling, the barman's yours. He can't take his eyes off you. Believe me.'

Julia looked again. I couldn't tell if there was blood in her veins or not. I didn't know much about her. I took no interest in her personally. I'd have guessed she was forty. She had great skin so it was hard to tell. She could have been married for all I knew. But she did look good; I wasn't having her on. There wasn't much to her, but what she had was perfectly suited to the little black dress and strappy stilettos.

'You'll call me next week about Helen?' she asked, then glanced again at the barman, who smiled at her.

'See, I told you so. Live a little,' I said. 'And yes, I promise to call you.'

Someone began tapping the side of their glass with a fork. I looked across and saw Liam standing in front of a large banner for Val's new book, *Out of Bounds*. The speeches were about to begin. I pushed my way through the crowd, taking Josh's hand as I passed him, and dragged him with me. He knew what I was about and led me through the back of the basement into an office. There was no time for niceties. He lifted my dress, ripped down my G-string, bent me over the desk and fucked me. We hadn't even spoken. It was hot, and over as soon as it had begun.

'I'm keeping this,' he said, and pocketed my G-string. He led the way out. The speeches were still going on. Liam was speaking. I let go of Josh's hand. He went one way, I went the other. I joined the crowd and clapped when they did. My legs were giving way. I leant against a bookcase.

Liam's speech was winding up. He was introducing Val. His speeches are never long. We must only have been gone for a few minutes, tops. A real quickie.

I needed another drink. I looked around for more champagne and found Liam's eyes. Had he seen? It didn't matter. I wasn't his wife. I was his lover. Very different. He could fuck off if he thought I should be loyal to him.

If Gail hadn't come up for the launch, Liam would probably have expected me to join him, Val and Michael for dinner after the event. And after dinner, Liam would have expected to take me back to his office. The idea of being with two different men in such a short space of time was interesting. Especially if Liam knew and still fucked me.

Scanning the room I suddenly saw Helen over by the stairs. For some reason my heart skipped a beat. It was like being caught masturbating by the housemistress. When I looked closer I realised it wasn't her. The two women looked nothing alike.

Josh drew near with a tray of champagne. He looked very pleased with himself. Grossly so. And I was struck by that feeling of collision again. I lifted a glass from his tray and took a sip. Josh tried to brush his hand against my bottom, but I evaded him. I watched him go. Nothing could spoil his mood.

Another waiter was carrying little quiches. But he was too far away. I was ravenous. I hadn't eaten anything all afternoon.

The champagne was going to my head. The champagne and the fuck.

The crowd erupted into laughter. I had missed what Val said, but I had heard her speak before. She's a good speaker. Always gets a laugh, too. Then it was over. Val made her way to the signing table and guests started to line up. I searched the room for Josh but couldn't find him. Julia was talking to the barman, I saw. Then I found Josh; he was speaking with Liam. This made my heart skip a beat. What the fuck could they be talking about? Liam laughed and patted Josh on the back, then they posed for a selfie. Afterwards Josh moved on.

I couldn't get to Liam easily, but he saw me coming and headed over.

'Who were you talking to?'

'He's another fan slash wannabe writer.'

So he didn't see me with Josh … Josh wanted to be a writer?

'Are you coming to dinner?' he asked.

'Are you asking?'

'Would you like to come to dinner, Amy?'

'Thank you for asking, but no, not this time.' I said this before I knew why I was saying it. Moments before I had wanted to go. In my line of sight the woman who wasn't Helen was getting her book signed by Val.

'We're not going down to the country tonight. Michael's flying to Berlin early tomorrow, so is staying at the Langham. I'll be staying in town. Will you be over later? Gail wasn't feeling well and stayed at home.'

I didn't like this. There was no need to mention Gail.

'No, I'm going to get an early night,' I said. 'The Helen Owen thing I told you about is getting messy. Julia is being a real bitch about it, too. They want the manuscript by next week.'

Liam wasn't happy being denied: it was written all over his face. He expected me to be in his bed later. But he didn't risk a second denial. Instead he asked, 'What about our work?'

'Already done. Sitting in your inbox.'

He gave me one of those smiles I had told him I find irresistible. I resisted it. Then, feeling the spirit of mischief enter me, I said, 'By the way, check out Julia. She's by the bar. I think she's going to fuck the barman.'

'Is that Julia? Our Julia? She looks different.'

'She looks hot.'

'She does.'

'Perhaps I'll see if she'll come to dinner.'

'Don't fuck the boss, Liam.'

'Don't fuck the waiter, Amy.'

# Chapter 18
# A Little Charity

Amy hadn't realised just how old Malcolm was until she agreed to walk with him to Waitrose. She was a fast walker who liked to get where she was going. She quickly realised the average speed of Malcolm's stride was glacial.

This was disconcerting as she had left her phone in the flat and Malcolm hadn't spoken since they left the house. She was already regretting her decision.

'Shall we get a cab?' she asked.

'What? Why? It's just around the corner.'

'How long does it normally take you to walk?'

'I don't know, I've never timed myself. Am I going too slowly for you? Should I pick up my speed?'

'Is that possible?'

'Probably not.'

'You're not that slow. I'm just a fast walker.'

'Did Helen tell you Daniel called? He might be around tonight for dinner.'

'I'm out tonight,' lied Amy. She'd hide out in the flat to avoid meeting Daniel again.

When they reached the high street Amy could see how far along Waitrose was and sighed. As they made their way, Amy had time to look at everyone and everything. She even had time to pop into Costa for a takeaway coffee and catch Malcolm before he reached Waitrose. In Waitrose, Malcolm was all business. There was no time for browsing; he went straight to the products he needed and then back out of the door.

Amy had thought the walk to Waitrose was long. Malcolm's pace halved when he was carrying shopping bags. And he wouldn't let Amy take them all, something she was eager to do.

And then Malcolm surprised her by turning into the Oxfam bookshop.

'You find gems in here,' he said, leading her to the back of the shop. 'But you have to be vigilant. They go quickly.'

Amy had never spent much time in Oxfam bookshops, or any second-hand bookshops. She'd never needed to. Her favourite bookshop was Daunt Books in Marylebone. They could get anything she needed. She wasn't a fan of online shopping. She loved to be served.

The books on the shelf in the Oxfam bookshop looked dirty and old to her. Malcolm only saw treasures. He handed her a copy of *Cecilia* by Fanny Burney. It was a very thick Oxford Classics paperback. She placed it back on the shelf. It felt grimy.

'A lot of book for a pound,' he said, watching her set it down. 'I haven't read it. Jane Austen read it. Admired it, I think. So it can't be all bad.'

Amy placed her shopping bags on the ground. Malcolm did so, too.

She watched him scan the shelves one after the other.

'Malcolm?' The young man who had been behind the counter approached.

'Yes? Who was that?'

Amy moved out of the way.

'We have a box of books I think you'd be interested in over by the counter. It just came in. I'm pricing them now.'

'Okay. Okay. Thank you, Asher. I'll be right over.'

He lifted his shopping bags and made his way through the shop to the counter. There was no one else in the shop. Amy looked around her. Saw titles she recognised. Some she had worked on. And then spotted a shelf full of Jack Cade novels. She went over to it. They were hardcovers and looked a little the worse for wear. She straightened them up. But the sight of them affected her. She didn't like to see them here. They were her babies, after all. And these ones had fallen on hard times.

She picked up a copy of *The Night* and took it across to Malcolm.

'This is one of mine,' she said, popping it on the counter.

Malcolm glanced at it. 'I know. They're everywhere.'

'But he's been rejected by his owner.'

'There are often a couple of mine here, too. Don't take it to heart.'

'I loved that book,' said the guy behind the counter, Asher, pointing to *The Night*.

Malcolm looked at him and said, 'Really?'

'Yes, I've read all of Jack Cade's books.'

Malcolm laughed. 'Asher, this is my friend Amy.'

'Nice to meet you,' said Asher, who was probably about twenty-five.

Amy thought he looked unwashed. His long hair was greasy and pulled back behind his ears. And his face glistened. Definitely Slytherin.

'Amy is Jack Cade.'

'What do you mean?'

Amy stared at Malcolm and then at Asher, who seemed perplexed.

'I work with a guy called Liam Smith to write the Jack Cade books.'

'You're shitting me. Really? That's amazing.' Then he paused and looked at Amy and Malcolm, searching their faces. 'Nah, you're shitting me, right?'

'Asher, why is it so hard to believe?'

'But I've met Jack Cade. He signed my book.'

'You met Liam Smith. Look it up. Jack Cade and Liam Smith are the same guy. And I helped Liam become Jack.'

Asher pulled out his phone and googled Jack Cade and Liam Smith.

'Hey, Asher, you know who your good mate Malcolm is, right?' asked Amy. She was smiling at Malcolm because he was trying to get her to be quiet.

'No, who?' he asked, while reading Wikipedia.

'The author Malcolm Taylor. He's longlisted for the Man Booker.'

'Holy shit, you're right! Jack Cade and Liam Smith are the same dude. But it doesn't say anything about you, Amy.'

'Which is exactly the way I like it. I'm a silent partner. Will you keep my secret?'

'Sure. Sure. My mind is blown. I can't tell you how weird this all is for me.'

Malcolm paid Asher for a copy of *Levels of Life* by Julian Barnes and then led Amy out.

'Do you think he believed me?' Amy asked as they walked along the high street.

'About me or you?'

'About me. I don't think he even registered what I said about you.'

'Probably. I don't know. He's a strange kid.'

They walked on in silence for a bit.

'Why don't you write your own thrillers? Why take the back seat?'

'It's just how it worked out,' said Amy, taking one of the bags from Malcolm. He had almost stopped moving altogether.

'And do you write for yourself ever? Do you have anything I could take a look at?'

'No. I mean I wrote a novel when I was at university, but it was rejected by nearly every publisher in London. I wrote it before I knew what I was doing. I'd do things differently now.'

'How so?'

'I don't know. I just wouldn't invest in it. Not in the way I did. I put everything I was into that book. It nearly killed me. And then for it to fail. It was awful. I think I could write with a bit more distance now. There's no pressure anymore. I've done it. I've helped write a string of bestsellers. We've been number one in the UK and US; it doesn't get much better than that.'

'Doesn't it?' asked Malcolm.

'No, it doesn't.'

'If you say so.'

Amy hated the way Malcolm said that. It was so smug. She wanted to hit him. But she restrained herself.

They walked the rest of the way in silence.

When they arrived back at the house, Daniel was there chatting with Helen. Amy was still angry at Malcolm and couldn't stand the sight of Daniel, so she went downstairs.

As she opened the door to the flat, she suddenly realised why the conversation with Malcolm had so unsettled her.

He sounded just like Max. That's what he had sounded like. Max.

# Chapter 19
# Whatever Is Necessary

Helen checked her inbox. There had been no reply to the email she had sent to Clarissa. She had waited a week before sending the same email again. And now another week had passed since resending that. And this was phase two. Her phone calls, and the messages she had left, had gone unanswered, too.

Their relationship was officially at an end.

Helen stared at the inbox. It was 5 am. She slept for just four or five hours a night now. The screen was the only light in the room. She closed the lid and sat in darkness until she noticed the faint hint of light coming through the edges of the drawn curtains. Then she stood and opened them. The dark cloudless sky above gave no hint of the coming dawn.

Thinking about this new Clarissa was painful.

She could happily recall their working life together. Opening up to her had been a long process – a few books before Helen could share her writing in the raw, her ideas still unclothed by art. Their partnership, for that is how Helen considered it, was based on mutual trust. To have Clarissa handle her work with such care and consideration was reassuring. Clarissa's edits and comments were couched in respect. Helen had always considered the work as being more intimate than friendship.

Over the years Helen had counted on Clarissa for more than just editorial advice. She learnt to consider her a confidant. In moments of doubt she had called on her, meeting for lunch or evening drinks. She had shared her domestic affairs, she had discussed her relationship with Malcolm, her anxieties about Daniel. Clarissa had responded to these with the same care and consideration. She had offered sound advice, or reassurance, whatever was necessary.

Helen turned on the desk lamp and started unpacking one of the three boxes that had been by the door for a week. They contained the files she had rescued from Malcolm's paper shredder. She switched on her printer, which was also a scanner, and arranged a selection of folders on the desk. Opening her laptop she saw there were no new emails.

Acknowledging the one-sided nature of her relationship with Clarissa pained Helen. She had considered Clarissa a friend while Helen was just work to Clarissa. One of her many writers. Now that Clarissa was retired she wasn't required to keep in contact. So she didn't.

Reviewing their working life under this suspicion was altogether too painful. And mortifying. She would not do so. What it said about her was awful. She had always had a good opinion of herself. Not to say she was narcissistic or a great egotist, but she had always assumed she was a good and likeable person whom others wanted to know and be acquainted with. But when she looked at the bare facts of her life she saw that this wasn't the case.

Twenty years they had worked together. But she had to admit that her relationship with Clarissa was all one way. Clarissa knew everything about Helen. What did Helen know of Clarissa in return – only that she was married to Hugh, they had three daughters, Cyn, Ali and Liz, lived in Putney and had a share of a villa in Provence.

Helen had never met Hugh, nor had she visited the house in Putney. She remembered Clarissa's daughters' names because she had made use of them in a novel. Framed photos of them had cluttered Clarissa's desk at Sandersons. Early on, Clarissa had invited Helen over for dinner, but there had never been time. And Clarissa stopped asking. She only remembered the villa in Provence because when Clarissa had mentioned she was going away for a month to the south of France, Helen had resented it. The editor holidays in France while the writer can't justify the cost of a weekend away in Brighton.

And Clarissa had been Helen's only close female friend. But it wasn't friendship, though, was it?

What Clarissa did outside their shared work wasn't relevant to Helen. She knew Clarissa was well respected in the publishing world and that she had mentored other editors and had written a few books on editing novels, but this only served to convince Helen she had the best editor in the UK. She didn't want to discuss different approaches to editing with her. Just as she wouldn't discuss paper quality with the printer and she wouldn't discuss RAM with the guy who sold her laptops.

Helen began to scan the contents of Malcolm's files.

She sighed. How blind she had been. And how ironic her failure was. Her novels were all about female relationships. She was admired for her depictions of female friendship. Clarissa had even said as much herself.

Clarissa's abandonment hurt because she had assumed they were friends.

But how could they have been when her commitment to her work and Malcolm was total?

Her marriage was a wall blocking intimacy with others.

Big love, true love, and complete compatibility were all-encompassing. To find a man like Malcolm who was also a writer – an intellectual who shared her obsession with perfection, with good work – was beyond her early expectation. To then remain in perfect harmony with him for another fifty years was exceptional. In her delight and excitement, she neglected all others, even, since he left home, her own son.

But now …

Malcolm was drifting away from her. And she had no one to talk to.

She was holding a loose sheet of foolscap, empty but for a little three-verse poem. It was written in the tiniest script, as if Malcolm had been ashamed of its contents. It was a filthy little thing. She remembered him writing it. A product of their first hungry months together. They were different people now.

She felt desperately sad, but no tears fell. Her heart felt dry.

Did she want a public record of the poem? Or was it something just for them?

She scanned it. There was no them. That is why she was doing what she was doing. None of their work was theirs anymore. Malcolm didn't have the right to destroy his work and she didn't have the right to censor it. Good and bad would be saved for posterity.

His behaviour recently had verged on the bizarre. The attempt to destroy his work. The hilarious but ultimately self-defeating radio interview. His refusal to accompany her to the awards night. His watching of daytime TV. It was all strange and upsetting. And the way he was with her. Courteous, obliging and good-humoured. More like hired help than a husband. And he wasn't writing. He wasn't reading. He lay about listening to records.

There was no denying it. The very moment Clarissa ended their working relationship, Malcolm had begun to drift. The cause was the same, that damned book and what motivated it, but whereas Clarissa could cut and run, Malcolm could not. Malcolm shared Clarissa's idea of Helen and both had been disappointed, that was evident. She now wondered if he shared her disgust, too. Because it had to be disgust. Nothing short of disgust would compel a decent woman like Clarissa to behave so abominably towards her. If Malcolm were merely disappointed, she might win back his respect. But if he were disgusted, like Clarissa, the break would be final. He would continue to drift further and further away.

Malcolm would never leave her. He felt he had a duty to himself, and to her, to remain. But merely remaining was just *not leaving*, which she wouldn't endure. She needed more from him. Love. His love had always been entwined with respect. If she had disgusted him by her actions, then there could be no respect. Which is why he seemed recently to refer to her in the past tense. Helen had always ... Helen used to do this or that ... You used to like ... But especially so when describing her as a writer. He used a tense that prohibited a future.

The house was all she had. She had been dreaming of such a house for all of her adult life. She loved it with an ardour that surprised her. Malcolm was wrong to detest the house. The house was an end and was distinct from the means. The novel was the means, the advance was the means, even the decision to write such a book was the means – detest all of the means, but the house itself was just a house, clear of any wrongdoing. She wanted him to love the house. If he loved the house she could endure his loveless toleration of her.

Helen wanted to keep the house, to mend her relationship with Clarissa and to force Malcolm to love her. That was why she had written the two new versions of the novel. The last version was more herself than anything she had written in the last ten years. She thought it her best work. But neither would read it.

Amy had read it.

But Clarissa and Malcolm would not.

# Chapter 20
# Amy's Decision

There was a loud knock on the connecting door.

Amy used her phone to turn down the music, and called out, 'Come in!'

The door opened and Malcolm, while remaining at the top of the stairs and thus out of sight, called down to Amy, 'Will you be joining us for dinner?'

'No, thank you. I'm going out for dinner. Sorry, I let Helen know earlier.'

The connecting door closed.

He was abrupt, Amy thought. But lovely in his way.

Malcolm probably knew that Amy had promised to give Helen some feedback today. It wasn't going to happen. She'd have to go upstairs before she left to let Helen know she still wasn't ready.

Amy poured herself a drink. And undressed.

She didn't want to go to dinner. Liam had organised it. Gail would be there, as well as the scriptwriter who kept telling Liam he wanted to turn Mark Harden into a Netflix series. They had been clever until now, and had kept the film rights. Liam had tried writing his own screenplays, but none were successful. Now, as the sales of the books escalated, and their dominance of the *New York Times* Best Sellers lists was impossible to ignore, the opportunists were circling.

Amy cautioned against acting in haste. She cited *Jack Reacher* with Tom Cruise. He came back with *Game of Thrones*, *Harry Potter* and *Outlander*. She returned with James Patterson's *Alex Cross*. He with *Gone Girl*.

Liam was growing impatient. He needed a big name to back the project. The truth was he was annoyed that Idris Elba was considering playing James Bond, when Mark Harden was a perfect fit. He'd sent Elba his treatment but so far no interest had been shown. Which hurt. Liam had Elba in mind as he wrote the books, he said. Amy always had Liam in her mind. Liam was Mark Harden in many ways. That's how Amy wrote him. Elba's eyes were too kind. Mark Harden wouldn't get far with kind eyes. Besides, she had read that Elba was tied up with filming Stephen King's *Dark Tower*. That could drag on for years.

She'd go to the dinner. It was unavoidable. She couldn't have a screenwriter whispering sweet nothings into Liam's ear. He was susceptible to flattery. He was an enthusiast when it came to film. He could easily waste weeks rewriting or co-writing scripts that went nowhere. She needed him to keep to their tight writing schedule if they were going to meet their deadlines.

Besides, Gail was going. She couldn't stand her up. She'd been the one who had insisted Amy come.

*

Amy was in the shower when there was another knock at the inner door. She turned off the water and listened. Helen was calling down to her from the top of the stairs.

'I'm in the shower,' she called out.

'I'll come down later,' replied Helen.

She turned the water back on. She loved the showerhead Helen had chosen for the flat. It was generous. Large and round, like in shampoo adverts. That was one thing her lifestyle failed to deliver.

Good showering experiences. Josh's shower, for instance, dribbled lukewarm water over her.

Josh. Try as she might to stop herself, her thoughts kept drifting back to Josh. He was a disturbance in the force. He had no right to be in her life. Or at least, no right to her thoughts as well as her body. Just last night, she'd waited at the bar for hours like a pathetic groupie until he had finished work. He couldn't keep his hands off her in the cab back to his place. As soon as they were through the door he undressed her roughly and pushed her onto the bed. He stood above her and undressed, rubbing his cock until she couldn't stand it anymore and took him in her mouth.

Afterwards, he fell asleep immediately. Distant is a strange word to use considering the nature of their relationship. They weren't emotionally connected; it was still largely physical. But there had been a connection of their natures the first and second time around. His nature had been open and accepting, hers had been hungry and demanding. This time he was evasive and uncommunicative. Or was it she who had changed?

He woke when she was leaving, but instead of stopping her, he let her go.

The tables had turned. He had grown complacent. Expected her to return. She had handed him control without realising it.

He was supposed to be her plaything. Her fuck buddy.

But it no longer felt like that.

Where had her self-confidence gone?

The best way out, the best way to retain her dignity, was to not see him again. To go cold turkey. No more Josh cock.

But even after thinking this, if she went to dinner, she knew she'd have to stop herself from going around to his place afterwards. She knew she would find this difficult. She could feel the pull of him even now. But it wasn't his cock that she wanted. The way she was feeling, a fake boyfriend was better than no boyfriend.

Ten minutes later Amy was standing in briefs and bra at the bathroom mirror applying her makeup, when there was another knock on the inner door.

'Come down,' she called out, in response.

Expecting to see Helen, Amy continued at the mirror applying her mascara, and said, 'I was going to come up before I left. Would you like a drink?'

There was a pause.

'Yes,' came the delayed reply. It was a male voice. Amy glanced at the mirrored reflection of the doorway. She could see Daniel standing at the bottom of the stairs from where he had a good view of her near-naked form. The look on his face was enough for her to hiss, 'Get out!' and kick the door shut with her foot.

'Helen asked me to invite you up for a drink before you left,' he said through the door.

'Go away, Daniel. I'll come up before I go.'

She leant against the door. She was so angry. Where did this guy get his confidence?

And now she would have to go upstairs and sit with him while she had a drink with his parents. She stepped into her dress. It was too short and the neckline plunged too deep for dinner with Gail or a drink with Daniel. But it was gorgeous. She felt gorgeous in it.

She opened the door and found Daniel seated on the bottom step. She turned her gaze away from him too quickly to note his apathetic slouch.

'Who the fuck do you think you are?' she said, giving him a wide berth. She sat on the edge of her bed, casting anxious glances over her shoulder in case he moved, and slipped her heels on quickly. 'Do you have any idea how repulsive you are? How out of line this behaviour is?' She stood up.

He just shook his head wordlessly.

'Get out of my way, I'm going up.'

Daniel stood slowly and walked up the stairs. Amy left him in the kitchen.

She found Helen and Malcolm in the front room. The television was on and they were watching the BBC news. Malcolm switched it off as Amy entered.

'You look stunning, Amy,' said Helen. 'Stunning.'

'And tall,' added Malcolm as Daniel came into the room behind her. In her heels, she was noticeably taller than their son, who looked tired and frumpy beside her.

'Where are you going for dinner?' asked Helen.

'The Dorchester, I think. Not sure which. I know Liam likes the Grill but he's not paying, this time. A scriptwriter from LA is taking us out. I can't remember his name. So it's probably Alain Ducasse. Americans always choose it. The Michelin stars blind them.'

'Daniel, would you mind getting Amy a drink?' said Malcolm.

Daniel departed promptly.

'I'm sorry, Helen, but I'm still not done,' said Amy, sitting on the edge of the couch, her knees together.

'What has M&R said?' asked Helen, her face revealing her anxieties.

'I've put them off for another week. They have confidence in me. More than I have in myself, I must admit. And I blame Malcolm for this.'

'Me? What have I done?'

'You gave me good advice.'

'Well, I'm sorry for it. I'll try to offer poor advice in future.'

'What did you tell her?' asked Helen.

'You were there, Helen. He told me to read your other books. Fatal. I'm ruined.'

'Told you so,' said Malcolm.

Amy laughed. 'You did.'

'So, you have a foot in both camps now,' said Malcolm. It wasn't a question.

Daniel returned with a glass of white for Amy and a beer for himself.

'I won't stay if it's going to be book talk. I've had enough of that to last a lifetime.'

Amy took the glass and downed half the wine in one sip.

'What would you like to discuss, Daniel?' asked Helen.

Daniel smiled and then laughed, weirdly. He looked at the carpet, then said, 'That's put me on the spot.' His face reddened and a sob escaped him.

Amy, Helen and Malcolm all exchanged glances.

'Geraldine's leaving me,' Daniel said, raising his face to them. His eyes were wet. 'She's met someone else. It's been going on for some time. A client. Fucking him while the boys were in the house. But she says she's been unhappy for a while.'

'Oh, Daniel,' said Helen.

Amy drank the rest of her wine. She needed to get out of this family crisis immediately.

'Is that why you're down here?' asked Malcolm.

'I've been looking for a job in London. I can't stay up there.'

'What about the boys?' asked Helen.

Amy stood up. She didn't want to know about the boys. She didn't want to feel any sympathy for the man. She was definitely on Team Geraldine, whoever she was.

Daniel looked at her. 'Are you going?'

'I have to. Anyway, I'm in the way here. We'll talk more tomorrow, Helen. Bye, Malcolm.'

With that she exited. Moving quickly through the house, making her way downstairs, locking the inner door behind her. If she came back to the flat that night, which she hoped she wouldn't have to, she didn't want a grieving loser breaking in and molesting her in the middle of the night.

She grabbed her coat and her handbag and left, walked down to the high street and took a cab to Park Lane. The night air did nothing to clear her head. There was way too much going on in her life. She had to rid herself of the Helen problem as soon as possible. Move out and get back to living the life she was good at.

In the cab Amy checked her phone. Liam had sent through the screenplay the American had written. She googled the guy's name. Goran Kovac. He'd done nothing she recognised. She opened the attachment and read the opening scenes of the pilot. They were better than anything Liam had written himself. But she couldn't see Hollywood getting excited. Not that she knew anything about that world. It was a hunch.

Malcolm's assessment of her predicament returned to her – a foot in both camps. It was true. Here she was going to dine with one of the UK's bestselling authors and discuss turning his books into a Hollywood blockbuster or TV series, while all that day she had been thinking about version one of Helen's novel, the one Maxine Snedden had paid a fortune for, deciding, along with Helen's previous editor, Clarissa Munten, that it wasn't worthy of the great Helen Owen and should be shelved.

A foot in both camps.

But she couldn't give Helen that advice, because Julia and M&R would move to take back the advance and Helen and Malcolm would be ruined. The advice she'd have to give Helen was – give them what they want.

The first manuscript is the one the publisher paid for.

Amy told the driver to let her out at Marble Arch. She was half an hour early. She'd walk down Park Lane. It would kill ten minutes. But as soon as she was out of the cab she knew she had been an idiot. It wasn't a pleasant evening. The traffic was atrocious, a slow procession of tail-lights. The exhaust fumes were overwhelming. And her shoes were new. She cast her gaze down Park Lane. The road curved to the left. She couldn't tell how far she had to walk. It had been years since she'd walked here. She could cross over into Hyde Park but she wasn't sure if she could cross back at the Dorchester. She remembered having fallen for that trick years ago. Besides, the park looked dark and menacing from where she stood. At least Park Lane was well lit.

Resigned to her fate, she wrapped her Burberry trench coat more tightly around her and started to walk. Her high heels were strappy and her long legs were bare. She felt underdressed and wished her coat were longer. She felt naked under it and probably appeared to be. More naked with every passing sweaty tourist. Men and women each stared boldly at her like she was an exhibit. What had she been thinking getting out of the cab? She could have waited at the bar. Liam and Gail were probably there now.

This Helen thing was getting to her. Making her do stupid things.

Why had she taken Malcolm's advice? Because of him, she'd been with them more than a month – a month! For the first time in her career she'd neglected her work. She'd just kept up with the Jack Cade edits, but hadn't made any of their Thursday sessions. Liam wasn't happy. And she'd only been in the M&R office at odd hours. She'd been consumed by Malcolm and Helen's work. There were emails gathering unread in her inbox. Her cubicle buddy, Valerie, was fielding calls from concerned authors, and she was compiling a stack of sticky notes. Kathy Lette's agent had left word for her not to worry getting back to her as she'd found another editor. Valerie said her absence was being noticed. Even though she didn't need the work at M&R, she'd be sad to lose it. She had loved M&R under Maxine's leadership. And leaving would mean Julia would rule unopposed, and she couldn't stomach that.

A whole month had gone by and she'd read all the versions of Helen's new novel, some of her previous novels and some of Malcolm's novels, including his latest, *A Hundred Ways*.

And what had she achieved? Nothing practical. Not a thing of use to anybody. It was as though she was on holiday with friends. She was wasting everyone's time. More hindrance than help. And, as Malcolm had originally suggested, she was in over her head. She had entered another tier of publishing and of writing, a higher one, where her qualifications weren't required. She was reading these books as thousands of others had, as a reader, as an admirer.

Helen's and Malcolm's books didn't invite her professional persona in. They had no need of her skills as an editor. They were complete. They were books she wished she could discuss with Max.

Version one was different, of course. Malcolm had known that Amy would come to recognise this in time.

Last week she had re-read version one quickly, and was filled with doubts. She could no longer see it as she had first seen it — rich, compelling, romantic and heartbreaking. Now it was slow, ponderous and obvious.

Malcolm's prophecy had indeed come true.

Julia had wanted Amy to turn Helen Owen into Jojo Moyes. But now Amy saw that the task at hand was the complete reverse. If she was going to do anything to the manuscript, it would be to make it more Helen Owen, not less. She thought she might be able to do that without losing too much of its commercial appeal. And that way, she hoped, she might be able to ease Helen's concerns and even, if she did a good enough job, get Malcolm's blessing for the project.

But working with the printed manuscript wasn't possible. She'd never worked that way. And this task was outside her comfort zone as it was.

So she had picked up her laptop and had begun typing out version one of the novel. She wanted to get inside Helen's head. Typing it out manually was definitely the slow option, when she might have scanned it in, or been more devious and logged in to Helen's computer when she wasn't around. The password was probably 'Daniel' or 'Malcolm'. But typing books out had always helped her understand a writer better. She would become immersed in a work, reconstructing it line by line according to the writer's vision.

This time she marked up the novel as she worked. So by the end of the long process she had a file called Version Helen and a file called Version Amy. Amy's version was tighter and more focused. She'd cut at least a third of it as she went. She thought it flowed better because it was less explanatory. And though she was pleased with what she had done, because now she felt she had contributed by strengthening its commercial appeal, she wasn't satisfied. The 'something' that was missing in Version Helen was missing in Version Amy, too.

But did that matter?

Back when Amy had first read version one, she now recalled, she had been convinced of its commercial potential. That Amy had come straight from the real world and wasn't yet influenced by Helen and Malcolm's world. She should now just trust old Amy's opinion on this. Helen wouldn't be the first literary author to offer the world a gripping story to pay the rent. Granted, most had been catastrophic failures, but Helen's worked as commercial fiction. Helen's would succeed.

But now she wasn't sure. This afternoon, on re-reading the opening chapters of Version Amy, she had become convinced it had no commercial potential. She was more confused than ever.

The one person she thought might be able to help was Liam. They'd come to share a sense of what worked, what the general reader wanted from a novel. And he was free of the atmosphere of Helen and Malcolm's literary world.

Now she had a digital copy, it would be so easy to send.

*

Dinner was a disaster.

Amy arrived early regardless of her efforts. She found herself a place at the bar and ordered a glass of champagne. She never minded waiting in a bar. Bars were her natural environment. With access to endless alcohol and nuts, accompanied by the easy chatter of a handsome, attentive and well-mannered barman, she was content.

By the time Goran Kovac turned up, three-quarters of an hour late, she had read his screenplay, read everything on the net about him and scrolled through his social media. She decided not to introduce herself. He was clearly drunk. He walked up to the bar like he owned the place, greeting the barman as he would a brother. He sounded Russian, but Google had told her he was Hungarian. He had been living in LA for ten years.

He was a large man, with a heavy beard, a mad mop for hair, a barrel chest and strong shoulders, though he was not particularly tall. He was wearing a dark suit with a white shirt open at the neck. Amy noticed his shoes when he first walked in. They were blood-red, cap-toe Oxfords. Which were matched by a splash of the same red in his suit pocket. He was no shrinking violet.

A drink in hand, Kovac looked at Amy for a long time while she pretended to be busy with her phone. In fact she was typing *Don't come near me* over and over again. There were other lone women in the place. She was really hoping one of them would attract his eye.

Then he said loudly, to the barman, to the bar, to whoever was in earshot, 'I'm here to meet with the author Jack Cade. Is he here yet?'

The barman looked at him as though he were speaking another language. Amy was in an awkward position. If she didn't speak now, he would soon find out she had consciously avoided introducing herself.

'You don't know who Jack Cade is?' he asked. The barman shook his head.

Kovac downed his scotch.

'You know Jack Cade, don't you?' he said to Amy.

'I should, I'm his editor.'

Kovac had been so loud that everyone in the bar was watching him. Now all eyes were on Amy. It seemed that the only person who didn't know Jack Cade was the barman.

Liam was now almost an hour late. He would normally message to let her know. But she had nothing.

'You're his editor!' shouted Kovac, and slapped his forehead. Then moved towards her. He motioned for the barman to give him another drink, lifted the bottle of Bollinger from the ice bucket next to Amy and refilled her glass. 'I have heard about you.'

'I hope not.'

'Yes, yes. I have a friend in publishing. When she heard what I was doing she said that you were the brains behind Jack Cade. That's what she said!'

'Don't let Liam hear you say that.'

'But that's what she said. And she said everyone knew. But I didn't know it. She said that you would have the final word on my script.'

'Who said?'

'I cannot say. But is it true?'

'You won't have to ask once you've met Liam.'

Kovac scrutinised Amy for a moment.

'Here he is.' Amy stood up and took a few steps towards Liam and Gail, who had just entered the bar.

'Sorry we're late,' said Liam. He looked exhausted.

Amy gave a frosty Gail a kiss and a hug.

'So this is Jack Cade!' boomed Kovac from behind Amy. She moved out of the way and dragged Gail with her.

Kovac introduced himself and gave Liam a bear hug.

Amy asked Gail what was wrong. But Gail shook off her enquiries.

Liam looked across at them. There was definitely something wrong, Amy saw. Something had spooked him.

Gail wanted champagne. Liam wanted a lager. But before the drinks arrived they discovered they had lost their reservation due to their lateness. The maître d' was being difficult, so Liam suggested eating at another place. Within minutes they were all in Liam's Aston Martin racing through the London streets, Amy and Kovac in the back. Liam was on the phone speaking to a friend he knew would pull a few strings for him. He wanted somewhere private.

'I did not know Aston Martins came in four-door,' Kovac revealed. He was like a child, touching all the buttons and running a hand along the finishes.

'Not quite Bond. But Gail insisted. Didn't you, babe,' said Liam, putting his hand on her knee.

No answer came. Gail was staring through the window at the passing streets.

After fifteen minutes of driving and with no callback from the trusted friend, Liam did an illegal U-turn and sped off south, crossing the Vauxhall Bridge and racing towards Clapham. The mood in the car was tense. Amy could only see the side of Liam's face, but his jaw was clenched, as it was when she criticised his work.

Amy had no idea where they were. There had been slow traffic on the A3 so Liam had turned off and was racing through residential streets. The muted roar of the Aston was exhilarating from within the car, deafening without. Liam had been raised in Brixton; these streets were well known to him.

Sharp turns, left then right. Roaring acceleration, hard braking. His passengers gripping the handles above their doors.

Amy saw that Liam had made a miscalculation. He approached a one-way bridge blocked to traffic from his direction. Liam swore and caught Amy's eye in the rear-view mirror. He looked ready to explode. He put his foot down and sped through the no entry signs and onto the narrow bridge, made narrower by the addition of a wide bike path. Gail gasped and Kovac wooted.

As soon as he was on the bridge and over the rise, it was clear a car was approaching the bridge from the other side. A little Renault, it swerved and braked, honking its horn and flashing its lights as Liam came through. The Aston swerved, and honked in return before roaring past them. Almost as an afterthought, Liam slammed the brakes and took a hard left. He straightened and accelerated rapidly to eighty miles per hour down the narrow side street.

Kovac laughed loudly and exclaimed, 'It's what Mark Harden would do. Isn't it? Isn't it?'

'You're a fucking child, Liam,' said Gail. 'Slow down.'

Liam sped up. The phone rang and Liam answered.

'Too fucking late,' said Liam, before the friend could answer, and hung up.

He came to a sudden stop.

'We're here.'

Amy looked out of her window and couldn't work out where here was. Liam got out. A laughing Kovac did, too.

Amy was about to open her door when Gail turned in her seat and said, 'I'm leaving him.'

Before Amy could say anything in reply, Gail got out.

Amy exhaled, relieved. She'd been apprehensive about the cause of their dispute, but as Gail's tone was friendly, Amy knew she wasn't the cause. She opened the door and climbed out.

The night certainly wasn't going as she had imagined. She wondered if she might get an Uber back to her studio. She certainly didn't want to go back to Helen and Malcolm's, not with miserable Daniel lurking about.

Then tattoo boy entered her mind. She didn't care that she was now his bitch. As soon as she could, she would excuse herself and find him.

As she crossed the street to join them, she messaged Josh: *Do you have the energy?*

Walking around a rubbish skip, she looked up and read the sign above the door Liam had entered – 'The Manor'.

'Where the fuck are we?' she asked no one, glancing down the street and vaguely recognising the high street at its end. She followed the others in.

The woman behind the counter knew Liam, kissed him on the cheek and led them to the back. Amy smiled at the self-conscious grunge of the place. Pure hipster. They were given a corner table and Kovac asked to see the wine list. They had a drinks list, the woman replied. Did they have champagne? Yes. French? All champagne is French. Then bring two bottles on ice.

While Kovac was negotiating drinks Gail hovered around the table but didn't sit. Liam studiously ignored her. She walked off to the bathroom. Amy gave Liam a look that said *What the fuck have you done?*, stood up quickly and followed.

The bathroom wasn't large. Black walls, dimly lit. Gail was standing in front of the mirror staring at herself when Amy walked in.

'Tell me what's happened,' Amy said rather forcefully.

'I'm tired of it all. He's so driven, so busy. I never see him. And when I do, he treats me like he treated his mother. I'm someone he loves and cherishes. He's all cuddles and affection. He buys me gifts. He sends me off to day spas. He organises shopping trips to Paris. But I want to be his lover, not his mother. And he lies to me just as he lied to his mum. And his lies are so transparent.'

'And you've said all this to him?'

'In part, but he doesn't listen to me. The way he talks to you and listens to you, he never does with me. He listens to your advice. He respects what you have to say. He hasn't heard a word I've said for years.'

'But I only talk to him about our work. There's more to the world than books.'

'Not to him. He can barely keep his eyes open if I talk about my day, or what I've been thinking or doing. We're going to renovate the house, but I can't get him to sit still and approve the architect's plans. We're going to tour South America, as we've never been, but when I try to get him to confirm dates, he won't. The only thing he wants to talk to me about is babies. He's obsessed with the idea of starting a family. That's what started all of this. He thought we were trying for a baby, he thought we'd agreed, but I hadn't agreed. He never listens to me. He ignored my concerns. He's ready, so I must be. Then he found my pill. I hadn't been hiding it. It was in my bedside table drawer. He was so angry. So upset.'

'Do you want a family?'

'Do you?'

'Not yet!'

'Same. I'm in my early thirties; I have plenty of time for all that. I'm still hot, aren't I?' said Gail, glancing at herself in the mirror. She was a beautiful woman who always dressed well and as a former beautician knew how to accentuate her qualities. She had put on weight in the last few years but no one could say she wasn't attractive. Amy thought the weight suited her.

'I'd fuck you.'

'That's what I thought, but he's marked me out as the mother of his children. I don't want that role. I certainly don't want to get stuck down in Surrey raising kids while he's living it up in London and New York fucking everything in a skirt.'

'Do you love him?'

'Of course I fucking do!' There was real fire in her eyes. 'And he loves me. You should have seen his face when I told him I was leaving. He was distraught. He loves me and only me. I'm certain of it. But right now I'd rather not be loved by him. I'd much rather be his lover than his wife. I'd rather be you, Amy.'

'Why me?' asked Amy, her heart missing a beat.

'Because you get his respect and his cock.'

Amy blanched. Her mouth went dry.

'Don't worry. I wouldn't mess with what you have. Without you, where would we be?'

'But ...' Amy's mind was racing to find a neat exit.

'I've always known. A wife knows. The man is a terrible liar. You're good. I'd never have known if you were my only source of information. You can lie to my face without a trace of it anywhere. You amaze me. Totally amoral. But he can't. He gave you away in the first few days. For a time he was infatuated with you. He was like a teenager. I knew something was wrong because he was fucking me all the time. Like when we were young. But watching you together, I realised you didn't love him. That was important.

You were all business. You knew how to get the best out of him and you milked it, literally.'

Amy felt the full force of Gail's assessment of her. *Totally amoral*, she'd said. Amy's hasty attempts to rationalise her behaviour stalled. All exits vanished. This was Liam's wife speaking. Flesh and blood. Not some idea of her. The pain visible now on Gail's face had been there all along, if only Amy had bothered to notice.

'I'm so sorry, Gail,' she said, resting her hands on the bench and looking at Gail's reflection in the mirror. She felt nauseous. The shame she had felt all those years ago with Max, the shame she had tried to drown in being shameless, returned.

Gail held her gaze for a moment. She resented the note of understanding in Amy's tone.

'There's no sorry for what you've done,' said Gail. 'Back then I hated you. I might have stabbed you. You were always so beautiful, so privileged, so smart, so friendly, so white. But I'm done with all that. I am. I've had years to get used to you and Liam. It's just business. You're collaborators. Without him, you're nothing and without you, he's nothing. Of course he was going to fuck you. And you him. He's gorgeous and brilliant, like you. And the money you two have made. It's extraordinary. Growing up we never dreamed of having so much money.' Gail was repeating the story she had told herself every day. The story that kept her upright. 'But he loves me. Always has and always will. I'm under his skin. I'm home to him. The only one he has. But I won't be the fat cow looking after the fucking kids. I won't.'

There were tears in Gail's eyes, but none fell.

'I've caught you by surprise,' said Gail, touching Amy's arm maternally.

Amy took a deep breath but said nothing. She stood up straight again and caught her reflection in the mirror. She looked as stunned as she felt.

A young woman entered the small bathroom. She stopped dead on finding Gail and Amy deep in conversation. Then, seeing the empty stall, entered and closed the door.

Gail leant close to Amy's ear and whispered, 'You must have known this would happen. One day. You must have.'

'I don't know what to say.' This was all too real for her. She was for flight. She had no fight in her. To fight would be to acknowledge the wrong she had done Gail. To own up to it fully. But she wasn't that strong. She just wanted to say the words Gail wanted to hear so she could get out of this night in one piece.

Gail's voice was trembling when she next spoke. 'I didn't mean to say anything tonight. I promised myself I never would. This isn't about …' Her voice failed her. She paused to breathe in deeply. 'I'm not jealous anymore. I'm not.'

Amy wanted so much to believe this. She took Gail's hand in her own.

The loo flushed and the woman left as quickly as she had come, making no attempt to get to the sink to wash her hands.

'The strange thing is,' Gail continued, having recovered herself slightly, 'even though you're fucking my husband, you're one of my closest friends. Really. You shouldn't be, but you are. I admire you. What you've achieved. And I trust you more than almost anyone. Even now. Can you believe that?'

Amy dropped Gail's hand and turned her face away. These words stung. She had only ever played at friendship with Gail, in order to mask her deceit. She liked her, but had never considered her a friend.

How ugly everything is, Amy thought. How ugly I am.

'I just wish …' started Gail, before being unable to speak. She caught her breath and tried to hold back the tears, but they fell regardless.

Amy took her hand again. She felt useless.

'This isn't about you, Amy. It isn't. I promise,' Gail said, losing her fight and sobbing uncontrollably. 'I don't hate you,' she said, between breaths. 'But it's hard. I want his children, I do, but I want him to be true to me. I love him so much it hurts. I said to him … I said … Be true and I will have your babies. Be true.'

Gail was overcome and turned away.

Amy walked around and, kissing her wet cheek, hugged her tightly.

How could it not be about me? Amy thought. I'm the one fucking her husband. Of course it's about me. I'm a fucking bitch. A fucking bitch.

*

When they returned to the table, Liam and Kovac welcomed them back as though they had been gone a few minutes. But the table told another story. The men had ordered a selection of starters and had demolished most of them.

Amy went to sit beside Liam, but Gail touched her arm gently. As soon as Gail sat down, Liam put his arm around her. Amy poured Gail and herself champagne. They held each other's gaze as they downed their glass in one. They followed it with another.

Amy noticed that Gail's hand was shaking slightly, then noticed the tremor in her own. How many nights had Amy shared with Gail like this assuming her secret was safe? How much pain had she inflicted on her? Day after day, night after night? Liam out with his wife and lover. It was awful. Everything was awful.

Now she was exposed, the future was a blur. She couldn't see how the night would end.

'I'm so happy to be sitting with two of London's most beautiful women,' said Kovac, in a good-humoured attempt to resurrect the night. Amy wanted to stab him.

Gail smiled politely, but all light had gone out of her eyes.

'I read your script, Mr Kovac,' said Amy, in a bid to lead the conversation away from the rocks.

'Call me Goran.'

'I read your script, Goran. It's good. I'm impressed,' she lied.

Kovac couldn't hide his pleasure. He clapped his hands.

'I am so pleased. I am such a fan of the novels. I have read them all a number of times now. Jack, I mean Liam, was just telling me about the one you're both writing now.'

'I'm writing. Amy is my editor.'

'Right,' said Kovac, glancing at Liam and turning back to Amy who sat beside him. 'It sounds complicated.'

'We're having difficulty with it,' said Amy, 'It's unusual for Mark Harden to be in love. He's such a loner. We haven't really tried romantic elements in the past. Sex, of course, always a bit of sex to break up the endless fighting. But no love.'

'We consciously avoided it until now,' said Liam. 'I never liked it when James Bond fell in love. Love weakens a hero. Makes him vulnerable. He shouldn't be vulnerable.'

'But the story led Liam there. Mark Harden sometimes does his own thing. We're just spectators,' Amy heard herself saying, making it up as she went. She was always in control.

'Goran was just extolling the virtues of HBO. He's convinced that if they pick up the series it will be done right.'

'The violence of the books must be converted to screen as is,' said Kovac, passionately. 'No censorship. The sex as it is – raw, brutal and erotic. It has to be unadulterated Jack Cade.'

'It's what viewers expect these days,' said Liam.

'How tame does *Game of Thrones* look now?' asked Kovac. 'We have become immune to its sex and violence. It looks like a cartoon now. But how shocking was the red wedding when it aired? We need Mark Harden to be grittier and more realistic than *True Detective*, more perverse than *Hannibal*, more erotic than *Versailles*. Have you seen *Bosch*?'

'Books are always better than the film or series. It's a fact,' said Amy, reaching out under the table and taking Gail's hand.

'Doesn't have to be so,' said Liam. 'Goran was thinking of doing an eight-part series for each novel. Be true to the books. As far as is possible.'

Amy smiled indulgently. Liam was kidding himself. Their novels didn't have enough to them for an eight-part series.

'Did you see what they did to Jack Reacher?' asked Goran. 'Not just the Tom Cruise thing. But the story. Lee Child had the story – why not start with *Killing Floor*? Millions of people had loved that book. Why not make a film of *Killing Floor* instead of taking elements from a few books?'

So the night filled up with words. A couple of hours went by. Food came and went, bottles were opened and emptied. Gail sat silent throughout. When at last it was time to go, Liam paid and then led the way out to the car, his arm around Gail's waist.

Liam was too drunk to drive, but hopped into the driver's seat, anyway. They were only going to the flat, not back to Surrey.

Gail hugged Amy, holding her a little tighter and longer than she would normally.

Amy felt compelled to say something. She had done so much damage to this woman over the years. When Gail ended the hug, Amy took her hand and whispered a promise into her ear. Gail replied by kissing her then opened the door and sat in the passenger seat beside Liam.

Kovac, seeing an opportunity, grabbed Amy and gave her a bear hug. With some difficulty she managed to force him into the car. He had wanted to see Amy home, but she was having none of that. She was getting an Uber.

Josh hadn't replied to her message. But she would go past his place anyway. It was only midnight. The Aston roared off. She was alone in the street. She had drunk a lot as the men talked and talked. She felt unsteady on her feet. She was looking forward to being manhandled by Josh. Her phone told her the driver was only a few streets away, but it was cold, so she stood rubbing her arms. Her feet were frozen.

The Uber arrived. Fifteen minutes later she was standing outside Josh's place. Her confidence had plummeted in the back seat of the car. He hadn't answered her original message, so she'd messaged again. No answer. She made the Uber wait. She buzzed repeatedly. Again she could hear the buzzer in Josh's room from the street. She took a few steps back and looked up. His lights were on.

She buzzed again. And again. She was getting annoyed.

Finally a woman answered, 'Go away. He's not here.'

In the Uber on her way back to Helen and Malcolm's place, Amy stared out at the passing streets. Josh's rejection had sobered her. It reminded her of Max and the tears and the stupor. Josh wasn't Max. Josh meant nothing. Fuck Josh. She needed a drink. She made the driver stop at an off-licence. She bought a small bottle of vodka and got back in the car. She hated vodka but it warmed her up. It fuelled her anger and her disgust.

She drank half the bottle. She was grotesque. Gail knew it. Fuck Gail. Liam relied on it. Fuck Liam. Josh was clear about it. Fuck Josh. Both Helen and Malcolm suspected it. Fuck them, too. But it was Max who had first discovered it. The award should go to him. Fucker.

She messaged Max: *Where want to meet?* She would see him. She owed it to him. Whatever he wanted she would give him. She read what she had sent. She grimaced. And sent a second: *Drunk. :-) Where DO YOU want to meet?*

The car lurched around a corner and Amy's vision blurred. She felt awful. She was exhausted. Her eyes were heavy. She rested her head against the glass. The movement beyond the window was hypnotic and nauseating.

'We're here. Hey, we're here,' said the driver, reaching around. He had his hand on her knee and was shaking her.

Amy woke. She'd slumped in the seat. Her dress and coat were lifted. Legs exposed to the hip. The radio was on, the volume down low. 'Smells Like Teen Spirit' was playing. It sounded weird. She sat up.

The driver's eyes were gentle. He was speaking softly. 'Don't leave anything behind. Have you got everything?'

She collected her handbag, found her phone and the bottle then paid the driver. She gave him a big tip. A fifty. He had touched her knee. She could still feel the warmth of his hand. He could have taken her anywhere, done anything to her.

'You're a nice man,' she said. 'Thank you.' She took a photo of him with her phone and thanked him again. She was leaning against the car. Unsure if she could walk the ten feet to the door. She slipped off her heels.

'Miss, I have to go.'

She steered herself towards the steps down to her flat. The Uber drove off. The street was very quiet after the sound of the Uber died away. The soft growl of traffic on a distant motorway the only sound. The pavement was freezing underfoot. Amy negotiated the stairs. Clutching her shoes, phone, bottle and handbag to herself, she gripped the rail tightly with her free hand. The key went in but try as she might she couldn't get the door open. She shoved it, tried other keys, swore at it. Nothing. She sat on the step and tried to stop her head from spinning. She might have been at the wrong door. That could be it. She picked up her things, stood up and climbed the stairs unsteadily.

On the pavement she looked at the houses. They all looked identical.

'Amy!' came a voice in the night. A whispered shout. She spun around. It was coming from the other side of the street. 'Amy, over here.'

She walked towards the noise.

Daniel was standing in the doorway of a house on the opposite side of the street.

'Daniel!' said Amy, in her normal voice. It sounded very loud.

'Shhh! Come on. What were you doing?' he asked. He was opening the gate for her.

'Going to bed.' She passed him and entered Helen and Malcolm's house.

'That was the wrong house,' he whispered, closing the door behind them.

'How do you know?'

'We're standing in the right house.'

'I want to go to bed.'

'I'll take you down. Have you drunk any water?'

'I don't like water.'

Amy wandered into the front room where the TV was on and sat on the couch.

'You can't sleep here.' He took her hand and lifted her onto her feet. He picked up her bag, shoes and the bottle. She held her phone.

'Sleep.'

He used her key to unlock the door and led her downstairs. There she got her bearings. The main lights were on and everything was very bright. She looked back at Daniel. He was dressed differently. He was in his pyjamas and dressing gown.

'You're in pyjamas,' she said and laughed.

'I was getting ready for bed. It's late.'

'Did you wait up for me?'

'No.'

She examined his face. It was blotchy. Like he'd been crying.

'You're funny-looking,' she said, as she made her way into the bathroom. She didn't close the door.

'Thank you,' he replied.

She pulled down her knickers and sat on the loo. He turned abruptly away as he heard the stream of pee hit the toilet water and began to climb the stairs.

'Where are you going?' she asked, from the loo.

'I was watching a film.'

'*Jack Reacher*?'

'No, *Ben-Hur*. It's been going for hours.'

'I liked *Jack Reacher*,' continued Amy, from the loo. 'I've told people I didn't like it, but I did.' Amy came out of the bathroom, lifting her dress over her head. She strode past him in her bra and knickers, saying, 'I'm so fucking tired.'

'Get into bed then,' he said, staring at her as she pulled back the covers. He switched off the main lights. The bathroom light was still on. He turned on the light at the top of the stairs so he could find his way out, then crossed to turn the bathroom light off. When he turned back, he expected to find her under the covers but Amy was standing by the bed naked.

'I thought I was repulsive.'

'You are. You're fat, old, bald and lecherous. You look like Bernard from *Four Weddings and a Funeral* minus the moustache. But you're a man with a cock and that's what I want right now.'

He took a step forward.

'Turn off the light.'

'I want to keep it on,' he said.

'Your view is better than mine, turn it off.'

*

Amy woke at 5 am. She switched on the bedside lamp. She was alone. She remembered what she had done and did not repent. She deserved degradation. She was an awful person. She discovered the bottle of vodka on the bedside table and took a swig. It burned. She took another. She kicked the bedsheets from her and looked down at her naked body.

He was all over her skin. Saliva, sweat and cum. He had worshipped her. Praised her with extravagant words. Thanked her as he touched her. Kissed her everywhere. It was like being the centrepiece of a religious ceremony. His breath was in her breath. She had given herself to him. To his lusts. He had taken her again and again, insatiably. She was disgusted by it all. His touch revolted her. His cock revolted her. His tongue revolted her. And yet she acquiesced to it all. She welcomed him again and again. Encouraged him, even. She had sucked his cock back to life so he could go again. Her body felt broken, beaten, diseased.

She rolled out of bed and pulled on her dirty underwear and then her jeans and a T-shirt from yesterday. She wouldn't wash yet. She would keep him with her. Disgusting man. Disgusting woman. Grotesque man. Grotesque woman. There was no escape from the plain facts. She was an awful person. She had done awful things.

She started to cry, but made nothing of it. She wouldn't give herself sympathy she didn't deserve. The tears fell and she ignored them. She took another swig of vodka. The bottle was now empty.

After a pee, she opened her laptop. Helen's manuscript. She had promised to give Helen her advice today. Stupid tears fell again. Everything she did was hateful. She didn't want to be herself any longer. She didn't have any advice. She only had what Julia wanted.

She wrote a short email to Liam. All business, no mention of personal matters.

*Subject line: Urgent.*
*Read this and tell me if you think it has legs. It's by a friend. I'm*
*too close to it to tell. Don't show anyone else. Delete when done.*
*Get back to me today please. Urgent.*

Amy attached the Word document of Version Helen then paused. Helen had expressly told her not to share the manuscript. She had been staying with Helen and Malcolm because of that rule. No digital copies were to leave the building.

Wiping away her tears, Amy pressed 'Send'. There was no other way. She could never be trusted. She was an awful person.

She lay back on the bed. Her life had taken a wrong turn when she agreed to meet Helen. Everything was fine until then. Or at least she thought it had been fine. No, she corrected, it *had* been fine. Now it was shit. Shit. Shit. Shit. Everywhere she turned there was judgement. Everything she did was judged. Helen and Malcolm judged. They looked down on Amy from on high and judged.

And they were harsh judges. They made her see.

She didn't want to see.

She pictured Daniel and Gail and Alan and Josh and Julia and Liam and Max.

Painful tears fell. Her chest hurt. Her breath was short.

She tried to fight back. She tore the sheets off her bed and threw them into the corner of the room. But she couldn't stop crying, so she took herself off to the shower and washed. Daniel was everywhere. Nothing would come off. No soap could clean her. Her tears fell, mingling with the hot water. She got out and dried herself. The tears would not dry.

She found her phone. Max had messaged back in the night.

There was no escape. The past was never gone.

She sent a reply: *Yes.*

# Chapter 21
# Did You Say a Million?

'Jesus, Trevor, what time is it?'

'Six. Why?'

'It's very early for a call.'

'So, you're awake aren't you?'

'I mightn't have been.'

'You mightn't but you are. You've probably already had your first cup of tea.'

'Trevor, you've probably woken Helen and Daniel.'

'Daniel's there?'

'Yes, long story.'

'I have time.'

'I don't. It's bloody early, it must be important, why did you call?'

'Look, stop complaining. I've been up since 4 am. Sleep at my age frightens me. The less I have the better. Listen to me. A friend from the US who is in touch with a friend in the UK who is friendly with one of the judges on the Booker let it slip that you're most likely going to be on the shortlist.'

'Idiots.'

'But you know what this means for you?'

'Trouble.'

'Sales. I've been here before. Shortlisters sell. Front window of every good bookshop. Book clubs. It's very fashionable to have read all of the shortlisters.'

'When will it be announced?'

'Soon. A few weeks. In September, I think. Sorry, Malcolm, I don't seem to have the date with me here.'

'I won't do interviews.'

'It doesn't matter. You've gone viral. Do you know what that means?'

'Do you?'

'Not until Zoe explained it to me. Going viral is good, Malcolm. We're seeing an increase in sales already. You're a meme apparently.'

'Is that good, too?'

'Yes. And you know what? The podcast of the radio interview has a million downloads on iTunes. I'm quoting Zoe again. She left some notes with me. She's a good girl. Her mother is still trouble, but by giving me such a clever granddaughter she redeemed herself.'

'Did you say a million?'

'A million. You've hit a nerve, Malcolm. That awful book is just what the young want.'

'God.'

'They're reprinting, too. I had a note from Graham. Ten thousand. I'm so happy we went for the high-spec hardcover. That extra cost will pay big dividends if this takes off. You might actually make some money out of this horrid little book. Wouldn't that be a surprise.'

'What sort of money?'

'Proper money, Malcolm. You've uncovered the zeitgeist of our age. The kids love this stuff. You're today's Hermann Hesse. This is your *Steppenwolf* or *Demian*. You're cool, Malcolm.'

'Could it win?'

'Don't be daft. But that won't matter. The kids like you, Malcolm. The kids! I'll send you some examples of the memes.

They're very good. Funny. Your profile has never been this high. I personally thought your interview disgraceful. Shows how out of touch I am.'

'I'm serious about interviews. I won't do them. I'm busy.'

'I don't want you to do interviews, either. Let that first one stand. Let them get excited about it. Leave them wanting more. To them you're an iconoclast. To them you're a rebel, Malcolm.'

'A rebel in a dressing gown and disposable pull-up incontinence pants.'

'Rebels come in all shapes and sizes. Goodbye for now, Malcolm.'

# Chapter 22
# I'd Forgotten His Ways

I left the flat early. Just past seven in the morning.

I knew I'd be out all day and was dressed for all weather – trainers, jeans, T-shirt and my new favourite hoodie. Something I usually wore around the flat. It was too big for me and was really baggy but it had fleece on the inside and was comforting.

Before I left I pulled my hair back in a ponytail and popped my cap on. I checked myself in the mirror. My face looked puffy, and there were dark patches around the eyes. Fuck it. After the night I'd had, the point was to look sexless. Completely and utterly sexless. With my sunglasses on, I was anonymous, too. Perfect attire for meeting Max.

As an afterthought, I grabbed my gym bag, emptied it and threw in my laptop, purse, phone, some changes of underwear, my makeup bag, sandals and a fresh tee. Then I added a dress. Anything could happen. I might never return.

Helen and Malcolm were already awake; I could hear faint noises in the kitchen upstairs. Helen would be waiting for me to come up and talk to her. It wasn't going to happen. I had to buy some time. Liam would get back to me, eventually. Even if he only read a few sample chapters while taking his morning shit. He was usually quick with his assessments. They weren't always right but they generally pointed in the right direction, which was helpful.

And then I was on the street moving quickly. I felt hounded. No one was following me, but I could feel the weight of Helen's reproaches. I could feel Daniel's idiotic hopes. I could feel Malcolm's censure. I could also feel the truth bearing down on me. The one I would not allow or admit.

I slowed my pace once I was out of view of Helen and Malcolm's place and was nearing the tube station. I was meeting Max at the V&A at eleven. It was his favourite meeting place, being a short walk from his office. But I had hours to kill before then. My default time killer was the National Gallery, but it was too early.

The tube took me to Sloane Square where I had breakfast at Côte Brasserie. It wasn't busy so I opened my laptop and did some work for Liam. I ordered another coffee to make it last, but the waitress eventually grew tired of my presence. I felt uncomfortable under her gaze and moved on.

I had never strolled down the King's Road so early. None of the shops were open. It was depressing. I crossed the street to look at the books in Waterstones' windows. There were our books: a neat little pile of the older titles in paperback beside a larger display of the latest hardcover, *No Going Back Now*. They were stickered with 'No. 1 Bestseller'.

And in the next window were all of the Man Booker longlisters. Malcolm's book was there. Each book was accompanied by a photo of the author and a quote. The standard author photo of Malcolm – taken about twenty years ago – was accompanied by a quote from the radio interview: '*A Hundred Ways* isn't about anything. That's why no one wanted to publish it. It's just a tiny blood clot. That's all it is. And it's travelling along an artery towards our collective brain – culture. Now I just want to live long enough to see the surprise in the eye of mankind as the aneurysm strikes.'

I was about to keep walking when Waterstones opened. I went in.

I stupidly decided to buy the other longlisters. Thirteen books. And then made another poor decision, which was to walk. By the time I reached the V&A my arms were about to break. It wasn't far, but I took a couple of wrong turns and the bags were heavy.

I arrived at the V&A early. I left the books in the cloakroom and walked through to the inner courtyard. This was my favourite spot in the V&A. Years ago, when Max would drag me here to exhibitions, if it was sunny, I would let him go around without me and I'd wait for him, lying in the sun with my feet in the paddling pool. Now, there were people already doing what I had once done. I stood looking for a spot when I heard my name.

Max was seated behind me, near the south wall at a small white table half in and half out of the sun. He was in the shade and the Penguin Modern Classic he'd been reading was resting open face down on his knee. I don't know how he knew it was me. I had passed my reflection in a shop window and had stared at it. I thought I looked completely anonymous.

I'd forgotten his ways. He was always early. It caused him great anxiety to be late; to counter that he habitually arrived at least half an hour early for things. It used to drive me nuts and was the cause of many arguments. We'd often end up arriving separately.

There are moments in your life when you know you've taken the wrong path. Meeting Helen had been a wrong step. Seeing Max seated at a table with a coffee and a bottle of mineral water in the V&A garden was confirmation of my error. I felt convinced that we were meeting because of that choice. The life I was living now with Helen and Malcolm was a shadow of the life I had lived with Max. The same centre of gravity. The same ambitions. I had re-entered his world by stepping through Helen's front door.

But I thought I'd left all that behind. I'd put years, millions of words and many men between me and the Amy who hung on every word that left his lips.

I didn't go to him now. I stood firm and stared.

I'd forgotten how petite he was. He'd grown in my memory. He wasn't exactly short – he was taller than me – but he was small: slight hands, thin wrists, narrow shoulders, no hips. Not an ounce of fat on him. He was wearing dark suit trousers, brown leather belt, matching brogues and a pink shirt. His suit jacket was hanging on the back of his seat. His shirtsleeves were rolled up, and his top button was undone, which was his concession to the sunny day.

There was a moment when I thought I would just walk off. He was suddenly alien. I looked at his face. His lips. His eyes. The slight stubble. He wasn't the same. It wasn't the Max I'd known. The Max I knew didn't need to shave. The Max I knew had a light in his eyes, an eternal optimism. A hint of laughter on his lips.

He must have sensed I was edging towards flight. 'Amy,' he said again, and stood.

I closed my eyes and took a deep breath. It was a mistake. I saw him naked. I saw that slight figure standing at the end of the bed. The pale skin. The patches of dark hair on his chest and the thick pubic hair. I remembered his cock and the weight of his body on mine. I remembered his hand on my hip as he slept, the nights in his arms while we read. I remembered how he held my hand on the street. I remembered how I had wanted him.

I opened my eyes. There were tears in them, but I brushed them aside. He wasn't the Max I had known. He was older. He was more reserved. He was a stranger.

I placed my sunglasses on the table, read the title of the book, *Extinction* by Thomas Bernhard, then I sat opposite him in the sun.

'There is no us, so don't even mention the past,' he said straight off. He might have slapped me. That was the effect. My cheeks reddened. I stared at him in disbelief.

'Would you like a coffee?' he added. I shook my head. Still smarting.

The hoodie was too warm now. But I couldn't take it off. I really didn't want to be me in front of him.

'You're different,' I said.

'Of course I'm fucking different,' he said. He looked at me very directly. 'And you know why.'

There was no denying anything he said.

'You owe me,' he added.

I knew what it was for him to say this. He didn't want anything from me back then or since. Something had changed.

I nodded.

'The magazine is in trouble. I need something big. Something that will sell physical copies and something that will get people to beyond the paywall online. An article that might get syndicated in the US.'

'Surely one article won't save you if you're in financial trouble.'

'The backers are getting anxious. A small uptick in sales would settle them down and give me another six months. It'll also raise my profile and give me a platform to leap from if it came to that.'

'So you want access to Liam?'

'I can get access to Liam, for Christ's sake. Anyone could. He's on tour most of the year. He's overexposed. No, I don't want access to Liam.'

'What do you want then?'

'I want the black man.'

At first I didn't catch his meaning. Then I remembered Val McDermid's book launch.

'Liam doesn't see things like that.'

'Bullshit.'

It was bullshit. 'Why would he talk to you about it?'

'Why not? Especially if *you* introduced the idea to him. You know, while sucking his cock.'

'Hard to talk with cock in your mouth.'

'You know what I mean.'

I turned around to look over at the children playing in the fountain. This wasn't going the way I imagined. He was being brutal, something he didn't know how to be when I had known him.

My face still turned away, I said, 'Liam despises guys like you. He says you're the cock-blockers of literature.'

'Is that what he says?'

'No, I was paraphrasing.'

'What does it mean – cock-blockers of literature?'

'What it says. There's a ton of great new writing out there, and Liam thinks writers like you denigrate it without reading a page.'

'There isn't much truth to that accusation. Besides, he probably reads as much of my writing as I read of his.'

'You're wrong there. Liam reads everything. He'll eat you alive if you give him a hint of that shit. Really, it won't take much, a drop of elitist blood in the water and you'll be dinner.'

'Still, he can't be that bright, if writing what he writes satisfies him.'

'Fuck you, Max.'

He was being awful. There was so much anger in him. I hadn't expected it. I thought he would have moved on. He seemed to have moved on. There had been no contact.

'Do you still write this shit down?' asked Max.

'If you mean my diary, yes.'

'Do you ever re-read the bits about us?'

'No. I don't look back.'

'You got it all wrong, you know. You're going to get this wrong, too, if you think it worthy of recording,' he said, pressing the tip of his index finger against the tabletop. 'I read it, you know. All of it. That's how I found out how corrupt you really are. You aren't honest enough to record the truth. Aren't smart enough, either. All the great diarists have an unworldly capacity for revelation. They hit on universal truths almost by accident. You write fiction. You rely on tropes and clichés. Your psychological assessments were way off. Your worries and concerns. Your childish hopes and dreams. Fantasies. And you wrote terrible things about me. But at least that was interesting. Reading a fictional Max, with fictional motives and anxieties.'

'I thought we weren't going to talk about the past.'

'And then you also wrote in detail about fucking Liam. Like it was an erotic novel. So much detail. Why would you do that?'

'I got off on it,' I said, wanting to land something on him.

'The sex scenes in the Jack Cade books are just as banal; I bet you write them, too.'

I said nothing.

'I tormented myself for a week before I got the courage to confront you and throw you out. I got to observe you that whole week knowing what I'd learnt. It changed you in my eyes. I knew where you'd been, could see what you were seeing. You behaved atrociously towards me. You revelled in the deception. Got off on it. Lied to my face. Day in, day out. Not only to me, to Liam, to your work, to your friends, to yourself in the diary.'

Even though I was angry at the way he was treating me, I deserved every word of it. The tears started to fall so I put my sunglasses back on and pulled my hoodie over my cap.

It was a beautiful setting for a horrible fucking conversation. All around us people were chatting; the kids paddling in the fountain were shrieking with delight.

'And I fucked you after I knew. That was the worst bit. That's the bit I regret. I shouldn't have. But I loved you so much and it was ending. Everything we'd shared up until that moment had been intact till then. As soon as I fucked you knowing that Liam had probably fucked you that morning, or afternoon, or both, all of our past years crumbled to dust.'

My shoulders were shaking. I raised my hand to my mouth in order to smother any noises I might make.

'I read some this morning, to remind myself.'

'You made a copy of my diary?'

'Yes, and I read it to remind me what you're really like.' He handed me his handkerchief. 'Because try as I might, even after all this time, and after all I know of you, I can't stop loving you.'

I looked at his face hopefully, but found only animosity in his eyes. His jaw was clenched and he spoke the next words as though spitting out poison.

'I hate you and love you in the same breath. Reading it reminds me to hate the more.'

I had done all of this to a man who loved me. If he were a changed man, I had changed him.

But the diary wasn't the whole story. Diaries never are.

We sat in silence for a long time. I wiped my eyes and eventually stopped crying. I couldn't look at him, so behind my sunglasses I closed my eyes.

I was the first to speak. 'How much does the magazine need?'

'Are you going to invest? Is that what you're suggesting?'

'Yes, why not?'

'Because I'd rather close it than take money you've made writing that shit with him.'

'How much do you need?'

'I know you can fix it. I know that. But I don't want you to fix it like that. Do you understand? All I need is for you to get Liam to agree to talk about race and racism in Britain.'

'He won't do it. It's too risky. Popular writers stay out of politics.'

'I've been researching black writing in Britain and I've interviewed a number of literary authors, most of whom struggle to make ends meet. I really need to get the perspective of a successful black writer.'

'Perhaps part of his success is due to not discussing his race.'

'His hero, Mark Harden, is black!'

'Don't you think that's awesome enough? He's got white readers all around the world invested in and cheering for a black man. That's political, don't you think? That's a bloody achievement.'

'But I want him to say as much.'

My phone rang. I searched in my gym bag and dug it out. It was Liam.

'Sorry, I have to take this.'

I walked quickly away from the table to the far corner. I took a very deep breath and answered, hoping to mask all that I was feeling. 'Hi, what do you think?'

'Whatever you said to her last night worked. She's not going to leave me.'

'Oh, Gail, right. Good. I meant the manuscript.'

I turned and looked back across at Max. He was reading again.

'I emailed a response ages ago. What have you been doing?'

'I'm having coffee with Max.'

'Oh, fuck. How did that come about?'

'Long story. So is the manuscript money?'

'Yep, it's money. I'm going to finish it tomorrow. But it's money. No doubt. Whose is it?'

'One of Julia's finds.'

'Really?'

'Yep. She'll be happy to hear you think it's good.'

'I'm meeting her later. I'll let her know,' said Liam.

'You're meeting her?'

'Yeah, we're having dinner. Her suggestion.'

'Without me?'

'Yep, she wanted it that way. Says you hate her. Do you?'

'Of course I hate her – she's inhuman.'

'I'll say you said, hi, then.'

'Don't you fucking dare. And don't mention the manuscript. I want the cred on this one. She's still my boss.'

'Why the fuck do you bother with all that? You don't need to be on the payroll there.'

'I like causing trouble. Delete the manuscript when you're done. I wasn't meant to show anyone. I have to go.'

'Hey, do you know it's been at least three weeks since we last fucked? I miss you.'

'It can't be that long.'

'It is. I'm counting. What happened to every Thursday? You need to find time for me. I miss you. I want you.'

'We need to talk, Liam.'

'That sounds ominous.'

'It is. But we need to discuss this face to face.'

'Shit, Amy, tell me now.'

'No. Goodbye. I have to get back to Max.'

I pressed end.

When I looked towards the table, Max was gone. My backpack was slung over the chair. I hurried over to it before the bomb squad arrived to blow it up.

# Chapter 23
# Publish This

Helen had spent the day scanning Malcolm's work. It was taking longer than she expected, partly because there was so much material, and partly because she kept finding writing she had forgotten about. There was so much unpublished writing. Good writing, too. Sketches, poems, essays and short stories. A few abandoned novels. She was falling in love with him all over again. Here was a writer's life. She had been moving chronologically, and in doing so she was watching him grow and develop. There were things in the young Malcolm that she hadn't realised she missed. A recklessness that was gone from the present Malcolm. He once wrote without a thought for the consequences. She now recalled how often Malcolm's writing had hurt her. She was hurt again by some of it. But she could see beyond that to the work itself. The wife might shed a tear and wish the words unwritten, but the reader in her appreciated Malcolm's honesty. It was a clearer record of their relationship than anything in her miscellany.

Helen had always sought to obfuscate the episodes she'd taken from life. While Malcolm would transcribe experience with a boldness that horrified her at times, she would dismantle a scene from life, break it into pieces, find what was universal in it, then reassemble it using imagined elements. His was the more effective method, but also the more difficult for those close to him to read.

'Helen.'

Helen didn't respond at first to the voice from the door of her office. She was reading. It was the original version of a scene in one of Malcolm's most admired novels, *Not Lost*, about the disintegration of a marriage. This original version was the record of one of Helen and Malcolm's arguments. Helen vaguely remembered reading it before. Back in the days when they read every word that either of them wrote. She'd been more resilient then. But it struck her powerfully now, because she had forgotten their arguments. She'd thought they'd had very few, but this page was awakening other memories and now she recalled that in the seventies, when Daniel was a child and they were still rather social, there had been arguments – bitter arguments.

'Mother,' said Daniel, from the door.

Helen lay the page down. She felt exposed. Caught in a private moment with the past. The habit of her mind to rewrite the facts of the past disturbed her as much as her inattention to the present. The mind strove for equilibrium, sorting memory as it saw fit, even against her own wishes.

Daniel touched her on the shoulder. 'I don't wish to intrude, but are you all right?'

'I'm fine, Daniel. These are your father's original manuscripts, notes and miscellany. I'm trying to make a digital record of them. But the scanner is slow and there are thousands of pages.'

'What will you do with the originals?'

'Protect them.'

'How will you do that?' asked Daniel, picking up a manila folder and opening it. It contained the foolscap pages covered with pencilled paragraphs he remembered well from his childhood. The pages that were in the office, the room he wasn't allowed to enter. Which he did when unobserved. He'd sit at his mother's desk and pretend to use the typewriter. Pretend he was like them. Sometimes pretending to smoke using a pencil. He was far more interested in his mother's typewriters and then bulky word processors than his father's foolscap pads. He never read anything he found in there. The words didn't interest him, but the hours they'd spend away from him did.

'I don't know what I'll do with them, Daniel.'

'Would anyone buy them?'

'I'm not going to sell your father's literary legacy.'

'Then what are you doing this for?'

'I woke early one morning to discover him putting his work through a paper shredder.'

'Did he say why he was doing that?'

'I didn't ask. I threw all of the papers I could find into boxes and dragged them in here. Then I hid the paper shredder. His behaviour lately has been very odd. Have you not noticed?'

'I don't know either of you well enough to judge whether you're acting oddly or quite normally.'

Helen couldn't find a reply to that.

'What about your papers?' Daniel asked.

'Most are digitised and on hard drives. But I do have the manuscripts I worked on with editors over the years. My letters, as well.'

'Did you or Malcolm keep diaries?'

'No, though now I wish we had.'

'Malcolm's papers will be worth much more if he wins the Booker.'

'I'm not looking for a buyer. Besides, he's not going to win the Booker. Since 2014 it's been open to the Americans. But none has won yet. They'll award it to one of them. More newsworthy.'

'You don't believe the winner is chosen according to merit?'

'Do you?'

Daniel wandered over to the bookcase to Helen's left, then to the windows beyond the desk. 'This is a lovely office. From your desk I bet you can see out over the park. You might be in the country.'

Helen was watching her son's movements with interest. He was clearly agitated; his gestures were jerky and quite random, as were his thoughts. But his face was bright and cheerful. Which ran contrary to her expectations after the previous night's revelations. That Geraldine had taken a lover wasn't much of a surprise to Helen. She and Daniel had been unsuited from the outset. And their age difference and diverging interests had made rupture inevitable. Malcolm had said as much the first time Daniel had introduced her to them. And this knowledge had caused them both to be more reserved towards her than they already would have been.

'Are you still set on moving to London? I don't think you've thought this through,' said Helen, stopping her work. 'How will you see the boys?'

'I'll fly up on weekends.'

'Can you really afford to do that? And where would you stay? Hotels? More money.'

'I'll need to rent a flat.'

'I don't think you've thought about this at all.'

'I have. I have. I can't stay in Edinburgh. I can't. I'll see her everywhere. It isn't like London where I could move a few streets away and never see her again. It's like a small town. And her family is everywhere. Her friends. It's impossible.'

'So is leaving your boys, Daniel! You need to think of them. A long-term plan. From nursery school to university. They're so young. You need to brave it out, for them.'

'I know what I must do. There are many musts in my head, not all of them achievable. When I think of the boys I think of her and when I think of her I think of him. And I can't allow myself to think of him. I don't have a long-term plan because there is no long term. I can't think long term.'

'Then what are you going to do now? Today. Tomorrow. Next week?'

'I don't know. I'd move into the flat below. But Amy is very comfortable down there. She's entrenched. You won't get her out easily.'

'She can go tomorrow if you'd like to move down there. I think she's done what she came to do. She's promised to make her recommendations to me this evening. I'm expecting her any minute now.'

'I don't want her to leave, at least not yet. She's at odds with the life you and Malcolm have made for yourselves. She's doing you both good.'

'How do you come to that conclusion? You said earlier you don't know us.'

'She's chaos. You're order. You need each other.'

Helen thought about this for a while. Her life didn't feel ordered.

'I heard you help Amy downstairs last night. Was she very drunk?'

'She was and she wasn't. I found her trying to enter the basement of your neighbour across the road, but then she was quite lucid in her speech.'

'She drinks too much. Malcolm and I can't keep up with her. She has the capacity of a problem drinker. Personally, I don't know what to make of her. She behaves in a manner that's alien to me. She lives like a gypsy and yet she has more money than the Queen.'

'Self-destructive, perhaps?'

'I don't know. I don't know how her mind works. She's clearly bright and astonishingly beautiful – more so now after we've been giving her regular meals – but she sullies both these attributes continuously by the choices she makes.'

'So she's self-destructive, as I suggested.'

Helen placed another page on the scanner.

'I heard you both go downstairs late last night but I didn't hear you return,' she said. This had just occurred to her.

'We talked. She didn't want to be alone.'

'I saw her leave early this morning. She looked like she was going to the gym. But she never returned. An hour ago I received an email saying she'd been waylaid by friends and was on her way home.'

'Did she write – home?'

'No, I don't think she did.'

'Be careful, Helen.'

'What are you saying?'

'Amy, she's probably only healthy in small doses. Too much Amy could be toxic.'

'Only for some.'

# Chapter 24
# Because You Owe Me

After Max disappeared, I sat for a while at the table watching the children play in the fountain. The sun was hot and lovely. I took off my cap and hoodie and thought about taking off my trainers and putting on my sandals, but remembering the dress I'd thrown in, I decided to change. I took myself off to the bathrooms.

Afterwards, I did what I had wanted to do when I first entered the garden: I went over to the fountain and sat with my feet in the water. The pool was shallow and the water was warm. The sun was directly overhead. Soon I was lying back with my eyes closed. The sun had warmed the stone beneath me. Now I was being warmed from above and below, within and without. In a sundress, in the sun, I was beginning to feel myself again. The horrors of the night, Gail's anguish, Daniel's desperation, and the trials of the day, Max's cruel retribution, were dissipating.

With my eyes closed I listened to all of the voices around me. The children talking and laughing, the couples taking selfies, the students who sat on the grass behind me. They were speaking in Italian. The noises melded together forming a comforting backdrop to my thoughts, which were of nothing and everything. Free form. One moment of Helen's writing, then Max's slender hands, the next of my parents who had emailed to say they were going to visit Antarctica and inviting friends to join them, which by default included me. Iceland, yes. Antarctica, no. Then I wondered why I never visit the places I dream of visiting. I've never been to Norway, nor even Greece. Or further afield. I haven't travelled. I'm not a traveller. I like London. I'm a Londoner. I've never set foot in Wales, even. Never been to Land's End.

I opened my eyes and lifted myself onto one elbow. There was a group of boys, not older than twenty, seated close to me. They hadn't been there before. All of them were looking at me. I smiled and lay back again. Let them look. They won't find the courage to say anything. Even though I'm alone. Even though I smiled. They'll find courage too late.

When I next opened my eyes they were gone.

As lovely as it was lying there in the garden with my feet in the water, I had to get back to Helen, who was waiting very patiently. I had nothing to fear in returning. Daniel wasn't a threat anymore. My self-loathing had disarmed him. I knew what I was going to say to Helen, too. Liam had helped there. I knew now my initial impressions were the correct ones.

I went straight to the cloakroom for my books. Max was there. 'I thought you'd gone.'

He was handing the attendant his chip when I spoke, and replied, as he turned around, 'I was back in the office before I realised I'd left my laptop here.'

I could see his brain adjust to my change in clothes. He was looking at me in the way I had prevented him doing by wearing my jeans and hoodie.

'You look amazing, Amy.'

I took the compliment, as it seemed completely involuntary on his part. He was probably wishing the words back in his mouth as soon as they were spoken. But they were said. I'd heard them.

'You look the same,' I said.

I handed my chip over and the man returned with my Waterstones bags. He handed them across. They were still heavy. Which I should have guessed they'd be.

'Are you going back to the office?' I asked as we exited the building.

'Yeah, what are you going to do? Have you had lunch?'

'No, but I'm running late. I'm going to deliver Helen Owen news she won't want to hear.'

We were on the front steps. He had started to edge away in the direction of his office.

'You're working with Helen Owen? That's a change for you.'

'That's why I can't introduce you to Liam: you have to be an arse about everything.'

'What did I say?' He took a few steps back towards me.

'That's a change for you,' I said.

'I didn't mean it that way.'

'But I heard it that way and so will Liam. There's an assumption in your tone that everyone agrees with your assessment of the writing world, in your classification system.'

'Most do.'

'Most don't and I have the bank balance to prove it.'

'Most serious-minded people do. Helen Owen would. You once did.'

I almost smacked him in the face. It was a very strong impulse, too. I stared at him, smarting from his words.

'You're wrong about Helen. She's coming around.'

'Under your influence, I suppose. Wait, is she still married to Malcolm Taylor?'

'Yes,' I said and put the bags down. They were cutting off the circulation to my fingers. One of the bags fell over and the top two books fell out. Paul Beatty's *The Sellout* and *Hot Milk* by Deborah Levy. Max bent down quickly to pick them up and set the bag against the step so it couldn't fall again.

'You've got the entire Booker longlist here. It's a bit late in the day to be reading this sort of stuff, isn't it?'

'Max, you can go fuck yourself.'

'Don't be like that.'

'Oh, fuck off. You're a shit. Why should I do anything for you?'

'Because you owe me.'

'Bullshit. I don't owe you anything. Really. If I'm the person you think I am, I should tell you to go to hell.'

'You're going to get angry at me? You don't have the right. You broke my trust and my heart. You fucking destroyed me. I'm not the man I might have been. I'm damaged. And you damaged me.'

Just at this moment we were interrupted by the sudden appearance of Alan, whom I hadn't seen since he proposed in the Sound Bar.

'Calm down, kids!' he said, pushing his smiling face between us both.

Max and I took a moment to adjust to this change in direction. Alan shook Max's hand and gave me a kiss on the cheek.

'Have you been up to the exhibition? What did you think?'

'What exhibition?' I asked.

'The one my firm is sponsoring,' he replied, and pointed to a banner hanging not five feet from both of us. 'Legally Binding', it said, 'The Accoutrements of Law Down the Centuries'.

'No, we just stopped by for a coffee and a chat,' said Max.

Alan's face fell. 'Well, come up now and I'll show you around. It's very exciting.'

Max shook his head. 'I have to get back to the office.'

'I have to go, too, Alan. Sorry.'

Max turned and walked away.

Alan watched him go and then turned to me and said, 'I couldn't believe my eyes when I saw you two together. But I gather it wasn't a pleasant chat.'

'No, it wasn't.'

'You look lovely. Much fuller in the face than when I last saw you. Less gaunt. Did you take my advice after all?'

'No, I've been living a half-life with two septuagenarians.'

'It suits you.'

I didn't say anything. I was looking at his face. He had so many opinions about me and how I looked. But his face was just a face. He wasn't a handsome man, yet he wasn't what I'd call ugly. He was just Alan.

'Hey, I re-read your novel the other day.'

'That's creepy.'

'I missed you. It's still brilliant.'

'It's angsty crap. I have to go.'

I started to move away but stopped short, caught in a fog of thoughts about Max.

'Have I always been a fucking bitch?' I asked, and then added, before Alan had time to formulate his response, 'No, don't answer.'

Alan breathed in deeply and scratched the tip of his nose.

'I mean I must have been to fuck Liam, right?'

'Max wasn't right for you. You weren't as happy together as you now make out.'

'What the fuck would you know?'

Alan looked off in the direction Max went. He was clearly hurt by what I'd just said. But he'd voiced something that rang too true after talking to Max.

'Was I different then? With Max? Was I a different person?'

Alan sighed and brushed back his hair. 'You were younger, that's all. You made some mistakes. We all did. You need to forgive yourself.'

'Stop. You sound like Dr Phil.'

'You didn't give yourself time to find out who you were. You went straight from school into a serious relationship with Max. And then you moved in together. It was a big commitment.'

'It was the most natural thing in the world.'

'You need to stop romanticising your time with Max. You wouldn't put up with his shit now. You're a strong woman. Max was always ...'

I waited for him to continue, but he just looked at me blankly.

'Max was what?'

'I can't find the right word. "Controlling" isn't right. Neither is "manipulative". But he was always trying to improve you.'

I thought about this for a moment. He was always trying to get me to read the books he liked. But then I pictured him reading *Twilight* because I'd asked him to. Remembering the pained expression he had worn then made me smile now.

'I was always trying to change him, too,' I said. 'We didn't agree on a damned thing.'

'You're complete opposites,' agreed Alan.

'And it was perfect.'

'Then why did you fuck Liam?'

I stood processing what he had said. I didn't have an answer. After a time, I said, 'You're a bastard.'

I moved off towards the road. 'Don't forget your books,' he said, lifting the bags and handing them to me. Then he said, 'Have you thought any more about what I said?'

I had no idea what he was talking about.

He pulled the little box from his pocket and held it up.

'Really? You're bringing that up again now?'

'You never return my calls. You never answer any of my messages.'

'It feels like a lifetime ago. It really does. So much has happened.'

'Well?'

I'd been keeping an eye on the road. A cab was coming. 'Be real, Alan. Stop with this fantasy. I'm bad news. Forget me.'

I hailed the cab and, clutching my bags, got in, leaving a visibly bemused Alan on the steps waving goodbye.

# Chapter 25

# So You Think I Should Publish It?

When Amy entered, Daniel was photographing Malcolm's papers with a digital camera and tripod. Helen was watching him.

'Oh, sorry, I thought you were alone.'

'Daniel has just made my job much easier. I'd been scanning each document in and it was taking forever. This is much better.'

'Hello, Amy,' said Daniel, turning and trying very hard to look casual. He even perched on the edge of the desk, but found that uncomfortable and stood straight.

Amy thought he looked more like Bernard from *Four Weddings and a Funeral* than ever.

'Hello, Daniel,' she replied, looking at him, trying to convince herself that what had happened had happened, so implausible did it seem at that moment.

Helen looked from one to the other and had her suspicions confirmed. Daniel's whole manner had shifted immediately on Amy entering the room and Amy was unusually self-conscious. Something *had* happened between them.

There was a moment of silence. Not quite silence: snoring could be heard through the open door. Malcolm taking a nap, presumably.

Daniel felt he had to say something, so asked, 'Nice day?' but couldn't muster the warmth needed to make it seem natural. He'd convinced himself during the hours of her absence that nothing further would ever happen between them. The joy he'd experienced then only heightened his self-loathing. She'd offered herself to him out of pity and that was that. She was right to: he was pitiable.

He had since renounced all claims to her.

But the sight of her in her summer dress had shaken his resolve.

'Yes, thank you, Daniel.'

Her feet were bare, he noticed, revealing her to be a true member of the household. She was perfection.

'Doesn't she look lovely, Helen?' he said, weakly. He had never desired anyone more in his life. She was life. Unless he was suffering under cruel delusion, he had kissed her body. He had tasted her. He had fucked her. It was an extraordinary thing to have done. He wanted to reach out and touch her now. The slightest touch would serve as proof that it had happened.

'Yes, she always looks lovely. It's her burden,' said Helen, feeling distinctly uncomfortable. 'Are you ready to talk about my book, Amy?'

'Yes, I am. I'm so sorry it has taken this long. Should we discuss it here or down in the flat?'

'I'd like to stay here. Daniel, can we have a few minutes?'

Daniel looked from Amy back to his mother. And caught an unmistakable expression of disgust on Helen's face, which she hid by quickly turning away.

'I'll bring up some drinks,' said Daniel, persisting where it was hopeless.

'No, we'll come down when we're finished,' said Helen.

It was extinguished.

Daniel glanced at Amy and then left. He had hoped to brush past her, but she was quick to move well away from his trajectory.

Helen followed her son and closed the door behind him.

'Well?' asked Helen, turning.

'What are your priorities?' asked Amy, sitting on Helen's desk. She pushed the dress between her thighs and placed her bare feet on the seat of the chair.

Helen watched her. Was about to ask her not to sit on Malcolm's papers, but reconsidered. She was old, Amy was young, and it was too exhausting to teach youth how to behave. Amy's youth and beauty and her casual disrespect angered her.

'Don't talk to me about priorities,' she said, crossly. 'What are your thoughts about the three manuscripts? You've read all three and more of my work.'

'All three manuscripts would find a publisher, Helen. If it were up to me, I'd publish all three. There's great value in them being read together. Variations on the same theme. So different in their way, but circling the same big ideas.'

'But you don't have your way, do you?'

'No. There are considerations here that have nothing to do with art.'

Helen sat down on the couch by the door. She'd known this was coming. The weeks that had passed, the agonising wait, had been futile. She had only postponed the inevitable.

'Version one is very commercial,' said Amy, thinking of Liam's assessment. 'It will appeal to the largest audience. Version two is literary, and unless it wins an award, its audience is limited.'

'And version three?'

'Version three is sublime.'

'And that isn't good in your world, is it?'

Amy thought about this for a moment. It sounded like something Max would say to her. But Helen wasn't being intentionally rude. She was asking in good faith, asking Amy about the commercial viability of her novel as she would ask a foreigner about the customs of their country.

'I don't think Julia will recognise its potential, so no. But I may be wrong.'

'To make all of this go away I should give them version one.'

Amy nodded. 'That's the one sure path out of this mess.'

Both women sighed. Amy on having to repeat what she had said on day one. Helen on hearing her sentence.

'I'm sorry, Helen.'

'I'll lose this house if I don't publish it. I'll lose my reputation if I do.'

Amy almost mentioned her leaner and meaner rewrite of version one, but held her tongue. She only had a digital copy. What if Helen wanted to see it then and there? Her duplicity would be exposed. She avoided Helen's eyes by scanning the bookshelves while concluding that her version was irrelevant to the current discussion. Her edits had only increased its commercial appeal, the very thing Helen was struggling to deal with.

Instead Amy said, 'I wonder if they'd publish it under a pseudonym?'

'I have considered that.'

'And?'

'Robert Galbraith.'

Amy smiled.

'They always find out.'

'Why not own it then, like John Banville? He won the Booker but writes crime under the name Benjamin Black.'

'And he hasn't been a contender for the Booker since.'

'Does that matter?'

'Not in itself. His recent work mightn't be any good. But I tend to doubt that. Writers of his stamp generally get better with age.'

'Like you and Malcolm.'

Helen didn't say anything to this, and said instead, 'But by writing both literary fiction and genre he has confused matters. It's just easier for any critic to assume the worst.'

'Surely it doesn't work like that?'

'Are you aware of all of your prejudices? Do you know how they were formed? I don't know how all mine were formed. I'm sure I have them. They make up my taste in literature to some extent. I don't know whether, were I to read John Banville now, knowing he also writes crime fiction, my judgement would be sound.'

Helen stopped and looked up at the bookcases near her head.

'But don't listen to me. I've had theory after theory about the Booker and their judgements. When your best work isn't recognised, year after year, you start to let the whole thing get to you. You end up a little cracked.'

'Does it play on your mind so much?'

'How are any of us to tell if we're writing well? I've been fortunate. I've had Malcolm Taylor's opinion throughout my writing career. One of the country's best literary critics shares my life. So I shouldn't grumble. Because of him, I generally know when I'm doing good work. I'm in a better position than most. But he's also my husband. And is the man who says I look beautiful when I can see my own face in the mirror. So I seek the opinion of my peers. But my peers aren't reading everything I publish, just as I'm not reading everything they write. They're probably doing what I'm doing, re-reading the books they read when they were younger – Proust, Richardson, Eliot, et cetera.'

'So the next best thing is the Booker?'

'Yes, the judges sift through the recent writing and give a lucky few writers a nod. Which is the best we can hope for.'

'Are writers generally supportive? Have you ever sent fan mail to a writer?'

'Yes, and I've received my fair share, too. I wrote to William Trevor, Iris Murdoch, Doris Lessing and others. Patrick White, too. Magnificent writer. All but forgotten now. Many of them I stayed in contact with. Oh, and then there was the letter I wrote to John Fowles! It was right after I read *The French Lieutenant's Woman*, back in the early seventies. I completely understand why he ignored my letter. It was a declaration of my love for him as well as the novel. I basically offered myself to him.' Helen laughed.

'*The French Lieutenant's Woman* is one of my ex's favourite books. Max. But he could never decide if it was literature or not. It tormented him.'

'Of course it is!' said Helen passionately.

'Max is suspicious of success.'

'So am I, but *The French Lieutenant's Woman* broke all the rules. It was caught in that no man's land between commercial fiction and literature. Indefinable, really. But if pressed, I'd have to say it is literature.'

'I think that's where your new novel sits, on the literary edge of commercial fiction. It has bestseller written all over it, but it will also make people think. And because of that it will sell extremely well. I'm sure of it. Most people won't know whether it's literature or not. And if it's a success it will draw thousands more people to the rest of your work.'

'Which worries me. Until recently I've had one reader in mind, Malcolm. I never needed to spell anything out for him. My preferred readers need to know as much as he does. They have to bring something to the table. If you come empty-handed or empty-headed to my novels they shrivel up and die. Just read some of the more recent reviews on Amazon. One-star reviews because readers don't know what's going on. But this new book bulges with unnecessary explanations, grotesque foreshadowing, detailed descriptions of things that need no descriptions. It's almost two hundred thousand words. The second version is half that. The third almost a novella.'

'Couldn't this new book serve as a bridge to your other writing?' said Amy, pushing away thoughts of her own version of the book.

'Imagine if it's all the things you say it is. Imagine if the world declares it the best thing I've ever written. My magnum opus. Imagine if my whole life's work gets eclipsed by this novel, which is at its heart a cynical grab for cash. Something I wrote in a moment of weakness.'

'Books aren't written in a moment. You wrote this over months and months. You knew what you were doing and you did it extremely well. This book isn't one of Helen Owen's best, but it's a far sight better than most writers writing today could write. That's a fact. I know authors who would kill to publish this under their name.'

'So you think I should publish it?' asked Helen, smiling.

This stopped Amy. She had just been enthusiastically imagining a future where the book was published and didn't harm Helen's reputation, when the last few weeks she had been thinking to herself, Fuck the house, Helen. Rent a shitty little flat and keep producing brilliant work.

'No.'

Helen's heart sank. She had been buying into Amy's vision. She could imagine herself as Umberto Eco, publishing her *The Name of the Rose* to rapturous global applause. He kept his reputation, kept publishing serious work in semiotics, because everything he did was drenched in irony. *Foucault's Pendulum* wasn't a richly plotted thriller, a precursor to *The Da Vinci Code*, it was literature.

'Fuck,' said Helen. And smiled again. She rarely swore and enjoyed her transgressions. 'I thought I was going to publish my *Name of the Rose*.'

'Max hates that book with a passion. And books like *The Shadow of the Wind*, *The Poisonwood Bible*, *Atonement* and *The Life of Pi*. They sell millions of copies and get mistaken for literature. He hates that.'

'I'm with Max. So what do we do now?'

'I'll meet with Julia tomorrow and offer her version three.'

'You said Julia wouldn't recognise it for what it is.'

'I wasn't thinking straight. You keep talking to me like I'm one of them, so I've been thinking I'm one of them. I know you've got three complete versions of the novel. But they haven't got a clue.

If I take version three in and tell them it's version one, they'll have no reason to doubt that claim.'

'And if Julia rejects it?'

'Julia will hate it because it's brilliant. She sent me in to talk you out of being brilliant. I was meant to turn you into something acceptable, that they could sell in the supermarkets. So by delivering version three I will have failed her. But so what? I'm on team Helen, not team Julia.'

Helen smiled sadly. 'I don't know …'

Amy waited for her to say something else.

'Should I give Julia anything? The way you talk about her … She sounds horrible.'

'I know, I know, but she'll think she'll have the book her predecessor paid two million pounds for at auction. That means something to her.'

'But she won't have it.'

'But she'll think she has. Version three will get the royal treatment. It will be their lead title for Mother's Day. Though they may decide to hold onto it for next Christmas.'

'What will happen if I give them nothing?'

'Vikram Seth failed to deliver *A Suitable Girl* and came to some arrangement with Penguin. I don't think he gave the entire million-pound advance back. But he gave them something, I think. You never get to know all the details of these kinds of things. The worst-case scenario for you would be M&R demanding the full amount plus interest. Initially, Julia seemed reluctant to do this, because throwing you and Malcolm out onto the street would be a bad look. Now that Malcolm's Instafamous it would be even more difficult for them. But it's two million pounds. It isn't lunch money and this isn't Julia's mess; she has deniability. This happened before the merger, before she was in the job. This is someone else's legacy. She can blame Maxine Snedden for signing the deal.'

Helen covered her face with her hands.

'So I go in with version three?' Amy asked.

Helen thought long and hard and finally nodded. Then she removed her hands from her face and looked at Amy.

'How did it all come to this?'

'You did what few literary authors have been able to do. You wrote a bona fide blockbuster.'

# Chapter 26
# I Think They Cleared Your Desk

Amy: *Can I book a meeting with you tomorrow? Around 3 pm?*

Julia: *Do you still work here? You haven't been in the office for weeks.*

Amy: *Yes, I have. I've just been avoiding you.*

Julia: *Are you sure? I'll have to run that past HR. I think they cleared your desk.*

Amy: *Haha. I need to chat about Helen Owen.*

Julia: *I'm out of the office tomorrow. Can we meet next week?*

Amy: *You haven't got time for me until next week?*

Julia: *Unfortunately, no. Shall we say 2.30 pm Thursday?*

Amy: *Okay.*

# Chapter 27
# You Wouldn't Say That

Amy stared at the screen. And then took the glass of wine Malcolm was handing her. She took a sip and scrolled through the short exchange with Julia.

What was she playing at? One moment she was desperate for news of Helen's book, the next she couldn't care less. And why was she so perky?

'Is something amiss?' asked Malcolm. He sat at the kitchen table facing Amy, who was sitting on a barstool. Helen was putting together a plate of olives, bread and cheese.

'Everything is amiss, Malcolm. Especially your use of "amiss".'

'What is amiss about my use of "amiss"?'

'You wouldn't say that.'

'Wouldn't I?'

'Not if I had anything to do with it. I'd replace it with "wrong". "Is something wrong?" I'd have you say.'

'But if I'm me, an older literary chap, mightn't I say "amiss"?'

'Most likely, but why risk alienating the reader by using a word they're not familiar with? Especially when there's nothing to gain and a lot to lose.'

'What's there to lose?'

'The reader could close the book. And that would be that. The *you* in the book is terminated over one word in one hundred thousand.'

'Where's Daniel?' asked Helen, interrupting.

'He went out. Said he'd be back for dinner,' said Malcolm.

'Shall we go into the front room?' suggested Helen, who was already making her way to the hall carrying the plate of nibbles.

'Amy, Trevor says I'm a meme.' He was following her down the corridor.

'I know! You're Instafamous. There was a crazy quote of yours in the window of Waterstones. Something about a blood clot.'

'Yes, that's right. That's what Trevor said. Stuff I said on radio is being used.'

'I bought all of your competitors while I was there, the other longlisters. I'm going to try and read them all.'

'Can you lend them to me afterwards? I haven't read of any of them, yet. I mean, I know Coetzee. *Disgrace* was good. But I don't really know any of the others. A.L. Kennedy sounds familiar, but I'm not sure I've read him or her. I feel so out of it.'

'We can read them together,' Amy said as she sat down in the front room. 'All three of us. We'll have our own Booker.'

'I'd better win that.'

'Shoo-in.'

'Have you told him?' asked Helen.

'Told me what?' asked Malcolm, sitting.

# Chapter 28
# This Is My Inheritance

Daniel was lying on the sofa bed in his father's office listening to Neil Young's *On the Beach*. He hadn't heard the album for forty years, at least. He had forgotten it existed.

Only minutes before he had been idly flicking through Malcolm's LP collection and scoffing. Jazz, folk, sixties and seventies rock'n'roll – some artists he knew but most he didn't. He'd always been repulsed by his father's choices. Back then he'd preferred ABBA, Boney M and the *Grease* soundtrack to the stuff his dad played. Then he spotted the cover of *On the Beach* and memories flooded back to him. He stared at it and recalled doing the same as a child. It had been so strange to him then. An outdoor table and chairs on a sandy beach, replete with fringe-edged yellow umbrella, beside a buried fifties Cadillac, with only its fins and brakelight visible, like the tip of an iceberg. In the background stands a man looking out to sea. It was still strange now. And it annoyed him. It was purposefully eccentric and implied meaning it just didn't contain. Like so much of the culture Malcolm enjoyed. It seemed designed to make you feel stupid if you didn't get it, or didn't *pretend* to get it, which is what Daniel suspected most people did.

*On the Beach* had been one of his father's favourites. At least he remembered seeing the album sleeve on top of the record player often. But he couldn't remember anything of the music.

That's why he had removed the disc from the sleeve and had popped the record on the turntable. But he found he didn't remember the music at all.

As he lay on the sofa listening to it, he felt more and more disheartened. For some reason he thought by playing the album he'd unlock some key to his past. Something to fill the ever-deepening void he felt within him. Staying with Helen and Malcolm had focused his attention on the life he'd shared with them as a child. They were asking him to look again. To reassess. But instead of changing his views, he seemed only to confirm them.

He remembered Malcolm would only ever play his music when Helen was out. This was something he'd never questioned until now. But it meant she hadn't shared his taste in music either. And though his father really enjoyed music, he had to wait for an opportunity to play it.

Daniel had always supposed it was because Malcolm, when not sleeping, was either writing or reading, and he required complete silence for both. But it was because Helen was always there with them.

And those days when he would hear the music were the days when it was just him and his dad at home. But apart from the music, he couldn't recall anything they did together that was different from all the other days.

The silence of all the other days. That is what he remembered most clearly from his childhood. Living in dread of disturbing Helen and Malcolm. He closed his eyes and once again felt the oppressive weight of that silence. Children are not silent. And they shouldn't be expected to be silent. He would never think of asking his own boys to be silent all day. And yet his parents had yelled at him for making the slightest sound. Then they would send him out to play with the other boys.

An exile for art's sake.

Malcolm entered the room. 'You remember this, do you?' he asked Daniel.

Daniel opened his eyes and looked at his father. 'What?' he asked, contrasting the man before him with the man of his memories. The Malcolm standing in the room was softer, more reasonable and gentler than the man he remembered. As though all the hard edges had been worn off over time.

'The music. Why are you playing it?'

'I don't know. I was flicking through all that fucking Bob Dylan you have and then I spotted this,' he said, lifting the album sleeve off the bed. 'Something about the cover art. I think I remember you playing it.'

'I used to. Side two, really. I rarely played side one.'

Daniel sat up, reached across to the turntable and flipped the disc. He heard the scratching needle and, sitting back down, listened intently as the music started.

'Oh, yeah,' he said, lying back on the sofa. 'I remember this. Jesus. When were you into it?'

'I don't know. Sometime in the seventies. That was when I made friends with some of the Californians at university. They would have introduced me to Neil Young.'

'I can't believe it. It has to be forty years, but I remember the sound so clearly.'

'I used to listen to it if your mother was out, just after I put you to bed. You never seemed to mind.'

'I remember you playing it pretty loud.'

'I couldn't play it loud, the neighbours would come knocking. You remember what that was like, don't you?'

'I remember lying in bed with the lights off listening to the mournful guitar and sad drums.'

Malcolm didn't say anything. He walked to the chair at the desk and sat down. They listened for a few minutes as the song ended and the next began.

'It's bleak, Malcolm.'

'Do you think so?'

'Well, it's not ABBA, is it?'

'I've never thought of it as dark.'

'Well, it is. It's damned depressing.'

'There's an optimism in the lyrics, isn't there? Things are shit, but we'll get through it.'

'It's not very convincing,' said Daniel, and he reached over and turned it off. 'Makes me want to slit my wrists.'

Malcolm smiled grimly but didn't say anything.

'I'm not built like you,' said Daniel, sitting up. 'You have no fear of the dark. You stare into the void for kicks. The music you listen to is depressing. The books you read are depressing. The books you write are depressing.'

'Some say *A Hundred Ways* is quite funny.'

'If you're the Grim Reaper, maybe. It's fucking awful. It's darker than anything you've ever written.'

Malcolm stared hard at his son.

Daniel put his head in his hands. 'I don't know how you two do it. This fucking life is hard enough without holding every speck of it up to the light for examination. Don't you ever wish you could turn your head off for good?'

'Never,' said Malcolm, though without much conviction.

'You must have such a high capacity for pain. I don't. I have no capacity for pain. None. I have to be so cautious. Everything in this life frightens me.'

Malcolm felt as though his son had punched him in the stomach. He could barely breathe, but knew he must say something.

'You just need time to adjust, Daniel,' he said, but it was more of a whisper.

'What? What did you say?'

'You need time to adjust.'

'Adjust to what?' asked Daniel, standing. 'Geraldine leaving?'

Malcolm nodded. He wanted so much to take the pain away from his son.

'I'll never adjust to that. There's no adjusting.'

Malcolm stood, intending to try to embrace his son, to give him some comfort, but he took longer to rise than he expected and the moment had passed. Daniel had already left the room.

# Chapter 29

# Sorry, but It's Too Hot in Here for Clothes

Liam answered the door wearing shorts and only shorts.

'Sorry, but it's too hot in here for clothes.'

He gave me a chaste kiss on the lips and then turned back down the short passage to the living room. I hadn't seen him near-naked for a month or so. It wasn't the way I wanted this meeting to go. He was every bit as fit now as he'd been when a soldier. Probably more so, having gained weight and muscle as he aged. I have seen pictures of the nineteen-year-old soldier; he looked like a boy. Liam was all man now.

All the windows were open, but there was only a faint breeze. Looking around I couldn't fail to notice the place was a mess. I was trying to remember how long it had been since I had been there.

'Yeah, it's a pigsty. I haven't had time to clean up,' he said, following my gaze.

'Gail hasn't been here in a while, either?'

'She won't come here anymore. We've got ourselves a townhouse in Holland Park.'

'When the fuck did that happen?'

'The day after we had dinner. She insisted on me buying a house suitable for raising a family. She's sick of being stuck in Surrey.'

'So you just bought a place?'

'Yeah. Well, no. Gail had been working on it for ages. She just forgot to tell me her plans.'

'Are you sure? Perhaps you were just half listening to her?'

'Probs.'

'Probs?'

'Yeah, probs.'

'Are you going to get me a drink?'

'It's just gone two and we haven't done any work yet.'

'I didn't come here to work. Get me a fucking drink.'

'You have a problem, you know. Don't fuck all this up by becoming an alcoholic.'

'Become? I've been a high-functioning alcoholic for years.'

He went into the kitchen and asked, raising his voice, 'Yeah, but you're not high-functioning at the moment are you?'

'Who says?' I said, rounding on him where he stood in the kitchen opening a bottle of Moët.

'Julia. She's ready to sack you over this Helen Owen thing. She just needs an excuse. Rock up to work drunk again and she'll turf you out.'

'She's chicken shit.'

The cork popped and hit the ceiling, causing me to jump.

'Well, if you give her a chance, she'll fuck you over. Seriously. Listen to me.'

'Shut up.'

He poured out two glasses and walked up to me, almost barging through me, his arm touching my shoulder as he walked back into the living room. He stood holding out a full glass to me.

'You reading that?' I said, taking the glass and pointing at the copy of Ian McGuire's *The North Water* lying open, pages down.

'It's brutal. Visceral. I'm fucking loving it.'

'It's on the longlist with Malcolm.'

'I know. I've read Malcolm's book, too.'

I raised an eyebrow.

'Fucking hated it,' he said, smiling broadly.

I laughed, and said, 'Each to their own.' Then, taking a sip of the champagne, 'Tell me about your new house.'

'Gail's new house.'

'Okay then, tell me about Gail's new house.'

'I'd rather bend you over that table and fuck you till you pass out.'

The way he does that. It's like a lightning bolt through me: the tone of his voice, the look in his eyes. There is nothing like it. I shouldn't be so susceptible to it but I am. I suppose the force of it is compounded by the hundreds of times he has fucked me into oblivion.

There was time to breathe. He put down his glass. That gave me a second to gather myself. He stepped towards me and took hold of my wrist. I took a step back. His movement brought with it his scent. It was overpowering, gorgeous and I had missed it.

'Let me say something.'

'After.'

I looked down. I could see his cock thicken in his shorts, which weren't big enough for him. His cock pressed against the fabric.

'Fuck, Liam. Stop. I promised Gail I wouldn't.' I reached out and pushed against his chest with all my might. He didn't move. My hand looked small and frail against the broad mass of flesh.

'Wouldn't what?' he asked, grabbing my hip and spinning me around. He pulled my body against him, his cock pressing against my back, one hand on my hip, the other grabbing my breast.

'She knows. She's always known.'

'Knows what?' He lifted my dress. And I felt myself being pushed forward. I steadied myself by grabbing the edge of his writing desk.

'She knows about *us*. She promised not to leave you, if I promised not to fuck you.'

'She doesn't know anything. She played you and won.' He began to pull down my G-string. He did it slowly, crouching as he reached my calves. I could feel his hot breath against my butt.

'She knows. And if she asks me, I won't be able to lie. Not anymore.' I lifted my left leg and he pulled my G-string over my stiletto.

'Don't lie, I don't care. She's threatened to leave a million times. But she hasn't. She fucking loves that place in Holland Park.' He parted my legs and pressed his face between them.

'Oh fuck, Liam. You're a bastard. A fucking bastard.' His tongue entered me from behind. I lowered my head and rested it in my arms. 'I'm a fucking awful person.'

Liam stood, ran the tip of his cock against my wet lips, then grabbed my hips.

He said, 'Yes, you are,' as his cock slid into me deliberately slowly.

*

I lay on the bed as he showered. After a while, I reached to the floor and picked up my dress.

My life isn't perfect, I thought. I'm not perfect. I've done things I regret. But Gail can go fuck herself, really. Why should she dictate my pleasures? She married a man who turned out to be a bastard. Her doing, not mine. I fuck him and get out. Bastards are lovers, not husbands. Rule number one. Everyone knows. She knows it, too. She wants her cake and all.

And why would I give this up? Why wouldn't I want him to destroy me whenever he wanted to. He just came twice. I'm covered with the stuff. It's on my face, in my hair, on my fingers. I rubbed it all over my breasts. He's a sex god. He knows how to make me come with cock alone. I shudder at his touch. His cock was designed for me. I can't resist, and shouldn't be expected to.

And we have a brilliant working relationship. We're successful and this is how we got there.

What is a wife in all of this? Nothing. Nothing.

Fucking Liam is outside normal life. It doesn't count. It's part of the creative process. Necessary to it, even. Gail said as much herself.

Max hadn't thought so, though, when he found out.

I climbed off the bed, threw on my dress and began looking for my things.

'I'd leave her and marry you,' he said, emerging from the bathroom door as I was stepping into my G-string. 'You know that, right. You're the woman I should be with. You're the one I can't stop thinking about. You're the one who inspires me. I do all this for you. You challenge me to do it. To be better and better.'

I went into the bathroom to avoid having to say anything in reply. I checked myself in the mirror.

I always look my best, I think, just fucked. My dress creased, hair messed, face smudged, cum on my skin. There's something about my eyes, too. A cock-crazed glint. And my lips are fuller, as well. Sucking cock beats collagen. My movements are different. They're jittery, quick, dangerous. In stilettos the effect is devastating.

I looked at what I was wearing. I'd never intended to keep my pledge to Gail, had I?

I left the bathroom, grabbed my bag and checked my phone. I was consciously ignoring him. I needed to go. I downed the last of the champagne and turned. He was stretched out naked on the bed. His cock was beat, but lay semi-erect against his thigh.

'You're a gorgeous specimen, Liam.' I took a photo with my phone.

'Delete it.'

'No. It's mine'

'Delete it!' he said, almost shouting.

'I'll crop it. No face. Just that gorgeous body and that hard-working cock.' I turned the phone to him to show what was left. He seemed mollified. 'It's a gorgeous cock, Liam,' I added. Then I saw it move. 'Did that thing just stir?'

'You're leaving too soon. I have fight in me yet.'

'I've got to go,' I said, watching his cock thicken. 'I do.'

'Only you can do this to me. No one else. How many times have I come?'

'I've really got to go.'

'You can't leave this,' he said, gripping his cock. 'I know you. You're thorough.'

He rolled off the bed and approached me. I didn't move. His cock was hard now. He took my phone out of my hand, held it up and started filming me.

'Suck my cock, Amy.'

'You're going to film me, Liam?'

'Yes. Suck it good for posterity.'

He'd never done this before. This was new. I'd been filmed hundreds of times, but never my face and never by him. Here he was saying my name and filming my face. Madness.

But it was hot.

*

He was leaning against the doorframe watching me tidy myself up in the bathroom again. He was naked. There wasn't much for me to do; he hadn't even bothered to undress me. After I sucked his cock he had filmed himself fucking me from behind. He'd just lifted my dress, pulled my G-string aside and fucked me hard and fast. I'm certain the neighbours heard that one. The windows were open, it took him a long time to come and he was brutal. By the time he came, I was screaming with every heavy thrust.

'Marry me,' he said.

'Not a chance.' My hand was shaking as I tried to reapply my lipstick.

'I'm serious.'

'So am I.'

'So you're saying no.'

'I'm saying no,' I said, looking at him in the mirror.

'Why?'

'You're a bastard to women.'

'I'll change.'

'You already have. From nice guy to bastard.'

He smiled.

'And we don't love each other,' I continued. 'Love is important.'

'I love you, Amy.'

'Said your cock.'

'Seriously, I love you. Not being with you for so long has made me realise it.'

'Being fucked for three hours made you realise it. You're under the spell of my cunt. When I'm gone, spray some air freshener, take a cold shower, watch some football and all will be well.'

'Don't play with me, Amy. I'm trying to tell you I love you.'

'I know what your love looks like. You love Gail. That's love and that's the best you have to give. You may love me as a friend, as a fuck buddy, but you love Gail with all your heart.'

I left the bathroom and picked up my phone. I'd arranged to see an estate agent about selling my studio. I quickly texted him that I'd be late. Then took a quick peek at the video Liam had just made. Fuck.

I suddenly felt myself again. This is the world I belong in, I thought. This is my natural habitat.

Liam was all sincerity.

'I love you as you are,' he said, sitting on the edge of the bed.

'Well, that's a problem because I don't love you. I love to work with you. I love to fuck you. I love to be your slut. Your porn star,' I said, showing him the footage he'd taken of me taking his big cock all the way into my mouth. 'But I don't love you.'

He looked glum for a moment, then said, 'Love's not everything. We understand one another. That's so important. We share goals. We're both ambitious and creative. We could have an open relationship. You could fuck hot waiters and homeless guys and I wouldn't say a thing. We could move to France or Italy. Get out of all of this and live large.'

'You're not that guy, Liam. You think you are. But you're not. You want a family. You want a home to come back to, with a loving, chaste wife and adoring kids. You're that guy, really. This is my fault. If I hadn't come into your life you wouldn't have a mistress – it wouldn't even have occurred to you that you could have one. It certainly wouldn't have occurred to you to fuck your fans, publicists and fellow writers. I brought this to you. I corrupted you.'

'We corrupted each other.'

'No. I kissed you first. Remember how innocent it all was in the beginning? Even if you had wanted to kiss me, you would never have tried. I kissed you. And you kissed me back, but then our feelings of guilt kept us from doing anything more for weeks.'

'I wanted to.'

'But you didn't. And you wouldn't have done anything more. You married your childhood sweetheart. You were a good boy. You were a soldier. You had principles. I fucked you and Gail over. You don't love me. You shouldn't even *like* me.'

'But I do.'

'That's unfortunate. Try to forget it and I'll try to forget it, too. Because I don't want to know that you think you love me. It will make things awkward. You need to be the bastard I've taught you to be. You lose that, you lose me.'

And with that I left. I felt mean. I felt ungrateful. He'd fucked me so well. But I also felt right. And although I had betrayed Gail again, I had fought for her, too. He didn't love me, he loved Gail. He needed to hear it. He needed a slap. We had something unique and we were fucking lucky to have it. But it wasn't unbreakable.

# Chapter 30
## Too Good for Them

The pages of Malcolm's notebook were fluttering in the breeze. The beautiful afternoon was turning bad and people were packing up their picnics and collecting children. The park hadn't been very busy, but there had been enough activity for Malcolm to forget his purpose and give himself over to people watching. But now the temperature had been dropping steadily and the breeze had turned to gusts. When the sun went behind one of the fast-moving clouds, Malcolm felt distinctly uncomfortable. But he did not rise from his bench.

Recently, he'd been writing more and more. He was being compelled to write. He took no enjoyment from the work. In fact, he was feeling deeply unhappy. The book was about loss, and it was affecting him terribly. It was difficult, but the words flowed.

He placed his hands on the fluttering pages of the notebook Daniel had given him. The pencilled words he saw there depressed him. Pages and pages of them. They were all about a writer called Malcolm Taylor who had been married to the writer Helen Owen. Malcolm was having great difficulty coming to terms with Helen's death, but was having more difficulty because he had decided he needed to write about it. Memoir seemed too close, so he had decided to write a novel. But he couldn't decide upon a name for his fictional Helen, so he had begun calling her Helen. Having done that, he had begun calling his character Malcolm, because it was easier. Yet it was a novel, and not a memoir. That was decided and unchangeable. But by doing this the lines between fact and fiction were blurred. And the Malcolm in the book was succumbing to depression.

Malcolm closed the notebook. He needed to get out of the wind. His phone rang.

'Malcolm Taylor.'

'I haven't caught you at a bad time, have I?'

'No, Trevor, I'm at the park.'

'I haven't seen you for a while and wondered if anything was wrong.'

'No, no. I've been writing.'

'The same thing?'

'Yes. It's very dark and complicated. You'll probably hate it.'

'You don't sound too good there, Malcolm. Are you sure you're okay?'

'I'm just so sad,' he said, and tears sprang unexpectedly from his eyes. 'The man in my book has lost his wife and has no one left in the world,' he said, taking out his handkerchief and wiping his eyes. He felt awful, like his heart was broken. He started to sob and hung up the phone. A woman passing by stopped to ask if he was okay.

'Sorry, I'm fine. I lost my wife recently. I'm fine. Thank you.'

She touched his shoulder, smiled and walked on.

Malcolm's phone rang again.

'Malcolm, we got cut off.'

'My fault, sorry. Someone was asking directions.'

'Now, Malcolm, are you sure you're all right?'

'No, I'm not all right. I don't know what I'm doing with this book. It's drilling a hole right through my heart. It's killing me.'

'Then stop writing it!' demanded Trevor down the line.

'I can't. It's good. Very good.'

'But if it's causing you distress ...'

'I can tough it out. I have to. I have no choice. It comes to me with such force. It's so real. So painful.'

'Can you send me some pages?'

'No, no. No one is seeing this one. It's private. I don't even know if I'll get it published.'

'But you said it was good.'

'Too good for them.'

'I see.'

The clouds had completely obliterated the sunshine and the park was looking bleak.

'Malcolm, are you still there?'

'Yes.'

'I'll call you when I hear whether it's true you've been shortlisted. I'll hear later today or tomorrow.'

'Thank you, Trevor. Look after yourself.'

The park was empty and Malcolm sat shivering as the first drops of rain fell. The tears had returned and his shoulders rose and fell with his sobs. Minutes passed before he suddenly shouted, 'Stop it, man!', gathered himself and stood up. He tucked the notebook under his arm and, as the rain fell more heavily, hurried out of the park.

# Chapter 31
# You Know Me Better Than Anyone

Max and Amy talk on the phone:

'Have you heard the news?'

'What are you talking about, Max?'

'I've been told Malcolm Taylor is on the shortlist.'

'We all heard that rumour days ago.'

'We all …'

'Malcolm, Helen and I.'

'And you didn't think to let me know?'

'Why would I?'

'I told you why. He's not doing interviews.'

'So?'

'I need something big to keep the magazine going.'

'Which is what to me?'

'From what I've heard he's the last widely recognisable author on the list. Coetzee and Strout are out. You just get me into the house. I'll do the rest.'

Silence.

'I'm sorry. I'm going about this all wrong. I'm under a lot of stress. I need your help.'

'I spoke to Liam. He's willing to talk to you.'

'Liam? Oh, thanks, but right now, Malcolm is the main game. It would make my reputation if I could secure the interview he won't give.'

'But I spoke to Liam. He's expecting —'

'That story is on the back burner. Why are you being like this?'

'You tell me, you read my diary, you know me better than anyone.'

Silence.

'Please, Amy, the things I said at the V&A were unfair. I was angry. Hurt.'

Silence.

'The diary captures you at your worst, it's true, but it also reveals you for who you really are.'

Silence.

'I told you I re-read the diary because I wanted to hate you.. That isn't true. Not really.'

Silence.

'Amy? Amy?'

'Yes.'

'I'm trying to say I'm sorry.'

Silence.

'Amy?'

'Be here tomorrow at six. I'll message the address.'

# Chapter 32
# He Couldn't Tell

Daniel had been woken early by the sound of raised voices. When he went out to investigate he realised it was much earlier than he'd supposed. The house was still dark. He switched on the landing light and went upstairs. He found his parents' door closed and heard the distinctive sound of Malcolm's snoring. When he returned to Malcolm's office, where he'd been sleeping on the sofa bed, he saw that it was exactly 4 am. He sat on the edge of the bed and listened to the night.

He could hear voices. And then laughter.

The noise wasn't coming from the house, but from the street. Malcolm's office overlooked the street. Daniel turned off his phone, which was giving off a low glow, and went to the window. Malcolm's desk was in the way and he had to squeeze in beside it.

There was an Aston Martin blocking the street, headlights on, idling with a low rumble. A black man was standing by the open driver's door resting his elbows on the roof of the car, talking to someone who was too close to the front of the house for Daniel to see.

He pressed his head against the glass, but saw no one. He guessed it was Amy.

The black man was gesticulating as he spoke, but the window muffled his words.

Daniel lifted the window an inch. The cool night air and voices entered.

The black man said, 'I'll park this and walk back.'

'No, go away. Gail was expecting you home ten minutes ago,' Daniel heard Amy whisper.

'She's probably asleep. You know that. Let me come in for five minutes. One drink and I'm gone.'

Daniel saw Amy now; she'd stepped out from the basement steps and rested her hands against the front gate.

Still whispering, she said, 'It was a great night, Liam. A great party. Go home.'

So this was Liam Smith, thought Daniel.

Liam walked around the car, leaving the driver's door open. He was powerfully built.

Daniel had read a few Jack Cade novels long before he'd met Amy. He enjoyed them. Found them addictive. He'd always pictured Idris Elba as Mark Harden. But now he realised Mark Harden was Liam.

When Liam reached Amy, Daniel couldn't hear what they were saying. They were so close. Whispering. But he saw Liam's hand move a few strands of hair from Amy's face and saw him kiss her. She kissed him back, the front gate between them.

Daniel watched as Liam lifted Amy over the gate. His hands were all over her as they continued to kiss. He lifted her dress and she pulled it back down. Then he pulled out his cock and Amy took it in hand.

Daniel couldn't believe what he was seeing. The car was idling in the street. They'd probably woken more people than him. Eyes would be watching them. He suddenly thought to grab his phone. He'd record it.

When he returned Amy was stroking Liam's cock as they kissed, her dress was up around her waist, underwear halfway down her thigh. Liam had his hand between her legs. Daniel started filming.

It was dark, but there was enough light from the streetlight a few houses down to see what was going on.

Then she knelt right there on the street and took his cock in her mouth. Daniel started to stroke his own cock as he filmed. She was so gorgeous and yet so depraved. He simply couldn't compute it. And he had fucked her, too.

Liam lifted her from the ground and placed her on the bonnet of Daniel's Citroën. Then he began to fuck her. Amy stared up at the camera. Did she see Daniel? He wasn't sure. She made no sign that she had seen him. But then, would she? He couldn't tell.

Daniel came suddenly against the windowsill.

But they weren't done. Liam turned Amy around and fucked her from behind. But he completely obscured Daniel's view of her. All the camera could get were Liam's fast and furious thrusts.

Then Liam growled and came.

Never in Daniel's life had he ever seen anything like this. He'd watched porn. But never could he imagine people got away with this stuff in real life. His sexual life had always been so careful. Until Amy, he had never really done anything out of the ordinary. He was unerringly loyal in his relationships. Without effort. And experimentation in the bedroom had never seemed necessary. Why risk losing what he had by sharing his fantasies?

Watching Amy opened his eyes. Now he understood how easy it was for his wife to stray. He could now imagine exactly how it would happen. How his wife could fuck one of her clients.

He watched Liam do up his trousers then stand back and survey his work. Amy hadn't moved. She was lying face down across Daniel's bonnet. She was completely exposed. Liam stepped forward and slapped her bottom then walked around Daniel's car to his own.

'Bye, gorgeous.'

Amy lifted her hand slightly and waved.

The car roared off and Amy stood up slowly. Pulled her underwear up and dress down. She stood in the street looking up at all the houses with a dazed expression in her eyes and a slight turn to her lips that wasn't quite a smile. She leant back against Daniel's car and looked up at him. She blew him a kiss, then walked back through the gate and down to the basement.

# Chapter 33
# Not Like Hers

Liam and Julia on the phone:

'I've just read it, Liam.'

'What do you think?'

'You're right, it's good. Very good. The others all agree, too.'

'Have you spoken to Amy?'

'I keep putting her off. We were meant to speak last Thursday. I'm glad I dodged that one.'

'What are you going to do, Julia?'

'Try and publish it.'

'How? Amy shared it with me in confidence.'

'I'll say we found the original manuscript. The copy Clarissa Munten and Maxine Snedden read.'

'But aren't you just back at square one?'

'No, Legal have been in touch with Helen. They're tightening the screws. She'll give in. Anyway, I'm going to call her myself.'

'It's a great book. Deserves a large audience. Why wouldn't she want to publish it? I don't understand her.'

'She has principles, standards.'

'So do I.'

'Not like hers, Liam.'

# Chapter 34
# We Tried Our Best

The cleaners had just left and Helen was making her way around the house inspecting their work. She wasn't very happy with them. They were impossibly quick. In and out in under an hour. Four of them. Each racing off into different rooms. One does bathrooms, one vacuums, one dusts and wipes the tops of tables and benches, bookshelves, and the last takes on the kitchen and then mops the floors in the bathrooms and kitchen and flat.

She didn't like strangers in the house. They touched everything. They went through her most private spaces – her bedroom and office. They moved her things, never putting them back as they were. They shuffled Malcolm's pages, upset the piles of books. Left things in strange places. She once found her reading glasses on top of the loo. Why would they move them at all?

This was the second company of cleaners. The first was exactly the same. So she was reluctant to try a third group. She just wanted them to do what they said they'd do. It wasn't challenging work. The objectives were clear. She'd even offered them more money to take more time. But this was rejected as unnecessary. She didn't understand this conclusion.

They were gone now, though, and the bathroom smelt clean. She wouldn't look in the corners.

She just didn't have the energy to clean such a large house. The flat had been much easier to maintain. These stairs were a problem, too. She felt it now. Their bedroom was on the second floor, their offices on the first. It was a difficult climb to the top some evenings.

She imagined a day when neither of them could reach the second floor. She imagined they would use the ground-floor front room as a master bedroom. Too old to visit the upper floors of their own house. Thank goodness there was a ground-floor lavatory.

She stood at the top of the stairs and looked down. She heard noise downstairs and wondered if Malcolm had returned with Trevor. They were having Trevor to dinner to celebrate Malcolm's shortlisting.

She went into their bedroom to change. On the bed she found a letter she'd hidden down the side of the mattress. The cleaners must have found it and thought it lost. It wasn't. She opened it and read it again. She would lose the house. There were no two ways about it. They didn't even seem to want the book anymore. Just the money. And the papers were saying house values were dropping. She sat down on the bed.

'Helen?'

'I'm in here.'

Daniel pushed open the bedroom door.

'It's so hot out there!'

'Is it?'

'Haven't you been out?'

'No, not yet.'

'I picked up all you asked me to get. I bought a cake, too.'

'Thank you, Daniel.'

'Is anything the matter? You look a bit out of sorts.'

She handed him the letter.

Daniel read it and said, 'Can they do that?'

'They seem to think so.'

'I don't understand. It says "failure to deliver"; I thought you gave them the book. That's why you have the house. You sold out.'

'It isn't that simple!' she said crossly, taking back the letter. 'Forget it.'

'Have you repented the decision? Is that what's happened? Is this about your integrity?'

'Go away, Daniel. Forget about the letter. Don't mention it to Malcolm.'

'He doesn't know?!'

'About the letter? No. He knows I'm debating whether to give them the book.'

'He'll join the dots.'

'I know he will.'

'What's done is done. Give them the book. Why lose the house over this? You think anyone will know the difference between this book and your others? They won't.'

'Malcolm knows the difference. I know the difference. The difference is the whole point!'

'Then you shouldn't have written the book.'

'I was tired of Brixton. Of never having enough money! I needed to do something. I was writing my best work but no one was paying any attention to it. The papers were full of debut authors getting astonishing publishing deals. Always young, always attractive. My work was irrelevant. I needed to do something.'

'So you did sell out,' he said, smiling. He sat down on the dressing chair by the wardrobe, his hands on his thighs.

'Why does that make you happy?'

'Because you've always been so bloody holier than thou.'

'Daniel, you say such horrible things.'

'I only say them. You do them.'

Helen looked at him, uncomprehending.

'Neglect, Helen. Your work was always more important than I was. You never had time for me. You were always home and always absent.'

Under Daniel's gaze, Helen looked at the carpet.

'I understand what you were doing now. You were being the great writer. But it was impossible for me to understand what you were doing then. Impossible. You and Malcolm treated me like a little adult. A tiny literary gent. You never spoke about anything I could understand. Nothing was simply as it seemed. Everything was complex. Everything had meanings beyond my grasp. And you were continually disappointed that I didn't rise to the challenge. You couldn't hide that from me.'

'We did our best.'

'Perhaps. But I don't think so. I don't think you could stomach the ordinariness of parenting. You were above such things. You'd worked hard to crawl out of the sea of mediocrity, and the repetitive needs of a child, those stark unchanging realities of a child's development, were dragging you back in. You were adept at talking to Kingsley Amis but couldn't find a way to talk to the parents of my schoolfriends. You didn't know how to speak to my teachers. You were bored by all of them and bored by me. The needs of your own child bored you stiff.'

'That's just not true, Daniel. We have always loved you. We delighted in all of your achievements. We were always available to attend school events, unlike other parents. Your friends were always welcome at home. We were a minding service for many of them. Their parents appreciated our help. We went to every game of football you played, every concert you were in, every play. We arranged for violin lessons when you requested them. We found the money to allow you to go on an exchange to France. We tried our best.'

'That's not how it felt.'

'You're so bitter, Daniel. I don't know where your resentment comes from.'

'I just told you.'

'But none of it's true. Your allegations don't bear scrutiny. Your feelings must have some other source.'

'There you go again,' he said, rising.

'I haven't done anything.'

'You just pushed my experiences of life off the table,' he said, throwing his arms across in front of him as though knocking things off a table.

'No, I didn't, I suggested you might want to re-examine them.'

'Because you can't be wrong? Your thoughts on this matter can't be re-examined?'

'You forget that I was an adult throughout your childhood. You were a child. Perhaps, just perhaps, your memory is muddled. I remember a happy child. A child with friends. A child who excelled at school and who rose to challenges. I remember a child who would sit on the floor listening as adults spoke. You didn't need to do that. The television was on in the other room. There were games and puzzles. There were children's books to read. You chose to sit by our feet and listen. And on occasion you would surprise us by adding to our conversation.'

Daniel didn't say anything to this. He had moved to the window with his back turned to her.

'I agree with your father when he says your problems began when you left our world and entered the real world. You set yourself unrealistic goals, do you remember? But set out to achieve them in a desultory manner. Your university career was unspectacular, and as a result of these initial setbacks you recalibrated your goals. Even then you might have become an academic with a bit of effort, remember, but you accepted that role in university administration.'

Daniel turned abruptly.

'So I chose financial security. I didn't want to live hand-to-mouth like you and Malcolm.'

'We didn't live hand-to-mouth.'

'I remember the arguments about money.'

'Everyone has those.'

He smiled bitterly. 'Do you have any idea what effect money worries have on a child?'

'So we're to blame for you switching degrees? We were supporting you financially while you were at university. You could have gone on to do a PhD and we would have backed you all the way.'

'Where would I be with a PhD in semiotics? Driving a taxi.'

'Teaching?'

Daniel scoffed and said, 'What does a teacher earn?'

'Respect.'

Daniel's eyes widened at this remark. Helen saw the colour drain from his face.

'Nothing is ever good enough.'

'I'm sorry, Daniel. I didn't mean that. It just came out.'

'You both had great expectations, but I didn't know what I wanted to do. I had no vocation. No passion for anything. You and Malcolm have always known you were writers. I used to dream of writing a book to make you both proud of me. But that was impossible. I knew that early on.'

'We just wanted you to be happy.'

Helen waited to see if Daniel would say anything.

'I easily understand the detrimental effect Malcolm and I could have had on you once you were an adult. Malcolm has that effect on me. Every year he raises the bar and I must either lift my game or quit. He has such strength of character. He never wavers and never tires. He'll continue the struggle until his last breath. And that's exhausting. If I'm honest, I know how you must feel, because I stopped fighting, too. I feel a great deal of resentment towards Malcolm, even though I have no right to feel anything but love and pride. It's like watching someone continue on towards the summit without you. You want them to go because you love them and you want them to stay because they should love you enough to forgo their dream.'

'I wasn't fit for the path you two took,' said Daniel, his voice breaking. 'I couldn't keep up. I wanted you to turn around. I wanted you to give up all your dreams and stay with me.'

Helen stood up and went to her son by the window. She turned him around and kissed him, then hugged him to her, something she hadn't felt permitted to do for many a year.

'I'm so sorry, Daniel.'

# Chapter 35
# Tuesday, 13 September 2016

Usman had no difficulty carrying a very dapper-looking Trevor from the car to the front room. Malcolm watched Usman as he had always watched powerful men, with envy. On these occasions, he always recalled the brief moments when he had felt powerful. They were rare, for he'd never tested himself in sporting endeavours. He'd never fought another person. Overall his life had been largely devoid of any physical accomplishment.

Once, when Daniel was still a boy, a friend had offered them his cottage in Cornwall for the weekend. It had been very cold and the stove burnt through a lot of wood. Malcolm found himself being sent out by Helen to chop wood, to keep them all warm. He'd never chopped wood before and stumbled in his initial attempts, but soon found a rhythm and enjoyed the satisfaction that came with successful physical work. The axe coming down on the blocks, with the weight of his body behind it, splitting the log and sending the two pieces flying, was like nothing in his experience. He always returned inside with an armful of wood, flushed with pride.

Watching Usman carrying in the collapsed wheelchair, holding it in front of him with one outstretched arm, evidently so it wouldn't scratch the doorframe or the walls, impressed him deeply and made him yearn for such strength. For Usman's strength was like Amy's beauty: it gave him a confidence he probably didn't know he had, and had an effect on others that it wasn't necessary for him to appreciate. He lifted Trevor from the sofa into the chair. Then straightened his bow tie and made him comfortable.

'I will come back for Mr Melville at ten,' said Usman as he turned to leave.

Malcolm followed him out to the front door. It had reached thirty degrees Celsius that day and was still very warm.

'Thank you, Usman.'

'Even though I told him it was hot, he insisted on wearing the tuxedo. It is too large for him but he wouldn't wear anything else.'

'It's fine. We're celebrating tonight. He always was one for spectacle.'

'Congratulations, Mr Taylor. Mr Melville told me of your good fortune.'

'Thank you, Usman, see you at ten.'

Malcolm closed the door. He stood for a moment and listened to the house. Silence. He walked past the front room into the kitchen. There was no sign of dinner being made but there were three bottles of red on the counter. They hadn't been there before. He checked his watch. It was six.

'Malcolm?' shouted Trevor from the front room. 'Are you there?'

'Sorry, Trevor, I'm coming.'

Malcolm walked to the bottom of the stairs and looked up them.

'Daniel!' he shouted. 'Helen!'

He waited for a response. When none came he walked back to the front room.

'Would you like a drink, Trevor?'

'Isn't anyone here? Have I got the wrong night?'

'We'd both have the wrong night in that case. No, I spoke to Daniel as he was going out to Waitrose. He was planning to make dinner with Helen. He's come back; there's wine on the counter. But I don't know where they are now.'

'If the worst comes to the worst we can order Indian and get right royally drunk.'

'That doesn't sound too bad, does it?' said Malcolm, with a short laugh. 'I'll get us drinks at least.'

When he reached the kitchen the door to the flat was opening.

'Amy, at least you're here.'

'Why, where's Helen?'

'I don't know. But Trevor has arrived in a tuxedo and we have no dinner for him.'

'I'm no help with that. I can't cook. Hopeless. But I can organise takeaway if that's a help.'

'Thanks, I'll give them another fifteen minutes. Trevor normally eats at six; he'll be dead by seven.'

'Malcolm, a friend of mine – actually, an ex-boyfriend – popped by to see me this afternoon. He's still downstairs, would you mind if he joined us tonight?'

'As there's no dinner made, there's no chance of him upsetting any plans, so why not?'

'Thanks, I'll let him know.'

She disappeared downstairs.

*

Daniel and Helen were making their way down the stairs when Daniel remembered something. He stopped and looked up at Helen, who was a few feet behind him.

'I forgot. I did a bit of research for you. Apparently the British Library bought Graham Swift's papers for a hundred grand a few years ago. It's not much, but maybe they'd do the same for Malcolm's papers and yours, too, of course. It could help save the house.'

'Graham is in a different league, Daniel. Booker winners always are. I doubt whether the British Library would be interested in our work. I was thinking a private collector or library. And I wasn't thinking of so much money.'

'I'll contact the British Library for you. It doesn't hurt to enquire.'

'Thank you.'

Laughter could be heard coming from below.

'It sounds like the party has started without us.'

'What is the time?'

'Half six.'

'I don't think I'm up to this.'

'Neither am I.'

*

Amy was uncomfortable. Malcolm and Trevor had welcomed Max with warmth and generosity but she knew his real purpose. She had presented Max as a friend. He wasn't a friend. Not anymore. By letting him in, she was betraying Malcolm and Helen. And herself. Just as she had once betrayed Max.

She stood by the bookcase and sipped her champagne. It was done now.

And she knew Max was adept at making friends. He opened the conversation with, 'I thought the Booker was an award for fiction. There's not an untrue word in *A Hundred Ways*. How is it eligible?' Obviously rehearsed, but forgivable because entertaining. Trevor took the bait and soon they were deep in discussion.

This ability of Max's was self-taught, not instinctive. He had been a shy, introverted boy who had been ignored at school. Invisible even to bullies. His reading had isolated him from his peers. He formed obsessions with long-forgotten writers of the first half of the twentieth century and collected them in cheap second-hand paperbacks. His bedroom in his parents' house was stacked with hundreds of them by the time he left school, all read, few digested. He entered university a walking anachronism.

A confusion of moral archaisms, political phantoms and artistic dead ends.

He caught Amy's eye in their first year of university by his absence. She would see him in lectures and hear him speak weirdly and often brilliantly in tutorials, but would never find him in the bars or cafes. He never attended the parties or the gatherings. When she did see him on campus, he was with mature students or lecturers.

To Amy he was aloof, interesting, out of reach. He was unlike the other boy-men. He wasn't loud and boisterous, he wasn't drunk or dishevelled. He spoke with confidence in tutorials but not aggressively, and not because he liked the sound of his own voice. And he dressed unusually. He was a little middle-aged man at nineteen. He modelled himself on writers of the forties and always wore a suit, even in summer.

Amy had thought him gay until one evening at the gathering of one of her friends, he appeared. He sat beside her and delighted her with wonderful nonsense. And it became clear that as she had been observing him, he had been observing her. He remembered things she had said in tutorials, remembered the books she admired and those she hated. He had even read part of the novel she had been writing and sharing with friends. Which embarrassed her at first, but then, when his views on it were critical and correct, caused her to burn with indignant rage. He cooled her temper with the help of his self-effacing humour when describing his own attempts at fiction. Then, quite surprisingly, he'd kissed her.

Soon after their first kiss, Max started writing for the student paper and was forced to interview his subjects. The work opened him up to the world. He read contemporary writers to review them and through them discovered how to speak to his peers. But he was never one of them. He took on a role, which still hadn't entirely left him, of observer, of commentator. The relationship he had with his peers was like that between an embedded war correspondent and the troops.

And Max never mentioned the first thing most men commented on: Amy's beauty. He saw it, but it wasn't what interested him. He appreciated her beauty. He was attracted to her beauty, he said. But he was far more interested in the strength of her will, which marked her out in a crowd. She was determined to get into publishing and showed it by topping all her subjects. And she was a voracious reader. Reading biographies of famous editors, publishers and even histories of publishing houses. And then there was the fiction. Books that Max disdained, she'd fly through. The latest bestsellers. The zeitgeist books of the last fifty years. And they'd all end up filled with notes in the margins and Post-it notes protruding from the pages. She dissected them, examined them, discovered their secrets. And then she would argue with him. He would make her read Hermann Hesse's *The Glass Bead Game* or Virginia Woolf's *To the Lighthouse* and she would break his heart by drawing his attention to their inadequacies. And then would take him to task for his outdated thinking, tease him for his unrealistic ambitions, and ridicule his obsession with the idea of a golden age of writing, which she said had only ever existed in the minds of an elite few.

Their passion for each other was born out of these intellectual tussles. Neither had met with such sustained and well-argued opposition before. Each was flattered by the potency of the other. Their intimacy grew as their indefensible prejudices fell. Delighted, they returned again and again to the fray, their minds afire with perfectly phrased arguments and sharp rebuttals until the heat of their words was lost in the conflagration of their bodies.

When they moved in together, they might be found entwined in bed, him reading Dorothy Richardson, she reading Georges Simenon. They were both fascinated by the dichotomy of publishing, each representing a warring party. She was intrigued by writers whose work appealed to millions upon millions of people and who seemed to speak for a particular epoch. He by those who spoke for all but reached only a few.

Daniel and Helen appeared at the door. Trevor, Malcolm and Max were oblivious to the change, so engrossed were they in their discussion about Boris Johnson. Max had worked for him briefly as a researcher when Johnson had been editor of *The Spectator*. Malcolm thought him a dangerous buffoon, but Max and Trevor demurred.

After Daniel went off to get drinks, Amy, who had been listening but was taking no part in the discussion, drifted over towards Helen, who was still hovering by the door.

'Are you all right, Helen?' she asked.

'I've heard from M&R again. Lawyers.'

'Julia is avoiding me. She hasn't been in the office. I don't understand what she's up to, but it's not good.'

'Who is that man?' asked Helen.

'Max. He's my ex. He popped over this afternoon.'

'He seems a strange choice for you.'

'I did say ex.'

Helen said nothing.

'Have I told you I'm selling my studio?'

Helen shook her head.

'I was wondering if I might rent the flat on a more permanent basis.'

'There is no permanent anymore, Amy.'

'I know. I'm sorry. At least until … then.'

'Daniel was thinking of doing the same.'

'Oh, then forget what I said. Daniel is family.'

'But I want him to return to Edinburgh. He needs to be near his boys. They need their father.'

'You're right, they do.'

Helen placed her hand on Amy's wrist and drew her nearer. In a near-whisper she said, 'A neighbour knocked on our door this afternoon. Vanessa. I know her to smile and wave to; she has three little children. She's a pleasant enough woman and spoke up reluctantly. I'd say her strong Christian feeling compelled her to come.' Helen smiled grimly. 'She seemed to think a prostitute was working from this address and wanted to warn us. She said she knew we'd recently taken in a lodger and thought, as we're an elderly couple, we might be being taken for a ride.'

Now it was time for Amy to smile grimly.

'Last night she saw a white woman with a black man in front of our house. She said they had oral sex on the pavement and intercourse on the bonnet of a car. She was very particular about these details. Do you know anything about this? Is this part of the trouble you warned me about when I asked you to stay?'

Amy thought she might die on the spot. It was one thing to catch Daniel masturbating at the window and quite another to hear Helen speak to her about oral sex and intercourse.

'What did you tell her?' was all Amy could manage to say.

'I told her it was unlikely to be a prostitute. And more likely to be someone who'd had too much to drink. She took this explanation well and with great composure fled. The whole thing was mortifying for both of us. But once she'd gone, I couldn't help laughing.'

'I'm so sorry, Helen.'

'I'm no one to you, not family, not really a friend, and as a feminist I should keep my mouth shut – your body is yours to do with what you will – but I suspect a darker reason for your behaviour.'

'I drink too much and do silly things.'

'On the street in front of our house?'

'It was 4 am and lasted no more than five minutes.'

'What lasted only five minutes?' asked Daniel, as he handed his mother a G&T.

'The phone call I had with Prince Harry,' said Amy, without missing a beat.

'You know Prince Harry?'

'Not well. We met at a party and danced together. He asked for my number.'

'I'm sure he did,' said Daniel.

'And he called you?' asked Helen.

'Yes, but as I said, it lasted no more than five minutes. It would appear I bored him. Never heard from him again.' They were looking at her open-mouthed. 'Never really fancied redheads, anyway.'

Max came over and introduced himself to Helen and Daniel. Trevor called out that he was starving. And after a brief discussion, it was decided to order Indian, as it was Trevor's favourite.

\*

Amy and Daniel were out on the street; they were walking to pick up the Indian. Delivery would have taken an hour and as it was only a five-minute walk away, Amy had decided to pick it up. Daniel couldn't resist the chance to be alone with her so had followed her out.

'How warm it still is!' said Amy. 'It's lovely.'

'That Max is a ponce.'

'Said the ponce.'

'Am I a ponce?'

'No, not really, ponces usually have an ounce of self-belief.'

'So I'm pathetic?'

'Exactly.'

They turned the corner and caught sight of the park. In the evening light, the trees were prematurely golden.

'Don't take it to heart. Helen just said a neighbour came over today to warn her that her lodger might be a prostitute.'

Daniel laughed. 'You do act the whore, Amy.'

'Show me then.'

'What?' asked Daniel, instantly aroused. What was she suggesting? He looked across at the park. He had read about dogging. It was still light. There was no telling what Amy might do next.

'Me being a whore. I know you filmed it. That's how I saw you in the dark window. The light from your phone's screen lit your face.'

'You want to see it?'

'Of course!'

Daniel took out his phone and started the video. He held it up for Amy to see.

'Oh, shame it's so dark. You can hardly tell it's me,' she said, taking the phone from him. 'I'm such a slut! Now I'm on my knees. So sordid. But look at me go!'

Daniel was unsure what to say to that. He adjusted his cock, which had grown hard and pressed uncomfortably against his trousers.

'He's a big guy. He really pounds you hard,' said Daniel, hoping Amy was thinking what he was thinking.

'He would break your neck if he knew about this. But god, he's a gorgeous specimen.'

Amy watched to the end as they walked in silence.

'Have you watched this today?' asked Amy.

'Yes,' said Daniel, quietly.

'Did you jerk off again?'

They were waiting for traffic to clear before crossing the high street. The Indian looked busy.

She crossed before him and he looked at her bare legs, the hem of her very short dress rising in the wind. He crossed soon after and Amy repeated the question as she handed back the phone.

'A couple of times,' Daniel said, hoping that the revelation would lead to more intimacy.

'Well, I'm glad you got something out of it. Wait here.'

As Amy entered the crowded shop, Daniel walked to the edge of the pavement and looked up and down the high street. A group of young men were smoking outside the King's Head. Through the window next to them, he could see the large screen showing the football. A lot of green.

Bored, he looked at his phone and checked his emails. Nothing. His wife was still his wife according to Facebook. He wondered when her status would change or he would be unfriended. He flicked through her photos. There were very few of them together. If he was in a photo it was because he was with the boys. He closed down Facebook: he couldn't bear to see pictures of the boys. Everything was fine, if he pretended the boys didn't exist. The boys complicated matters. He'd been dumped before. She was much younger than he was. He'd been surprised that she had loved him. That she had agreed to marry him. He'd been very fortunate. But she was always going to leave him. They always did, in the end. He hadn't factored in the boys. The boys were something completely unexpected. Losing them was impossible. So he drove them from his mind.

While playing with his phone it suddenly occurred to him what Amy had been doing. He was such an idiot. He opened his videos. Gone. Deleted.

He was an idiot.

Amy came out and handed him the two bags containing dinner. They recrossed the high street.

'You deleted it?'

'Of course I did.'

They walked back in silence.

*

After Usman had come for Trevor, Helen and Malcolm remained seated in the front room chatting to Max, whose company they really seemed to enjoy. He had always had an old head, and tonight it had really paid off. He was familiar with Helen and Malcolm's work, and had read their peers and even their influences. But it was his interest in novels about writing and writers that had them talking. Max mentioned Gissing in passing. Malcolm had been fascinated with George Gissing's *New Grub Street* as a young man, and had only recently re-read it. He had found so many parallels with his experience of the writing life. He knew the characters, had lived some of their trials. Then Max revealed he was considering writing a book about these kinds of books. Malcolm and Helen suggested a few: Balzac's *Lost Illusions*, Knut Hamsun's *Hunger*, John Irving's *The World According to Garp*. They then debated whether to include Willa Cather's *The Song of the Lark*, which was about a singer, and Theodore Dreiser's *The Genius*, about a painter. Weren't they just ways for the author to mask their interest in themselves? asked Malcolm.

While Trevor was with them, the conversation was more inclusive, but now Daniel and Amy were left out of this discussion. Daniel took himself off to bed but Amy felt she had to stay. She was too lazy to walk into the kitchen to open another bottle of champagne, so she poured herself a glass of whisky from the bottle on the coffee table.

She was only half listening to their conversation. Max's close proximity, the sound of his voice, the intensity and eloquence of his speech, took Amy back. She was transported to their flat. The nights when there would be a group of people – usually writers, students and artists – talking and drinking into the small hours of the morning. She remembered being front and centre in many of these discussions – being very outspoken and full of ideas. Everything had been important, then. She'd been as passionate about ideas and books and literature as Max. And passionate about Max, too. Such nights would fire her up. She would sometimes get so worked up she'd throw everyone out so she could drag Max to bed and ravish him.

Amy realised she had nodded off. Malcolm was standing and saying good night to Max. Helen, still seated, was looking straight at Amy.

'Are you still with us?' she asked.

'Just.'

'It's after twelve. Time for bed,' said Malcolm.

'Amy, I left my bag downstairs,' said Max.

'Thank you for celebrating with me. Good night,' said Malcolm.

'Nice to meet you, Max. Be sure to drop in again,' said Helen and followed Malcolm out.

Amy knew how drunk she was when she tried to navigate the stairs to the flat. She judged herself to be drunker than she ever remembered being on those steps. Drunker than the night she'd fucked Daniel.

Parts of her passage down were obscured from her. Her brain no longer seemed committed to full consciousness. One moment she had trouble with her heels. The next she was barefoot.

Max was talking. She couldn't focus on him now. Moving from the sofa in the front room to the bottom of the stairs had been too much for her. All she could focus on was climbing into bed. She saw the bed. But needed to pee, so made her way unsteadily to the bathroom.

*

'What time is it?' Amy asked, rolling onto her side.

Max was seated on the bed fully clothed with his laptop on his lap. The bathroom light was still on. She could smell bleach.

'Four.'

'Why are you still here?' It all felt so familiar. As if no time had passed.

'I was worried about you. You vomited and ...'

'I'm so sorry,' she said quietly over his words.

'... then went into a bit of a stupor. I thought you might vomit again. I didn't want you to go the way of Jimi Hendrix, so I stayed.'

'Thank you, Max.'

'You'd do the same for me,' he said, closing his laptop. 'At least I hope you would.'

'I would, you know I would,' she said, reaching out and touching his hand briefly, before bringing hers back under the covers. He was here in her room, almost in her bed. How natural it felt.

'Here, drink this,' he said, giving her a glass of water. She lifted herself to one elbow and drank the whole glass.

'I have to pee.' She jumped up and ran to the bathroom. She was still in the dress she'd worn last night. She took it off and sat on the loo. Then she went to the sink and washed out her mouth with mouthwash. She checked her hair. Disaster. She took off her underwear and threw on her bathrobe. Then she switched off the light and ran back to bed. As she got under the covers she cleverly disrobed in one clean movement.

Max had opened his laptop again. He half closed it on Amy reappearing.

'Feel a bit better?' he asked.

She nodded. It was like old times. He was so normal. Max how she remembered him. She used to wake in the middle of the night to find him working. She learnt her bad sleeping habits from him.

'Writing down notes on last night?' she asked, snuggling into the duvet.

'More trying to frame the story. The marriage is interesting, isn't it? And their son, what an oddball.'

'Be kind to them.'

'I'm in love with them both already.' He clapped the laptop shut and looked as though he was going to get up, but then leant closer to Amy. She thought he was going to kiss her, like he used to, but he stopped short and said quietly, looking her in the eye, 'You have to stop this.'

'What?'

'This. Your drinking. It has to stop.'

'What do you know about it? We haven't seen each other in years.'

'People talk. Besides, anyone can see you drink too much. You had more than your fair share of three bottles of champagne over dinner and then sat on the couch and had two very large whiskies. You don't even like whisky. Or you didn't. Who knows, now?'

'I was celebrating Malcolm's success.'

'When you nodded off upstairs Helen said something, too.'

'What?'

'That you drink too much.'

Amy rolled over, turning away from Max.

'They both care about you, Amy. I can tell. And it's a wonderful thing to be loved by such people.'

She said nothing.

'People are worried about you.'

'They can fuck off.'

'Why are you doing this to yourself?'

She didn't answer him.

'Look, I'm going to go.' He got off the bed and put his laptop back in the bag. 'Malcolm has agreed to do the interview, so I'll be back later today. Thank you for getting me in the door.'

She said nothing.

'They're both great. I understand why you're staying here. I would if I could.'

Max stood at the end of the bed and watched Amy to see if she would say anything. Nothing came so he walked through the lounge area to the front door.

'Max.'

He couldn't be sure he heard his name or whether he just wished to hear it.

'Max.'

He went back to the bed.

'Max, don't go. You needn't go. Sleep here. I know I'm a mess. It's all right.'

He crouched down by the bed and brought his face in line with hers.

'I can't.'

'Kiss me.'

'I can't.'

'You loved me once.'

'I did. But I can't stay.'

'Kiss me, Max. Just once.'

'No. You're not mine anymore.'

She reached out and took hold of his hand.

'Stay with me, please. I want to be with you.'

'As much as I would like to, I can't. And I won't. We're both different people now. We'll never be as we were.'

She let go of his hand.

He closed the street door quietly behind him.

# Chapter 36
# Nothing to Be Ashamed of

Malcolm was making breakfast. He had been to Waitrose early and had bought bacon, eggs, tomato, baked beans, thick-cut bread, and Cumberland sausages. He didn't normally drink whisky and had had a few with Trevor the night before, so he awoke feeling the worse for wear. He wanted a big breakfast and assumed the others would all come running as soon as they smelt the bacon frying.

Not long after Malcolm started cooking, Daniel came down the stairs and entered the kitchen.

Malcolm looked at him and smiled. Daniel said nothing but started cutting up the tomatoes.

A few minutes after Daniel's appearance, the door to the flat opened and Amy appeared in her bathrobe and bare feet. Her hair was a mess and her face was pale and blotchy. It was obvious to both men that she wasn't feeling the best. It looked like she'd been crying.

'What's cookin', Mal?' she asked, shyly.

'The lot. Are you hungry?'

'Famished.'

'Has Max gone?' Malcolm asked.

'He's my ex-boyfriend,' she said. 'He went home last night. Can I make some juice for everyone?'

They both nodded.

'Is Helen coming down?' asked Malcolm.

'She was on the phone in her office when I passed her,' said Daniel.

Malcolm checked the time. Just after nine.

*

As they ate their breakfast, Malcolm was telling Amy and Daniel stories about Trevor. In a previous life, Trevor had been an actor. He had walked the boards with Olivier and Gielgud. He had once wooed Maggie Smith. And his first wife had been a famous Greek actress he met while starving in Greece during the war.

Amy was wolfing hers down, as was Malcolm. Daniel was taking his time. He didn't usually eat much in the mornings. The instant coffee Malcolm had made him wasn't coffee at all. He didn't know what it was. He added another teaspoon of sugar.

They all heard Helen coming. Amy jumped up, took her plate from the warmer and placed it next to Daniel at the table. Malcolm poured her some tea. When she entered the kitchen, it was clear something unexpected had happened.

'I've just spoken to Julia,' she said, and sat down. 'They found the missing copy of the original manuscript in a drawer last week. She said they've all read it and love it. She was telling me how great it was, how proud she would be to publish it, how all of the editorial team were behind it, how the heads of marketing and sales were behind it one hundred per cent.'

'But ...'

'She also said she was assigning someone called Valerie Hodges to the book to replace you, Amy. She said you'd resigned.'

'What!?'

'I don't think she knows you're living here.'

'We need to fight this.'

'No, we don't. I'm done. They can publish it. Leave it alone.'

'But if it isn't what you want ...' said Daniel.

Helen was silent. She looked as exhausted as she had sounded.

'It's a good book, Helen, and nothing to be ashamed of,' said Amy, trying to make the best of it. But she felt hollow. She didn't believe Julia had just 'found' the manuscript. It was too much of a coincidence. Liam must have given it to her. 'As I said before, I know fifty writers who'd throw their mother under a bus to have their name associated with that manuscript.'

'It means we get to keep the advance and the house,' said Helen, smiling bravely. 'That's a relief.'

Malcolm hadn't looked up from his plate since she had entered nor the whole time they had all been talking. Helen glanced at him, expecting him to raise his eyes on this news. He didn't.

'It's a lovely house,' said Amy, filling with self-loathing. Helen looked demoralised. And Amy knew it was because of her actions. Helen had trusted her. Amy had betrayed that trust. Amy had placed her trust in Liam. He had let her down in turn. And now Julia had succeeded in taking the fight out of Helen. And even though this was the perfect time to admit what she had done, the fear of being asked to leave Malcolm and Helen's life was suddenly too great. Without examining her reasons, and with the rationale of the coward, Amy chose to be silent. She would fix things before Helen and Malcolm discovered the truth.

Amy said with forced cheerfulness, 'I still want to look into whether we can get the second and third versions published. I think the three books together would make for an interesting study.'

'Why?' asked Daniel. 'You're in a privileged position, you've read all three. I haven't read any of them.'

'The three books are variations of the same theme,' said Amy, eager to leave the table but unwilling to do so while Helen needed her.

'Like the versions of *Lady Chatterley's Lover* Penguin used to publish?' Daniel asked. 'I remember them from my university days.'

'I don't know those,' admitted Amy.

'They were more drafts of the same novel,' said Helen. 'Mine are completely new novels. Each distinct from the last.'

'But they share the same DNA in a way,' added Amy. 'Like brothers and sisters. If you're told they're family you see the similarities, but not knowing them, you wouldn't guess their connection.'

'When I started, Daniel, I knew I could tell the story I had in mind a number of ways. I just decided to write it for a general audience, as you know, in the hope of making some money. I'd spent most of my writing life with the brake on. Carefully choosing every movement forward. This time I rolled with it and reached speeds I never thought I could. Completely uninhibited writing. I did one rewrite and I was finished. The whole process took a quarter of the time I normally take. And as a result, the manuscript was huge. Almost two hundred thousand words. Later, when I decided not to publish version one, I returned to write the second version from scratch. I inhibited my imagination. I wrote with precision, with patience, entirely conscious of every choice. The story shrank considerably. Characters vanished, scenarios, too.

'The third version was different. I wrote as I'd never written before. I can't quite describe that process. I suppose one way would be to say I wrote at a molecular level. But that sounds ridiculous.'

'That's the version you should read, Daniel. And so should you, Malcolm,' said Amy.

Malcolm looked up from his plate. He seemed surprised to find himself spoken to. They saw that his face was wet with tears. Daniel had never seen his father cry before and it shocked him. Helen turned away. And Amy said, 'Malcolm, oh dear, what's the matter?'

'I don't know,' he said, his shoulders shaking, 'I feel so sad.'

Amy hugged him as Helen left the table and then the room.

Daniel picked up a sausage from his mother's untouched plate and took a bite.

'This sausage is good, but everything else is fucked,' he said, chewing.

# Chapter 37
# Max's Notes I

Strangest meeting with Malcolm Taylor today. Last night we had talked about my interviewing Malcolm and Helen Owen, a larger piece about the couple, their careers and the effect the shortlisting was having on them.

Today I arrived and Helen was nowhere to be found and when I sat with Malcolm in his office, he told me that the interview would have to be short and centre on *A Hundred Ways* and the Booker shortlisting.

Then, as things progressed and talk turn to Helen, he consistently referred to her in the past tense. At one point I saw that he was getting upset. I looked away for a moment and he recovered himself. But throughout the rest of the interview he wiped his eyes from time to time.

This was very different from the Malcolm I had met the night before. Seated with his long-time agent, the irrepressible, nonagenarian Trevor Melville, Malcolm had been voluble, warm, entertaining and forthright.

We discussed novels about novels and writers, and Malcolm pointed out that both Hesse's *Gertrude* and Maugham's *Of Human Bondage* feature heroes with a disfigured foot, suggesting that artistic sensibilities are an infirmity, a burden. And Trevor reminded us of the role tuberculosis plays in the novels of the nineteenth century and how often it is the poet or the artist dying slowly and gracefully in the corner on a chaise longue. Art as a disease society needs to excise.

They both teased me good-naturedly, too, Malcolm referring to a book I had never heard of, *Enemies of Promise* by Cyril Connolly. In it, I gather from what they said, Connolly lists all of the things one ought not to do if one wishes to succeed in literature – become a critic, a journalist, write paid reviews, edit literary magazines, teach writing etc. All of which I have done and still do.

But this morning, it was as though we were meeting for the first time. Last night had been wiped from the record.

When I asked Malcolm what he was working on now, he said it was too distressing to talk about. Too raw. So we turned back to *A Hundred Ways*, which he seemed to know next to nothing about. He couldn't recall the names of the characters, the story or the process of writing it. He acted like a poor student who has been asked to speak upon a book he had not read. I say acted; he *was* that student.

My knowledge of the book interested him and he took his cues from me. I reminded him of the radio interview that brought him some level of fame and he chuckled for the first time. Trevor had told him all about it, he said. As though the interview hadn't happened to him.

I had two hours with him, which went surprisingly quickly. I will listen to the recording again, but I don't think I got anything of use. At least, it's not the story I want to write. I will speak to Amy to see if I can get access to Helen.

There was one bright spot, but this was off point, and confusing. I went to my recording for this, because it's very particular. He said that he doesn't think my generation, including me, capable of understanding literature, or history, or philosophy, as we were raised in the internet age, which has applied a filter on us. A filter that confirms my own preconceptions at every turn. He says his contemporaries had a chance, but only discovered they were deceived late. Their vision had been impaired by the generation before. Now, the world could only be seen through the lens of irony. Nothing could be taken at face value.

I don't quite understand what he means by all that. But he's got me wrong. I'm not that guy. My experience of literature etc., comes via books, not the internet. I thought I had more than proven that the night before.

# Chapter 38
# It's Perfectly Fine as It Is

I didn't announce myself or knock, I just walked straight into Julia's office. There was someone with her. A man. In a suit. Bald. Lean. Mid-thirties. I don't know who he was or what he was doing there. But as soon as Julia saw me standing in the middle of her office, she finished up with him and ushered him to the door. He nodded to me as he left. I walked to the chair in front of Julia's desk and sat down.

Julia made her way back to the desk, slowly.

'Well, look at that. Books. Liam's book, too.' There was a pile of hardcover Jack Cades on the end of her desk. 'Now you're a publisher.'

'I've just spoken to Helen,' she said, as she sat down.

'I know. That's why I'm here.'

'Before we start, I should tell you things have changed around here. There's been a restructure. Your role has been made redundant.'

'You think I give a shit?'

'You should. We're taking Helen away from you.'

'And giving it to Val. Helen told me.'

'No, Val said it wasn't her thing.'

I smiled. Loyal Val. I loved her even more in that moment.

'We're giving one of the young guns a go.'

'Good plan. Did you think that up all by yourself?'

'I had help,' she said, smiling, flashing impossibly white teeth. I didn't like that smile. She was very pleased with herself. I remembered the impulse I'd had the last time I was in the office. The impulse to smash her teeth in with the corner of her laptop.

'You know I don't need the salary I get here, right? And I can get a job anywhere I want?'

'Are you sober?' she asked, ignoring my words.

'It's eleven in the morning.'

'Would you be happy to take a breath test? New company policy.'

'Liam said you'd try something like this. You've just said I've been made redundant, you've probably cleared my desk, I no longer work here. What good would a breath test do?'

'Make it harder for you to get another job.'

'In publishing? You're not serious. People get fired for being sober in this industry. Face it, there's nothing you can do to me, and no point either, you've got what you wanted. Helen's book is brilliant, in your sense of the word, and will sell millions. It's your *Pillars of the Earth*. Congratulations. Where did you find a copy of the manuscript?'

'In a drawer.'

'Riiight.'

Julia placed her hand on the pile of Liam's books.

'We're also taking Liam away from you.'

I snorted. Let's call it a snort of contempt.

'Does that worry you?' Julia asked, caressing the spine of the top book.

'I work with Liam. Co-authors. We have a contract between ourselves. M&R have a publishing deal with the both of us. I'll be working with Liam on the books for as long as we agree to write them, regardless of the views of this office.'

I smiled as Julia's smile paled.

'I didn't know that.'

'Yes, you did. You must have known.'

'I didn't. I thought you brought him to us, but I didn't know about the contract you have with him.'

'How did you get this job? I mean really!'

'That's all before my time. It was an acrimonious handover. Maxine Snedden's refusal to cooperate has made my life very difficult.'

'Knowing nothing has made your job difficult. But at least Maxine left you Helen's manuscript, right?'

'Right.'

'Bullshit. Did Liam give it to you?'

'Give me what?'

'Helen's manuscript.'

'What are you talking about? It was found here. It had been filed incorrectly.'

'Riiight. I'll speak to Liam. He'll tell me.'

Julia, reverting to her old ways, took a deep breath and gave me a banal smile.

'I couldn't help but notice a lot of new faces out there,' I said casually as I stood to leave. 'Young faces, too.'

'Restructure, as I said.'

'Julie Gibson gone? Sandra Fullerton? Susan Churchill? Gary Shorten? Curtis Small?'

'All gone.'

'I heard they quit.'

'It was time for a change anyway.'

'They were the most experienced publishers you had. Well done. You know they'll take their authors with them, don't you?'

'It's been very good for M&R. Cleansing. We were getting stale.'

'So it's just me and Valerie left?'

Julia drummed her fingers on the top Jack Cade.

'And you want me gone.'

Julia smiled.

'If I go, I'll take Valerie with me. You'll just have the newbies. The ones I thought were interns.'

'A young, hungry team is just what M&R wants right now.'

I laughed. 'Look,' I said. 'My first impulse was to try and convince you not to publish Helen's book, but she doesn't want me to do that. I came to find out how you got yourself a copy of the manuscript. You've answered that. Liam gave it to you.'

Julia ignored me again.

'What happens now? Is there a little cardboard box with my stuff in it? Do I need to speak to HR or sign any papers?'

'We'll be in touch.'

I stopped at the door. 'You know Helen's manuscript needs a bit of work, right?'

'My team didn't think so.'

'The kids out there? What's their track record with this kind of thing?'

Julia didn't answer me.

'I'm sure it will be fine. They know what they're doing. But it would be a shame to stumble at the finish line. There's a lot of money at stake.'

'I've read it, Amy. It's great.'

'All of it? Really? Good for you. It has some pretty big words in it.'

She ignored me. 'We're pushing for March 2017. In time for Mother's Day.'

'That's a quick turnaround.'

'Strike while the iron is—'

'Julia, it's not all marketing. Without word of mouth these books don't reach their potential. Readers must feel compelled to thrust it into the hands of other readers. They need to become evangelists for the book.'

'It's perfectly fine as it is.'

'No, it isn't. I've read it a few times now. I've made some important changes. Like I do for Liam. Much-needed changes.

But don't take my word for it, ask Clarissa Munten and Maxine Snedden. They both knew it needed tightening up. Even Helen's agent said as much before he died.'

'We know what we're doing.'

'Good to hear.' And then I left her office.

I went to my desk and found all of my things as they were. Valerie was typing away as usual. HR hadn't done a damned thing. Julia was all bluff.

'Would you come with me if I jumped?' I asked Valerie, but got no answer. Then I realised she had her earphones in. I tapped her on the shoulder and she squeaked.

'Fuck! You scared me,' she said, taking out her earphones and looking up at me.

'Julia's being a fucking bitch. Would you come with me if I jumped?'

'I've been in talks with Hachette,' said Valerie, shyly.

'You'd leave me?'

'I've hardly seen you at all. You don't answer your emails or my messages. Besides, Julia said you weren't coming back.'

I fell into my chair and said, 'I'm so sorry, Valerie. Will you ever forgive me?'

She shook her head slowly, but smiled. 'You know what you need to do?' she said. 'You need to take Julia's job. You'd be a great publishing director.'

'Maybe,' I said, not warming to the idea.

'With your money, you could start your own publishing house. Have you ever thought of that?'

I stood up and kissed Valerie's forehead.

'I've got to go.'

'Think about it. I'd come with you if you jumped in that direction.'

She blew me a kiss and popped her earphones back in.

While waiting for the lift I received a text from Julia.

*Send me your edited version.*

*No fucking way.*

*What do you want?*

*Your job.*

*Not possible.*

*Good luck then.*

And then as the lift doors were closing, Julia thrust her hand in and stopped them. They opened slowly. If I'd had more presence of mind, I would have taken a photo of her. She was a different person. My words had done their job; she was a bundle of self-doubt.

'Amy, we must be able to work something out.'

I was pressing the button for the ground floor. 'You know my terms. Call me if you need me.'

'I need your help now. I need to get this done before I go on maternity leave.'

'You're pregnant?'

'Liam didn't tell you?'

'Why would Liam tell me?'

Julia smiled.

The doors closed.

I descended.

# Chapter 39
# All the Light Had Gone Out

Dr Aldington had been Helen and Malcolm's GP for the last fifteen years. He was only in his late fifties but looked venerable. Especially when compared with his GP colleagues at the practice. None of whom, according to Helen, looked old enough to drive, let alone practise medicine.

But she had remembered thinking the same of young Dr Aldington when he had replaced elderly Dr Grant, who had died suddenly one afternoon while seated at his desk. Thankfully, he had done so between appointments.

Malcolm was in with Dr Aldington and Helen was in the waiting room. She stared first at the white featureless walls, then the grey neat carpet, then the blank-faced youth staring at his phone, then at the pile of magazines, and finally at the flat-screen television playing a loop of ads promoting blood-thinning medicine, incontinence pads, cough mixture, fungal cream and the like. No windows. No natural light. Helen didn't like the new premises. Neither did Dr Aldington, for that matter. He had been rather comfortable in the Georgian townhouse the practice had occupied for one hundred continuous years. The young doctors had all voted for the change.

The door to the passage that led to the consulting rooms opened and Dr Aldington followed Malcolm out. The doctor smiled reassuringly on seeing Helen's anxious expression. Malcolm walked straight to the counter and spoke and laughed with the receptionist. Helen overheard him make another appointment before Dr Aldington spoke to her.

'He's fit as a fiddle. We'll run a few tests, of course, but as far as I can tell you have nothing to fear. His mind seems as sharp as ever.'

This was not the news Helen was wanting. His tears that morning had shocked her. Surely he was unwell. Not himself.

Walking with Malcolm back to the tube she wondered whether Dr Aldington had been duped. Malcolm could turn it on when he wanted. As when he spoke to Max. But what would Dr Aldington say if he saw him now?

She stole a look at his face as he walked beside her. All the light had gone out. She knew so well the faces he would present when angry, when sulking, when despairing, proud, anxious, calm and tired. Each in their way had some hidden architecture to them, some frame holding the flesh in place. Glancing again at his face but staring too long and hard, for Malcolm turned to look back at her, she was saddened to see no such architecture there. The flesh of his face hung slackly from the bone but his eyes were afire.

Her head filled with questions, but she was too frightened to speak. What if he answered them? What if he told her he was dying? What if he told her he no longer loved her? What if it was Alzheimer's? What if he told her he was going to take his own life?

He said nothing and turned back to focus on the footpath ahead of him.

As they descended to the tube, Helen made no effort to wipe away her tears. She followed Malcolm to their platform, where they both sat on a free bench to wait the four minutes for their train.

# Chapter 40
# The Truth Is Just Fucking Fine

Liam wasn't answering his phone.

I didn't doubt that he had fucked Julia. But that she was pregnant by him? That was bullshit. Wouldn't happen. Couldn't happen.

I walked quickly away from the M&R office in the direction of Waterloo Station, trying his number a couple more times as I went. I didn't want to message him: *Did you knock up Julia?* I needed to speak to him. In person, if possible.

I rang his publicist. Nothing. I called M&R reception and was told where he was.

I'd forgotten he was signing at the warehouse. I fucking hate signings.

But Liam loves them. A book signed is a book sold, he says. The guy never signed more than a few thousand and we sold two hundred thousand of each book in hardcover in the UK alone. It made no sense. The hardcore fans appreciate it, he said. Which was probably true. But then, they were exhausting.

That's one of the reasons Liam found warehouse signings easier than the public signings. The strain of public events took their toll. The people who lined up for hours for a few seconds with him – quick hello, selfie, personally signed book – were devoted to his fiction, and they often knew more about it than we did. Their questions and queries more often than not stumped us. And

Liam especially didn't like looking a fool. But it wasn't just this. Liam had nailed it when he said, 'Each fan takes a tiny little piece of me away. Soon there won't be anything left.'

I stood in the main hall of Waterloo Station with the whole population of the world buzzing around me. I couldn't make up my mind.

I wasn't his girlfriend or wife. What was it to me if he got Julia pregnant? He was reprehensible. I was reprehensible. No change there. I'd betrayed Gail since promising not to, and I'd do it again, so I wouldn't be rushing to tell her about Julia. She'd find out the hard way.

But *Julia*, Liam? *Julia*? And just when I thought I had her, too. The fucking soulless bitch. She'd been on her knees. At my mercy. But she had one last card to play. Bitches always do.

And it was a good one. She'd probably been fucking him since Val McDermid's book launch. Jesus. And I'd been sharing him with her. Well played, Julia, well played. Did she know she was deceiving a wife and a lover?

It was all getting too messy. Liam was getting messy.

I didn't mind being his slut. I enjoyed that role. He could bend me over whenever it suited him. But only a few days ago he was making out that he loved me. That he wanted to run away with me. What was going on in his head? What if I'd said yes?

I had to see him.

Were Julia and this kid a problem he didn't want to face?

While waiting for the train I scrolled through my emails. I found one from Liam. No subject line, just an empty email with an attachment. The first chapters of something with the working title *Tangential*. Tellingly, the author of *Tangential* wasn't Jack Cade, but Liam Smith.

I couldn't believe the timing of this. He *was* losing his mind. Mid-life crisis.

One of the most difficult aspects of our very successful union was Liam's desire to be respected by people he respected – by writers like John le Carré, Ian McEwan, Zadie Smith. Which meant convincing them that his thrillers were literature – an impossible challenge – or Liam writing something completely different, an award-winning literary novel – just as unlikely.

From time to time Liam would disrupt our very tight and well-orchestrated publishing schedule by sending me a few chapters of a literary novel. These chapters usually meant work had stopped on the new Jack Cade. When Liam did this I always found him hard to deal with.

My harsh and critical edits of his Jack Cade novels often meant he wouldn't speak to me for days. He was a million times more sensitive about his literary efforts.

I read the pages on the tube on the way out to the M&R warehouse. The pages weren't bad. But they weren't fucking Julian Barnes.

*

I was ushered into the room the warehouse staff set aside for book signings and found Liam surrounded by a team of people, most of whom I had met before on previous signings.

There was someone new, however.

'Hi. Where's Fiona?' I said, walking across to Liam and giving him a chaste kiss on the cheek.

'What are you doing here?' he asked, looking up and signing at the same time. The books were being moved under his pen and removed in a seamless process by two young women, one on either side of him. I had to get out of the way. They were all so intent on the business at hand. He had five thousand books to get through. A day's work. They were to be a Waterstones exclusive edition.

'I got your email,' I said, having skirted around to the other side of the large table. 'I read most of it on the tube on the way here.'

The warehouse doors opened and a guy I'd met before brought in a two-metre-tall pallet-load of boxes. I returned his nod hello and moved out of the way again. Matt, the guy usually in charge, was hurriedly unpacking the boxes and placing the books in neat piles. He smiled and raised his eyebrows. Another guy was putting them back in boxes when they'd been signed. It was some process. They were all sweating.

Liam stopped signing. 'What did you think?'

I knew this was coming and I had a lie ready: 'It's great.'

He was satisfied with that. His whole body relaxed and he got back to signing.

The person I didn't recognise as I came into the room had removed herself to the quietest corner and had been enjoying one of those phone conversations that seem impossibly silent. She was now finished and moved proprietarily towards Liam. Standing behind him and placing her hands on his shoulders, she looked boldly across the table at me. She wasn't beautiful but she was slim, blonde and she couldn't be more than twenty, which combined to make her attractive.

'Fiona's on maternity leave. Remember? This is Vanessa, her replacement,' said Liam, not looking up.

Vanessa smiled and squeezed his shoulders.

He'd fucked her, too. Fucking publicists.

He was out of control.

I leant across the table and shook her outstretched hand. 'I'm Amy.' She could try to work out what I was to Liam herself. I walked over to Matt, knowing her eyes would follow, and asked to open a box. There is nothing like seeing a book you've worked on come into being. But better than that is to open one of the boxes. Matt knew my need and handed me the blade.

'Not too deep, you don't want to cut the books,' he cautioned.

I slit the box and pulled out a copy of *Moving Target*. To be honest, I couldn't quite remember what it was about; we had written it two books ago. With half the cover taken up by the name Jack Cade and a silhouette of Mark Harden walking down a deserted street, it was sure to sell at least a million or two worldwide. I kissed the cold cover and placed it back in its box.

Looking up I caught the publicist staring at me. Her hands were still on his shoulders. Very protective. Was I ever that young and that dumb? Did she really think she was going to be Mark Harden's girlfriend?

'Hey, Liam, have you thought more about my plan?' I asked, trying to sound like I had a reason for being there. 'The series of YA books?'

'I don't have time.'

'Sure you do, I'll be doing all the work.'

'What kind of return is there? I mean Baldacci, Grisham, Coben, Patterson, Reichs and a few others have done it. Get me some numbers. Personally, I think it takes away their edge. What was Jack Cade doing at seventeen? Probably fucking a cheerleader in the back of his dad's car.'

'We'll make it an erotic series for teens, then. Beat E.L. James to the idea.'

This made Liam laugh.

'Besides, I wasn't thinking about us writing new stories. Just sanitising the original books for a younger audience, like Dan Brown will be doing soon with *The Da Vinci Code*. Did you hear about that? The Jack Cade brand would do all the work. Probably lead to more backlist adult sales, too. Kids wanting to read the real thing, with all the sex and violence, like you used to. Young Adult didn't exist when you were growing up, remember.'

Liam stopped signing. He was about to say something when his publicist interrupted.

'Don't forget to sign one for my mum,' said Vanessa. 'She's your biggest fan. She nearly died when I told her what I was doing today.'

Jesus, Liam, you met her today? That's fast work. Where'd you fuck her? In the back of the hire car on the way?

'I won't forget,' he said. He couldn't cope with the look I gave him. He returned it with one of his most devious grins then continued signing. He did fuck her on the way! Bet he knew the driver would've watched the whole thing. I had created a monster. He'd been a fucking choir boy when we'd met. Now look at him.

'How is *Girl on Girl* going? You haven't sent any pages through since we wrote the outline.'

'Been busy. *GOG* is on the back burner. I'm busy with *Tangential.*'

The two young women kept passing the books through and he kept signing.

His fucking dreams of literary greatness again.

'What's *Girl on Girl*?' asked the publicist.

'Do you have time for that?' I asked, ignoring the girl.

'Yes.' It was final. Cold. He didn't look up. In a warmer tone, he said, '*Girl on Girl* is the working title of the new Jack Cade. It's a joke. *Girl on the Train. Gone Girl. Girl with All the Gifts. Girl with the Dragon Tattoo.* We thought it was time for a bit of *Girl on Girl.*'

'That's funny, they do all have girl in the title. I hadn't noticed that.'

'And they're all about women,' he added.

Now it was time for my tone of voice to shift. 'Don't you think you need a break?' I asked. He noticed immediately. He stopped signing.

'Are you all okay if I take five? How many do I still have to do?'

'We're about halfway. Take all the time you want, Liam,' said Matt. 'I might see if we can't rustle up some afternoon tea for us all.'

*

Liam led me outside through a fire door, which he propped open with a brick. We were in a space between two warehouses. An identical fire door was directly across from us. A concrete path ran down between the two buildings to the street. This area was evidently a refuge for smokers, as there was a ceramic pot against the wall filled with sand and cigarette butts.

Liam lit up.

'You're smoking again? What the fuck is going on with you?'

He didn't answer with words, but he exhaled with a brutal contempt.

'What am I to you?' he asked, standing straight, chest out.

I paused before answering. Not because I didn't have an answer but because I had many and needed to know what had prompted his question. Surely it couldn't be love. I'd made myself abundantly clear on that front. And we had ratified the agreement on the bonnet of Daniel's car. My suspicion was that Julia had got to him, had found his weakest point and had pressed it with a meticulously manicured finger.

The way he was holding his body was aggressive, and ready for battle. But the look in his eyes was vulnerable and he was biting the inside of his lips, which he only did when he was anxious.

'What are you to me? A golden fucking goose,' I replied, knowing this was the one answer he feared most and one, if I were Julia, I'd have encouraged him to believe.

'You would say that. Perfect.'

The fight went out of his body and he fell back against the wall, sliding down until he looked like he was seated on an invisible chair.

'What would you prefer?'

He took a long drag on his cigarette. 'The truth is just fucking fine,' he spat out, smoke issuing from his mouth.

'You think that's the truth?'

'I know it is.'

I wanted to kick him. This mood was new. It was defeatist. So unlike Liam.

'We need to put things into perspective.'

'Do we?' he asked, exhaling and looking down at the ground.

'Yes, you shit.'

'I have to think of the future. This won't last forever. Jack Cade will go the way of Len Deighton and Frederick Forsyth. It could happen without warning, too. Changing geopolitical factors can fuck me overnight. Like the fall of communism for John le Carré and Tom Clancy.'

'Both of whom survived the fall.'

'You know what I mean. I'm exposed. I need to ensure I can continue writing beyond Jack Cade.'

'*Tangential?*'

'Yes, maybe. Why not?'

'Oh, come on, Liam! Neither of us is ever going to win the Booker but together, as Jack Cade, we can continue to entertain millions of people. Our readers can rely on us. We're a brand. You know how rare that is in publishing?'

'It's just work. I have no love for it. It's soul-destroying.'

'Christ, Liam, neither of us need work again. We've each made a fuck-ton of money. We can quit now. You can go and write *Tangential* and I can …' I paused. I had no idea what I could do beyond Jack Cade. I smiled, slightly embarrassed. 'I don't know what I'll do but I'll find something.'

He looked at me. It was a strange look, I couldn't quite understand it. But it unnerved me and I said, rather cautiously, 'I like doing what we're doing, I really do.'

'I can't work like you do. The schedule we agreed to is too tight. And you work too quickly. Always emailing me, demanding more. Like it's a race. There's way too much pressure on me to deliver.'

He was exhausting me with his negativity.

'I need time to think, to read, to travel. I need a break,' he added.

'Fuck it. Take a break. You need one. You're all over the place. I'll write the next one without you. You can edit it at the end.'

'As if you could. You need me more than you'll ever admit. The meat of Jack Cade comes from me; you're just the warm plate, the veg and the gravy. You've never fired a gun, you've never beaten someone to a pulp, never been beaten to one, never experienced battle, never been shot at, never lived on rations or even slept on the ground in the open. The reader will know the difference.'

'You forget, I went to boarding school,' I said, trying to lighten the mood, even though I was upset by what he'd said.

'You call that living?'

'You've said all this before. It doesn't hurt me anymore. It's just boring. Good writers make shit up. Like Jeanette Winterson and Venice. Shakespeare and everywhere. You think Tolkien ever visited Hobbiton?'

'He was at the Battle of the Somme, Amy. The man had lived. You're a smart cookie but you're a rich, impossibly beautiful white girl who hasn't travelled, doesn't know her history, has little interest in politics or science or technology … You're one of the privileged. You haven't suffered.'

'Why are you being such a fucking cunt?' I asked, feeling the tears well up.

'You need me, I don't need you.'

He had said it. That's what the weird look had been about. But his words took my breath away.

'If we're being honest,' he continued, 'I don't need a break from the work.' He looked me in the eye and said, 'I need a break from you.'

I slapped him. I'd never slapped anyone before. It felt good.

He'd been slapped before, however. He barely moved. I wanted to do it again. But he stood up straight and looked at me with such contempt I reconsidered.

'Thank you,' he said, coldly.

'For what?'

'Showing you care.' And then he walked back inside.

'Hey, fuckwit,' I called after him.

He stepped back outside.

'Congratulations.'

He looked puzzled.

'Julia told me her exciting news. You're going to be a father.'

'Go away, Amy.'

'And you gave her Helen's manuscript, too, didn't you, you cowardly piece of shit.'

'Go! I'm done with you.'

'I'm done with you.'

'My lawyers will be in touch.'

# Chapter 41
# Daniel on the Road

Daniel didn't really know where he was. Or if where he was had a name. He supposed every foot of England was named by now, but whether anyone had named the spot where this particular Shell service station on the M6 was he did not know. While he filled his car with fuel, he took out his phone with his free hand and checked Google. They called it Welcome Break at Charnock Richard, which was an odd thing to call a place. Charnock Richard. And then he saw that he wasn't strictly in Charnock Richard, which was a few miles away.

He'd been here before, he recalled. A number of times. Never had it occurred to him to wonder where he was beyond noticing it was a Shell service station. According to Wikipedia it was the first service station on the M6. There you go.

The petrol pump was taking forever. He didn't know what the capacity of his fuel tank was. He assumed sixty litres, because that's what his last car had. He'd never been on empty in this new one. But he'd just filled past sixty litres, so he watched the numbers climb. It stopped at sixty-four litres.

He went in to pay.

Inside he browsed the shelves. Considered getting coffee. Then a Cornish pasty. But felt slightly nauseous. He didn't need anything. Still he lingered. He didn't want to drive on. He was between things. Between London and Edinburgh, between parents and wife, between doubt and certainty.

He'd left London in the middle of the night. Without ceremony. Without goodbyes.

The previous evening Malcolm had said he wanted to drive north with him whenever he left, but Daniel thought that was taking things too far. He wasn't Malcolm's son anymore. Or, more correctly, he was possibly more his son than ever before. The past Daniel had known and relied on had been repudiated by them both, Helen and Malcolm, each separately. And Daniel had conceded as much. So he wasn't the son they'd known. He wasn't the son he'd known himself to be. The resentful son – the unloved and the unseen.

After scanning the products in the car maintenance section of the shop thoroughly, he was now loitering in front of the sweets. He picked up two Curly Wurlys, thinking of the boys.

While in London, Daniel had become a new son. He had been reborn. And he'd had no choice in the matter this time, either. Helen and Malcolm had expected him to love them back with his newborn heart. To see them with his newborn eyes. To embrace them with his newborn arms.

But he was completely alien to himself. And felt nothing.

He stood in the queue to pay and glanced out of the window to see which number pump he'd used. The man in front of him smelled of something familiar, but he couldn't think what it was. There was a deep blackhead on the nape of his neck.

Malcolm and Helen saw everything. They knew everything. But their great faith in him was misplaced. He couldn't do new. He was too old, too tired. Failure was his due. A comfort. A conclusion. For him, there was no second chance.

The literary giants didn't know everything after all.

Daniel had reached the front of the queue. 'Six, please.'

'Did you want the Curly Wurlys?'

He had handed over his card but had held onto the sweets without thinking. He looked at the woman behind the counter for the first time – she wore a look of incurable boredom – and then tossed the Curly Wurlys onto the shelf with the chewing gum, saying, 'Sorry. No.'

He waited for her to hand his card back, but the woman just stared at him.

'What?' Daniel asked.

The woman shook her head and swiped the card.

'Do you want me to put them back?' he asked.

She shook her head again, more dismissively this time, and placed his card and receipt on the counter while looking to the next customer over his shoulder, signalling to Daniel that their business was done.

He stepped to one side and replaced his card in his wallet, staring at the Curly Wurlys he'd abandoned so thoughtlessly.

'Where are the toilets?' he asked, suddenly, desperately. Those in the queue looked at him. The woman behind the counter said nothing but indicated with a nod of her head.

Daniel found all of the toilet stalls busy and, having no choice, vomited loudly in a large yellow bucket on a cleaning trolley, covering the mop with his waste. Afterwards there was complete silence. No one made a sound. No one asked if he was all right. The stall doors remained shut. Washing his face and rinsing his mouth at the sink, he noted the look of horror on the face in the mirror staring back at him.

On his way back to the car, he felt light-headed. The woman behind the counter kept her eye on him even as he passed through the door to the forecourt.

Outside, the air was noxious. He paused. He didn't want to leave the safety of the service station. The nausea persisted.

He would move the car to the parking lot.

As he walked towards it he clicked the button in his pocket and the orange indicators blinked. Watching the daylight reflected in the car's polished curves as he drew nearer, he noticed something.

A handprint on the bonnet. Amy's handprint. He stopped short and just stared at it.

Images flashed before his mind.

Ignoring the car that had just pulled in behind his, he approached the handprint carefully. Then he saw the other marks. Life had happened on his car bonnet. Life that Amy hadn't hesitated in seizing greedily for herself. The same life that Geraldine must have craved and was now enjoying. The life that he had not suspected existed. The life that would never be his.

By the pump was a paper dispenser. He took a handful of paper and scrunched it up. He lifted the watering can from its place. Then, pouring water over the bonnet, he wiped away the remnants of life.

The young woman in the car waiting to use the pump honked her horn.

He got hurriedly into his car.

On the drive from London, he'd been half-listening to one of Geraldine's audio books, *The Power of Now* by Eckhart Tolle. As the narrator started again, he turned it off. The past, present and future were all equally appalling. Now, he didn't want to think about anything.

He merged back onto the M6 and turned on cruise control.

As a child he had developed a technique to deal with moments of high anxiety: he sang 'Puff, the Magic Dragon' softly to himself. He thought of this now, but didn't sing. It began to rain. The windscreen wipers started automatically.

\*

Four hours later Daniel was sitting against a tree in Braidburn Valley Park, just near the back gate to the house he'd shared with Geraldine. He was hoping to catch sight of the boys. And maybe talk to Geraldine herself, if the moment was right.

He had come at four because it was the time Geraldine often stole an hour with the boys in the park. Recently, they had become obsessed with the Braid Burn. The shallow stream fascinated them. And worried their mother. But Daniel loved to watch them dance excitedly on the bank when they had thrown a leaf or a twig into the water. If left to their own devices, the boys would have played beside the stream all day long.

Geraldine wasn't happy with this obsession. She needed to be so vigilant. She had visions of finding one or both of the boys face down in the stream under the bridge. The boys could get through the back gate if it was left unlocked and into the park. Samuel was fearless and would climb the back fence and sit atop it. He hadn't yet found the courage to jump down the other side. But they were both growing up so fast.

Daniel had promised Helen he'd return to Edinburgh and look for a flat. He'd taken compassionate leave from work, but knew they couldn't afford to have him gone for much longer. They were understaffed as it was. He'd have to call them.

But the thought of doing anything of the sort exhausted him.

As he leant against the trunk of a tree, the sunny breaks, the familiar scent of the grass, the sudden brief shower that passed as rapidly as it had come, the beautiful green prospect, were all one to him. The nausea of Charnock Richard had turned into a heavy weight in his stomach, like a boot pressed menacingly against him.

When the boys did run into sight, he hid himself. The only thing that had mattered on the drive up was seeing them, but on seeing them he realised this was no longer true. They looked like another man's children. That man would give them Curly Wurlys. He blew his nose on the receipt he'd been given at the service station, threw it on the ground and wiped his eyes with the back of his hands. Then Geraldine emerged from the garden, closing the gate behind her. She was shouting after the boys.

She looked the same. She was wearing the dark jeans she always wore, the muddied Hunter boots she pulled on for the park, the overlong black cardigan she wore over her T-shirt when she was unsure about the weather.

As she passed him, he looked at her face for signs of change. Her expression was the same as she always had when unobserved. Beautiful, contemplative, slightly anxious. She'd never been observant. And so didn't notice him now. Most of her attention was directed inwards. As much as she spoke about living in the moment, the outer world had always been a distraction.

She shouted again after the boys to stop.

They ignored her.

From the trees, Daniel watched her as she walked with quickening steps down the hill after them. On the drive up, Amy and Geraldine had merged lazily in his mind. But now there was no chance of confusing the two. Geraldine wasn't a libertine. She wasn't a risk-taker. She was a woman who needed to be loved, who needed her family close, who needed to be listened to and respected.

The whole of his marriage to Geraldine he had supposed he had been unloved and unlovable. Loving hadn't come easy. He wanted so much to be the husband and father Malcolm hadn't been. But it was forced. Fuelled by resentment. He loved Geraldine with a weight that negated the effect. Love wasn't to be bullied into greatness. Love suffered under his heavy-handed approach.

Geraldine loved easily and beautifully. He'd lived under her loving gaze in the beginning. How dearly he had needed the warmth of her gaze and touch. His joy was easily mistaken by her for love returned. But Geraldine was not to be mistaken forever. She had stopped loving him. The warmth had turned into a kind of distilled panic. A nervous energy. A devotion to children, to cleaning, to work and to her family.

And this had suited Daniel. This was what he had sought without knowing. The outer veneer of happiness. But it wasn't enough for Geraldine. It wasn't enough for her family, either. They knew she was unhappy. They were the first to speak to her of divorce. She hadn't considered it possible. With Geraldine's family working against the marriage, it was only a matter of time. An alternative future had entered Geraldine's mind. When one of her clients' compliments carried a different tone, she welcomed the change and reciprocated. The dam on Geraldine's heart was breached.

Helen had asked Daniel to speak to Geraldine. To work out arrangements for access to the boys, to make the transition as easy as possible for them. He might have crossed the park now and had that chat. She was there. He was there. The boys were running around like madmen. They'd be happy to see him, he assumed.

But there was no crossing the expanse of greyish-green grass. There was no discussing the future. He would be playing a part. Speaking words he must say but would mean nothing. Such words would only prolong the deception.

She would speak from the heart. She always had. She probably always would.

She believed in things. In the soul. In love. In hope. In forgiveness. In a life beyond.

He watched her retie her hair as she turned to face the breeze. Wisps of rebellious hair corralled into a hair tie.

He was on the wrong side of the glass. Life was on her side. He was sure of it.

He was being left behind again. But he would do nothing to prevent it. The thought of crossing the field exhausted him. Geraldine's gaze would be turned upon him. The joy of the boys on seeing him would be too great a weight and would crush him. This was what life at its core was for him. It was overwhelming. He hadn't fought hard enough. He hadn't forged his own life. He wasn't fit for the challenges. The resentment that had sustained him for so many years, and had given his life purpose, was gone. He had made peace with the past and was now empty.

He sat on the ground, being sure to keep out of sight, the boot pressing ever harder against his stomach. They'd have to go back inside before he could think of getting back to his car unnoticed. He made himself as comfortable as possible. He was prepared for a long wait.

# Chapter 42
# Max's Notes II

The time I spent with Malcolm this morning was stranger than our first interview. He was distracted. Very upset that his son Daniel had driven back to Edinburgh without him. He said they had talked of doing the drive together. He was confused at being abandoned by him. He spoke of being all alone now. Though Helen had let me in and I could hear her on the phone in her office.

I don't know how to approach this story. Malcolm is not cooperating at all. Not strictly true. He seems not to realise what I'm trying to do. I make every effort to alert him to the fact that my visit isn't a social one, that I'm here to interview him, but he manages to confuse this after a few minutes of talk.

When I try to bring the conversation around to his work he evades me by discussing politics – he is obsessed with Trump. He says the world deserves him and hopes he wins. I don't know whether he's serious or not, but I suspect he is.

Malcolm did say something, which I record here verbatim.

'My fear, and I feel it strongly in myself, is forgetting higher thinking. The memory isn't infallible, it needs to be reminded of such things, it needs someone reading the lines in the dark, a prompter. I can read or watch or listen all day long to contemporary literature and media and never hear one whispered line from the dark. Higher thought is silenced not by arguments but by forgetting, or worse, never knowing.'

When I asked him what he meant by higher thought, he stood up and went to the shelf behind me. He took down an old Penguin paperback edition of George Eliot's *Daniel Deronda*. He handed it to me and said, 'There's some in there. I just don't remember where, exactly. It's been a long time since I knew such things.'

I flicked through the pages of the thick book and saw that a passage had been underlined. I showed it to him. 'I bought it second-hand,' he said, 'that wasn't me. I look after my books. I'm only a custodian, after all.'

I said it was quite pertinent to his career and read it to him.

Quote: 'I am not decrying the life of the true artist. I am exalting it. I say, it is out of the reach of any but choice organisations – natures framed to love perfection and to labour for it; ready, like all true lovers, to endure, to wait, to say, I am not yet worthy, but she – Art, my mistress – is worthy, and I will live to merit her. An honourable life? Yes. But the honour comes from the inward vocation and the hard-won achievement: there is no honour in donning the life as a livery.'

After I read it, Malcolm surprised me by saying, after a pregnant pause, 'I don't even know what that means. I have now forgotten more things than I can hope to know in the future.'

He is perplexing. Not what I expected at all. I have re-read *A Hundred Ways* over the last couple of days and the book sparkles with wit and humour. His satire hits its mark. It's dark and uncomfortable, too, but has a good heart. Which is important. But Malcolm himself has no spark at all.

'Do you believe in genius?' I asked at one point, despairing at his lack of clarity. 'Enough to marry her,' he answered. I liked that. It wasn't an answer I expected but it was good all the same.

He went on to talk about the difference between his writing and Helen's writing. They were representatives of two great opposing literary traditions, he said. The 'is' tradition and the 'ought' tradition.

This confused me, so I asked him to clarify.

He said that writers like George Eliot and Jane Austen were examples of the 'ought' tradition. They were always writing about how we *ought* to live. And Helen was the daughter of that line. Her writing sought change. While Malcolm was the son of the 'is' tradition. So he was at pains to describe the world as he found it.

I asked which two authors represented his lineage.

He thought for a moment and then said, 'Thackeray and Fielding.'

\*

After I left Malcolm, and started on my walk to the tube, I found Helen walking just ahead of me. I caught her up.

'I'm very worried about Malcolm,' she said, almost straight away.

I told her he seemed a little distracted and a touch depressed, but that I was not a good judge as I had only just met him. She asked if he had anything to say about her. I said he was very proud of her. Much more comfortable discussing her work than his own. She told me about her new book, about the trouble it had given her, and Malcolm's opinion of it. This was the book Amy had been working on. Helen had been conflicted about it, she told me.

'May I read it?' I asked.

She shook her head. 'It isn't literary,' she said.

We parted at the high street. She was off to the supermarket. Before she left I asked about Amy.

'We haven't seen her,' she said.

\*

Is this what genius looks like? Is this how it continues to produce well into old age?

I have met and interviewed many writers; they wear their writing in some obvious way. Even if only in their transient enthusiasms – as when they are in the midst of research. But Helen and Malcolm travel incognito. Unrecognisable. Nice, educated people, but nothing extraordinary.

But their work burns. They have genius.

I just looked up a line by Matisse I thought was 'Live as the bourgeois, burn in your art' and discovered I had misremembered it and misattributed it. The author of the advice/rule was Flaubert in a letter: *Soyez réglé dans votre vie et ordinaire comme un bourgeois, afin d'être violent et original dans vos œuvres.* The translation Google offered was, 'Be regular and orderly in your life like a bourgeois, so that you may be violent and original in your work.'

My line is better.

# Chapter 43
# Sometimes It's Hard to Let Go

I was asleep on the floor in the corner of my empty studio when the front door opened and the estate agent, Gerald, walked in accompanied by the two new owners.

There have been better moments in my life.

I shouldn't have been there. The new owners were well within their rights to be put out. We'd exchanged contracts; it was no longer my studio.

Gerald said something to the new owners that I couldn't make out and ushered them back into the hall. Then he came over and crouched beside me. I was sitting up and wiping the drool from the corner of my mouth by this stage.

'Sometimes it's hard to let go,' he said, as if finding the previous owner sleeping rough on the floor of their sold studio was a common occurrence.

I went with it. It seemed a good option, in the circumstances.

'I'll miss this place so much, Gerald,' I lied, getting to my feet. 'After the removal men left I gave the place a thorough clean and then I just couldn't leave. I must have fallen asleep.'

'They say that moving is one of the most stressful things we do in life. You were probably more exhausted than you thought.'

Gerald was a good agent; he'd got me a great price for the studio, but he wasn't too bright. Which was fine with me. He did

274

what he did well and looked good doing it. That's enough in this world. More than enough.

Having sold the place, I'd been living there to sort through my crap and either throw it out or pack stuff up. But I could easily have hired someone to clear it out. I was really avoiding Helen and Malcolm and Max. Mostly Max.

I left Gerald's side and walked quickly into the bathroom, checked my face in the mirror, pulled my hair back in a ponytail. I still looked like I'd slept on the floor.

'Amy,' said Gerald from the other room, 'I came over about seven last night to check everything was in order for this morning. You weren't here then. And the power was off.'

'I was taking the last bits and pieces to my new place,' I said, making it up as I went along. 'I came back around nine.'

I returned to a puzzled Gerald and kissed him on the cheek.

'Sorry about this. Apologise for me, won't you?' And with that I got the fuck out of there.

I had ended up sleeping on the floor of my studio because I'm a drunk. No other explanation will do. And I'm cool with that. It's me. It's what I do. But I had intended doing something completely different. After sorting the studio out, I had intended heading straight to Helen and Malcolm's place. It was my fault Julia had Helen's manuscript, and I wanted to tell her. She had said no digital copies and I'd ignored her.

But on my way I stopped off at the Regency for a drink. To fortify myself. One drink became two. And even though I wasn't looking very glamorous in my cleaning gear – faded, paint-speckled jeans, stinky T-shirt, ugly grey sweatshirt and old trainers, all of which I had commandeered from Max years ago – I was invited to join in on a game of pool. Then dinner was ordered. More drinks. A bit of flirting. Then the boys' girlfriends turned up. More drinks. Jealous words. A bit of a fight. More drinks. Then the pub closed and I staggered out onto the street friendless.

Once I opened the door of my studio I knew I had made a mistake. I should've left immediately. But I was tired and drunk and I really couldn't face the stairs, the street, the search for a cab, the talk with the receptionist at some hotel, the going up the lift to my floor, the working out how to open the hotel room door, the pulling back of the tightly tucked-in sheets and then the undressing and the climbing into bed. So I lay down on the bare floor. Just to rest a while.

The floor wasn't very comfortable but I slept soundly enough for a time. In the middle of the night I woke shivering. I looked around confused, then pieced things together. I was sleeping on the floor, in my studio. I sat up and checked the time on my phone. Four.

I felt stiff and sore and nauseous and drunk. I sat up and leant against the wall. There were no curtains on the windows. The yellow glow of London lit the room. I checked my phone. A message from Daniel. *I'm sorry*, it said. I replied, *For what?* And one from tattoo boy, which was a surprise.

Josh hadn't been ignoring me after all; he'd been in Greece. A writers' retreat. No internet, no phones, no TV. He'd finished a novel he'd been writing for years. Could I help him get it published? He added a link to a Google doc.

I crawled into the very clean bathroom and threw up into the toilet. I rested my head on the edge of the bowl. I felt much better. I flushed, then switched on the heat lamp. No electricity. I sat on the loo. No toilet paper. I flushed again and pulled up my jeans.

I took myself off to the corner of the room and sat on the ground.

For the briefest of moments I thought some gold had fallen into my lap, a writer who could replace Liam in work and pleasure, but my hopes were quickly dashed. Josh was talentless. The novel was atrocious. It wasn't a novel, really. More a collection of thoughts, none of them interesting. And worse, they were poorly expressed. It was embarrassing.

Then I wondered if it was just literature. Maybe he was an artist. Maybe he was inventing some new form of expression. I read on. Nope. It was shit. But just to be on the safe side, I emailed it to Max with the question *Is this avant-garde or just shit? I'm drunk and can't tell.*

If it was literature then that was something to work with; if it was shit, and I was pretty sure it was shit, then seeing him again just wasn't an option.

I lay down again and rested my head on my arm. I opened the video Liam had taken of me sucking his cock. I stared at the screen. I wished I had the video Daniel had taken. I wanted to watch that again. I should have sent it to myself before deleting it. Now it was gone. Liam was gone. I'd never experience that again. At least I had this little video. I replayed it again and again. I just wished I could see more of Liam in the video. I should have taken the camera from him and filmed him.

I wondered what Max would make of the video. I was tempted to send it to him. He said he'd never be with me again. Maybe I could torment him. Maybe he'd change his mind if he saw me at work. Liam had intimidated the hell out of him. And Max had left me because he had discovered I was fucking Liam.

Sending him the video was an idiot idea. I was still drunk. How would Max watching a video of me sucking and fucking Liam help me in any way? I watched the video a few more times, trying to get myself off, but only ended up frustrated, sore and angry. I watched the video one more time, deleted it and then fell asleep.

Only to be awakened by the new owners.

# Chapter 44
# One Hundred Per Cent behind the Book

Helen read the email again. She had to be careful with correspondence from people she didn't know. The English language was changing rapidly. Familiar words were being given new meanings. Some were losing their meaning altogether.

This email was from Julia O'Farrell, Publishing Director at Morris and Robinson. The woman she had spoken to on the phone. The woman who had sent Amy.

At first glance the email was an invitation to visit the M&R offices to meet 'the team' and to discuss their plans 'moving forward'. But Julia had been unable to resist repeating much that had been agreed to by Helen over the phone. She seemed to think there was some doubt. To counter that doubt Julia assured Helen again that the team was one hundred per cent behind the book in its current form. And further, she rejected the suggestion that the manuscript required extensive rewrites. Julia wrote this as though Helen had been involved in such discussions. She hadn't been. It was the first she had heard of extensive rewrites. She assumed Amy had been in contact with Julia. But Amy had said nothing of rewrites to her.

The email was meant to be reassuring but it had the opposite effect on Helen. Julia's smiling tone was disheartening. To read that Julia had 'socialised' very early cover treatments with 'key stakeholders' just depressed her.

She didn't like thinking about an office full of people busily making plans concerning *that* book. She didn't want to be shown a range of draft covers, she didn't want to agree on a title, she didn't want to read through the copy edits, she didn't want to have her photo taken for the publicity department. Or want to be paraded around the country, visiting bookshop after bookshop, library after library, festival after festival. She didn't want to meet her new readers. She didn't want anyone to say anything pleasant about the book.

She thought with horror of being made to go on *The One Show* or having to talk about the book on radio. All the extra duties that modern publishing required hadn't even entered into her deliberations about the book. She had been so focused on whether to publish or not, whether to keep the money or return it, she hadn't considered what agreeing to publish entailed.

She wrote, *Dear Julia,* and then paused. She wondered if she should talk to Amy before replying. But couldn't see what that would change.

The pain she felt when she thought of Malcolm, the man she had relied upon her whole adult life for good advice, was sharp and made her wince. Her eyebrows knitted together and she raised her hand to her brow, rubbing it roughly to ease the pain.

'Where are you, Malcolm?' she asked in a whisper.

Then quickly typed: *Do what you like with the book. I don't care anymore.*

And pressed 'Send'.

# Chapter 45
# Max's Notes III

I am getting nowhere with Malcolm. He is very patient and has allocated two hours every morning for me. But none of my questions are being answered in a way that is useful for my piece. He spoke about his childhood at length this morning. But I couldn't shake the suspicion that he was fabricating much of it. Why he should do so I have no idea. He will not speak at length about *A Hundred Ways*. I saw it was in the bestsellers lists and told him so. He didn't seem to think that was a good thing. The trouble is, Malcolm is so obliging, so pleasant, so easygoing. I find it hard to press him for more details. With other authors it's hard to get beyond what they want to tell me, their agenda, to get at what I want to hear. But with Malcolm, it's different; he causes me to doubt myself.

I am here to interview a potential Booker winner, a man who has gone silent just when he was becoming interesting. Dozens of journalists would kill for the opportunity and I am failing.

I tried a few things to get him talking. I asked if he believed, like Will Self, that the novel was dead. He retorted, 'Was it ever alive?' There was no smile on his lips. I prompted him. He said, 'The novel has never held a position of importance in society. This importance is a fantasy of novelists, their publishers, their critics and their most earnest admirers. Even amongst the privileged minority who read regularly, the novel is regarded as a form of entertainment only. As entertainment, the novel is very much alive. More novels are being read today than at any time in our history. They're just not the kind of novels I, or Mr Self, would choose to read.'

'Why do you think that is?'

'There's uphill reading and downhill reading. As you can imagine, uphill reading requires more effort. Downhill, less so. Readers will do both in their reading lives. Most will tend to favour downhill reading. It's thrilling to race headlong through a book. Uphill reading is more taxing and requires a certain amount of humility. We need to accept that we won't always enjoy or even understand all we read. It can be a hard slog at times. The ego takes a battering. But the rewards are great.'

I brought up the Nobel Prize. I told him Helen Owen was being listed on the betting sites as a chance. He didn't think she was eligible this year. I assured him she was. And told him she was considered the best chance the UK has, ahead of A.S. Byatt, Kazuo Ishiguro, Julian Barnes and Ian McEwan.

And he said, 'I like when they give it to a writer no one has ever heard of. That always makes me chuckle.'

'Why do you think you're never seen as a chance for the Nobel, Malcolm?'

'I don't know why. I don't even know the criteria. I remember looking at the list of past winners and being unable to make much sense of it. I'd read many of them but at a glance I couldn't discern any unifying characteristics. And many great writers are missing from that list, which defeats the purpose, I think, if the purpose is to promote and honour literature. If someone is on the list they're literature and if they're not, they're not. It's reductive. Imagine not reading Leo Tolstoy or Willa Cather because they didn't win the Nobel. I'm sure it happens. People are drawn to these lists like life rafts. Lists make it easy for people who haven't got the time or the wit to discover great writing on their own. But we're talking about literature, anyway. No one can agree on what it is. How can you begin to work out who to honour when we can't agree what it is we're all trying to do? What I think is literature will differ greatly from what you think is literature.'

'Are there any certainties? You mentioned Tolstoy. Can we say with conviction that *War and Peace* is literature?'

'You and I might. But many years ago I overheard a man in a bookshop saying he preferred the abridged version to the unabridged.'

'Shakespeare then. Surely everyone can agree that Shakespeare's plays are great literature.'

Malcolm gave this a moment's thought and then said, 'Tolstoy didn't think much of Shakespeare.'

# Chapter 46
# Malcolm Taylor Is Here

'Hello? Am I speaking to Helen Owen?'

'Who is this?'

'Marty Raymond. You don't know me. I live in Brixton, in the flat you once lived in.'

'Yes?'

'Malcolm Taylor is here.'

'What?'

'He's been here a couple of hours. He said he missed the old place and asked if he could step in for a moment. I knew who he was. When we moved in the estate agent said you both had lived here for many years. I've just read *A Hundred Ways*.'

'What's he doing?'

'We chatted for a bit while he went from room to room but he said he wanted a minute alone in the room where you both wrote together. It's now our spare room. He's in there just sitting on the end of the bed staring out of the window. He seems reluctant to leave.'

'I'm so sorry.'

'Nothing to be sorry about. He can stay as long as necessary. I just thought I should let you know.'

'How did you find me?'

'I googled Malcolm and found his agent's email and reached out. Someone called Zoe rang and gave me your number.'

'Thank you very much for taking the trouble to let me know. Malcolm hasn't been himself lately. I'll come and fetch him.'

'See you soon.'

Helen hung up. Feeling unsteady, she made her way quickly into the front room and sat on the sofa. She stared at the carpet. Her mind had gone blank. She felt numb. After a while, she lay back on the sofa and closed her eyes.

She took a few deep breaths. And moaned involuntarily.

He'd gone back to the flat. He was in their room. Their writing room. Had he lost his mind?

Since Daniel and Amy had gone, the house had been quiet. It had been awful. She and Malcolm were rarely together in the same room for more than a minute. The longest they were together was for the nightly news bulletin. But that wasn't together; neither ever spoke. The horrors of the US election played out in silence. Even meals were being arranged separately.

He seemed to blame her for Daniel's departure. But hadn't said as much. All she got from him were pleasantries. Nothing more. He went to bed before her, woke before her. He made her tea in the morning and gin and tonics in the evening. He brought back meals from Waitrose. He spent hours with Max in his office and then hours out of the house by himself. She found him once in the park and had walked off rapidly before being seen.

They hadn't spoken about her book. They hadn't spoken about the house. They hadn't spoken about Daniel. They hadn't spoken about their relationship. They hadn't spoken about him.

She was in the dark about Malcolm. Didn't know if Daniel had spoken to him in the way he had spoken to her. She didn't know what he and Max were speaking of when they met. She didn't know if he was writing. She didn't know what he was thinking. She knew he was depressed, listless, thin-skinned, exhausted and frailer than he had ever been. She also knew the doctor would be no help.

Now this. She didn't want to fetch him. They would have to travel back together. The silence then would be too painful. But she had no one to call. It was the cold truth. She had made Malcolm her world. With him, she hadn't needed anything. Without him, there was nothing. Nothing.

The young man who called would be waiting. Malcolm was her problem. Not his. She had to get up. She had to call a cab. She had to get going.

After calling for a cab, she went into the kitchen for a glass of water and thought she heard music coming from downstairs. She knocked loudly on the door to the flat. No reply. She opened it. The music wasn't very loud at all, but it was on. She walked down the stairs.

'Amy?' she called when she reached the final step. There was no one in the room. She went to the bathroom door. The shower was on. 'Amy?'

'Helen?' came the reply from within the bathroom. 'I'll be out in a sec.'

*

They sat in the cab together barely saying a word.

Helen had been grateful and relieved when Amy had said she would come with her to pick up Malcolm. She had hugged her warmly and kissed her cheek. But now, as they drew ever closer to Brixton, Helen felt physically sick.

He was in their writing room. He was making a point whether he knew it or not. She had disrupted fifty years of continuity. She had been the one to break a shared train of thought. Not him.

And now she couldn't even recall the moment when she had discussed the move with Malcolm. She couldn't remember his reaction. Perhaps he hadn't reacted. His silence had been approval enough for her at the time.

She had been offered more money for one book than she received for the others combined. Of course he was happy for her.

Of course he would want to share in her good luck. Of course he would come with her. Of course she hadn't given him a thought.

The cab passed row after row of apartment blocks but then slowed and turned through a gate and drove down a narrow lane into a larger square before stopping at Helen's request near the entrance to a five-storey building. Helen looked out of the window at the charmless block and shivered at the sight of it. So many years had gone by stranded within its solid brick, prison-like walls. A lifetime.

She paid the cab driver and got out.

Amy was already out of the cab and looking around. They were in the middle of some estate. She had no idea which building Helen and Malcolm had lived in. She certainly didn't recognise the area. She had never spent much time in Brixton. A couple of trips to the markets with Max and occasional dinners with Liam had been the extent of it. The area certainly didn't look like Helen and Malcolm at all. She couldn't fathom the idea of them living in this estate for so long. She couldn't picture Daniel living here either. It was all so out of character. National treasures didn't live like this.

'It's better now than it was,' said Helen, reading Amy's thoughts.

'I can't believe you lived here,' she replied, frankly.

'It was all I could afford at the time. It was just after university. I shared the flat with a couple of girlfriends. Before I met Malcolm. Girls on their own in a rapidly changing neighbourhood. But they all gave up the fight. Went home. I stayed on. Made ends meet. I was doing well. And then I met Malcolm. He moved in with me. I got pregnant and as we both wanted to write full-time, this was all we were able to afford for many years to come.' She stopped talking and looked around. She assumed most of her old neighbours were still here. It was all so familiar but removed. 'We were novelists; our income was never secure.'

Helen looked up at the building again and it seemed at once familiar and strange. In the past, while writing a book, she might travel to the proposed setting of a newly conceived novel. She'd walk the streets, sit in tearooms, visit the local church or post office, catch the local buses, talk to the older residents. Then she would take these experiences back to her room and revisit all she had seen through the prism of fiction. The setting could occupy her imagination for years. Normally she would never revisit these places. But on occasion, by accident, many years later she might return and the strangest feeling would come over her. It was as though she were uncovering repressed memories or a past life. She'd recall conversations and actions on the corner of certain streets that felt so real she was left confused as to what was true. Like being woken mid-dream.

Now the estate felt like the setting of an old novel pushing itself to the front of her mind. Malcolm and Daniel were like vivid characters. She remembered important scenes – birthdays, fights, celebrations – and certain conversations, some mundane, some life-changing. It didn't seem like one of her more interesting novels.

Amy was real. She was with her now. Helen reached out, touched her shoulder and said, 'In the seventies and eighties it was considered a rough area, but it wasn't really. There's always more good than bad in places like this. There was a strong sense of community. We all looked out for each other. While Daniel was growing up, he never lacked friends.'

They entered the brick building to their right and Amy followed Helen up two dimly lit flights of stairs. The walls were newly painted but the stained concrete stairs revealed years of varied and unsavoury use. It was all so squalid, Helen could see plainly now. She was compelled to explain it all to Amy, who looked more and more out of place with her expensive shoes, thousand-pound jeans and perfect face. And Daniel's complaints seemed more justified now. What *had* they been doing here?

She stopped at a nondescript door and said, 'I think Daniel still thinks we chose this life. That we could have written more successful novels if we'd tried. I suppose it was confusing for him. Everyone used to visit us here. Even people he saw on television. He'd see our photos in the newspaper and occasionally, we'd be on television, too. People on television didn't have to live like us, surely?'

'But Daniel was right.'

'How so?'

'You could have written a more successful novel if you'd tried.'

Helen looked to see if Amy was smiling or not. She wasn't. There was a sharpness to Helen's tone when she said, 'I wrote that by *not* trying.'

She knocked on the door.

The door opened and a man with a pleasant smile said, 'Thank you for coming, Helen. I'm Marty. Come in.'

Helen felt distinctly ill at ease crossing the threshold. The flat claimed her immediately. Gripped her tightly with vivid memories. All she wanted to do was run.

Amy stepped in behind Helen and returned Marty's smile.

'I'm Helen's friend Amy,' she said, looking around the flat. The flat wasn't what she'd expected. It was bright, clean and quite modern.

'You've painted and had new floors put in,' Helen said.

'We didn't, the landlord did, then put up the rent. A lot of the flats are being renovated and sold off. We're concerned the landlord might want to sell this, too. Two doors down went for five hundred thousand pounds, can you believe it?'

Helen gave him a look of surprise.

'It's true!'

Helen headed to the spare room without waiting for an invitation. Marty said nothing. She stopped at the door and looked in. Malcolm was still seated on the end of the bed as Marty had described on the phone. The last thing she wanted to do was go in. She looked back down the hall at Amy and held out her hand. Amy took it in hers. They went in together.

'They've cut down the plane tree,' said Malcolm, before he even looked at Amy and Helen.

'Yes, they have,' replied Helen.

'It's a shame. There's no privacy.'

'There never was in winter, either, remember.'

He turned his head slightly and looked at both women. Then turned back to the window.

'This is where Helen and I wrote our best work, Amy. The room seems small now. Much smaller than I remember it being. I wonder how we fitted all the books in here and the two desks. But we did.'

'The whole flat looks smaller now. I think it's the new floors,' said Helen.

'They shouldn't have changed a thing.'

Helen glanced at Amy. She didn't know what to make of Malcolm's behaviour.

'We need to go now, Malcolm,' said Helen. 'Marty has been very patient.'

'This place makes sense to me still. Even though it's changed. It's more mine than anywhere else on this earth. The books I have read here, the books I've written. The conversations. The love. Daniel as a boy. All mine. And these walls, this small space, so meaningless and mean, are mine. We might have chosen other paths. But we didn't. Money didn't matter as much as the work we were doing. And the work was good. It's still good. And they all came to visit us here. They didn't judge us because our circumstances were ordinary. They judged our conversation, our writing, our hospitality.'

'We need to go, Malcolm. This isn't our flat any longer.'

'Amy, can you imagine us here? Sitting across from each other?'

'Only because I've seen the photo in your office. But I doubt I could otherwise. It's a very small room. None of this seems like you.'

'Because you met me there. That place is insidious. It compromises me. To you I am that comfortable house, that uniform street, I am the pristine Waitrose, the litter-free park, the graffiti-free high street. That's who I look like now. Like a middle-class tosspot. Like a kindly grandfather. Like a retired doctor. But this is me. Brixton is me. The estate is me. These neglected streets. That other place is nothing. It's ill-gotten, it's corrupt, it's a lie. Do you think I could have written *A Hundred Ways* there? No way. Not now. I'm grubby now. Complicit in the deception. I didn't protest. I didn't chain myself to this flat. I didn't make my objections to the move known. I went unwillingly but in silence. I'm corrupt, too. I'll never write another honest book.'

'Stop talking, Malcolm. It's done. This isn't your home anymore. You're not a child. You shouldn't be here. Get off that bed and come with us now.'

'The thing is, Amy, I thought she was happy here. Or if not happy – none of us is ever happy – committed to the place, attached to it, connected in ways that are indescribable. Rooted. We'd done everything here. It isn't a palace, but it was ours. Little did I know what was going on in her head. I should have known better. I should've read the signs. I didn't know she desired such things. I just didn't know.'

'It's not terrible to want nice things, Malcolm,' said Amy, noticing Helen's tears. 'It's not a crime to want to be rewarded for your work. You two have worked hard all your lives; you deserve the spoils. You do. You both do.'

'It's ugly. It's little. It's sad to want such things. It gets in the way of what we're doing. She knew that, too. She knew it. We were free, intellectually free, as long as we stayed here. Nobody owned us. Nobody could say a thing about our choices. I worked when I wanted to. That was the luxury our life here bought. Writing always came first. My teaching and my critical work were all cast aside when inspiration struck. She never had to work at all. Because we weren't burdened by mortgage repayments or high rent. We were free. We were immune from their influence. Those idiots. Those fools. Those parasites. She knew that. We were free.'

Helen left the room. Amy heard whispered voices and the front door of the flat open and close.

Marty came to the door of the spare room.

'Can I stay the night here, Marty?' asked Malcolm.

'Umm ...'

'That won't be necessary, Marty,' said Amy, 'Malcolm is coming with me.'

'Where are we going?'

'You're going to show me your Brixton.'

Malcolm stood up. Amy had said the right thing.

'Thank you, Marty. You've been very patient with me. I appreciate it. I do.'

He stuck out his hand and shook Marty's.

'Would you mind signing my copy of *A Hundred Ways*?' asked Marty.

'I'd love to. Yours will be the only signed copy. I never sign books.'

They returned to the living room and Malcolm was handed the book and a pen. Marty watched Malcolm sign in silence. And then, as they moved to the door, said, 'It's a shame the blue plaque scheme doesn't honour the living. This building needs something on the front letting people know that you and Helen wrote so many of your books here.'

'Would you mind if I dropped by from time to time?' Malcolm asked, ignoring Marty's comment.

'Just email me before you do. I don't want you coming all this way to find us out,' he said, handing Malcolm his business card. Malcolm noticed it said Direct Design, before he put it in his pocket.

'Thanks again,' said Malcolm, and then led Amy down the stairs. When they reached the courtyard there was no sign of Helen. They walked across the yard and through the opposite building into another courtyard and then across a patchy lawn towards a road.

'This is where Daniel and his friends used to play football,' he said, stopping and looking back across the lawn towards the estate. He looked Amy up and down. 'I can't see this place as you see it. You're the epitome of privilege. My father drove a truck. This place was a step up for me. This place took me in. I know everything about it. There are no secrets here.'

'It looks like a hundred other estates to me. One entirely indistinguishable from the other.'

Malcolm looked around, trying to see it with her eyes. And then across the road up at the dark building looming in wait there.

'He said they should put a plaque on the wall to say we'd written our books there. Who for? Everyone here knows that. Just as they know that when he was a kid Les Lowden, the footballer, lived up there in that flat, the one with the Union Jack in the window. And that Paul Clive, who lived opposite us, died fighting for ISIS in Syria. Granted, these are exceptional bits of news. They stand out. But we all knew a million smaller bits of news, too. Life is lived in the open here. It's all the same shit other communities experience, but it's impossible to hide here. A kid fell ill, we knew it. We knew which family was doing well, and which was falling apart. We could tell the kids who'd end up getting into trouble from those who'd managed to get out in time. We had kids stay with us when they just couldn't go home.'

He returned the wave of a woman who was pushing a buggy. The child in it was fast asleep.

'She's a great-grandmother, if you can believe it. She doesn't look much older than fifty. But I suppose she's as old as I am. Her first daughter, Macy, had her first kid at fifteen. But she turned out all right. She was working as a teacher last I heard.'

Amy looked at him in silence. She wondered why he was telling her all this.

Sensing her confusion, he said, 'We are the writers we are because of this place.'

# Chapter 47
# Liam Messages Amy

Liam: *I hate you.*
Amy: *I hate you, too.*
Liam: *Be at my apartment at five.*
Amy: *Fuck off.*
Liam: *Be there.*
Amy: *Why?*
Liam: *You know why.*
Amy: *No fucking way.*
Liam: *You'll be there.*
Amy: *Fuck off.*

*

Liam: *Are you on your way?*
Liam: *Amy?*

# Chapter 48
# A Bridge Too Far

'I read the manuscript. I know it's Helen's, so there's no need to keep up the charade.'

'What do you think?'

'It's extraordinary. She's never written anything like it.'

'How did you know it was hers then?'

'I was her editor for twenty years.'

I was having afternoon tea with Clarissa Munten at Galvin Demoiselle at Harrods. Her choice. I had never been there before. I can't remember the last time I joined anyone for afternoon tea. I asked for a glass of champagne. The place suited Clarissa, though. She looked like many of the other ladies enjoying their tea that day.

'I'm sorry I lied to you. I wanted you to read it and thought you mightn't if you knew it was Helen's work.'

'How did you get hold of it?'

'I've been working with Helen.'

Clarissa's expression revealed the thought she was too polite to voice. She took a sip of tea.

'On the other book?' she said, at last.

'Yes, and they still haven't decided on a title.'

'And you work for M&R?'

'Yes and no. I worked with Liam Smith on the Jack Cade thrillers. Editor slash ghostwriter slash co-writer. I don't really need to work for anyone anymore. But I love editing. I like turning books around.'

'And is that what you're doing for Helen? Turning her book around?'

'I thought I was. But I realised I was in way over my head with Helen and Malcolm. M&R are going to publish the original manuscript, the one Helen originally sent you. Probably in March 2017 ahead of Mother's Day.'

Clarissa cut a minute morsel from her éclair and lifted her fork to her mouth. I watched as she took her time chewing and swallowing. Then she took a delicate sip of her tea, before asking, 'Why has it taken so long?'

'Helen lost faith in the book. Largely due to you and Malcolm.'

'I did nothing to dissuade her from going ahead with the book.'

'But you refused to work on it.'

'I just didn't think it was worthy of her.'

'And you said as much?'

'Of course, as her editor.'

'Do you think of her as a sellout?'

'The advance they offered was substantial; she would have been a fool to refuse it.'

'But?'

'I thought she was above such things, if I'm honest. And I think Malcolm did, too.'

'Well, she's been made desperately unhappy by her decision. By way of penance, I think, she's gone on to write another two brilliant novels. The manuscript you've just read is the second of those, which is the more accomplished of the two.'

'What does Malcolm think of the new work?'

'He won't read them. Their relationship has broken down. They don't talk.'

'That's awful. I was always jealous of Helen's relationship with Malcolm. They seemed the perfect literary match.'

'He's miserable too.'

'And just when he's been rewarded for all his hard work. The Man Booker shortlisting was long overdue. He's a brilliant writer.'

'Not as brilliant as Helen, though.'

'That's always been my opinion. And his, come to think of it.'

'I've been living with them for the last few months and I've fallen in love with them both. It's desperately sad to see what's happening to them. I'm caught in the middle a bit and don't know how to help. Helen confessed to me that she had tried on a number of occasions to get in contact with you.'

'I feel terrible about ignoring her. But I just couldn't face her. I was too disappointed in her. She shook my faith in … I don't know what.'

'Literature?'

'No. My faith in her, I suppose. We'd worked together so long – I was a priestess in the church of Helen Owen. Working with her was a privilege and the highlight of my career. I believed in what she was trying to achieve with all my heart. The fact that I couldn't articulate what that was made it all the more important. She was striving for some intangible other. Something higher than us. My only talent was I could feel when she was close.'

'And this new book?'

'Is the reason I'm still talking to you,' she said, reaching into her bag and pulling out the manuscript, which she placed on the table. She rested her hand on the pages. 'This is the real Helen Owen. This is the book I've been waiting for.'

'Would you be willing to meet with her?'

'Ah, that's a bridge too far, I'm afraid. I'm retired. My husband and I are just about to spend a month at our villa in the south of France. It's my sixty-fifth birthday next week and we're expecting the girls and their families to join us for a week. The weather is still lovely down there.'

'Can you send her an email?'

'Look, Amy, it was nice to meet you but I have to go.'

She reached into her bag to get her wallet and I waved her away, saying, 'I'll get the bill.'

Clarissa stood and then sat back down. 'Helen broke my heart. Do you know what that feels like?'

I nodded.

'Then you know how hard it is for me to even talk about her.'

I said nothing. Clarissa stood again.

'Thank you for sending me the manuscript and tricking me into reading it. It hasn't healed the wounds but it has dulled the pain a little.'

She moved away but stopped after taking only a few steps. I stood up. She turned. I could see that she was upset, on the verge of tears. I walked to her and touched her arm.

Clarissa looked me in the eye, and said, 'Don't let them publish that book. Promise me you'll try to stop them.'

'There's nothing I can do.'

'I don't believe that for a second.'

# Chapter 49
# Amy Messages Max

Amy: *I need to see you.*
Max: *Why?*
Amy: *I don't know.*
Max: *Please, Amy, don't do this.*
Amy: *Just dinner.*
Max: *No.*

# Chapter 50
# How Are the Boys?

The phone had been ringing for a while now. Helen lifted her head from the pillow. She had assumed Malcolm would pick up. It stopped. She lay her head back down and closed her eyes. The pill she had taken was trying its best to do what it was made to do. She fell back to sleep. How long she had slept before she was woken by the sound of the phone ringing again, she couldn't tell. Her head felt heavy and she was finding it difficult to keep the sound of the phone from being absorbed by her dreams.

She roused herself and sat up unsteadily. The clock by the bed said it was almost 5 pm. She had been sleeping for a few hours. The phone stopped ringing. She regretted taking the sleeping tablet. Her night would be sleepless, but there was no other way to get through the day. She preferred sleep to everything now.

Malcolm had withdrawn completely from her. He was so unlike himself as to be a stranger to her. Since the Brixton episode he had taken to sleeping in his office, on the sofa bed Daniel had used.

Helen raised herself slowly from the bed and stood on the carpet in her bare feet. Her head felt like a bowling ball. Her neck struggled to hold it steady. She went through to the bathroom and started running a bath.

The evening stretched out before her. It was unbearable. The BBC news. Then something to eat. Then she might read. If she could focus her attention. Lately, as Amy was keeping much to herself downstairs, she had joined Malcolm watching endless inane reality TV shows, sitting in silence drinking their gin and tonics, then red wine. Night would announce itself when he took himself off to bed, and then the empty hours would loiter about Helen with their maddening silence. Last night she had grown so impatient for dawn she had risen and in her dressing gown had gone out into their tiny back garden then, growing ever colder, had waited for the sky in the east to lighten.

Now she opened the bathroom cabinet and looked at the little bottles of pills she had collected. As a child of the austerity years, she never thew out what might be re-used or repurposed. She remembered being prescribed Valium years before. She had never taken them. Not after the first time, when she felt her mind soften around the edges. But now she hunted them for exactly that purpose. The gin did not silence the mind. Valium would.

Helen undressed and clutching the bottle, climbed into the bath. The water was very hot. Her body reacted as it always did, like it was undergoing a trial by fire. Soon the worst was over and she grew used to the heat. She read the label on the bottle and took a full tablet then dropped the bottle on the floor. She made herself comfortable and closed her eyes.

Her mind was caught in a terrible loop. Like a large animal in a small cage pacing round and round. Each of the four walls repeatedly examined for a missed route to freedom. Each wall disappointing her in turn. Malcolm. Clarissa. Daniel. Amy. Malcolm. Clarissa. Daniel. Amy.

How narrow her life had become. Where had her friends gone? Where had her family? Her colleagues?

Malcolm. Clarissa. Daniel. Amy.

She had always preferred being alone. She was a reader, a thinker, a writer. Being alone was her default setting. It had always driven people away. Except Malcolm. He had intruded on her isolation. But being with him was no burden. He was alone with her. He had defended her space from intrusion. He had managed her needs. Forced her to be social for her own good on occasion, but let her retreat just as readily.

Now he was a burden. His presence was an intrusion. His absence was an intrusion, an irritating background noise. Now she was never alone. Never happily alone. Malcolm. Clarissa. Daniel. Amy. Every path to true solitude blocked.

The telephone rang again. She let it. It rang out twice. Malcolm wasn't home, obviously.

Malcolm wasn't an irritating background noise like the telephone. He was a cardboard cut-out of himself pointing to his own absence. Reminding her incessantly – what was, is no more. Love gone. Friendship gone. Affection gone. Respect gone. In their place, an abyss.

She began to wash herself and then emptied some of the water out before refilling it with more hot water.

The pill she had taken hadn't done anything. Her thoughts were with her still.

She reached down and found she couldn't get to the bottle. She stretched out her arm, lifting her bottom from the base of the bath and tapped the bottle closer to her with the tips of her fingers.

What would two or three do? She had researched it for a novel years ago. But couldn't remember what she had discovered. She vaguely recalled that it wasn't as dangerous as she'd hoped.

She took three more.

The bathwater cooled quickly. She turned the hot on with her toe and watched the water rise and rise. She watched it run over the edge of the bath.

She turned the tap off with her toe. And, raising her knees, lowered her head under the water. As a child she would try to hold her breath forever and, her eyes opened wide, would imagine her mother finding her dead in the bath.

Helen found it surprisingly easy to hold her breath. There was no pressure to breathe. She lay there staring up at the moving ceiling. She wondered if she had always been able to breathe underwater. She heard a strange sound. Very slowly, she raised herself out of the water. The telephone was ringing again.

The strange thing was she was dressed and standing in the hall. She looked at the floor and the front door and the photo of Daniel on the hall table. She raised her hand to her head and found her hair dry. She looked at herself in the hall mirror. Everything was as it should be.

Someone said, 'Malcolm.' Someone said it again. She looked back down the hall towards the kitchen. He wasn't anywhere.

Helen was in the front room. There were two gin and tonics on the coffee table. One was empty. Now she was sitting and now she was standing. The television was on. The news was on. She couldn't hear what they were saying. Both glasses were empty. The telephone was ringing.

'Hello?'

'Helen! Where have you been?'

'Hello?'

'Helen? Is that you?'

'Yes, it's me. I'm Helen. Who is this?'

'Geraldine.'

'How are the boys?'

'The boys are fine, Helen. I've been trying all day to reach you.'

'I've been here.'

'Is Malcolm there?'

'Yes.'

'Can I speak to him?'

Helen covered the phone with her hand and shouted, 'Malcolm? Malcolm?'

'No. He isn't here. I thought he was.'

'Are you all right, Helen?'

'I'm fine. I had a nap. And a bath.'

'When do you think Malcolm will be back?'

'I don't know.'

'Is anyone else there?'

'Amy might be downstairs.'

'Who's Amy?'

'My editor.'

'Can you get her, please?'

Helen put the phone down and walked slowly out to the kitchen. She opened the door to the flat and shouted down, 'Amy!'

*

'Hello, I'm Amy.'

'Is Helen all right?'

'She seems a little confused. Who is this?'

'Geraldine. Daniel's wife. I have some terrible news and I wanted to make sure Helen had someone to look after her. Do you know where Malcolm is?'

'No. What's happened?'

'Daniel. Can I speak to Helen again? She should hear this from me.'

*

'Hello, this is Helen.'

'Helen, it's Geraldine.'

'How are the boys?'

'They're fine, Helen. I have some terrible news.'

'Why are you crying?'

'I've been trying to reach you all day. The police came this morning. They found Daniel's car. Helen?'

'Yes?'

'They found Daniel, too. Oh, Helen. Daniel is dead. Daniel is dead. I'm so sorry. So sorry.'

'Daniel isn't dead; he was just here the other day. He stayed with us.'

'He's dead, Helen. The police came this morning. I've been in to identify him. He's dead, Helen.'

Helen handed the phone to Amy, then went into the front room and sat on the sofa.

Amy heard the TV turn on. The BBC news.

'Hello?'

'Is she all right? She didn't seem to understand. Her son Daniel is dead. He killed himself in the back of his car.'

Amy couldn't speak. In one ear she could hear Geraldine sniffling, in the other a voice from the TV telling Helen the weather forecast.

'Hello?'

'Sorry. No, I don't think she understood. She's behaving strangely. Like she's on something.'

'Did you know Daniel?'

'Yes, we met when he came to stay. Are you all right?'

'No, I'm not. It's my fault. What can I tell the boys?'

'It's not your fault. I'll try to track down Malcolm and look after Helen. Do you have someone there?'

'My parents are here. Thank you. This is awful. Awful. Goodbye.'

Amy stared at the phone and then at the photo of Daniel on the hall table. She couldn't fathom that he was dead. It didn't seem possible. He didn't seem to her the sort of person who'd kill himself. He had every reason to do it but so did most people. Few actually went through with it.

Amy went into the kitchen and poured herself a wine. She'd been horrible to Daniel. She downed the glass and poured herself another. She'd said such horrible things to him. And then she remembered the message she'd received from him. What was he sorry for?

Helen's behaviour had rattled her, too. Her son was dead and she was high as a kite. Or so it seemed. Amy wasn't trained for this kind of thing. She wasn't someone who knew what to say in terrible circumstances. She wondered where Malcolm was. He was normally home at this time. She didn't want to be the one to tell him. He would be devastated. He had mentioned Daniel so often since he'd left.

She went downstairs to get her phone.

'Max.'

'Hello, Amy.'

'I need your help. Helen and Malcolm's son Daniel has died. I'm here alone with Helen who doesn't seem to understand what's happened and Malcolm is missing. She doesn't know where he is.'

'Malcolm's with me. We're down at the King's Head having dinner.'

'Oh, thank god! Don't say anything to Malcolm, but can you get him back here as soon as possible?'

'We'll leave asap.'

Amy went back upstairs to the front room.

Helen was sitting on the sofa bolt upright. The TV was muted and she looked at Amy as she came in. Her eyes were wet.

'Amy, something has happened.'

'I know, Helen. I'm so sorry.'

'What happened? It was terrible. I know.'

'Geraldine rang. You spoke to her on the phone,' said Amy, trying to get Helen to recall the conversation rather than being the one to tell her.

'I feel so confused, Amy. I took something to help me sleep. I had a nap and a bath. Now I feel strange.'

'What did you take?'

'Valium.'

'Do you remember what Geraldine said?'

'Daniel's dead. But he's not. He was here today. You saw him. He was helping with Malcolm's papers.'

Amy sat down and put her arm around Helen's shoulders.

'That was a while ago, Helen.'

'Where's Malcolm?'

'Malcolm's coming home. He has been with Max. Do you remember Max?'

'Does Malcolm know about Daniel?'

'No. He doesn't.'

'Why didn't Geraldine tell him?'

'He wasn't home.'

Amy heard the sound of the front door being opened. She jumped up and went out to meet Malcolm before Helen could. She led him into the kitchen and sat him down. Kneeling on the floor in front of him, with her hands in his, she told him the news.

# Chapter 51

# In the Newspaper

**Edinburgh Evening News**

*The body of Daniel Taylor, son of acclaimed writers Helen Owen and Malcolm Taylor, was discovered in a car in Comiston this morning by NSL staff. Local residents had reported the car on a number of occasions. All attempts by the NSL to contact the owners of the car had failed. It was only after moves were made to impound the car that Taylor's body was found under blankets on the floor.*

*Taylor may have been dead for a week, say police. Results from an autopsy are pending but police believe there are no suspicious circumstances.*

*Taylor's wife, Geraldine Taylor, was unavailable for comment, but a source close to the family confirmed the marriage had broken down in recent months.*

*Taylor's relationship with his famous parents had been strained, a source said, with Taylor often heard describing the writers as cold and distant and his childhood as 'lonely'.*

*Daniel Taylor had not been reported missing. He was the father of two young boys.*

*If you're affected by these issues and need someone to talk to please reach out to the Samaritans, who can be contacted on 116 123.*

# Chapter 52
# Try Writing about It

Amy carried the wine out to Max, who was sitting on a bench in Helen and Malcolm's small back garden.

'Thank you for staying. It's been really difficult.'

'You've been great with them both.'

'I barely know them, though, really.'

Amy had thought to sit beside him on the bench. There was room. It might have been done casually. Like friends. But she had thought the better of it. And the moment had gone. She glanced at the other bench but it was a little bit too distant. Sitting there would draw attention to her predicament. Now she was stuck standing.

'You know them well enough. They've practically adopted you.'

'But this is ... huge.'

'There's no getting over this, either,' said Max. 'He was their only child.'

'The papers have been saying terrible things, too.'

'I know. I don't even know her but I feel for Geraldine.'

'Helen's asleep now. I gave her a sleeping tablet. I slept in her bed with her last night. She sleeps as poorly as we do. But she said she found comfort in my being there. Malcolm is still sleeping in his office. He hasn't spoken to Helen. I would have thought this would bring them together.'

'He thinks she's dead.'

'What?'

'Malcolm. He's convinced Helen's dead. It's what his new novel's about. And somehow the fiction has become reality for him. In his conversations with me, Helen is his dead wife.'

'That can't be true.'

'I've tried correcting him a number of times, but he gets as offended as a man whose wife has actually died being told she's alive. So I leave it. And we talk about her legacy and her novels as though she'll never write again. It's very strange. Unnerving, especially when you know what he believes and you see him interact with her. It's like he's trying to overcome mental distress, as though he's trying to convince himself that the apparition of Helen is just in his mind.'

'Oh god, Max.'

'He's suffering a double loss.'

'I don't know how to deal with that.'

'Try writing about it.'

Amy looked back at the door. The night was cool and she wasn't dressed for it. Max was fine in his suit. She finished the drink in her hand.

'I'm getting another, do you want one?'

He held up his full glass.

Inside, Amy looked around for her cardigan. Not seeing it, she grabbed Malcolm's jacket, which was hanging on the back of the kitchen chair. She filled her glass, put the jacket on and returned to Max.

He laughed.

'What? Don't you like my jacket?'

'Somehow, you pull it off. But then you'd look gorgeous in a Hazmat suit.'

'It's because it's a beautiful beige.'

'It's because you're beautiful.'

Amy tried not to smile and glanced at the bench.

'I forgot to say. That manuscript you sent me. The one you were too drunk to know whether it was good?'

'Josh's book. I'd forgotten about that.'

'It was rubbish. Utter drivel.'

'Thought as much.'

Josh seemed like another world. A film she had seen once. He made no sense in Helen and Malcolm's garden. He made no sense in Max's presence.

'Sit here,' Max said, shifting himself to the edge of the bench, making space for two Amys.

Amy stared at the bench and didn't move.

'It's a seat, not a marriage proposal.'

'I know,' she said, perching on the furthest edge from him.

They didn't speak, however. Max smiled at her, she smiled back. Finally, she stood up.

'I can't think when you do that.'

'Do what?'

'Be nice to me.'

'Are you so attached to thinking that you can't give it up from time to time?'

'I gave it up for years and look where it got me.'

'It got you here, with Helen and Malcolm.'

'And they've forced me to think in ways I'm not entirely comfortable with.'

'Thinking hurts, Amy.'

'So does feeling.'

Max was staring at her intently. 'Yes, you taught me that,' he said after a time.

'I can't bear to think of the hurt I've caused you, Max.'

'I was all in, Amy. Do you know what I mean?'

'I do. And I knew it then. I knew it then.'

Max dropped his head.

'I'm so sorry, Max.'

After a moment of silence, he stood up, and looked at her, giving her the slightest of nods. He said, 'I'd better go now.'

'Thank you, Max.'

'For what?'

'Smiling at me.'

\*

Later, as Amy climbed into bed beside Helen, she was startled when Helen suddenly roused herself and switched on the light.

'You don't need to sleep here tonight,' she said.

'I don't mind,' Amy replied, pulling the sheets over her. 'If you'd prefer I didn't, I can go downstairs.'

'I don't know what I want.'

'Then I'll stay.'

Helen switched off the light.

Amy closed her eyes and rolled on her side. Everything Max did was a question. He was never silent. There was always an unspoken conversation about the conversation while any conservation with him was in full flight. There were words in every pause.

She'd forgotten how to speak to him. And she wondered if she'd ever be able to again.

Everything had changed so much. She didn't know herself.

That morning, while shopping at Waitrose with Malcolm, she passed a young guy she recognised. He turned and smiled and was about to approach when Malcolm came up to her with the coffee he had gone in search of. The familiar face winked and wandered off. Following Malcolm with the trolley, Amy searched her memory to put a name to the face. Or even a situation. And it was then it occurred to her that the last time she had had sex was with Liam in the street. She couldn't remember ever going so long without sex. She couldn't remember ever not wanting sex. And she realised, as the name of the guy she'd seen popped into her head, that she didn't want sex.

Ehsan. That was his name. He was Iranian.

He was at the checkout ahead of Amy and Malcolm, and when he was finished he gave Amy an opportunity to speak by fussing with his bags. Amy now remembered the nights she spent with him. He was married. It had given the nights an extra thrill. But now there was nothing. She let the opportunity pass. With a quick wave Ehsan walked out.

And now, in bed, having spoken with Max, she felt nothing but exhaustion. She drifted off to sleep.

*

'You didn't have to sleep with him.'

Amy wasn't sure she heard the words. She opened her eyes and listened.

'Amy, did you hear me? You didn't need to sleep with him.'

'He slept with me,' she said, knowing Helen meant Daniel.

'It wasn't right. He was still married. He was confused.'

'He was a grown man.'

'You didn't need to do it.'

'Neither did he. Don't make me responsible for his death.'

'You need to be more careful with what you have.'

'I did not kill Daniel. Daniel killed Daniel.'

'Be careful what you say.'

'You be careful,' said Amy, sitting up and turning on the bedside light. 'I had nothing to do with Daniel's death. Nothing whatsoever.'

'We all had something to do with Daniel's death,' said Helen, her back to Amy.

'We all had something to do with Daniel's *life*. He was responsible for his death. End of story. Go to sleep.'

'We all had something to do with Daniel's life,' said Helen, barely audible.

'We all had something to do with Daniel's life.'

Amy turned off the light and lay back down.

'I sent him up to Edinburgh,' said Helen.

'It was the right thing to do. He needed to be with his boys.'

'I pushed him. He said he wasn't ready. I pushed him.'

'He went because he wanted to go. You didn't force him to go. He wasn't a child. He made his own decisions. You need to remember that.'

'We'd reconciled. We were better than we'd ever been. He felt obliged to do as I asked. It was too early for him and he knew it.'

'Helen, please go to sleep. We can't know. We'll never know. Do you want another tablet?'

'No. I think I'll get up.'

Amy reached for her phone. 'It's 1 am.'

'I'll watch television for a while.'

'I'll come with you.'

# Chapter 53
# Nothing

Malcolm and Trevor talk on the phone:

'I won't go to the funeral.'

'Your son's funeral, Malcolm?'

'What's a funeral? Nothing.'

'It means things to others. I'd go if I could. They'll expect you to be there.'

'What others? I'm alone in my grief. What others?'

'Geraldine? Your grandsons? Helen?'

'You talk as if Helen is still with us.'

'She is, Malcolm. And she's in as much pain as you are.'

'Mournful spectre. Let her go then.'

'Alone?'

'We all are, aren't we? Daniel was. For more than a week. More alone than any of us can hope to be.'

'You have to go, Malcolm.'

'I do not. I will not. I share nothing with anyone. I'm completely alone. Nothing is nothing to nothing.'

'Malcolm? Malcolm?'

# Chapter 54
## Who Were You to Him?

Helen was seated on the edge of her bed. Amy was doing her makeup. There was no talk. It was the morning of Daniel's funeral. Helen had only decided to go the night before. Luckily, Amy had been able to find a last-minute flight to Edinburgh for them both. She took business-class seats.

Malcolm still refused to go. He lost his temper when Amy tried to argue with him, so she let him be. After Helen's stress at hearing Malcolm's raised voice, Amy had only managed to get her into bed at 2 am.

Amy had booked an early flight. She'd set her alarm for 5.30. After only two hours' sleep, Helen had climbed out of bed. Amy was exhausted, but she climbed out of bed, too. She followed Helen downstairs to the kitchen and let her make a pot of tea for them both. Then they watched TV until Amy's alarm went off.

Helen was listless. But they needed to go. Amy felt compelled to do Helen's makeup, dress her and push her out the door.

Helen let her. Without a word.

In the Uber, as Amy stared out of the window at the waking London streets, Helen reached across the empty seat and took Amy's hand in hers. When Amy turned to look at Helen, she found her face turned to the window. Helen held her hand all the way to the airport. Then they made their way through check-in.

On the other side Amy forgot she'd paid business class and bought them each coffee and a pastry. After sitting at their gate for half an hour they boarded their flight.

Helen took hold of Amy's hand as the plane lifted off the ground.

Amy could only think in short painful bursts. Even with Helen holding her hand, she'd never felt more alone. Helen and Malcolm's grief was an impenetrable wall. And would remain so. She loved them both. Max had helped her see that. But did they love her back? Could they love her now?

She wanted to be there for Helen. She felt compelled to be there. She wanted to serve her in any way she could. She would stay close as long as she was needed. But this was all so new to her. This desire to serve. To love. To be loved. She felt exposed and fearful.

Amy hadn't spoken to her own parents in over a year. The last time she'd spent extended time with them was the week after her graduation. Two days at their house in Kent. She had divorced them effectively. And it had been largely amicable. From time to time her father would email her his thoughts on the latest Jack Cade. Occasionally her mother would send photos of the two of them on some beach, or in New York. But these photos weren't sent to Amy exactly, they were sent bcc. She never knew if her mother meant to send them to her or not. Nor could she begin to guess who the other recipients were.

Amy felt the tears on her cheek before she realised how sad it all was. She was flying with a woman she barely knew to bury that woman's son. Helen said she and Daniel had only just reconciled. They'd spent twenty-five years estranged. Twenty-five years.

Amy had been estranged from her parents for almost as long. Since they sent her off to boarding school. Was her mother now clutching the hand of a stranger, too? Did she have regrets? Would she welcome Amy back? Did she want her to sleep beside her, to comfort her?

The plane landed in Edinburgh and the taxi took them down the bypass before heading back up to Morningside Cemetery. The driver had said it was quicker. Amy had no idea where she was, so said nothing.

Helen clutched Amy's hand, holding it ever more tightly as they went.

The car drove along the east side of Braidburn Valley Park, and Helen said, pointing across the valley, 'Daniel and Geraldine's house is on the far hill there. I can't recall which it is, we were never asked to visit. I've only ever seen photos. I used Google maps for the rest.'

'Is that where the wake will be held?'

'No, Geraldine's parents' house, which is up there somewhere, too. Probably the biggest one.'

'They lived close by?'

'Geraldine's parents bought Geraldine and Daniel a house when they were married. They wanted to keep her close.'

'Have you met her parents?'

'At the wedding.'

Helen turned her head back to the window.

Soon the cab stopped and Amy paid the driver. They got out. Amy wasn't sure where to go. She assumed the cemetery was on the other side of the high stone wall, but there was no obvious entrance.

Amy also assumed there would be a church attached to the cemetery. Being so isolated from her own family she hadn't been to a funeral before. But that's how it always was on television.

Helen placed her hand on the cold stone. 'He's my son. How did it come to this? Why is he being buried in Edinburgh? He should be with me. I'll never see him again. They have him.'

'Who has him?'

'Geraldine's family held a service for him this morning. In a church. He wasn't a believer. He would never have asked for a religious ceremony. They've taken him from me.'

Amy had her phone out and was looking for an entrance.

'Why didn't we go to the service?' she asked, absent-mindedly.

Helen didn't answer her. She wanted to go home. She leant against the wall wearily as Amy concentrated on her screen.

'There's Geraldine,' said Helen, gesturing towards a woman in black getting out of a black Mercedes. She was with her parents and the boys. They were some distance off. Geraldine's parents glanced in Helen and Amy's direction. Neither acknowledged them. The small party disappeared. Helen and Amy walked down to where the Mercedes was and saw the entrance to the cemetery.

More people arrived. Helen and Amy joined them. All followed Geraldine and her family, who seemed to know where they were going.

By the time the coffin was being lowered, thirty or so people were standing around the grave.

Helen recognised none of them, but assumed they knew who she was. Daniel had told anyone who would listen of his uncaring literary parents. Her picture had been in the papers since Daniel's death. Now Helen was here without Malcolm. Which would confirm all the stories.

Prayers were said. Tears were shed. The sky was clear and blue. It was over.

Geraldine left the arm of her father, walked over to Helen and hugged her briefly. Helen followed the retreating boys with her eyes. No one else approached her. The mother of the deceased was a pariah.

Amy introduced herself to Geraldine.

'You're Amy?' she said, surprised. 'Why was Daniel sorry?'

'What?'

'The last message sent from Daniel's phone was to you. It said, "I'm sorry". What was he sorry for?'

'I don't know.'

'You don't know.'

'I don't know.'

'Who were you to him?'

Amy paused for a moment. She glanced quickly at Helen, who was examining Geraldine's tear-streaked face. Amy hadn't much liked the way Geraldine had spoken to her. She hadn't liked the way no one had spoken to Helen, either. Geraldine's parents hadn't brought the boys to their grandmother. She didn't much like the cemetery and what she'd seen of Edinburgh had depressed her. So she said, 'I was his lover.'

The look on Geraldine's face was worth the lie, Amy thought. It was a cruel thing to say and the wrong place to say it. Helen had gasped on hearing the words. But she thought Daniel deserved a tiny win. Geraldine had left him for another man. She'd taken a lover. Why not leave Geraldine with a different image of the man she'd betrayed?

'I don't understand,' she said.

'You wouldn't.'

Geraldine walked off.

'Why did you say that?'

'Because I've been her.'

'It was cruel and unnecessary.'

'Much is.'

Amy watched Geraldine rejoin her parents. She must have told them because they all turned and looked back at Amy. She blew them a kiss.

'She's quite beautiful, isn't she?'

'Geraldine? Yes, she is.'

'She's much younger than I expected, too.'

Helen murmured assent. Then she placed her hand on Amy's elbow.

'You didn't tell me Daniel messaged you.'

'I didn't know till now it was the last thing he sent.'

'Can I see it?'

Amy took out her phone and found the message. She saw her reply – *For what?*

Helen held the phone and then kissed the screen.

'I'm sorry, Daniel,' she said. Helen handed the phone back, made her way closer to the grave and stood there a while by herself. The rest of the mourners were walking back to their cars.

Helen decided at the last minute not to attend the wake.

Amy messaged an Uber, which took them back to the airport. They had hours to wait. She found a place for Helen to sit, then went off to find an earlier flight home.

When she returned Helen was in tears. She led her to a more private spot.

They sat side by side, knees touching. Helen dried her eyes. When she was done, Amy reached out and took both Helen's hands in her own.

'I just don't understand,' said Helen. 'His last message said, "I'm sorry". That was the only note he left. I'm sorry. And he sent it to you but you don't even know what that means. What could he be sorry for? What had he done to you?'

'Nothing.'

'Why didn't he leave a longer note? Why didn't he call me?'

'I don't know, Helen,' said Amy.

'Why message you? Why was he thinking of you?' asked Helen, desperately.

Amy was shaking her head slowly. Tears were in her own eyes now.

'Was it the last thing he did?'

She didn't have answers for any of Helen's questions. Nobody did. The full weight of Daniel's death was crashing down upon her now. She could finally feel it.

'Or were there hours between that message and his death? I need to know these things. I need to know,' said Helen, holding Amy's hands tightly in her own and looking at her with eyes glistening with tears. Her anguish was breaking Amy's heart. She wanted so badly to offer her comfort but her brain wasn't functioning as it should.

'I don't know why he messaged me. I'm so sorry, Helen. I wish I did.'

Helen was clearly disappointed.

Having just said she didn't know, Amy spoke again. 'Maybe he was worried he'd taken advantage of me. Maybe he was sorry that having just met me he was doing something so distressing.'

Helen's eyes widened like a child's, hungry for answers.

'Did he mean to send it to Geraldine, not me?' Amy continued. 'Or maybe he did mean to send it to me and maybe I'm meant to convey the message to others. To tell everyone that Daniel's sorry.'

Helen nodded slightly.

'I think it has to be that. Don't you think? He wanted everyone to know that he was sorry.'

Helen lifted Amy's hands to her mouth and kissed her knuckles. Then she hugged her and sobbed as she hadn't sobbed since Daniel's death. She broke down completely, Amy crying and holding her tightly in return.

No one took much notice of the two women sobbing and holding each other. Tears in an airport are not as unusual as tears in Tesco.

# Chapter 55
# Just One More Drink?

Amy messages Alan:

Amy: *I need to drink.*

Alan: *When?*

Amy: *Now.*

Alan: *It's three in the afternoon.*

Amy: *So?*

Alan: *I'm working.*

Amy: *Leave.*

*

Alan met me at the Sound Bar but he'd taken his time. I had been feeling like shit when I arrived but a couple of champagnes and the cute barman's Amy Special, a cocktail he had made up just for me, had lifted my spirits.

Alan was, as ever, immaculately dressed. But he looked paler than usual. And a little put out, which I tried my best to ignore. I wasn't there for him and his problems, I was there for me and mine.

As he joined me in the booth, I said, 'Oh my god, Alan. My life's a mess. I need your help. Personal and professional.'

'What can I do?'

'Tell me about your boring life, for starters. That will make me feel so much better.'

'Umm ...'

'Tell me about some clever terms and conditions you've devised. Fill the air with lawyer speak. Do it. Do something.'

'I'm getting married.'

'What?!'

'I'm getting married.'

'To who?'

'My partner, Sebastian.'

I stared at him, too surprised to speak. Then, as if I had been transported back to a time when we were both teens, I punched his arm and all but screamed, 'You. Are. So. Gay!'

'Bi,' he said, pertly. 'Both of us are. But we're in love and nothing's ever going to be the same.'

'When are you getting married? Why aren't I invited?' I slapped him on the thigh hard.

Alan seemed relieved by my exuberant reaction. His face brightened a little.

'Sebastian is super jealous of you. He thinks you're the devil incarnate.'

'So he knows about me?'

'Of course he does. You've met him, too. A number of times. Though you probably don't remember. He's not your type.'

I shook my head. I didn't remember him at all.

'He's my business partner and best friend. So I've been talking to him about you for years. On and on and on. He was so sick of hearing about you he decided to put an end to it. A few weeks ago he stopped my chatter by kissing me mid-sentence. That was a surprise!'

'Oh my god! This makes so much sense! So much sense.'

'He'd kill me if he discovered I was with you.'

'I can't believe you've surprised me, Alan. After all these years. Wow. I'm stunned. Stunned.'

I stopped talking and just stared at him. I was smiling for the first time in days. He was beaming. I'd known Alan my whole life. He'd always been gayish, but he'd been so set on marrying me. He'd proposed. And he'd fucked me when I was distraught after Max threw me out. I suppose I just assumed he lived on the gay side of hetero street. There were a lot of men like that in the publishing world so I'd learnt to distrust my instincts.

'This is so weird, Alan. So weird. Shall we celebrate with a ruinously expensive bottle of champagne?'

'I can't stay, Amy. I have to get back to work.'

'Really?'

'I'm sorry, but … Sebastian means the world to me and I don't want to fuck this up.'

'Oh.'

'Just being near you is trouble. I can feel it.'

He moved away from me. Whether consciously or not, I couldn't decide.

'Just one more drink?'

'I can't.'

I suddenly felt on the verge of tears. Alan had been a constant presence in my life. Sometimes front and centre, sometimes in the shadows. And it felt like this was the end. A goodbye.

'You look great, Amy. Even better than you did in front of the V&A. Whatever mess you're in, it's working for you.'

I opened my mouth to say something, but no words materialised. He was going for good. Tears welled up in my eyes and rolled onto my cheeks.

Alan straightened in his seat at the sight of my tears. 'I'll still look after you professionally. This isn't goodbye. Email me.'

He stood up and stepped back from the table in an awkward movement. From that safe distance he blew me a kiss and then left.

He couldn't even kiss me on the cheek.

I stared at the empty bar, and then at my empty drink. I was desolate.

There were so many bad things I could do. I could call Liam. I could call Josh. I could blow the cute barman in the Sound Bar toilets. I could sit there and drink myself into oblivion and let life roll the dice and choose my depravity.

I could walk to Westminster and throw myself off the bridge.

I left the bar and hailed a cab, which took me back to Helen and Malcolm's house.

Fuck everything.

# Chapter 56
# You've Been Sleeping

Trevor woke up and found Malcolm snoozing in the big armchair by the window. He wondered what time it was; his blinds were drawn and the room was rather dark. It was always a bit difficult to tell whether the light coming through the edges of the blinds was daylight or the lights of the grounds.

Trevor had been feeling terrible the last week or so. He was tired all the time. And couldn't keep his food down. They were feeding him intravenously. But most alarmingly there were whispered conversations around his bed when he was thought to be sleeping. His daughter had visited more often than usual. And Zoe had been visiting daily. None of this foretold a long and happy future.

'Malcolm,' he said loudly. And he smiled as he watched Malcolm wake. He was confused and disorientated and looked quite the fool for a moment or two.

'Trevor, what are you doing here?'

'You've been sleeping.'

'Have I?'

'You're meant to be visiting me. But you've been a terrible bore, snoring loudly and passing wind.'

Malcolm sat up straight and wiped a bit of drool from the corner of his mouth. He had really been dead to the world. He felt groggy. He touched his hair and straightened his shirt and jacket.

'Have I? I'm sorry. I must have dropped off. You were asleep when I arrived.'

'The bed in the next room is empty if you want to move in permanently. We lost one on Thursday.'

'It wouldn't be a bad idea,' he said, standing up and moving to the chair closer to Trevor's bed. 'How are you feeling, Trevor? I ran into Usman in the car park, who said you hadn't been well this last week.'

'I'm dying, Malcolm. I can feel it. It's over.'

'You can feel it?'

'Yes.'

'What do the doctors say?'

'Nothing direct. But I can tell you now, from experience, when death comes you know. Death's coming. He's probably parking his car as we speak.'

'So this is it, then?'

'This is it. The last time you have to visit me.'

'I'd better say something profound, then,' said Malcolm grimly.

'I thought the dying man said the profound things.'

'You get the last word.'

Trevor chuckled and coughed. Malcolm handed him some water. Trevor waved it away.

'Everything makes me queasy; that's why this is in,' he said, pointing to the drip. 'I'm yesterday's news. How are you, Malcolm?'

'My son is dead and I killed him. I'm fine.'

'And Helen?'

'No change there.'

'And your book?'

'Finished. It's the best thing I've ever written. Too bad no one will be around to read it.'

'It's bad form for me to die so soon after Daniel.'

'You might have arranged things better. But then, you might be wrong. You look well enough to me.'

'I might linger. But I won't rally. Can I read the new book?'

'I didn't bring it with me. And as this is my last visit, it seems not. Probably for the best. It's all about death.'

'I could take it with me.'

'It would certainly be appreciated on the other side.'

'Malcolm Taylor? I hear he's big in Hades.'

Malcolm smiled but said nothing.

'Can you believe they gave the Nobel to Dylan?' asked Trevor.

'It makes sense to me.'

'How so?'

'You've been following the election. They're all fucked. Dylan's music is the last gasp of American culture. He stands for something. Awarding it to him now is a political decision, frankly.'

Trevor coughed and waved away Malcolm's assistance.

'Trouble is, in the US, no one knew whether Dylan's irritating whining drone was something to be proud or ashamed of. Thanks to the Nobel committee, Americans can rest comfortably. He's been given a bona fide seal of approval.'

'He's always annoyed me.'

'You're too old, Trevor. You always have been. You're a jazz man. Personally, I don't doubt Dylan's brilliance. I just hope he doesn't accept the award. Like Jean-Paul Sartre.'

'You compare him to Jean-Paul Sartre?'

'You have to admit Dylan's unique. And consistently brilliant across fifty years.'

'But the Nobel?'

'What is it, really? Come on. You don't take it seriously, do you?'

'Not now. Not now.'

They were silent for a moment. Malcolm was thinking of Daniel. That night they had listened to *On the Beach*. Daniel had flicked through *all that fucking Bob Dylan*. The following day

Malcolm had made him listen to 'Visions of Johanna' and Daniel conceded that he had always liked the song. Now he was gone.

'Have you written your acceptance speech?' asked Trevor, moving slightly. He was uncomfortable.

'I won't win.'

'Write one, just in case. Will you attend?'

'When is it?'

'Twenty-fifth of October.'

'That soon? Well, I haven't won then, have I? I'd know by now, surely.'

'Would you? I think they only warn the winner when they're living abroad. I'll make enquiries. Zoe tells me the bookies favour Madeleine Thien's *Do Not Say We Have Nothing.*'

'I haven't read it. I only got through a couple of them.'

'The Duchess of Cornwall will be handing out the award.'

'I don't think I want to be there. They'll have to excuse me after Daniel's death. I'll send Amy in my stead.'

'Have you adopted her?'

'She's adopted me.'

# Chapter 57
# Retail Therapy

The morning after Daniel's funeral, as I lay in Helen's bed, I turned my smartphone into a dumb phone. I don't know why. But it felt the right thing to do. So I did it. I deleted my Facebook account, my Tumblr blog, my WhatsApp account, my Snapchat, my Instagram and my Twitter, and then I removed my email permissions.

None of these companies make it easy to escape. They kept asking me if I was sure. *Yes, I'm sure.* Are you sure, you're sure? *Yes.* This is irreversible. *I know.*

But it felt good killing them off one by one.

My phone was just a phone. And it was on silent.

I was free to do whatever I liked. I had the money to do what I pleased. But most days I lay on the bed in the flat watching Netflix on my laptop. I was binge-watching episodes of *Orange is the New Black*. And when I was finished, I planned to move on to *House of Cards*. Bingeing on TV was something I had never done before. But I quickly developed an insatiable appetite for it.

I didn't have to be idle. There was work for me to do. But since I'd given my phone a lobotomy, whenever I opened my email on my laptop I clicked highlight all and, after a cursory glance at the sender and subject lines, pressed delete.

I saw emails from publishing friends asking for favours. People I'd never let down before. But I didn't care. What had they ever done for me? Nothing. What did they know of my life? Nothing. There were emails from Liam and even a couple from Julia. Another from Josh. But they were deleted with the rest. I even saw an email from Max. Delete. He had my number.

Helen had been just as inactive, but she had more class, and had been binge-reading Jane Austen and E.M. Forster. Malcolm wasn't idle exactly; he was finally sorting through his books. But it was taking a very long time. Every volume was drenched in memories.

We were all in some kind of holding pattern until the Booker winner was announced.

In my Netflix-induced stupor, I'd been wearing yoga leggings and hoodies. A few days before the Booker dinner I realised I had nothing to wear on the night. I'd forgotten that most of my clothes were packed in boxes in a storage unit. I ran through the truncated wardrobe I'd accumulated while staying in the flat and found it entirely unsuitable for the event.

I didn't want to leave the flat, but I had to. There was no avoiding it. I didn't want to go alone. I went upstairs and begged Helen to help me choose a dress for the night. She lay down her copy of *Howards End* and looked at me long and hard. Then nodded.

We took a cab to New Bond Street and Helen followed me from shop to shop, offering me little help. She looked tired and out of place. Thankfully, I was known in most of the shops we visited, so we were treated well and Helen was made comfortable while they fussed around me. The money I had spent in Mayfair over the last few years was obscene. And today I was determined to be excessive.

Helen actually gasped when the assistant at Hermes mentioned the price of the coat I was buying. Then, a little later, she needed smelling salts when I bought a few pairs of shoes. I just couldn't decide on an evening gown, though. Nothing seemed right. I wanted to make a statement. The literary world was so dull. When they dressed up for black-tie events like this, they were even worse. The women were forced out of their comfort zones and chose outlandish gowns more suited to school formals. I didn't want something full length, though all of the shop assistants in Vuitton and Givenchy tried to talk me into full-length gowns. Some of them were divine but I didn't want class, I wanted eye-catching. And leg was going to do that. I needed something short. A cocktail dress. But nothing I tried on was suitable, though Helen eyed each with the same mild approval as the last.

We barely said two words to each other while this was going on. So I was surprised when we stopped for a bit of lunch and she said, 'If he wins, then my sacrifice will be for nothing.'

I was trying to arrange my shopping bags under the table while weighing up whether I would risk the cold and go bare legged, so didn't quite get her meaning at first. Shopping makes an idiot out of me.

'Sacrifice?'

As soon as I said it I comprehended. But it was too late then. And I could see it in Helen's face. I had messed up.

'He won't win,' I said, too late.

'Trevor said *A Hundred Ways* is already selling very well. Better than anything Malcolm or I have ever written before. He's already starting to make good money from it. Trevor's granddaughter is talking to US publishers. The German rights have been sold. Polish, Slovakian, Russian and Greek rights are in negotiations. A Booker win will make Malcolm an international phenomenon. Such sales would mean we could keep the house without publishing my book. The whole thing would have been for nothing.'

'He won't win, Helen. Trevor said he'd know by now. You know, if his author had won. He has spies everywhere.'

'But if he did.'

'He won't.'

'He hasn't spoken to me. He won't look at me. When I enter a room, he leaves. I disgust him just as I disgust myself, and for the same reason. I wanted what people like you had and I gave them what they wanted to get it.'

'People like me?'

'Yes, the successful. Look at how much you can spend on a coat. Thousands of pounds on a coat! I wanted to do that. I wanted all of it. It was so stupid. So stupid. And at my age.'

'What you did wasn't easy, Helen.'

'Yes it was. It was a letting go. I've always known I could write that stuff. It isn't rocket science even though you lot pretend it is. And then you have someone like Lee Child saying he could write a Booker winner if he wanted. Let's see him try. Like your friend, what's his name? Good luck to them both.'

'Liam?'

'Yes. Him. Didn't you say he wanted to write serious literature?'

'He's desperate for the kind of respect you and Malcolm enjoy.'

'We don't enjoy any respect. We *endure* respect. We endured fifty lean years of respect. It almost killed me, all that respect. And now I'll die because it's been taken away.'

'No one's taking it away.'

'Malcolm's lost his respect for me. And so have I.'

'I'll make him read version three. I'll stand over him until he does and then he'll be begging your forgiveness.'

'It's been on his desk for three months. Untouched. I check as soon as he leaves the house. He hasn't lifted the cover page.'

'How do you know?'

'A trick he taught me. We used to do it when we were starting out. Publishers used to send our manuscripts back to us in those days. It wasn't easy to make copies. So we'd booby-trap them. If they hadn't read them, it was easy enough to tell.'

'Sneaky.'

The waitress came over to clear away the plates. I ordered a coffee and Helen a tea.

I wondered if Helen knew what Max had told me. She seemed to allude to it, but I didn't dare ask her, 'Do you know Malcolm thinks you're dead?' Instead I took the easy way out and said, 'I think I like the black evening gown from the first shop best. Shall we just go back there and end our little adventure?'

'I don't want to go back home just yet.'

'You're not tired?'

'I am tired. Very tired. But it's a tiredness that rest and sleep won't cure.'

'Is there anything I can do, Helen? I want to help.'

'No. You've already been very kind to Malcolm and me. We're morbid company.'

'It pains me that you're not getting along when you both need each other the most.'

'I bet you didn't expect to be in the middle of all of this when you agreed to look at my book,' Helen said, with a pained smile.

'I bet you wish I'd never knocked on your door.'

Helen's face lost the remnants of the smile and she looked me in the eye. 'Everything that's happened was well underway before you entered our lives, Amy.'

'Really? You and Malcolm were still talking. Daniel was alive.'

'In my grief I've said terrible things to you. I don't believe you had anything to do with Daniel's death. It was wrong of me to say so. I'll never forgive myself for saying so.'

And I don't know whether it was what she said or the way she said it, but I couldn't speak and realised with unmixed mortification that I was about to cry. Helen's eyes held mine and I saw, in the depths of her pain, my reflection. Here I was trying to be strong for Helen when my own life was falling apart. Tears flowed and it was completely uncontrollable. When Helen took my hand in hers, the tears were accompanied by sobs. Heads in the quiet little cafe turned. Helen stood up and came around to the chair beside me. She hugged me to her as I had done to her at the airport.

'It's all so shit, Helen. You and Malcolm deserve to be happy. And everything is just shit.'

'You deserve to be happy, too, Amy. Do you know that?'

I couldn't answer her. The idea was strange to me. Why should I be happy? What had I ever done to deserve happiness? It seemed a strange thing to say of someone like me.

Helen held me for a very long time. And after a while she began to ask me questions under her breath. And I answered them quietly. She wanted to know about Max. She wanted to know about Liam. I told her everything. She wanted to know about my parents. The tears returned as I told her. I couldn't help them. A dam had burst and the tears flowed.

I just wish we'd been at home instead of in that cafe. I'm not one for public displays of emotion. The waitress came over at one point to see if there was anything she could do. It was mortifying.

I went to the bathroom, took one look at my red eyes and blotchy face and sighed. Things had to get better from here. They had to. I couldn't cope with this life. It was all too much. I wanted to get back to the flat and back into bed. I blew my nose, touched up my makeup and returned to Helen.

'Shall we go?'

'You haven't got a dress yet.'

Helen and I returned to the first shop and bought another dress altogether. A slip of a cocktail dress. My spirits lifted a little after they all said I looked gorgeous in it. Helen thought it was a bit showy, which was what I was going for after all. To be on the safe side, I bought the other one as well.

# Chapter 58
# Have You Written Your Speech?

'Hello, Trevor?'

'Malcolm?'

'Can you hear me?'

'Loud and clear.'

'So the reception is good on the other side, is it? The flames don't cause any interference?'

'Very funny.'

'So let me be clear about this, you're not dead?'

'I'm not dead. This is true.'

'Good to hear. I'm on speakerphone. Amy's here.'

'Hello, Trevor.'

'Hello, Amy. Zoe's here. Shall I put her on, too? How do you put this thing on speakerphone, Zo?'

'Trevor?'

'Hello? It's Zoe, Grandpa's phone is ancient. I think I have it on speaker. Can you hear us?'

'Yes we can. Hello, Zoe, nice to meet you.'

'You too, Amy. You're going to be my date on Tuesday night, I hear.'

'Yes, we'll be the belles of the ball.'

'Malcolm, have you written your speech?'

'I have it, Trevor. Sealed in an envelope with strict instructions not to read it until the night.'

'And I've told her to bring it straight back to me unopened, if I don't win.'

'If you get a chance, Amy, steam it open and send me a copy.'

'I wouldn't dare. But I am frightened about what it contains. I'll have to read it out if he wins.'

'Malcolm won't win. I've been sniffing around and there isn't a hint of an upset. They're certain to give it to an American this year. As a sign of good faith. There are two in the running. If not them, then I hope Deborah Levy wins. I loved *Swimming Home*, and *Hot Milk* is impressive.'

'Don't listen to Grandpa, Malcolm. You're going to win. I can feel it.'

'I think I'm going to win, too.'

'You'd think this would make him happy, Zoe, but he's been very grumpy these last few days. Grumpier than usual, that is.'

'Amy, Grandpa has set us up with Hayley Granger, Malcolm's publisher. We're to meet her in the Old Library where the drinks are held. Have you met her?'

'No.'

'Well, she's nice and all but old, like Malcolm and Grandad. And a chatterbox. And more than a bit eccentric. Is there any chance we can meet up beforehand and go in together? We could even meet for pre-drinks. A bit of Dutch courage?'

'Sounds like a plan. We've called from my phone, so you have my number. Text me.'

'Malcolm, Zoe's let everyone know you won't be attending. Because of Daniel.'

'Everyone?'

'I put out a press release. You're the people's choice, Malcolm. Social media has already crowned you. Win or lose, you win.'

'What are you going to wear, Zoe?'

'I don't know. What are you wearing?'

'Message me and I'll send you a pic.'

'Trevor, if you're not dead by Tuesday shall I come and watch the announcement with you?'

'Yes, if I'm not dead, I'd be honoured.'

'He's doing really well, Malcolm. The doctors now think he'll be around for a while. At least until Wednesday.'

'You joke, but it's my existence at stake.'

'Dying's the easy bit. Living without you, now that's hard.'

'Malcolm's right, Grandad. We only joke because ... Wow, Amy! That dress is gorgeous! That's so unfair. How can I compete with that?'

'You don't think it's too much?'

'It'd be too much for me. But Grandad says you're one of the most beautiful women he's ever seen, and he once took Sophia Loren to dinner, so I reckon you'll pull it off.'

'I didn't say that!'

'Yes, you did.'

'So, are we finished? Amy's going in my place. She has my speech. She'll meet you, Zoe, beforehand and you'll go in together. Trevor, you and I will watch together in your room. Right? Good. We're settled. Let's hope I don't win. Goodbye, Trevor. Goodbye, Zoe.'

# Chapter 59
# Booker Night

I was standing in the cold in the square outside the Guildhall wrapped in my new coat, wishing it were longer and that I'd worn stockings. My slender black ankle-strap heels had looked so good with my Tom Ford dress, but with the coat on I looked like a tarty Kate Middleton. Or Pippa Middleton. And I was freezing. My bare toes were turning blue.

Where was Zoe? We had canned our pre-drinks drinks as both of us were running late, but now she was late for the drinks. Watching the other invitees arrive, I was glad I'd chosen to wear my first choice, the more classic little black dress. My second choice was a low-cut, obscenely short red number. More footballer's wife than editor. Black was the right choice. The most daring colour I'd seen pass me was purple. And mine were the only bare legs to be seen.

Zoe finally arrived, a diminutive dark beauty with an enormous smile. She too was wrapped up in a woollen coat, but she was wearing closed-toe pumps and stockings. Very sensible. The first thing she did was take a selfie of us both and post it on Instagram. She spoke at a million miles an hour and I didn't get a word in as we joined the crowd entering the building. We handed in our coats at the cloakroom and had our photo taken on the way. Zoe then took more selfies. At least ten. She was bubbling over with excitement and compliments, which I returned and she beamed with pleasure. When we reached the reception, Zoe left me by myself for a moment while she went off in search of Malcolm's publisher, Hayley Granger. I opened my clutch and made sure Malcolm's envelope was in there.

I'd expected the Booker to buck the trend of literary events. It was the Booker after all. But it didn't. It was worse. The room was rapidly filling with a collection of dull, middle-aged frumps. Faces I didn't recognise. Fashion I didn't understand.

My sleeveless little black dress seemed to grow shorter with every second. There was more skin showing on my body than was to be seen on all of the other women combined.

But it was a room where a woman dressed as I was, looking as naked and as fabulous as I was, could stand all by herself until the end of time without being approached. There weren't even any lecherous middle-aged men. The room was filled with decent middle-aged men who wouldn't dream of boring a young beauty like me.

And the younger men were all too earnest, all too serious to let their minds wander from their intellectual discussions to the base temptations of the flesh.

When Zoe finally returned with Hayley Granger I was on my second glass of champagne, still all alone, and wishing I was dead.

Then I saw Julia.

Of course she would be there. I was an idiot for not even considering this. It was the Booker. She was publishing director of M&R. I was glad to see she looked horrendous in a pale-blue lace and satin gown. Like a runaway bridesmaid.

Hayley Granger spoke to me. 'How's Malcolm?' she asked.

'Fine. I think.'

Julia was laughing. Who was that with her? He looked familiar.

'I'm astonished that *A Hundred Ways* is a serious contender. You know I tried to talk him out of publishing it. What did you think?'

'It rattled me.'

Julia had put on weight, too. She was standing very close to the familiar older man with her. He was tall and lean and his face looked ravaged by loss.

'Is he writing at the moment? He won't return my calls,' Hayley persisted.

'It's been a difficult time.'

'Of course, of course.'

Hayley seemed like a nice enough woman, but nothing she could now do would get my full attention.

When Max joined our little group, I was so surprised I actually let out a little scream. He laughed and kissed my cheek. He introduced himself to Zoe and Hayley and started talking about the chances of an American winning. He was wearing a tux, and with his hair longer and a little unruly, looked a bit like Kit Harington. He certainly looked as tall as Kit Harington from my vantage point atop my ruinously high heels.

My glass was empty again. I looked around for a waiter. None to be seen. Hayley said she would join us later and left our group.

Zoe and Max discovered they knew a lot of the same people. And Max found, as I had done, that Zoe could talk. For every story Max told, Zoe had a better one. And if it wasn't one of her own, she was happy to borrow one of Trevor's. Trevor did know everyone. And all the while, without drawing breath, she took more selfies and posted them, typing away at a furious rate on her phone.

I looked over Max's shoulder at Julia and saw what I didn't want to see. Liam was with her now.

I turned my back on them, knowing he would know I was there. He never missed a thing.

I expected him to come and join us, especially as Max was with me, but he did no such thing. The next time I saw him was in the middle of a general movement of people towards the Great Hall. He had his arm around Julia's waist.

'Isn't that Liam?' Max asked as we followed the crowd.

'Yes.'

'Is that his wife?'

'No, that's my boss, or more correctly, *was* my boss, at M&R, Julia O'Farrell.'

'Never heard of her. And they're a couple now? Has he left his wife?'

'He thinks he's just fucking Julia. But she has other plans. As far as I know, he's still with his wife. We haven't spoken for a while.'

'Why? What's going on?'

'He's trying to terminate our contract. He wants to go it alone.'

'And what do you think about that?'

'I try not to think about that. But I know something he probably doesn't know yet.'

'What's that?'

'He's fucked.'

Max looked at me. I raised my eyebrows and mouthed, 'What?'

He laughed. 'Don't fuck with Amy ... noted. Where are you sitting?'

'I don't know.'

We went over to the seating plan together. Hayley Granger was ahead of us. Zoe was with her. She turned and said, 'Table eleven for us. I don't know where you are, Max.'

'Right at the back, I expect.'

*

By the time the winner was announced I was so bored I just wanted the night to end. I wasn't listening to the speakers. I had completely tuned out. Julia and Liam were on the other side of the room out of sight and Max was behind me somewhere in the gloom. My attention was focused on the last few breadsticks standing forlornly in the glass. The rest of the table was either whispering together or scrolling on their phones. I was jealous of Zoe; she had been on Facebook, Instagram, Tumblr, *The Guardian*,

Tinder and now Twitter. And she had been interrupting these by messaging someone the whole night. My phone was now just a phone.

So I didn't hear them announce that Malcolm had won. I missed it.

Zoe screamed, clapping her hands like a child, then laughed loudly before suddenly grabbing me and hugging me, her face pressed hard against my own, held her phone aloft and took yet another selfie. Hayley stood up. I shook off Zoe and stood up. Hayley kissed my cheek. It still hadn't clicked. I looked around the tables nearby. They were all looking at us.

'He fucking won?' I said quietly to Hayley.

'He fucking won,' she replied with a laugh. 'You'd better get your skates on. Do you have his speech?'

'Somewhere.' I looked around for my clutch. It was on the floor.

'Hurry, the Duchess is waiting.'

'Duchess?'

I opened my bag and took out Malcolm's envelope. I did not want to do this. When I'd said yes, it seemed there was no chance of me having to actually do it. I'd said yes because Malcolm asked with such desperation in his eyes.

Hayley pushed me in the right direction and I made my way through the tables. The Duchess of Cornwall greeted me.

I stood at the podium. The lights were not so bright as to blind me. I could clearly see the faces looking up at me expectantly. Faces I recognised, faces I didn't. All was quiet.

My mind was blank. Then I said this: 'Just in case there's someone here from the *Daily Mail* or *The Sun*, I want to be crystal clear, I'm not Malcolm Taylor.' It got me a few laughs but I have no idea where it came from. 'However, Malcolm has prepared a speech he's asked me to read,' I said in a faltering voice. 'I only agreed to do this because they all assured me he wouldn't win,' I said as I turned the envelope in my fingers and added, 'I've been drinking like a fish all night. Bear with me.'

There was a little polite laughter.

I then tried to open his envelope. It took a moment. I was finally forced to tear at it. I really should have opened it before getting on stage but Malcolm had warned me not to. And in the confusion of the announcement, I had forgotten.

Three handwritten pages emerged.

I read.

'My name is Amy Winston, the brains behind the Jack Cade novels.'

I stared at what I had just read.

'He wrote that here,' I said, holding up the page to the crowd for inspection. 'I'm just reading what he wrote. I am Amy Winston, by the way.' And I laughed and then abruptly stopped. I couldn't see Liam. There was utter silence. 'The speech begins now.'

'I thank you for this award. But I do fear the judges have made a catastrophic mistake. *A Hundred Ways* is not a work worthy of such commendation. It is a cancer of a book, which needs to be excised from the body of literature before it spreads. That it has gained such notoriety worries me. It may be too late.

'Some commentators have said it is the book this age deserves. But for me, this is the best of all ages. An age that deserves better than this. In fact, this book has nothing at all to do with what is occurring today. Trump and Brexit, the rise of the far right, are minor corrections in a general movement towards a more equitable future. I am not a doom and gloom writer.

'*A Hundred Ways* is a full stop, an end, not a beginning. I didn't want to start a conversation. I wanted to end one.

'I have been writing professionally for fifty years. I am nearly eighty. I speak from some experience when I say this is the best of all ages. Which is not to say it is perfect. It is not. It is very far from perfect. But it is better than past ages.

'*A Hundred Ways* is my full stop, a novel that closes the door on my apprenticeship. I feel ready to write now without the aid of my masters.

'The writers in the room will understand me. At least the good ones will. And yes, there are good and bad writers. Good and bad books. If you can't tell the difference you haven't even started your apprenticeship.

'*A Hundred Ways* should be published with a warning. I didn't realise this until it was too late. I didn't realise how attractive the book would be to the young and the uninitiated. Most of my peers recognise it for what it is: an ugly little book. They admonish me for writing it. But the young cradle it in their laps like a pet rat. They stroke and play with it, oblivious of the disease it carries.

'And it won't do any young writer any good to read it, either.

'But enough about *A Hundred Ways*. It has won the Man Booker. The deed is done. There is no going back. I can only apologise for writing it in the first place and ask that none of you read it.

'If you must read an ugly little book, read *The Sellout* by Paul Beatty, which would have been my pick for this honour. [Applause]

'Before I let Amy leave the stage, I'd like to speak of my wife, the great Helen Owen. The finest British writer not to have won the Man Booker. Shame on us all.

'Tomorrow will mark fifty years since we were married, which means I have been living and working beside one of the world's greatest thinkers and writers for over fifty years. And for that I am thankful. It hasn't always been easy. Helen does not rest. Helen does not bend. She is always evolving as a writer. Always striving to be better. Just being in her presence has made me a better writer. But it has been exhausting. At times I have felt like Muhammad Ali's sparring partner.

'And you guys have given me, the sparring partner, the Man Booker. What fools we all are. [Laughter]

'Helen taught me what it is to have integrity. She is an authentic voice in a sea of compromise. Hand in hand we have walked a difficult path, and we have been rewarded with a small but loyal readership who have kept the wolves at bay all these years. I want to thank the few for taking a little interest in us for such a long time.

With your help we have been free from the corrupting influence of success for all our working lives. Publishers, in the main, are people of integrity. And our publishers have been committed to the good work we always aspired to create. They gave us their unswerving support in a world where poor work pays the bills, giving us the time and the freedom to remain true to ourselves.

'I want to thank Hayley Granger, my publisher, who told me not to publish this book. I should have listened to you. And I want to thank my long-suffering agent, the legendary Trevor Melville, a man who never collected his fee because he said my work never sold enough to cover the cost of his accountant. You may want to collect on this one, Trevor. [Laughter]

'And finally, as I would not be standing here if it were not for my wife, I dedicate this award to Helen Owen. I love you, darling.

'Thank you.'

I read the thank you and stood there for a moment. I wanted to say something, to add something to Malcolm's words. While reading, tears had welled up in my eyes. They now fell unremarked. The audience was silent. Expectant.

But I left the podium without another word. Malcolm had said everything that needed to be said. The room erupted in applause as I was ushered out the back and given a minute to compose myself.

Then they made me pose for photos, which was odd. I'd had nothing to do with the book. I didn't even know Malcolm when he wrote it. Thankfully I was joined by Hayley Granger, who took over those duties. She answered the questions of journalists. She spoke with the Duchess. I made my way to the ladies' room.

# Chapter 60
# More Than Any Book

When Amy left the stage, Malcolm turned the television off. The room went dark. Hearing his words coming from Amy's mouth had been a strange experience. Though seeing her on television made sense. She was astonishingly beautiful. TV beautiful. The close-ups had caught the tears rolling down her cheeks.

Though he had been telling himself and others for days that he would win, on hearing his name announced he had felt sick. His double bluff had failed. Fate wouldn't be tricked. He'd only written the speech to ward off good luck. He had even insisted Amy read it as some kind of voodoo spell. She had nothing to do with the book, after all. But he had won, regardless. And the speech had been read.

Then it struck him that Trevor hadn't said a word throughout.

He looked at Trevor. The park lights shone through the edges of the blinds allowing Malcolm to see his face. He lay perfectly still with his eyes closed.

'Trevor?' Malcolm whispered. On getting no reply he rested his forehead against the metal rail alongside Trevor's bed. He supposed Trevor had been dead since the beginning of the broadcast. There was no chance a living Trevor would have restrained himself on hearing Malcolm had won the Booker. Malcolm admonished himself for not noticing for so long. He'd been so preoccupied with the horror of winning. But Trevor hadn't been alone. Malcolm had been with him. He looked at Trevor's peaceful face. He would have to get the nurse to come in but decided to wait a moment. As soon as he called they would spring into action and he would have no time with Trevor.

'I didn't mention Daniel in my speech. Did you notice, Trevor? There were no words for that kind of thing. Besides, Daniel had always been a private affair. It wasn't quite right for two intellectuals to have a child. But then Malcolm and Helen the writers didn't have him, Malcolm and Helen the ratepayers did. He had been our guilty pleasure. An irrational sidetrack. How we loved him, though. More than any book. How can I say any of that in a speech?'

Malcolm turned on the bedside lamp and poured himself a glass of water. He drank from it and placed it on the over-bed table.

'That he should take his own life at the age of nearly fifty. Suicide is a young man's game, isn't it? I can't make sense of it. I'm not supposed to, I know, but old habits die hard. I should be able to understand this. He was my son. My son climbed into the back of his own car and hid under a picnic blanket. He swallowed pills, placed a plastic bag over his head and died. His two sons were not a mile away from him. Sons I know he loved. Why would he do that to them? Why abandon them?'

Malcolm pressed the emergency buzzer.

'They'll come for you now, Trevor,' said Malcolm, standing and placing his hand on Trevor's for a moment.

'What?'

Malcolm looked at his friend. His eyes were closed. He hadn't moved.

'Trevor? Did you say something?'

'Did you win?'

Malcolm started to laugh.

'Why are you laughing?'
'I thought you were dead. I've pressed the emergency buzzer.'
'Good thing there's no emergency then.'
'Why?'
'The buzzer doesn't work.'

# Chapter 61
# Don't Do This

I sat on the loo and wiped my eyes. The chatter in the small bathroom was too loud. The cubicle was closing in on me. The hum coming from the Great Hall was no comfort, either. I'd have to go back out there. I'd left my clutch with Zoe. I'd have to find her and then leave. Malcolm's win had set tongues wagging as he'd been the rank outsider. Everyone would want to talk to me.

But I didn't want to speak to anyone. All I could do was picture Helen alone at home listening to me read those words. Fucking Malcolm. I had to get back to Helen as quickly as possible. I wiped and flushed, then pushed my way through the crowded bathroom to the sink. A woman spoke to me, called me gorgeous. Said I read the speech very well. I got out of there.

The narrow passage was blocked by a line of women desperate to pee, and then further along, Liam. I looked back the way I came and there was no exit. He was smiling at me.

Fuck. Fuck. Fuck. Fuck.

I threaded my way through the women and tried to pass him without speaking, but he took hold of my arm. He really chose the wrong fucking night.

'Amy, don't do it.'

His casual manner and smile had vanished. There was real fear in his eyes.

'Let go of me.'

'Amy. Please.'

He let go of my arm. I moved out of the way of a passing couple.

'You initiated this, Liam,' I said. 'You set your lawyers on me. You got M&R's lawyers involved. Not me. Everything was perfect. You fucked it.'

'Don't do this to me.'

'I didn't do it. You did. I have to go. Don't ever speak to me again.'

And with that I left him.

# Chapter 62
# The Notebook

Helen had been seated on the sofa watching the news for a while before she noticed the leather notebook on the sofa opposite her. She couldn't remember having seen it before. The next article on the news was about Trump, so she turned her attention back to the television.

The world was going crazy before her eyes. What she saw angered her and so she switched off the TV. The Booker wouldn't start for another hour or so.

With Amy on her way to the dinner and Malcolm with Trevor, the house was quiet and empty. She lifted a framed photo of Daniel from the coffee table. She'd been moving this particular photo from room to room with her since coming back from Edinburgh. She stared at his face. The photo had been taken in Braidburn Valley Park by Geraldine. They'd sent it to Helen for her birthday. It was her favourite photo of Daniel. For the first time in his adult life he had looked completely and unreservedly happy. It was before the boys were born, when he and Geraldine were in the first flush of love.

She thought the picture captured life at full stretch. That Daniel was no more seemed refuted by the image. He lived and breathed in the frame. He was there. Eternally.

She put the frame down.

The leather notebook caught her eye. It looked expensive and out of place. She stood up and reached for it. It was heavier than she expected. She lifted the notebook to her nose and sniffed it. It smelled expensive. She assumed it was Amy's and opened it.

As soon as she saw the neat pencilled script, she knew it was Malcolm's notebook. She flicked through the pages. They were full. She caught sight of her name. Then closed the book.

During the last few painful months, when she knew Malcolm was out, she had entered his office. She had been anxious to find signs of new writing. If he were writing she was certain he'd be all right. But in all of her searches she had come up empty-handed. She'd been looking in the wrong place, she knew now. Malcolm had changed, for some unknown reason, the practice of fifty-something years' standing. He had discarded his foolscap for this flashy leatherbound notebook. The kind of notebook a doting grandparent gives a spoilt teen who has decided to write a novel.

Malcolm had been very careful with it until this moment, Helen mused. She had no idea he'd been using it. She hadn't laid eyes on it before. He was being unusually secretive.

She had a couple of hours until the Booker announcement. She took the notebook upstairs to her office, intending to photograph every page. He was just as likely to throw it in the bin now that it was full. She wanted to make sure there was a record of whatever was there. She set up the camera as Daniel had shown her. But on reading the first page she changed her plan. She sat in her armchair and began to read.

# Chapter 63
# Knowing What We Know

'Are you going?'

I turned to find Max standing a few feet off. I nodded.

I hadn't been able to find Zoe to say goodbye, but bumped into Hayley who had my clutch. The man in the cloakroom handed me my coat. Max stepped forward and helped me into it.

'Ben Okri has invited a few of us back to his place for drinks. Would you like to come?'

'I have to get back to Helen. You can help me get a cab.'

A few more attendees were preparing to leave too. I started walking towards the door.

'I can't believe he won,' he said, walking beside me, 'I really can't.'

'Imagine having to get up there in front of all of them.'

'It was a good speech, at least.'

'You think? Knowing what we know?'

'At least he spoke about Helen in the present tense. That's a step in the right direction.'

We were crossing the square.

'I was thinking of her at home watching it on TV. She's by herself, you know. Malcolm's with Trevor. All that stuff about integrity and no compromise. It would have been like an acid bath to her. Malcolm's a bastard for saying all that stuff. He knows how to hit the mark.'

'No one but you and Helen would see it that way. The world saw it as a heartfelt tribute to Helen Owen the writer.'

'I don't care what the world thinks. Only Helen matters.'

We reached the street.

'Where's the best place to get a cab?'

'There'll be plenty along here.'

We stood on the kerb, each looking up and down the street.

'So you're not working with Liam anymore?' he asked.

'That's right. We're done.'

'So that's the end of Jack Cade?'

'It might be. I'm not sure.'

'What will you do?'

'Oh, there's one!' I stepped out into the road to get the cabbie's attention, but he drove right past. 'What the fuck was that about?'

'I don't know. They're a law unto themselves.'

'You'd think they'd be more attentive. With Uber around.'

We stared after the errant cab.

'So, what will you do now?'

'Finish watching *House of Cards*. Fuck, it's cold.'

'After that?'

'I don't know. *Game of Thrones*?'

'Seriously.'

'I don't know, Max. I haven't a clue. I just need a cab. And some pyjama bottoms. And some thick socks.'

'There's one.'

'Get him!'

I watched as Max stepped out into the street. The cabbie stopped.

'Your chariot awaits, miss,' he said, opening the door for me.

I climbed in. He held the door open and stared at me.

'I want to have dinner with you.'

'I thought you said no to all that.'

'I've changed my mind.'

'I'll think about it,' I said, smiling.

'Can I say how beautiful you looked up on that stage?'

I shook my head.

'Can I say how beautiful you look right now?'

'Hey, mate, are you in or are you out? You're letting all the cold air in.'

Max turned to look at the cabbie and I leant forward in my seat so that when he turned back to me he was close. He turned back and I kissed him briefly on the mouth. Then I fell back in my seat and said, 'See you later, Max.'

Without taking his eyes off me, he closed the door and stood back. The cab drove off.

# Chapter 64
# But Who Would Do Such a Thing?

The house was silent when Malcolm arrived home. He made his way straight to the kitchen, where he opened the fridge and took out one of the mince pies he'd bought that afternoon. He looked at the bottle of white wine in the fridge door and decided to have a glass. He had just won the Booker; he could celebrate with a mince pie and a glass of wine.

He popped the pie on a plate, placed it on the kitchen table and poured himself a glass of that wine. Then he sat down. He listened to the house. Nothing. He began to eat his pie.

He had finished eating when Amy opened the door to the flat. She was still in the dress she had worn to the Booker, but her feet were bare.

'Congratulations, Malcolm. You were right. You won. I know it doesn't make you very happy to have won. But congratulations anyway.'

She hugged him from behind, briefly. But as he remained stiff and unreceptive, she withdrew.

'Thank you for reading my speech.'

'Have you seen Helen?' she asked, lifting Malcolm's untouched wine from the table and taking a sip.

'Of course not.'

'You know all that crap about Helen being uncompromising was unnecessary, right?' she said, sitting down at the table opposite him.

'I spoke of the Helen I knew. The Helen I loved.'

'What if she agreed not to publish the book?'

'What's done is done.'

'It can't be like that, Malcolm. It can't. There has to be a way back for her. I need there to be some way back.'

'We were compatible because we shared one thing. Integrity. What that is I don't know. I feel it more than I know it. Like authenticity. We all have a sense of when something is corrupt. Like off meat or milk. We know before we've even tasted it.'

'Helen isn't off milk, you shit,' Amy said, standing. She made her way to the hall then turned back. 'You need to read that fucking book. Version three. It's been on your desk for months. Then you'll be on your knees begging for her forgiveness.' She placed her hand on the table and leant in menacingly. 'If you don't read it, I'll tie you to a chair and read it to you. I tricked that fucking snob Clarissa Munten into reading it. She said it was the best thing Helen has ever written.'

Malcolm seemed unmoved by Amy's outburst.

'She said it was better than any of your shit. And I agree.'

'Why are you so angry, Amy?'

'Because you're breaking her heart, Malcolm. Because you're being unnecessarily cruel to a woman you've loved for fifty years!'

'She broke my heart first. Can you see that?'

'And she's suffered for it. She *is* suffering for it.'

'She's beyond suffering now.'

'Oh, for fuck's sake, she's not dead. She's alive. She's probably upstairs in tears. I would be if I were her.'

'Stop it! Stop it!'

Amy grabbed Malcolm's arm and pulled him to his feet.

He was surprisingly light, she thought. She might be able to force him upstairs. She'd end this right now.

'Come upstairs.'

Amy walked to the bottom of the stairs. When she turned Malcolm hadn't moved.

'You're coming one way or another, Malcolm. Don't make me kick your arse.'

He seemed to smile, but grimly, with a hint of a determination not to be moved.

'This isn't the outfit for a brawl. Do you have any idea how much this dress cost? More than any advance you ever received.' She strode back to him and took hold of his arm. 'But if you want to rumble I'm willing to risk it.'

As soon as her grip tightened around his biceps, Malcolm felt the fight go out of him. Though slender, Amy had youth on her side. He had nothing on his side. When she tugged at his arm, he moved forward. Then steadily, but with unexpressed reluctance, Malcolm was led upstairs.

'She might be asleep. Wait here.'

Amy left Malcolm on the first landing and went up to Helen and Malcolm's bedroom. She pushed the door open carefully. As her eyes adjusted to the darkness she saw the bed was made and empty. She switched the light on.

'Amy!' came a cry from downstairs. It was Malcolm. Amy's heart skipped a beat and her head filled with dread. She ran downstairs as fast as her feet could take her.

'Malcolm?' she said, when she reached the first floor.

'In here.'

There was less anxiety in the tone of his voice now. Amy went into his office.

Malcolm was standing by the sofa bed staring at a mound of shredded paper.

Amy rushed forward and took a handful of it.

'What's this?' she asked, looking at him. He was crying silently.

'My book. Someone has shredded my book.'

'What book?'

'The best thing I ever wrote.'

'What book, Malcolm?'

'It didn't have a name. I just finished it. It was …'

'The novel about Helen's death?'

'Who told you that?'

'You did,' she lied, remembering that Max had told her.

'I did not. I haven't told anyone. It's been a private project. I wasn't even going to publish it.'

'You haven't been that discreet. You don't know what you're doing lately, Malcolm.'

'It's gone now so it doesn't matter. But who would do such a thing?'

'Helen.'

'Impossible.'

Amy had been lifting the shreds of paper and she noticed a larger piece fall to the ground.

'There! What's that?'

It fell at Malcolm's feet. He bent to pick it up. Amy took it from him.

She recognised the paper. It was from a pad on Helen's desk. She turned it over.

Amy read it and handed it to Malcolm. 'She's not fucking dead.'

He recognised Helen's handwriting immediately. The note said: *You know nothing of grief.*

'I have to find her.' Amy left the room.

Malcolm sat on the bed and pushed his hand into the shredded pages. He read the note again. And he broke down. Not for the loss of his book. But for the loss of everything he loved.

Amy went into Helen's study. There was the shredder on her desk. And the framed picture of Daniel that Helen had kept near her since the funeral. There was *Howards End*, too. And version three was there. She had brought it back from Malcolm's office.

The note Helen had left for Malcolm had given Amy a bit of a shock. But these signs of action on her desk calmed her. She went downstairs, suddenly realising where Helen would most likely be. Sue had come to use the back garden as a place of retreat. Malcolm never ventured out there. When TV didn't help, she would grab a blanket and head outside. Since the funeral, Amy had shivered beside her watching two days dawn.

But the back door was locked. She unlocked it and walked with feet bare into the yard. It was freezing. She saw both garden seats were empty. She ran back inside.

She checked her flat. She checked the front room.

Panicking, she ran back upstairs. She pushed open the bathroom door, turned the light on. And screamed.

'Malcolm! Fuck! Malcolm!' Amy was hysterical. 'Malcolm. Oh my god! Fuck! Malcolm! Fuck!'

Amy took a few steps into the bathroom. What she saw horrified her. She couldn't think. Her body was leaden. Helen was naked, seated clumsily in the half-full bath. Her head rolled along the curve of the bath towards the noise. Her eyes fixed on Amy's.

Malcolm arrived.

'Oh my god! Helen! What have you done?! Oh!' He was screaming, too. He fell to his knees beside the bathroom cabinet.

'Get someone! Malcolm! Do something! She's alive!'

Amy moved slowly. She didn't want to see more, but she had to help Helen. All of her instincts were for flight. This was too much for her. The horror in Helen's expression. She was alive. She was in pain. She was dying.

Amy rushed out of the room. She ran into Helen's office and dialled 999. She screamed down the phone that Helen was dying, that she had stabbed herself. There was blood everywhere. The woman at the other end tried to calm her to get the address.

Amy couldn't remember the address. She couldn't think straight.

'I don't know! I don't know!'

The woman on the phone told her to calm down. Amy saw letters on Helen's desk. She looked at them. Nothing. She opened drawers looking for letters or bills with the address on it.

'What's the fucking address, Malcolm!' she screamed.

Then she found a bill. She read the address to the woman on the phone. 'Come quickly.'

While the woman was still talking Amy slammed down the phone and ran back into the bathroom.

Malcolm was on the floor. He had dragged Helen out of the bath and she lay awkwardly across his lap, legs bent and head thrown back, unconscious. Her naked flesh was bleeding from numerous wounds. He was hugging her to him and rocking her, like she was a child. He was howling like an injured animal. Blood was everywhere. She had stabbed herself everywhere. A frenzy of stab wounds.

Amy stood still for a moment. She saw the knife on the floor for the first time.

The blood was on the floor. On the bath. On the wall. The bathwater was red.

Towels. She pulled the towels from the rails. She'd stop the bleeding.

'Oh fucking Christ!' she moaned. 'Fuck! Fuck!'

She didn't know what to do. There were too many wounds. Blood gushed from Helen's thigh. Amy could see it pumping. She was going to die. She'd been stabbing herself while Amy had been in the house. Amy was moaning uncontrollably. Her hands shook; she was light-headed.

She covered her mouth and turned away from Helen and Malcolm, vomiting in her hands. It spewed out over the floor. She rested on one hand and shook her head. It was a nightmare. A nightmare.

'Helen. Helen. Helen. Helen?' Malcolm repeated. 'Helen. Helen. Helen.'

Amy turned and pressed her hand on Helen's thigh. Trying to force the blood back. Trying to save her. It was warm. Her body was warm. She looked at Helen's face. It was white. Malcolm was kissing her and repeating her name. Blood drained from a wound on her neck.

She'd attacked herself with such violence. Amy couldn't cover all the stab wounds. She didn't have enough hands. Why would she? Why?

Then Amy heard banging on the door. The front door bell had been buzzing, she realised, and now someone was banging on the door. She stood up and moving unsteadily, her bloody feet leaving a trail across the landing carpet and down the stairs, made her way to the door.

They rushed past her and up the stairs. They followed the blood. When Amy reached the landing, Malcolm was outside the bathroom, kneeling on the carpet, staring into the room and absently wiping his bloodied hands on his trousers. Helen was stretched out on the floor with strangers around her. Two more pushed past Amy. Amy collapsed onto the top step and pressed herself against the wall. She stared, expressionless, downwards.

# Chapter 65
# Phone Message

'Hello, Malcolm. Paul Beatty here. I just wanted to congratulate you personally on your win. And thanks for what you said about *The Sellout* last night. You didn't have to, and I appreciate it. It just wasn't my year. Well, congratulations again. Oh, and best wishes on this, your fiftieth wedding anniversary. Perhaps if you're ever in the States we can have a drink? Bye for now.'

# Chapter 66
# Max's Article

*Draft Copy*

**The New Old Ways**

*The generation of readers raised upon the* Harry Potter, Twilight *and* Hunger Games *series will determine the direction modern publishing will take. At the moment these readers and the publishers are in a game, not of cat and mouse, but of cat and cat, as reader and publisher circle one another, watching and waiting, and stagnating, neither getting the upper hand, neither taking the lead.*

*There is money to be made from this book-loving millennial generation, and the multinational publishers want to maximise their returns. But with so much at stake, neither side willing to take risks, and neither showing any initiative, much of the industry is forced to tread water.*

*Which is good for some. The first beneficiaries of this stagnation are the 'forgotten' writers of the fifties, sixties, seventies and eighties. Boutique publishing houses are springing up everywhere with one goal: to unearth neglected modern classics.*

*Like the emergence of vinyl, these publications are gaining popularity among those who never experienced their like. These are not nostalgia hunters but archaeologists, seeing the artefacts for the first time. And it is having an effect.*

*Even before his recent Man Booker win, Malcolm Taylor had been surprised to see some of his earliest novels being republished with sixties- and seventies-style jackets. They were designed to appeal to the more discerning of the* Harry Potter *generation. The author thought they looked atrocious. But since the win, all of Taylor's previously out-of-print novels have been placed back on the shelves and are selling well.*

*Speaking to Malcolm Taylor just before his win, I was astonished to discover that he did not think much of his earlier work was relevant to the present age.*

*'I recognise that writers like Kurt Vonnegut, Italo Calvino and Russell Hoban have a continuing relevance, if only in their dedication to experimentation in writing, which serves to remind writers that boundaries do not exist, but writers like me, who failed to bring anything new to the form and structure of the novel, all I have is social commentary. I will go the same way as Malcolm Bradbury, Elizabeth Jane Howard and C.P. Snow. And even Vonnegut and friends have a use-by date. Writers like Elizabeth Bowen and Milan Kundera, and my wife, Helen Owen, should be championed by a new generation. Because these writers expand our understanding of ourselves. But then none of this is about what should happen, is it? It's about utility. And Calvino is more useful to modern writers than Iris Murdoch, say.'*

*That concept of writers being useful to other writers struck me as interesting. Taylor was referring to craft and not to content, I think. For all writing is useful to writers, surely. Whether you are J.K. Rowling reading* The Chronicles of Narnia, *or Tolstoy reading* David Copperfield. *One thing that unites all writers is their dependence upon their reading.*

*Taylor's own reading has been extensive. I had the pleasure of examining his book collection while interviewing him for this article. The thousands of books, mostly bought second-hand, were still in some disarray, as he had recently moved house. And though he had just 'thrown the books onto the shelves', I could discern some reading patterns there. For one, there wasn't a single book we might be able to call commercial.*

*I asked him about the large number of American writers on his shelves.*

*'How can you ask? America, that's where everything was happening. The fifties, and most of the sixties, in the UK were bleak. We all looked*

*to the US for the new. They were streets ahead of us in every way. They were born innovators, largely because they consciously ignored the past. They had cut their ties, while we were suffocating under the weight of the great tradition.'*

*Where does he think the young writers of today should be looking? India? Africa? China?*

*'They can work that out for themselves.'*

*And does he think the mass reading movements of recent times –* Harry Potter, Twilight *and* Fifty Shades *etc. – adversely affect modern writing?*

*'We're talking exclusively about serious writers, are we not?'*

*I nodded.*

*'They wouldn't have read them. So zero effect.'*

*Does he think the internet has a positive or negative effect on writing?*

*'Positive. It is a tool. A very good one for research. And it is bringing people together. It is opening our eyes to lives unlike our own. I have heard it said that the internet gives people the answers they want to find. But this is not exclusive to the internet. It comes down to the questions you ask. And your dedication to the task. In 1950s London it was easy to find answers that suited your beliefs, if your beliefs were those shared by your neighbours, but it was almost impossible to find answers to questions no one wanted asked in the first place. The struggle to find or establish alternative viewpoints was a daily one.'*

*When I turned the conversation around to his own work, Taylor was evasive. He was much happier extolling the virtues of his wife Helen Owen's novels. When pressed to speak about* A Hundred Ways, *his tone was dismissive. But this was before the Man Booker win.*

*Our interviews were postponed after the death of his son, Daniel Taylor. When next we met, some six months later, Malcolm had won the Man Booker and was celebrating his eightieth birthday in the reception rooms of the exclusive retirement village in Richmond where his long-time literary agent and friend, Trevor Melville, resides. Melville, who recently turned ninety-two, gave a moving speech to the audience of twenty or so close friends and fellow writers, which ended with the most recent sales figures for* A Hundred Ways. *It has sold a quarter of a million copies in the UK alone.*

*When I found a quiet moment, I asked Taylor what it was about* A Hundred Ways *that attracted so many readers.*

'Success like this, obscene success, is always a sign of some kind of failure. I could name twenty writers whose most popular book was their least successful artistically. A Hundred Ways *must be pretty terrible to be so loved.'*

*The last time we met you were just finishing a new novel. When can we expect to read it?*

'I destroyed it. It wasn't working.'

*That surprises me, as at the time you excited me by saying you thought it your best work yet.*

'Which was clearly a sign something was desperately wrong.'

*And something was desperately wrong. In a year when the world mourned the loss of David Bowie, Prince, Muhammad Ali, Carrie Fisher and Leonard Cohen, Taylor was mourning the loss of his son and then, a few weeks later, the death of his wife of fifty years, Helen Owen.*

*Malcolm Taylor has said nothing publicly about these deaths. And when I alluded to the subject he pulled away from me. We are left with the tribute to Helen Owen he made in his Man Booker speech, where he credited her with keeping him on the right path and called her 'one of the world's greatest thinkers and writers'.*

*After speaking briefly with Trevor Melville at the same event, I did learn that Malcolm was working on a couple of new projects. The first of these is the publication of Helen Owen's final novel,* All Too Human, *which he has edited, and then, early next year, a memoir,* Helen Owen: A Writer Observed.

*So, as many of the biggest publishers call in focus groups and analyse big data in an effort to anticipate the needs of a cashed-up new generation of readers, some of the country's remaining boutique publishers continue to do what they have always done – publish great work by great writers, like Helen Owen and Malcolm Taylor, and allow time and good taste to work their magic. You don't need to be a wizard to work out which approach will win the day.*

# Chapter 67
# All Too Human

Max and Amy talk on the phone:

'Thank you, Max, we've just read the article. Knowing what you know, you were very restrained.'

'Nobody needs to know any of that.'

'When will you publish?'

'Next week. But not in my magazine. You've heard, haven't you?'

'Yes. I am sorry.'

'Never mind. After all you've gone through, the passing of a literary magazine is nothing.'

'You had a great story. He still hasn't spoken to the media at all and you chose not to go ahead. It might have saved you.'

'I couldn't do it. It wasn't right.'

'It would've sold copies, though, and you know it. So thank you.'

'That's what it was all about, wasn't it? Choices like this?'

'In a way.'

'I did write about it, though. I just haven't shown you. And I promise, no one else will see it. It's not for publication. I had to get it all down. You and Helen. Daniel's suicide. Malcolm's weird novel, his false grief. Helen's three manuscripts, her guilt, his rejection of her, her suicide on the night of his win. It's so dark.

Later, in a few years, I'll write a book about it. A novel, perhaps. I'd love to see your diaries on it all one day.'

'No, you wouldn't.'

'Amy?'

'Yes? … Oh … No, don't say anything. I know what you're going to say. I need time, Max. That's all.'

'Where are you? It sounds like you're at the beach.'

'That's Malcolm. He's in the pool. We're in Tuscany, just outside Lucca. I've dragged him here to finish his memoir. I'll send pics. It's gorgeous here.'

'How's he doing?'

'He's a mess. We both are. But writing about Helen seems to be helping him. We'll be back in London in September. We're launching *All Too Human*. Did you read the proof copy I sent you?'

'It's extraordinary, Amy. You and Malcolm have done a brilliant job.'

'Helen was a perfectionist. Especially with this one. It meant the world to her. We hardly did a thing to it.'

'Even so, it must have been hard for both of you.'

'Harder for Malcolm. Helen wrote the book for him. She saw it as her salvation, a way of winning back his respect. She all but begged him to read it. But the manuscript had remained unread on Malcolm's desk.'

'I didn't know.'

'Malcolm was inconsolable when he first read it. I didn't think he'd recover. He lost weight and interest in everything. It was too much for him. He loved her – more than anything – and he knows his cruelty brought her to self-destruction. He isn't the man he was. He'll never be that man again. But the work has given him a focus. He won't let Helen down again.'

'*All Too Human* cements her reputation as one of the greats.'

'Stop, you'll make me cry … Sorry, I'll let Malcolm know you said so.'

'I've written a review for *The Guardian*. They'll publish it in September. I'll send it through.'

'No need. I trust you.'

'Amy, just out of curiosity, how much of the M&R mess was down to your influence?'

'I don't know what you mean.'

'You don't know what I mean? *The Bookseller* announces a record eight-figure deal between HarperCollins and Jack Cade, and you pretend to have had nothing to do with it?'

'That was their doing, not mine.'

'How's that?'

'After all that's happened they're still going to publish Helen's more commercial novel. They're planning to call it *The Winter Rose*. A friend sent me a draft cover. It looks like a fucking Maeve Binchy. Malcolm is understandably horrified and has urged them to reconsider, but ...'

'But ...'

'Julia is a fucking bitch. Even though we've offered to pay back the advance, she's still going ahead.'

'So you took Jack Cade from her?'

'After she tried to take Jack Cade from me first.'

'So you think Julia was behind Liam's change of heart?'

'Of course! She would have whispered all kinds of bullshit into his ear as she stroked his cock. She knows Liam loves playing the bestselling author. She knows he hates it when anyone suggests publicly that I've played any part in his success. Like Malcolm did magnificently in his speech. It's a sore point with him. That's why he calls me his editor and never his co-author. So she convinced him to dump me. Not knowing the true nature of our arrangement.'

'Surely Liam knew.'

'Liam should have known. It was all in black and white. He really should have read the original contract more closely. He was, essentially, a hired gun, after all. I now have three Liams working around the clock on the new Mark Harden thriller for HarperCollins. It will be the best one yet.'

'I doubt Liam's okay with that.'

'Publicly, he has to be. Publicly, he retired on his own terms. Privately, I don't give a fuck.'

'I don't think he has much "privately" anymore. The tabloids are loving his decline. Gail's interview with *Hello!* magazine was pure gold. Did you read it?'

'I helped write it.'

'You're the devil.'

'I wish I was. Then I'd find a way to stop Julia publishing *The Winter Rose*.'

'You'll think of something. You always do.'

'I have Alan going over the contract and the correspondence between M&R and Helen, looking for something Malcolm and I might have overlooked. Hopefully something will come up.'

'I'm sure it will. And what news of your own novel, Amy?'

'Who told you about that?'

'A little birdy.'

'It's coming along.'

'Can you tell me what it's about?'

'It's just a silly love story.'

# Epilogue

I was somewhere in Sydney sitting in the back row of an auditorium with Malcolm's Australian publicist, Melanie, watching Malcolm, Liam, Michelle de Kretser and the panel facilitator, Angela Meyer, mic up. The panel was called 'What is literature?' It wasn't part of Malcolm's programme, but Kate Atkinson had taken ill overnight and had emailed Malcolm's publicist personally to ask if he might fill in for her. The Sydney Writers' Festival organisers were understandably delighted with this solution. Kate Atkinson had been one of the stars of the programme and this was to be her last appearance. Her sessions had been booked out well in advance. Replacing her with the keynote speaker was a neat solution to the problem.

When I saw that Liam was to be on the panel too, I tried to talk Malcolm out of agreeing to the extra session. But this news seemed to amuse him. He said he had enjoyed reading *Tangential* and was looking forward to meeting the author. Noting the mischievous glint in his eye as he spoke, I let him have his way.

I was finding it hard to stay awake. I was still jetlagged. For the entire week of the festival I had been a bit of a zombie. I had never flown so far in my life. I now know we should have broken the trip with a couple of nights in Singapore as Trevor had suggested. But Malcolm had been for getting it over with in one go. So I relented.

Neither of us is a great flier. And then Malcolm got lucky on the second leg and slept most of the way from Singapore to Sydney. He managed almost eight hours' sleep, something he rarely got at home. But I just couldn't sleep. While he snored softly I sat watching terrible movie after terrible movie. The last five hours of the last leg had been the worst. They went by so slowly. The lights were dimmed. The rest of the plane was asleep. I felt trapped and on the edge of hysteria. I was so happy when we finally landed. I could have kissed the ground.

And we had flown business class. The poor fuckers in economy must have felt like they were in Abu Ghraib prison.

On arrival in Sydney I'd upgraded us both to a suite overlooking the harbour. But I still hadn't slept through the night. I was catching two or three hours at a stretch, whenever I could.

I rested my head against Melanie's shoulder. She was my new best friend. I did everything she told me to do.

Malcolm gave me a wink. I blew him a kiss back. The stagehand was fiddling with each of their mics in turn. The four of them were chatting amiably, Angela on the left of the stage with her notes on her lap, Liam beside her, then Michelle, and Malcolm on the far right. Malcolm looked to be the most relaxed of them all. In fact, the whole festival he'd been like that. Completely chilled. Even before giving the keynote address. He just had no fucks to give anymore.

Malcolm had only agreed to attend the festival because his programme was largely devoted to Helen's works. The first two sessions Malcolm had participated in were on his memoir of Helen, in which he had taken full responsibility for her suicide. They were emotionally draining for everyone involved. The third session was on Helen's last novel, *All Too Human*, and the fourth on his own work. Including the keynote, it was a full programme for any writer. And now he had agreed to this extra session. He was eighty-one years old. He seemed to have more energy than ever. Especially when talking about Helen.

And then there were the publisher dinners, the lunches with other authors, the drinks, parties and trips out to see Bondi Beach, the Blue Mountains and the Opera House, and the overlong harbour cruise.

I was his official chaperone, but I was useless. I couldn't keep up with him. I kept falling asleep on his or Melanie's shoulder.

The doors opened and the audience was ushered in. Most were elderly, it being 2 pm on a Friday, but there were a few young hipster types to break up the greys and variations of beige. There were about three hundred people in the audience. And a crew was filming the session and streaming it live onto Facebook.

Liam hadn't looked in my direction the whole time I had been in clear view, but now, as I was being hemmed in by pensioners, he glanced across and caught my eye for a second. I almost smiled. He looked nervous.

I had successfully avoided him the whole time we had been in Sydney. He was at some of the dinners and drinks, and he had been on the harbour cruise, too, but he'd kept his distance, and I had kept mine.

*Tangential* had been poorly received by the critics, but his name was enough to get him into the bestseller lists and invited to festivals. His fans on Goodreads, our fans really, had been generous in their praise. He'd earn thousands of five-star reviews, but I knew their praise wasn't what he sought. The literary world he aspired to join had been silent, neither praising nor damning the novel. Its response could be summed up in one word: 'meh'. The response all writers fear most.

I lifted my head off Melanie's shoulder as the session got underway. The panellists happily agreed with the facilitator, Angela, that it was a bitch of a topic to tackle. Amid general laughter from the audience, each writer openly confessed that they had no idea what literature was. Angela apologised to the audience for wasting their time and made to stand up, before turning to her panellists and asking them, 'as we're all here', if they could take a stab at a definition.

Michelle de Kretser handled herself admirably, keeping clear of the traps that lay in every direction.

Liam dived in recklessly and was soon out of his depth.

'It's subjective, really. What's literature to one won't be literature to another. Definition is impossible. It's ethereal. Inexpressible. Open to interpretation. And it must be. I won't be told what literature is, I must discover it for myself.'

'So how do we teach literature?' asked Angela.

'It can't be taught. You'd need defined characteristics to teach it, and we all just agreed, there aren't any.'

There was a moment of silence before Angela spoke again: 'Malcolm, is there any way out of Liam's paradox?'

'I don't believe everything is subjective. I think there are universal truths. Truths we can build upon. Building blocks such as the flesh and blood and bone of our beings. The mechanisms that allow us to breathe, to breed, to run in fright. Our biological selves. Our shared human nature. Our predictable psychological responses. These are far from subjective. And these objective realities give us a firm and consistent point of reference if ever we get lost.'

'Dr Johnson kicking the stone?' asked Angela.

'Yes, if you like. Sometimes we lose ourselves in our own cleverness. And we need the rude shock of a plain fact to wake us up.'

'So how would you define literature?' asked Liam, with no small amount of petulance in his tone.

'I don't know about you, but I burn with shame when Mr Knightley upbraids Emma Woodhouse for being unkind to Miss Bates. I have been guilty of such behaviour myself. Scoring a point at the expense of another. Via her novel, *Emma*, Jane Austen has been able to reach out from the grave, and across two centuries, to rap me on the knuckles. How could she possibly do that if everything was relative? Her point is a universal one. Her lesson is as valid today as it was then because at base we have not changed.'

'So literature is a collection of universal truths?' prompted Liam.

'I used to teach writing. I failed most of my students because the one thing I wanted them to learn was the one thing hardest to teach. I wanted them to see the world as it is. It's harder to do than it sounds. We're all encased in stories – those told to us and those we tell ourselves. I would say to them, in the safety of that classroom, that most novelists write by dipping their ladle into the great vat of past fictions. In that vat, stewing for centuries, are all the plots, clichés, tropes, themes, character types and common phrases ever used in fiction. Novels written using this method are usually quite successful because they ask nothing of the reader. The reader reads in a pleasant stupor of familiarity. A publisher might describe this kind of fiction as commercial fiction.

'The fiction I was trying to encourage my students to write was fiction written from direct experience of life. This kind of fiction is much harder to write and is, in turn, sometimes taxing to read. But often only at first. As readers we navigate by signpost, but in this kind of fiction the signposts are unfamiliar to us, almost as though written in another language. We stumble around, we get lost, we might even get frustrated, but there comes a time, if we're patient, when we learn to see the world anew, as the writer has learnt to see it, and suddenly all of the signposts become clear. And if we're very lucky, life itself becomes clearer.

'No one writes exclusively from the vat, just as no one writes exclusively from life. Writing is a series of compromises. Writers from life need to be understood, so they borrow from the vat. Writers from the vat need to be new, so they take from life.'

Malcolm stopped speaking.

The audience seemed to be leaning forward, just as Angela and Michelle were. They expected him to say something more.

He looked across at Angela, then over at me.

'I just thought of something Dylan Thomas said while giving a lecture,' said Malcolm: '"Somebody's boring me. I think it's me."'

The audience laughed.

'No, no, Malcolm,' said Angela, 'not at all. So you think literary fiction is the consequence of a particular combination of a writer's direct experience of life and their reading?'

'Well, of course it is,' said Liam. 'Literary fiction is ...'

'Literary fiction doesn't exist, Liam. Not the way you think it does. You set out to write a literary novel as though the word "literary" describes a genre the way the word "crime" does. Literary fiction. Crime fiction. But "literary" describes a quality. It defies genre because it can apply to all genres.

'I thoroughly enjoyed *Tangential*, Liam. But it isn't literature. It's a work written by a writer steeped in a particular kind of literary fiction. At a guess, I'd say your particular vat was filled with novels by Martin Amis, Ian McEwan, John Banville, Roddy Doyle and, for a bit of extra zest, Will Self. It doesn't mean your book isn't any good. It is good and thousands of people have already enjoyed it. And thousands more will, too. And that's a wonderful thing ... Bringing enjoyment to thousands of readers. It is, isn't it?'

Liam stared at Malcolm and nodded.

'We're all here because we love reading. Especially novels,' Malcolm continued. 'To be honest, I've never particularly liked the idea of literature. I'm still suspicious of the word. When I was growing up in London's East End, it always seemed to be a stick with which to beat the lower classes. As a teen I resented those who read and enjoyed the classics, who went to see Shakespeare at the theatre, who could drop quotes into their conversation. And I was right to. Many people did use literature as a weapon. And they still do. And I would hate for anyone to think that I thought of literature that way. To me, literature is the fastest and surest route to understanding something of this life. At eighty-one, I know how brief our lives are. Mine has flashed by. And any help making sense of the world is still most welcome. The quicker the better. What is literature? Literature is life's cheat sheet.

'As my beloved late wife, Helen Owen, said, "Great writing is rare. With so little time on this planet, shouldn't we spend at least some of that time getting acquainted with the writers most often acknowledged as exceptional?"'

And with that Malcolm placed his hands in his lap and was silent.

For a moment the audience was silent, too. His fellow panellists were looking at him, expectantly.

As the silence lingered, I had an awful feeling that I was the only one in the audience who appreciated what he had just said.

Then the audience applauded all at once. Some stood and whistled. His fellow panellists were applauding, too.

I stood up and raised my hands above my head, clapping like a child.

Malcolm turned and saw me, his face a smile.

# Further Reading

Recommendations from the principal players:

**Helen Owen**

1. *Middlemarch* by George Eliot
2. *Persuasion* by Jane Austen
3. *Howards End* by E.M. Forster
4. *Anna Karenina* by Leo Tolstoy
5. *The Death of the Heart* by Elizabeth Bowen
6. *The French Lieutenant's Woman* by John Fowles
7. *Night* by Edna O'Brien
8. *Stoner* by John Williams
9. *The Prime of Miss Jean Brodie* by Muriel Spark
10. *The Blue Flower* by Penelope Fitzgerald
11. *Death Comes for the Archbishop* by Willa Cather
12. *The Portrait of a Lady* by Henry James
13. *The Echoing Grove* by Rosamond Lehmann
14. *Brief Lives* by Anita Brookner
15. *The Tenant of Wildfell Hall* by Anne Bronte
16. *Three Lives* by Gertrude Stein
17. *A House and its Head* by Ivy Compton-Burnett
18. *Stories* by Alice Munro
19. *To the Lighthouse* by Virginia Woolf
20. *The Age of Innocence* by Edith Wharton

**Malcolm Taylor**

1. *Tom Jones* by Henry Fielding
2. *Winesburg Ohio* by Sherwood Anderson

3. *Emma* by Jane Austen
4. *Daniel Deronda* by George Eliot
5. *Wide Sargasso Sea* by Jean Rhys
6. *Buddenbrooks* by Thomas Mann
7. *Our Mutual Friend* by Charles Dickens
8. *New Grub Street* by George Gissing
9. *Lost Illusions* by Balzac
10. *Vanity Fair* by Thackeray
11. *Esther Waters* by George Moore
12. *The Turtle Diary* by Russell Hoban
13. *Earthly Powers* by Anthony Burgess
14. *Jude the Obscure* by Thomas Hardy
15. *If on a Winter's Night a Traveller* by Italo Calvino
16. *The Tin Drum* by Gunter Grass
17. *Parade's End* by Ford Madox Ford
18. *Absalom, Absalom!* by William Faulkner
19. *An American Tragedy* by Theodore Dreiser
20. *Slaughterhouse Five* by Kurt Vonnegut

## Amy Winston
1. Harry Potter series by J.K. Rowling
2. *The Adventures of Sherlock Holmes* by Arthur Conan Doyle
3. *Outlander* by Diana Gabaldon
4. *Alex Cross* by James Patterson
5. *The Thorn Birds* by Colleen McCullough
6. *Flowers in the Attic* by V. C. Andrews
7. *The Da Vinci Code* by Dan Brown
8. *Kane and Abel* by Jeffrey Archer
9. Jack Reacher novels by Lee Child
10. *A Song of Ice and Fire* by George R.R. Martin
11. *The Girl on the Train* by Paula Hawkins
12. *Me Before You* by Jojo Moyes
13. *Valley of the Dolls* by Jacqueline Susann
14. *The Girl with the Dragon Tattoo* by Stieg Larsson

15. *The Hunger Games* by Suzanne Collins
16. *Gone Girl* by Gillian Flynn
17. *The Godfather* by Mario Puzo
18. *Shōgun* by James Clavell
19. *The Pillars of the Earth* by Ken Follett
20. Maigret novels by Georges Simenon

## Liam Smith

1. *The Spy Who Came in From the Cold* by John le Carré
2. *For Whom the Bell Tolls* by Ernest Hemingway
3. *The Day of the Jackal* by Frederick Forsyth
4. *Roots* by Alex Haley
5. *London Fields* by Martin Amis
6. *On the Road* by Jack Kerouac
7. *White Teeth* by Zadie Smith
8. *The Sense of an Ending* by Julian Barnes
9. *Red Storm Rising* by Tom Clancy
10. *Infinite Jest* by David Foster Wallace
11. *Divine Comedy* by Dante Alighieri
12. *The Corrections* by Jonathan Franzen
13. *Captain Corelli's Mandolin* by Louis de Bernières
14. *Gravity's Rainbow* by Thomas Pynchon
15. *On Chesil Beach* by Ian McEwan
16. *The Stand* by Stephen King
17. *Crime and Punishment* by Fyodor Dostoevsky
18. *Devil in a Blue Dress* by Walter Mosley
19. *The Road* by Cormac McCarthy
20. *All Quiet on the Western Front* by Erich Maria Remarque

## Max Lyons

1. *Remembrance of Things Past* by Marcel Proust
2. *Ulysses* by James Joyce
3. *The Magic Mountain* by Thomas Mann
4. *Hunger* by Knut Hamsun

5. *Jane Eyre* by Charlotte Brontë
6. *Lolita* by Vladimir Nabokov
7. *Madame Bovary* by Gustave Flaubert
8. *Pride and Prejudice* by Jane Austen
9. *The Red and the Black* by Stendhal
10. *War and Peace* by Leo Tolstoy
11. *Rudin* by Ivan Turgenev
12. *Hamlet* by William Shakespeare
13. *The Alexandria Quartet* by Lawrence Durrell
14. *Remains of the Day* by Kazuo Ishiguro
15. *The Awakening* by Kate Chopin
16. *Austerlitz* by W.G. Sebald
17. *The Unbearable Lightness of Being* by Milan Kundera
18. *A Visit from the Goon Squad* by Jennifer Egan
19. *The English Patient* by Michael Ondaatje
20. *My Brilliant Friend* by Elena Ferrante

**Trevor Melville**
1. *The Razor's Edge* by Somerset Maugham
2. *Women in Love* by D.H. Lawrence
3. *Our Man In Havana* by Graham Greene
4. *The Naïve and Sentimental Lover* by John le Carré
5. *The Darling Buds of May* by H.E. Bates
6. *The Ginger Man* by J.P. Donleavy
7. *Flaubert's Parrot* by Julian Barnes
8. *Under the Greenwood Tree* by Thomas Hardy
9. *Silas Marner* by George Eliot
10. *The Pickwick Papers* by Charles Dickens
11. *The Pursuit of Love* by Nancy Mitford
12. *Gentlemen Prefer Blondes* by Anita Loos
13. *Memoirs of a Fox-Hunting Man* by Siegfried Sassoon
14. *A Room with a View* by E.M. Forster
15. *As I Walked Out One Midsummer Morning* by Laurie Lee
16. *Lucky Jim* by Kingsley Amis

17. *Kipps* by H.G. Wells
18. *The Enchanted April* by Elizabeth von Arnim
19. *A Moveable Feast* by Ernest Hemingway
20. *The Story of San Michele* by Axel Munthe

## Julia O'Farrell

Julia declined the invitation to submit a recommended reading list, so Amy, who knows her best, provided one for her.

1. *The Bitch* by Jackie Collins
2. *The Idiot* by Fyodor Dostoevsky
3. *Confederacy of Dunces* by John Kennedy Toole
4. *Pride and Prejudice and Zombies* by Seth Grahame-Smith
5. *Don't Read This Book If You're Stupid* by Tibor Fischer
6. *Malice* by Danielle Steel
7. *Mostly Harmless* by Douglas Adams
8. *Vile Bodies* by Evelyn Waugh
9. *Ignorance* by Milan Kundera
10. *The Beautiful and Damned* by F. Scott Fitzgerald
11. *The Insulted and Humiliated* by Fyodor Dostoevsky
12. *How to Lose Friends and Alienate People* by Toby Young
13. *Mantrap* by Sinclair Lewis
14. *Can You Forgive Her?* by Anthony Trollope
15. *You Can Heal Your Life* by Louise L. Hay
16. *All I Really Need to Know I Learned in Kindergarten* by Robert Fulghum
17. *The Burden* by Agatha Christie
18. *The Golden Fool* by Robin Hobb
19. *Eating People is Wrong* by Malcolm Bradbury
20. *Nice Work* by David Lodge

## The Author

1. *Middlemarch* by George Eliot
2. *Clarissa* by Samuel Richardson

3. *Persuasion* by Jane Austen
4. *Daniel Deronda* by George Eliot
5. *Jane Eyre* by Charlotte Bronte
6. *The Egoist* by George Meredith
7. *War and Peace* by Leo Tolstoy
8. *Wuthering Heights* by Emily Bronte
9. *Mademoiselle de Maupin* by Théophile Gautier
10. *The Return of the Native* by Thomas Hardy
11. *The Song of the Lark* by Willa Cather
12. *Sister Carrie* by Theodore Dreiser
13. *The Man Who Loved Children* by Christina Stead
14. *Maurice Guest* by Henry Handel Richardson
15. *Weymouth Sands* by John Cowper Powys
16. *Gertrude* by Hermann Hesse
17. *Confessions of Felix Krull, Confidence Man* by Thomas Mann
18. *North and South* by Elizabeth Gaskell
19. *Zorba the Greek* by Nikos Kazantzakis
20. *Stories* by Anton Chekhov

# Acknowledgements

My wife, Tamsin, is the reason this book exists. Without her love and support, and her stubborn refusal to read any part of it until I was finished, I would still be perfecting the first few pages. Thank you, my love.

And thanks to Catherine Milne, my publisher at HarperCollins, who had faith in me as a writer long before she had the chance to sign me up as one of her authors. You have helped my writing immeasurably.

Thanks to Simone Camilleri, my agent and friend, who took me on when no one else would.

Thanks to my parents, Pat and Terry Purcell, who encouraged me from the very first, even when, as a cocky nineteen-year-old, I sat down to write my autobiography. The best of parents, they let the world burst that bubble. And to my brother, Tim, who was one of the very first readers and loudest supporters – ta.

Thanks to Isabel for being awesome.

Thanks to Ben for all the material. And to Andrew Cattanach, my one-time colleague, my friend, my sounding board, thanks for your faith in me.

Thanks also to Sarah McDuling, who has been on this writing rollercoaster with me for years.

Thanks to the incredible HarperCollins team: patient Scott F., honest Alex C.; Nicola Y. and Claire G.; the indefatigable Alice and Sarah, wonderful Kate M., Michael W. supporting from the wings, James who steered from above, Emily and Tom, Hazel Lam for that cover, and many others.

For all those who have put up with my writerly pretensions

over the years: Anne, Jane, Matt, Dawn, Trish, Keith, Claire, Tina and many others – thanks.

Thanks also to my long-suffering work colleagues, some of whom read early versions of the book: Tania (pink), Ben, Rob, Olivia C., Jo (fashion consultant), Tanaya (meh), Bron E., Olivia F., Tracey, Angela, Kirsty, Hayley H., Jill, Liz E., Nick, Zia, Mark, Bron D., Sara, Elana, Sam W. and many more. It's a privilege to work with such great people.

Special thanks to Hayley Shephard for her Mr Bean GIFs and inspiring notes from abroad.

This novel about novelists wouldn't be the same without all the fictional cameos from real-life authors. Thanks to Val McDermid, Michael Robotham, Jeanette Winterson, Paul Beatty, Kathy Lette, Michelle de Kretser, Angela Meyer, Jojo Moyes and the dozen or so other novelists mentioned. I hope you all appreciate that this novel is a love letter to books and writers.

Thanks to Christopher Tomkinson for recommending I read *Catch-22* back in Year 12. This is all your fault.

I also want to thank all the people who have taken the time over the years to talk books with me – from the delightful oddbods who frequent second-hand bookshops to the writers who allow me to pick their brains every chance I get.

And finally, thanks again to my wife, Tamsin. Loving a writer is no easy thing.